A short review of
A Dozen Miles
of Unpaved Road:

"Pray explores the deep, honest, and raw feelings of working class life in the USA from the point of view of a Bogie-esque narrator. Each short story reveals a quickie view of the roughhewn underbelly of mundane life with characters from truck drivers, to transvestites, to convicts, to union organizers, and to company managers. A late in life author, Pray writes from his years of hard living in honky-tonks, truck stops, freight docks and rail cars, but always with a fast moving, dialogue driven plot. Reading Pray, one wants to experience this seedier, yet moral side of life. Each piece takes the reader down to a world unimagined but possible. Check this collection and live out fantasies you didn't even know you had."

—RW Klarin, author of *Living the Dream Deferred: A Boomer's Reconnaissance, Reflections, and Redemption on the Road to Reinvention* and *Expression Is Liberation* (a poetry collection)

A Dozen
Miles
of
Unpaved
Road

A Dozen Miles of Unpaved Road

**Trucks
Truckers
and Loaders**

**12 Stories
of Working
Life**

W.F. Pray

All company names and any character names used in this work are fictional.
Any similarity to the actual names of existing companies or persons,
either living or dead, is purely coincidental.

A Dozen Miles of Unpaved Road / William F. Pray
Working Class Literature
Firebird Publications

ISBN: 978-0-9863321-1-1

Art Direction: Susan Shankin
Design: Tim Kummerow

Printed in the United States

Dedication

This work is dedicated to all those working men and women who made it possible: all the truck drivers, loaders and dock workers I have known throughout my working life. Bless you, you make the goods and services of this world possible, make the world run smoothly and run on time. Also, to the couple of English professors I had early on in my educational career; you made one or two comments that stayed with me my entire life. And finally to the Rayman family, and especially to Holly Rayman. I knew you your entire life, Holly, and I miss you.

Acknowledgments

Writing is far easier than publishing. For the former I wish to thank Amanda Freeman. Her practical aid, insight and advice were invaluable. For counsel in the later I would like to thank John, Phil and Bob. And in a most general but vital way, I would also like to thank Mike for his support, Laura Z. for her emotional and spiritual comfort, and Samantha and Brandon Bernardy for their timely assistance, and The Rhino for being there at key times.

Oops, I surely can't forget my two children, Jack and Emma, for being there to make the very unreasonable most reasonable.

Contents

Preface

Each one of these twelve stories is based on an actual event. The event was either one in which I was a participant, and therefore was a first-hand witness to the unfolding; if not an actual participant, then the event was related to me personally by a highly reliable source. I have attempted to keep as close to the actual event as possible, letting the straightforward development of the occurrence deliver its meaning. If that meaning is typically outspoken rather than tangled in a morass of symbolism I think that is a symptom of the source, a frank and even blunt view of the world, and not a graceless lack of subtlety. Given those parameters, I believe that these stories certainly qualify as working class literature in the most authentic of senses, and I hope they are a contribution to an important genre that lacks serious representation.

W.F. Pray

Reno, NV, 2015

Queenie Tank

I had never been arrested, or ever found myself needing a cop. All that changed the evening before my twenty-fifth birthday, and that wasn't the worst of what went down that day.

"You know, Ace," L.T. Grimes was saying. "I gotta find the time."

"For what?" I asked.

Grimes grew quiet, frowning, gazing across the hood of the Freightliner at the sun baked Arizona highway rolling endlessly on ahead. He finally answered, "You know who I mean—Lucy."

I glanced at Grimes. He had turned off the air conditioning, rolled the window down, then jacked out the wind-wing. Maybe L.T. liked to sweat. The hot, dry desert air was blowing across his face, making his short hair bend back in a kind of nervous dance.

"Yeah, you know," he said more to himself than me. "I can't seem to stop thinking about her. But you know, I never made the funeral and I never visited the cemetery. Christ, I was always working."

I watched Grimes for a moment, watched him swipe at a thin rivulet of sweat trickling down in front of his ear. I had heard this before.

L.T. was speaking about his daughter, who had died of leukemia when she was around fourteen. That had to have been eighteen or twenty years before—way before I knew him. There were two pictures of the girl pinned to the driver's side visor. They were reasonably clear middle-school photos of a girl of twelve or thirteen, reddish hair, freckles, round face. There was nothing very remarkable about the girl, just an uncertain pretty face of common enough appearance. She meant nothing to me, of course, but when Grimes brought her up I listened respectfully, if mechanically.

L.T. shook himself. "There's something big about the way my life worked out. It got all messed up somewhere."

I was team-driving with L.T. and had been the guy's co-driver for the better part of a year. We got along okay—not real great, but well enough, which was crucial when living twenty-four-seven in the close quarters of a line truck's cab where the only place to get away from each other was the sleeper berth, and that only separates the two of you by a padded canvas curtain.

"I don't know, Ace," he went on. "I was never really there for her. I was always working. I wish I had known her better. The only thing I know for sure is that I was a disappointment for her." He laughed to himself, but without any joy. "But there's no do-overs in life, is there? Gotta get it right the first time."

L.T. Grimes was a big man, thick in the neck, with a face made of features that looked to be pushed together in a hurry. He had a real broad back, sloping shoulders, and arms that stretched the seams of his dirty t-shirt. Back in his early years, L.T. had played left tackle for a team up in the Canadian league. Now in his fifties, L.T. slouched, round shouldered when he walked or sat in the driver's seat. Despite being thickly muscled, L.T. looked old, and because of his bent size, twisted nose, and heavy lips, he was a thoroughly disagreeable looking guy.

"Yeah, Ace, all my life things seemed to go wrong . . . You know. My marriage to Lucy's mom? I do shit—things on impulse. Jesus I got married four times and I'm only fifty four. I don't know why I do shit. But Lucy came out of that one and it was the best thing that ever happened to me, only I didn't know it until she was gone. Why'd it happen that way? Why'd she have to die before I even got to know her? Nothing lasts, nothing makes any sense."

L.T. glanced over at me with a look that suggested he was surprised to me sitting there watching him.

"Sorry," he apologized, looking again at the highway. "I talk too much, Ace. Can't help it, I guess. It's like I naturally do shit I can't help. Don't know why." He switched hands on the steering wheel and thought for a moment. "I try to do right but mostly it seems to go wrong."

L.T. turned back and gave me a quick grin. He had a small gap in his front teeth that gave him a little-boy look. "Sorry, Ace," he apologized again. "I'm still talking too much."

I had no way to reply to L.T. He was right. He often rambled like that, talking to himself. I watched him give his shoulders a little shake. Except for the hiss of the tires and the wind blowing through the open window the cab got quiet again. I liked L.T. and liked to think that I understood L.T. about as well as I understood anybody, which at the end of the day meant I didn't understand him at all. It must be that I try too hard to understand rather than let the understanding happen.

"Hell," L.T. suddenly popped off. "Let's celebrate your birthday, Ace. You up for a burger?" He smacked his thick lips and glanced at me. "I know I can sure use one?" He slammed his hand down on the steering wheel. "Damn, Ace, twenty-five. Boy do I wish I was twenty-five again, except shit," and he laughed. "I'd probably make the same mistakes all over again."

We were both tired and the road ahead was growing dim, the sun passing behind the mountains west of Tucson. Except to change-over in El Paso, we hadn't stopped since Sweetwater. Grimes, his night vision going bad on him, had done the bulk of the daytime driving. Given that we were several hours ahead of schedule, a stop looked good to me before my turn at the wheel.

"Yeah," I answered. "I can stand to eat."

"We'll stop near the Air Force base just east of Tucson. I know a place."

L.T. was a drinker who knew lots of places everywhere. This stop in Tucson meant that L.T. was going to get a little more than shit-faced, then pile into in the sleeper behind the driver seat. It was my turn to drive anyway, so I wasn't put out by driving most of the rest of the way into L.A. No matter what, L.T. never laid off his work on me. Drunk or sober, I'd always found L.T. to be a stand-up guy. Of course, the company would fire L.T. if they found him drinking on the payroll, but I didn't mind covering for him. L.T. was who he was, and I am who I am, and we scratched each other's back accordingly.

"Yeah," L.T. repeated. "I know a great place."

That was how we got to the Horney Toad Saloon.

L.T. swung the rig into the lot next to the Toad and pulled around behind. He killed the engine and we got down from the cab, stamped our feet in the desert dust to get them awake, then stretched the kinks out of our backs and just stood for a moment in the warm late afternoon sunlight.

There were eight or ten chopped Harley hogs outside of the entrance, all shiny and polished. The bikes were not just flashy, but tricked-out gang style. Back in those days the biker gangs weren't the genteel riding clubs of retired business gents like they got to be later on. In those days chopped hogs meant Hell's Angels, the Mongols, Satan's Slaves, and other assorted drug dealing, extorting, strong arm criminal types just one step out of the jail house.

Inside the Toad it was dark and cool, and smelled vaguely of motor oil and stale beer. I stopped just to the right of the door and let my eyes adjust to the low light. I saw L.T.'s white t-shirt as he headed down the bar and was following him when I felt that kind of itch you get when eyeballs rake over your back. It made me turn and squint into a dark corner. I could make out six or eight bikers and a couple of women, all lounging in booths around a pool table. Their faces were shadowy and blurry, ranging out of the light cast from the lamp that hung over the green felt of the table. Even so, I knew they were unsmilingly taking our measure.

L.T. had bellied up to the bar and was quickly sucking down some suds and nodding appreciatively to the barmaid when she set down the quarter-glass of George Dickel, straight-up—L.T.'s poison of choice.

I pulled out a stool next to L.T. and waved at the barmaid for a 7-Up and a burger. One of us had to stay sober.

"Yeah, for both burgers and drinks," L.T. added and dropped small wad of cash in front of him. "All on me, Ace. Happy birthday!"

I watched the swing of her hips as the barmaid walked to the window opening onto the kitchen, then took a closer look around the place.

The interior of the Toad was lit by a row of soft lights behind a soffit running around the upper walls and a blue ceiling skylight, angled so that the frosted late sunlight cast a glow on a nearby

Moved

flanking wall that hid a jukebox and a dartboard. The pool table behind us was dim and, the players moving in and out of the shadows. Rather than cheerful and inviting the mood of the place was quietly depressing.

The barmaid brought us our burgers, and I carefully lifted my bun, examining what was under it. Not L.T. He leaped on his burger like he hadn't eaten in a month. I watched him take two big chomps and a swallow of George Dickel. I picked up mine, took a small bite and watched the action in the mirror behind the bar.

The several men and the two women around the pool table were dressed in that biker way—all denim and leather that was neither stylish or expensive, but looked like something worn till it would dissolve off the wearer in a hard rain. A couple of the men seemed to be watching us.

A second 7-Up was set on the bar in front of me and I looked again at the barmaid. She smiled at me, and winked.

"He said another round," she said, and nodded at L.T. "Don't get drunk, sweetie."

When she walked away I watched her swinging hips again. L.T. was busy finishing his whiskey and didn't notice the man coming up behind him.

"Hey, dude, you want to part with that money?"

Both L.T. and I glanced in the direction of the voice. One of the bikers was standing a few feet away from us, leaning on a pool cue. He was looking at L.T. He was thin, dark, hampered in looks by a sharp weasel-face and long, black hair braided coolie-style hanging over his shoulder.

Grimes half turned to the biker. "What's up, Ace?"

"You want to shoot some pool for a few of those?" The biker nodded at the several big bills on the bar in from of Grimes. One of them was a fifty. "Just to pass the time."

I couldn't see L.T.'s face, but I heard him say, "We just got here, Ace."

The biker did not move or lower his gaze. "Why not knock that burger back and grab a cue, maybe take some of my money."

L.T. was still turned away from me so I still couldn't see his expression. "Maybe in a sec, Ace."

The biker turned to me: "You shoot pool?"

Instead of replying I waved my uneaten burger at him.

The biker looked back at Grimes. "I guess it's just you, dude"

"Yeah," L.T. answered, shrugged and shoved the last of the burger in his mouth. "Sure, Ace."

"Then let's go."

L.T. got off the stool, kicked back the last of the whisky, then scooped up the bills on the bar with one hand and grabbed the beer with the other.

"What's your name, man?" the biker wanted to know as they walked away.

"Grimes."

"Okay, Grimes. I'm Angel."

"Call me L.T."

"Okay, L.T., call me Angel."

That name, Angel, and the biker's ugly, pockmarked face struggled in a vicious contest for control, with the face winning by a knock-out; the pointed, harsh features and neck had too many scars and jailhouse tattoos to ever present a saintly picture. Angel looked as though he had skipped his childhood and joyfully gone straight into low-life adulthood.

The two of them walked toward the pool table and the sea of denim and leather rolled apart to let them through. I turned back around, eyeing the barmaid over my burger. She was leaning against the register, watching Grimes and the bikers at the pool table. Her expression was flat, except for the tight little line of her lips. She looked as though she had bitten into something sour, or maybe she was seeing something I couldn't.

She sensed me looking at her and flicked her eyes in my direction. "I sure hope no trouble starts," she said. "Those bikers can be trouble and except for the cook, I'm here alone, and that skinny bastard ain't worth shit. He'll run like a rabbit."

I don't know if it was the tenor of the voices or the long silences between speech and the click of the balls, but when I was almost all the way through the burger my scalp started to tingle and pull at my ears, making the little hairs on the back of my neck stand up. I turned around on the stool.

Grimes was standing next to the table, his pool cue butt on the floor, him sort of half leaning on it, facing Angel. Grimes was tall enough that his head was out of the light from the table so I couldn't see his expression. Angel I could see, and he was plenty agitated. His body language made me lower my glass of 7-Up and get half off the bar stool.

"*Fuck*," I heard the barmaid hiss. "I really don't need this horseshit."

No one seemed to move, but quicker than hell L.T. got blind-sided from behind with a cue that broke against his neck and shoulder. L.T. was big enough that it was hard for anyone shorter to fully connect with this head, so the cue stick did little damage, and if L.T. felt the wallop, he ignored it and stepped forward, plunging his fist into Angel's face with a crack of bone that yelped against my eardrum. Angel went down hard and all hell broke loose. Two guys and one woman jumped on Grimes and he rolled around the pool table holding them up, all a tangle of pumping fists and scratching nails. L.T. was grabbing one biker by his long hair and at the same time trying to punch another greasy character who danced just out of reach. Several bikers were on their feet waving pool cues at Grimes while he struggled to dislodge the woman hanging like a monkey on his back.

The barmaid cut loose a gargle of half screams and half profanity, and raced for the phone on the far end of the bar. Me? I took half dozen steps forward to help L.T. and ran into a beer glass that came out of nowhere. It shattered against my cheekbone and eye. I flopped to the floor in a daze, blood and pain filling my eye, the roar of voices, breaking glass, and splintering wood rocking my head. I couldn't see anything through the blood. I covered my head, scared that my eye was gone, and crawled back toward the bar, hiding from sounds that were wild and confused.

I don't know where they came from, but in a matter of minutes it seemed like there must have been a hundred Pima County Deputies swarming into the place. I hunched over the bar and with my one good eye I saw the barmaid pointing a snaking finger my way and shrieking: "That's one of them! That's him . . . !" leaving me to wonder just what the hell she was screaming about. I was one of *who?* A couple of deputies snatched me off the stool and hand-cuffed me, leaving me to feel both confused and at the same time, rescued.

The emergency room stitched up my cheek, pronounced my eye good, and I was booked on assault and disorderly conduct, public drunkenness, disturbing the peace, and a couple other charges, but I had stopped listening. I asked the booking deputy if I could just pay a fine and he gave me the kind of look that flatly stated that if he got one more smart-ass in here today, he was going to quit, only not before he shot the prick.

Back in those days the Tucson lockup was a two-story, cinder-block and stucco structure that looked to have been built during the construction boom just after World War Two. It was loud and noisy, gray and damp and rank with the stink of an endless stream of human flotsam passing through. I was marched down a row of cells on the bottom tier and turned into the third cage. The first thing I noted was that there was only one double bunk, the top already occupied with a skinny guy who looked on me with complete indifference, and a fat man on the bottom who greeted my presence with a frown and a gob of spit flung at the toilet. He missed the toilet, the wad of spittle drooping on the wall by the sink.

There was a wooden stool in the corner next to the commode. I took it, feeling the sullen eyes of my new companions crawling over me. Neither looked like hardened criminals. Just a couple of down-and-outs; a fat middle-aged guy with three days growth of beard and a skinny young kid, pasty white and shallow cheeked, with his left eyebrow half cut away and poorly bandaged. The kid had drugs written all over him. The fat guy just looked like a Saturday night drunk.

The kid tapped his cheek with his finger and asked, "One of the cops clip ya?"

Involuntarily, I reached up and touched the bandage just under my eye. I shook my head. "A beer glass."

The fat guy grinned. "Which bar?"

"The Horney Toad."

The young guy cocked an eyebrow. "Oh, that fucked-up place."

"Yeah," I answered, "That fucked-up place."

"You busted on a drunk?"

"And assault."

"That's it?"

"And some other shit."

"Yeah." The fatso jerked his head at me wisely. "It's all that other shit that'll get ya."

I waited a second, then asked, "How long's it gonna take for me to get offered bail, or a fine, or whatever it takes to get out of here?"

The skinny kid on the top bunk replied, "Tomorrow, maybe. They'll take us all to the court room tomorrow." He seemed confident, sounding like an old experienced hand. "The judge is a Mex. An easy enough guy. A local. You local?"

"No. I'm a long haul line driver. My partner got arrested too."

Fatso got up and went to the commode next to where I was sitting. He bent down close enough for me to smell his stinking breath hissing between his thick lips. He plucked some toilet paper off the roll sitting on the floor.

He looked me over careful-like while folding the toilet paper. "If the judge hasn't never seen you before . . . . " He inhaled deep and blew his nose. "He'll for sure go light on you." He used the same paper to wipe his spittle off the wall and tossed the whole mess into the steel commode. "Me, I'll get ten days."

I didn't ask Fatso what the ten days was for, only watched him wipe the residue of snot from his nose onto his sleeve while he walked over to the open cell door to look outside.

He turned to me. "If you want to look for your pal, now's the time. The deputies'll leave the cell doors open until nine. They don't care if you walk around. So go look for him, if you want." He grinned, showing a missing front tooth. "Don't worry. We'll save your seat."

The Tucson lock-up had twenty-four cells, ten on the upper tier and fourteen below. After a quick search I found L.T. on the top tier, in a cell near the stairs leading down to where a doorway exited back into the booking room and holding-cells. L.T. was in the cell with three other men, two of them were the bikers who had jumped us in the Toad. One of them was Angel, who showed both eyes swollen nearly shut and turning a shiny blue and green. L.T. must have hit him pretty damn hard, but like old pals the two of them were hunched over a backgammon board when I looked in.

I leaned against the door of the cell and L.T. rolled his eyes at me. "What say, Ace? What'd you get booked on?" I could see the sweat glistening through his short, dark hair. It was hot in the cell house, and hotter still on the top tier. The temperature had to be spiking up into the mid-nineties.

I told L.T. the list of charges against me.

L.T. picked up the dice and tossed them. "Same as me, Ace." He squinted at the dice, counting. "We'll be out tomorrow," he added, and moved the chips on the board. "I got your fine covered, Ace. Don't worry about it. It's your birthday present."

I watched the two of them play backgammon for a few minutes. It looked mighty odd, what with them punching each other goofy just a few hours ago. Angel rolled the dice, cocking his head sideways. He had to work his gaze around the plaster bandage covering the hugely inflated broken nose Grimes had given him. I could see that L.T. had a nasty cut under his chin and his left ear was bandaged. His t-shirt was bloodied. I didn't brother to ask L.T. whose blood. I watched as Angel moved the chips and picked up the dice, handing them to L.T.

"L.T.," I asked. "What the hell started that fight anyway?"

He stopped rattling the dice and looked up at me. "Damn if I can remember," and he looked at Angel. "You remember?"

The biker laughed. "Shit no."

L.T. chuckled along with the biker. "I think you said something about my mother," L.T. started, "and then I said . . . " and suddenly the chuckle froze in his throat, his mouth open, his eyes all agog.

There was a quick, silent shift in the mood of the cell block. For a split second it was as if some wily prison knowing had crept from the gray walls to seize that tiny dead space between blinks, making the whisper of air itself stiffen and gasp, so that even the little shiny dust motes floating in the heat locked up tight in the sunshine. I got a real weighty, creepy feeling as I looked at the expression on Grimes's face. He was standing now, his eyes glued to something behind me, something way down the gangway. I turned my head.

Up the stairs she came—long, lanky, and very blond. There were two deputies walking behind her. One deputy was grinning, full of fun, all small teeth and winks and eye rolls. The other deputy was more deadpan, with only his eyes nasty and narrowed, as if peering at a suspicious turd in a dark corner. Both cops were sweating, the front of their uniform shirts dark around the neck and large half-moons under the arms.

But the tall blonde babe was cool, super cool, her head held high, proud, but not pleased. Her long face was tight, tolerant, controlled, fazed somewhere between irritated and resigned. Platinum hair, shoulder length, pink blouse, too-tight short-shorts, from which sprouted long and graceful legs tapering down into backless, black high heels, clicking a rhythm into the steel floor of the gangway, a tiny tip-tap rhythm that every man in the quiet block could feel poking him deep down in his belly.

Grimes and I had moved back into the cell to let the deputies and the woman prisoner pass, not believing what we were seeing. We weren't alone. Every jaw in that crazy-ass Tucson jail house was dropped open.

From behind me I heard a voice. It was one of the bikers, a guy with the long grizzled hair. "Hey, man," he was talking to Grimes. "You know that sweetheart's a dude, right?"

I didn't understand. "Huh?" I frowned at him.

"The *queen,* man," and he jerked his thumb toward the gangway running in front of the cage. "The bitch in the white shorts . . . she's a tranny . . . I mean, you know, the *bitch* is a *dude.*"

I poked my head out of the cell and looked down the gangway, looking again at the swinging blond hair, tight shorts and smooth, long legs. I blinked and looked back at the biker "You're shitting me. That's a *man?*"

"Well, hell yeah" he laughed. "*Some* kind of man. Got a cock, you know, but works the streets with her ass. A *tranny,* or maybe a CD, or some kinda weird shit. But she's got a dick, otherwise they couldn't put her in here with us animals."

"A dick," I said, mostly to myself, still puzzled.

A man leaning on the rail next to me said knowingly, "Naw, she's a TV, not a cross-dresser. Ya gotta look at the tits. That's some store bought shit there."

I snorted in disbelief and turned my eyes back down the gangway. The cops were looking in several cells, one hanging onto their captive.

"Yeah, a tranny," another guy agreed. "The cops catch the bitches selling their ass down at the bars on East Broadway near the Air Force Base. Give them fly-boys a blowjob in the shitter for a couple of bucks and a jolt of JD."

The biker next to me was grinning nasty now. "Yeah, man! A couple of JDs and who the fuck knows the difference anyway." He backed up laughing, pumping his hands as though he had a fist full of that blond hair, and rocking her head into his crotch. He gave me the best side of his leer. "Kinda gives you a chubby, don't it?"

I couldn't believe it. My eyes went to Grimes, who had also heard the uneasy chaff and banter. He looked at me deadpan, then went to the rail, with Angel standing next to him. An hour ago the two of them were scrapping. Now it was like they were joined at the hip, pals for life.

Looking at my fat cellmate, who must have come up the stairs behind me, L.T. asked, "But they let her in here?" Then spat out,

"What the fuck's the matter with 'em? She'll get killed in this zoo."

Fatso laughed. "Oh, yeah, man, they got a queenie tank in the next building—a kind of protective custody for the trannys, the queers and the weird-o's. But sometimes the deputies like a little fun." He winked. "You know how it is, being bored shitless and all. So they toss the queens in the pit with us fuck'n savages."

The biker next to me added: "Yeah, man, a little red meat for the lions—if you know what I mean." He laughed, but not convincingly. "*This* is the queenie tank tonight!"

Grimes glowered at him. "That's fucked up, Ace."

"Yeah, it sure is, man," he replied. "Way fucked-up."

I watched as one of the two deputies spoke to someone inside the last cage at the end of the gangway. They turned the tranny loose and push her through the opening. They said something to whoever was in the next cell, then turned away, coming back down the gangway toward us. Everyone parted to give them room.

"Man, I'm gonna be hating this shit, dude." Angel said it to no one in particular, then turned to L.T. "This is way fucked, dude," he said. "That bitch is gonna be screaming all night long with what's gonna happen to her down there. We won't get any sleep at all. I seen plenty of dumb-ass shit like this before."

L.T. found something in his mouth he didn't like and as the deputies approached ducked his head, spitting it out. I didn't like his movement or the expression on his face. He suddenly looked up and stepped deliberately in front of the first deputy.

"Hey, you can't put her in here," he snapped. "She'll get wasted down there."

"Yeah," the deputy replied. "Well, the she's a he, buster, and he chose his lifestyle, so let him enjoy it."

L.T. planted his face about six inches from the deputy's. He was a half a head taller than the deputy, who was clearly startled.

15

"Yeah, well he didn't choose this shithole," L.T. snarled. "You did, *buster*."

Both officers had stopped, halted by L.T. looming large in their path. The deputy in front was momentarily dumbstruck. The deputy behind him was quicker. He pushed around his partner and stuck his baton in L.T.'s chest. "Back fucking up, asshole!"

Grimes stood rooted to the spot. "Get that bitch outta here."

"What the hell's it to you?" The deputy pressed Grimes with his baton. "Get back in your cell!"

Grimes got a real ugly twist to his face. "Yeah, well, kiss my fuck'n ass!"

"Yeah, for Christ's sake," Angel unexpectedly seconded Grimes. "Get the bitch out of here before they fuck her up down there."

Now suddenly confronted by two inmates in his face, the deputy shoved L.T. harder with the point of the nightstick. L.T. reflexively knocked the club aside and everything after that went down so fast my eye followed it faster than my mind could record it.

In hindsight, and in the calm of a smoky interview room, this is what I told the investigators: it seemed that after Grimes knocked the club out of his chest the deputy raised the baton to strike L.T., which caused Grimes to quick straight-punch the officer in his face. It was a reflex move that rocked the deputy back into his partner, stumbling both of them to the ground. The sight of the two sprawled uniforms emptied the cells, bringing men onto the gangway, and filled the air with cheers, jeers, hoots and laughter. More humiliated than hurt, both deputies were up and plenty pissed, blood streaming from one of the officer's face. They quickly moved on L.T. and Angel, both swinging their truncheons wildly at them and anyone standing near them.

Along with a half dozen other detainees, I back pedaled into the cell behind me. Not the bikers. Nearly all those from the Horney

Toad who had jumped L.T. were now all in with him, piling on the two officers in a mass of fists and boots. A half dozen deputies quickly responded, rushing into the block, clubs swinging, bringing nearly the entire cell block into a full melee of shouts, punches and stomping feet.

The immediate aftermath was both predictable and fierce. With truncheons, blackjacks, and mace, it took maybe twenty minutes to subdue and arrest nine detainees, including L.T. Grimes. I didn't see him after he was led out of the block in handcuffs. He and the other jail inmates involved in the scuffle ("riot" as it was identified by the Pima County Sherriff's office) were moved by bus to another facility up in Phoenix. The next day I was fined and released. There was no way to reach Grimes and I had to get the rig and load to LA as a solo driver. After that the company fired Grimes and got me a run to San Francisco where I changed rigs and was hooked-up in a team for a long pull to Chicago and on to Syracuse. It took me a couple of weeks to find out what had become of L.T.

Grimes had been arraigned, tried and sentenced, on two or three counts, to eighteen months in a medium security prison in Maricopa County, just a little way outside of Phoenix. It took me the better part of six months to get back to Arizona long enough to pay him a visit. Back then, prison visitors in a medium security lockup were separated from the prisoner only by a table with a little rail running along the top, with a couple of guards looking on. I was able to shake hands with L.T. and give him the only thing I had that might be of value to him: the two pictures of his daughter.

"Oh, man," Grimes said to me, a half frown, half smile mingling his features. "You kept these." He gazed at them for a long moment, then looked up at me. "Thanks . . . these pictures of Lucy mean a lot to me. Thanks, Ace. I really appreciate it."

We spoke for a few more minutes about the driving work, recent changes at the company Grimes had worked for, about the conditions he was living under, about the bad food, the security at the prison, the small farm worked by the prisoners, some friends L.T. had made at the facility, and the weird and sometimes utterly zany behavior of those inmates who were obviously mentally ill.

Then, out of the blue, L.T. suddenly said, "Lucy, you know, I never liked that name much. I would have preferred Madeline, but I was never around to name her. I was always working." He added as though to no one in particular, "What do you think?"

I raised my hands helplessly. I had no idea what he wanted me to suggest.

L.T. was quiet for a long time, clutching the pictures and staring down at them. He was silent for so long that I was beginning to think I should leave when he looked up.

"But you know what, Ace?" he suddenly said in an upbeat tone, "After the shit went down in there they moved that tranny out of general and into the next building—she got the queenie tank. The shit went to shit, but I saved her ass."

The unexpected change of subject caught me off guard.

"What?"

"Hey—why I'm in here, Ace. The tranny." L.T. chuckled. "You remember why I'm in here, right?"

"Yeah." I caught up with him. "The tranny."

"They moved her to the queenie tank."

"That's something."

"I guess I made her day, huh?"

"I guess."

"Hell," he chuckled again. "I just might have saved her life."

"Yeah, maybe." I remembered the nastiness in the cell block. "Might have, L.T."

"And for a stranger and a weird-o to boot."

My only response was to nod my head.

"Now, Ace, ain't all that some pretty shit?"

I tried to smile. "Yeah."

"I was on autopilot, you know—when I hit that deputy. Just reflex, Ace, just instinct. Couldn't stop myself. I told you, I don't think. I just do shit. You understand?"

I nodded.

"I shoulda just gone back into the cell and looked out the window at the trees and the birdies, and minded my own damn business." L.T. wiggled his eyebrows, getting an icy half smile at the corners of his mouth. "But that's me, right? Always sticking my foot in the shit." He laughed. "I must be some kind of shit magnet."

I waited, saying nothing, and L.T. finally looked up at me hard, serious, frowning. "Don't come back here, okay," and he stood up, sticking out his hand. "Thanks for coming, Ace, I mean it, and thanks for these, but I don't want you to come back here, you know?"

I slowly took his hand, not sure what to say.

"You remind me of stuff, Ace, and it bothers me."

I dropped his hand, feeling sorry, only not sure for what.

L.T. signaled the guard, winked at me. "My life's a mess, Ace, but you know what?"

I shook my head.

He suddenly flashed a smile at me—big, the gap in his front teeth making him look fresh, young again. "You know what I really gotta do when I get out of here?"

I waited while the guard took his arm.

"I gotta get to the cemetery to visit her—Lucy. I think she'd really like to know that I'd visit her now and then. I'll make time, you know, I just don't want to disappoint her anymore."

The gap-toothed grin broadened as the guard started to pull him away. "And you know, Ace, this ain't just impulse. Not this time. I thought about it and I made myself a promise to her. I never told her that I loved her, not once, so I gotta do it better this time, Ace, and if I do, I know things'll turn out right for us."

Cannonball

Near to the eastern end of Gallup there was a filling station that was owned by an old guy named Chester Potts. Chester was a good friend to all us kids and would let me and my brothers, Tim and Andy, loaf in the shade of the station's overhang, sipping Cokes and watching the big rigs roar past on Old Highway 66. From out of the desert the great machines would streak, slowing in dark belches from air brakes, their engines straining, hulks looming with power and purpose. They would chafe at the timid city speeds, then lumber on ahead, regaining their flight. One after another they would pass in a stream of determination—the wiry flatbeds, the swollen tankers, the muscular tractor-trailers—with men sitting behind their wheels looking so remote, so aloof and preoccupied, that even when one of us waved, we rarely received so much as a glance of recognition in return.

I can't say that being ignored by them ever bothered us much, as we understood that truckers lived in a world apart. I mean, what with the destiny of the road at their fingertips, they would have little regard for such small-time as us. It seemed to us that they lived way beyond the place of ordinary mortals. My oldest brother, Tim, had patiently explained this to us, and he was the undisputed authority because once, over at Pa's shop, he had seen a real truck driver up close. Our Pa was a welder, and had a place up the street, around back behind Chester's station. One night, he kept Tim with him until the shop closed, which was about seven. The way Tim would tell it, he was perched on top of a stool at the workbench, busy scraping soot and carbon build-up from some tools, when he and Pa heard this rig pull up in the street beside the shop. Then this trucker came and in told Pa he had a trailer with a split seam somewhere. Pa put on his coolie cap, grabbed his mask and his cart with the gas cylinders, and started outside, with Tim right behind. All the time Pa was working, Tim was watching that trucker. He was trying to memorize every little detail, he said, so he could tell us about it later.

"He was big," Tim would say, "bigger even than Pa, and he walks like this," and Tim would strut up and down with a cocky swagger. "And he wore a red cowboy shirt and cowboy boots, and he smiled out of the corner of his mouth," and Tim would show us a tough, confident looking, and slightly crooked grin. Tim had even managed to get up the courage to ask that trucker where he was headed, and the trucker had answered him, "Baton Rouge"—which had a far away, mysterious and magical ring to it, and it might as well have been Mars, for all we knew of the world.

I guess there is nothing unusual about boys taking to the simple signs of manhood and power, so when Tim announced his decision to become a trucker, Andy and I not only glowed with understanding, we promptly seconded the idea. Just to imagine what it must be like to be in command of all that roaring steel and rubber made my head swell. To us, that the men and their machines never stopped, never tired, never got lost, that they just kept on going, on and on, straight into the night, and on into the next day, so that catching up with them would have been reaching for a fistful of next week. Those men had a real big edge on life—or so it seemed to us.

"King of the road," Tim would shout. "I'm going to be king of the road"—which was also the name of a café just down the highway from Chester's station, where the parking lot was always jammed with rigs. It got to be so that whenever Andy and I could not find Tim, we knew right where to look. Down at King Of The Road Café our big brother would be snooping around the rigs or peeking in through the glass of the café's front window, anxious for the day he could get that special license and join a meaningful way of life.

It didn't take long before we started to dress up like we saw the truck drivers doing. We each had one cowboy shirt and would wear it until our Ma would snip at us that it would turn into a rag on our backs, but we didn't pay any mind. We'd roll up the cuffs, exposing invisible tattoos, tuck the shirt tails into our jeans, put on the belts with big, shiny buckles, and strut around, just like we'd seen them do. I found out some time later that truckers mostly walked the way they did because of bad backs, or hemorrhoids, or some other ailment hammered into their bodies by the endless, jolting miles of asphalt, but at the time we were positive that they swaggered the way they did because they were tough and they knew it.

The years went by pretty quickly and Tim and Andy, because they were so much older than me, began to take on a change. They started wanting to be off by themselves and didn't want me around. Sometimes I'd force it and tag along, only to feel useless and rejected and sore as hell about it. Their behavior seemed so mysterious that I began sneaking around, spying on them. I'd stand in the shadows of the hall and watch as they'd swish Pa's bristle brush in the soap cup and spread the foam over their fuzzy cheeks. I saw the way they were trying to let their sideburns grow, and how they'd both bought cowboy boots. When they'd go off by themselves I'd run down the side of the highway and for sure catch them at the King of the Road Café. Of course, if they spotted me, they would only tell me to beat it, so I never let on that I was there, but just pressed my face to the window and watched them sitting like big shots at the counter, drinking coffee and jawing with the truckers. Their rejection made me so angry that I broke one of our strictest rules and told Pa, but Pa only glanced sideways at me and said, "coffee's better than whiskey, and there's worse folks than truck drivers"—which is when I realized something had really changed. Tim and Andy must be for certain grown up, if Pa was behaving that way, letting them get away with how they was acting. There seemed to be no recourse now but to learn to live with my new brothers.

One night, about the time it was my turn to try shaving, Ma sent me around to the public library to get a world atlas. After dinner we all scrunched around the table and looked for a place called Korea. It was just a little finger of land and didn't look very special at all, but Pa said that if Harry Truman thought it was important enough to fight for, then it must be important. My Pa liked Truman a lot and used to say that he was more of a regular guy than Roosevelt, but he liked Roosevelt plenty too. Pa used to say that you could always count on Roosevelt to be on the side of the working man, but even so, Pa still liked Truman better. Pa said Truman was more of an old fashion Democrat.

SPACE

Ma didn't say anything about Korea or Truman or anything else, only watched us in a kind of funny way. I could see she didn't like all the talk about fighting. The next day, she sent me back to the library with the atlas and never brought it up again. She made out that it was the end of it, but I could see by the set of her mouth that she was worried. I couldn't see what about until a couple months later when Tim got called up by the draft board—and around four months after that Andy was called up too.

If Ma had been tight lipped about it, my brothers were both pretty excited—especially Tim. He had said he was going to volunteer for the motor pool and let the army teach him truck driving. Suddenly, the war made real sense to me and I started gnashing my teeth. I was chock full of anger and jealousy. I wanted to go off to the army with them and learn to drive a truck. I hoped with all my might that the war in Korea would last that long, at least. Being forever left behind was looking like my dismal lot in life.

Pa never said very much about their leaving, except on the day we took them over to the bus depot. He told them to do like they were told, and not give anyone any trouble, try not to get hurt, and if they didn't write Ma he was going to whip 'em good. When the bus pulled out of the station, and Pa and me climbed back into the old pickup, he looked kind of strange. He seemed oddly pleased with himself. There was a tiny smile on his face that made cool shadows in the hollow of his cheeks. He turned to me as if he was getting ready to say something, only he didn't. He just stared at me for a moment, then started the engine, and we drove home in silence.

When we got home and walked in through the kitchen door, I saw Ma sitting at the table, her face hidden in the quiet dark of the shaded light.

"Ma," I said. 'I want to join up."

"No!"

"I'm old enough, if you or Pa will sign."

"I said, No!"

There was an iron in her voice that cut through me, her eyes brittle bright in the dark. I looked at Pa. He had quickly turned away from her, taken a step back and moved toward the sink, wetting his hands and reaching for a towel. He gave me a certain look he had and I knew not to bring it up with Ma again.

As I remember, Tim came home twice, and Andy only once. Andy had not made the motor pool, but Tim had been more lucky. My big brother sat on the sofa in the living room in his army fatigues and gestured frantically, showing us how it was to shift a five-by-three.[1] He gave a selfless promise to teach Andy and me to drive a truck, and we all three would head to Amarillo where there were more truck driving jobs than any other place in the country. He laughed and said that we might even meet up at King of the Road Café on our way through to our different destinations. We'd have coffee and look out for kids who wanted to live a life on the road. Maybe us old hands would even offer them a piece of advice about truck driving.

The fighting in Korea fast became old news. It went on and on; the reports were confusing and sometimes contradictory. It was hard to tell who was winning. I was in my second year of high school and working in a shop that built lawn furniture, which struck me as being stupid—I mean building lawn chairs in the middle of a war. One night, when I got home late, the place was real quiet. I squeaked open the screen door to the kitchen and

---

1. A five-by-three was a five gear main shifter, with a three gear auxiliary shifter. They were configured as two floor shifters, the main being the taller shifter of the two; this gave the truck fifteen forward gears and three reverse. This was a popular system until the 1960s when simpler shifting systems were developed.

stopped. Pa was sitting in the dark, alone at the kitchen table. Something told me not to turn on the light. I stood frozen in the doorway, staring ~~that~~ the dark shape of the coffee mug he held in his big, hard hands. ~AT

After an agonizing moment he lifted his head and said, "Your brother... Tim's dead."

At first I was sure I hadn't heard him right. I thought he had taken me for somebody else and was trying to make some sort of joke. I even went through the silly motion of looking over my shoulder to make sure no one was standing behind me laughing.

Only it was true, even if I would not believe it until the day Tim's body came home, and I looked into that casket. What I saw wasn't my brother. I mean, I knew inside my head what my eyes were telling me, but it wasn't him either. I suddenly felt giddy. The great ugly casket, all these people, the preacher with his face sweated from the heat inside the little church made me feel somehow on trial. There was something wrong and only I knew what it was. Tim wasn't there. Tim was out hiding somewhere having a good laugh at all these stupid people. My lips twisted with this silly little smile coming onto my mouth, and I turned my head and looked at Pa. I wanted him to glance back and wink, the way he did when he'd started some mischief. He didn't. His face was cold, austere and remote, looking like a second corpse in that church that day, and I realized then how much I loved Pa and didn't want to lose him.

Andy never made it for the funeral. We found out the day before Tim's body arrived that the army had reported him AWOL; then, a few days after Tim's funeral, we got a telegram that he was missing in action, and finally, about three weeks after we buried Tim, two soldiers came up to the house and told us that, like Tim, Andy was killed in action. The force of the second shock drove Ma to the brink of losing her mind. She would stay in bed all day, refuse to eat, and would break into long, racking sobs that would rattle the windows and tear through the house with a sorrow that would freeze you to the bone. At last, Pa and I had to take her to a hospital up in Albuquerque where she stayed for almost two months. She came around after that and gave every outward sign of having put it behind her completely and everyone, with a sigh, was careful not to bring it up again, but I'd catch her every now and then staring at me, tears coming into her eyes, and I'd get scared and wouldn't know what to do.

Tim and Andy getting killed had hurt us all, but not the way it had hurt Pa. I could see it eating at him month after month, twisting him into a tired and cynical old man. He spoke less, and in a way seemed more patient with me, calm and ready to listen, but it was all with ice burning behind his eyes. Sometimes I would glance at him working, hunched over his bench, look at his face when I knew he could not feel me watching. The skin of his cheeks was getting loose, and his shoulders seemed smaller, like he was being drained of his weight. There was hollowness to the ice in his eyes. The old Pa was still alive, but I only saw him once.

We had taken the pickup and were headed out to charge up three or four of his oxygen cylinders for the welding equipment. We had just made the stop alongside the filling station when Chester Potts leaped out of his chair and came bowling over toward us, hopping on his good leg and waving a newspaper in his hand.

"Hey, Farley," he shouted at Pa, "have you heard, Farley? That war's over—*That goddamn war's over.*"

My eyes were instinctively drawn to Pa. He sat there rock quiet in the driver's seat, gaping queerly at old Chester, watching him cover the last, short distance to the truck. The suddenly his head fell forward, cracking against the steering wheel with a deadening

THEN

28

thud. I caught my breath, sure he had died. I wanted to reach out to touch his arm, only I was too frightened to move. Then Pa's shoulders began to twitch, quaking in little snaps, and a heavy moan tore out of his chest, followed by another, and suddenly he popped upright, his face dark and filled with violence, his eyes bugging out with revenge and hate. He snatched at the steering wheel with both hands and shook it, swinging it, pulling at it with all his force, as though he wanted to rip it out of the truck, and all the while growling and snarling like a wolf caught in a trap, knuckles white, eyes bulging, spittle dripping off his lips.

God only knew what old Chester must have thought when he reached the side of the pickup and saw the two of us—me blubbering and Pa trying to tear the steering wheel out by the roots. I recall Chester mumbling something like, "Thought you'd want to know, Farley—Sorry," and seeing him shuffle back across the street to his gas station, his head drooping, the newspaper hanging sadly alongside his leg.

Pa died about a year later, just after I graduated from high school. A couple days after the funeral, I forced myself down to the welding shop to shift through the tired husk of his living. It was a mismatched museum, from old, grease stained Batman comic books to a woman's panties. The panties I held up to the light. The crotch had been burned out—with a welding torch most likely. I shivered and shook my head, realizing that there was a lot to my Pa I didn't know.

In his desk I began to turn up half started letters—hardly begun. I found a few others in a foot locker, and two in his tool chest. They all had a date at the top, an address heading, and *Dear Mr. Senator,* or *Dear Mister President,* with the rest of the page left blank. I found over twenty in all, written over the past two years, mostly during the winter, it looked like. Just the greeting and that was all. In a couple I could see where the pen had been pressed to the paper below the greeting, as though Pa had opened his mouth to speak, only nothing came out. He could not find the words or had been seized by a sudden helplessness. I stacked the letters all together and set the pile aside.

After I had finished in the shop, and was about to turn off the lights, I remembered the letters. I stared out at the street for a long moment and finally picked them up, though I had not the slightest idea what I was going to do with them. I locked up and walked down the street to Chester's filling station. Chester was pushing a broom around the front of the station when I showed him the letters. He set the broom aside and sat heavily in the chair outside the office, beginning to thumb through the sheets of paper. He nodded, then he nodded again, as if he could read some invisible writing on the empty pages.

Chester tuned *[TURNED]* his head in my direction, his narrow, sunburnt face set deep, his thin lips drawn tight together. For a moment I thought he was going to reach out and pat me on the shoulder, only he didn't. Then he sort of stared past me, his lips pressed more tightly, and he nodded one last time at something I couldn't see.

A single sheet slipped from his fingers and was caught by an evening breeze that whipped and tossed it toward the highway. Neither of us made a move to recover it, but only watched it lie by the roadside, fluttered about by the trucks hurtling past as they roared toward the sunset. For just a moment, Tim and Andy were standing there with me, watching the letter get lost in the dust and gusty winds of the highway, where there were only the great machines and their drivers. It startled me to think that me and my brothers had once thought the drivers so awesome and filled with the control of their own destiny, riding a cannonball for a grand and endless string of tomorrows.

Money

"Brian, why you such a paddy boy."

Daniel laughed. "Yeah, fool. How come you gotta be so fucking *white*, man?"

"Come on, paddy boy," Emilio egged me on. "You cool. Don't be afraid. We'll hook you up down at the Mayan and get you with some righteous bitches."

"Home girls, man!" added Daniel.

"Come on, dude. *Muchas bonitias*. Them's righteous bitches, man." Emilio paused to light a cigarette. "And trust me, Brian, they'll tie your little white dick in fucking knots."

I smiled at the good natured harassment from Daniel and Emilio. For a long time now the two of them had been at me, trying to get me downtown to one of Houston's Latin dance clubs, the Mayan. Houston had a huge Latin population, one that was uniquely segregated from the Anglo population. The divide was both social and economic, though by the late eighties the economic gap was showing strong signs of closing. Socially, however, the ethnic split was a different matter.

Maybe it was the era, as things seem a bit looser these days, but back-in-the-day—at least in Texas—the social segregation seemed to be largely by Latin choice and at the time I had little appreciation for the honor these guys were bestowing on me. To them, I was super- *güero*. Not the most flattering term for an Anglo, but accurate, I suppose—tall, slim, blonde, blue eyed. I wouldn't exactly fit right in at the Mayan.

I was raised by my grandfather in Dalhart, about ninety miles north of Amarillo, where Gramps ran a feedlot business. The town of Dalhart had a combined population of around seven thousand, with about ninety-five percent being white; the only Latinos I ever saw were day laborers and ladies who cleaned houses.

Moving to Houston for employment was an eye opener. On the job, Daniel and Emilo worked to pry me loose from my country consciousness. My background had left me unprepared for their quick brightness, their savvy ways and friendly eagerness to expose me to the Latin culture. In the face of their open honesty, my impression of them had quickly gone from a distant and fixed suspicion to affability.

Daniel Molina was a bit older than me and was my dock foreman; a man forceful at times and always straight-ahead with his words. Emilio Estrella was younger than me, just crossing the line of twenty-one, but he was already the lead loader on the swing shift.[2] Both guys had taken a bit of time to warm up to me, but now they seemed determined to give me a shove into the Houston Latin scene. Nervous though I was, tonight I would let myself be pushed into the downtown Mayan Club.

---

2. The swing shift is working hours that generally run from 2:00 pm until 10:00 pm.

The Mayan was a cavern of a place, four floors of throbbing Latin rhythm, all swallowed in an ocean of youth and energy and wrapped up in a stunning display of the latest and brightest fashion. Daniel and Emilio went in before me, pushing through the crowded lobby, laughing and greeting people they knew with hoots and jokes, and it seemed that between the two of them they knew just about everyone in the club. I lost count of the number of times I had been introduced, and was amazed at the fluid ease with which the people around me could switch back and forth between Spanish and English. I spoke little Spanish, a fact that I often regretted—a regret that became especially acute as my eyes tracked the stream of dark, beautiful women gliding softly past me.

Nor could I dance, another long-time regret, so when Emilio and Daniel had been sucked into the press of bumping and pulsating bodies on the huge dance floor, I was left alone, but was just as glad. I was growing exhausted with the introductions, with the rapid mix of Spanish and English, and smiling at all the faces I knew I would never see again. I had driven downtown in my own car and wasn't worried about being left behind at the close of the evening, so I drifted up to the top floor barroom where the view of the dance floor below, awash in sweeping floods of multicolored light, was nothing short of spectacular.

I ordered another beer from the bartender, and was watching the televisions above the bar that put most of the club on close-circuit display, when I felt a slight pressure at my elbow. I turned my head and saw that a small young woman had pushed her way up to the bar and was digging into her miniature handbag. She fussed and rooted, plucking out coins, laying them on the bar top. I knew she had to be at least twenty-one, as the bouncers at the door of the club had even stopped me and Daniel, but she looked younger, and also looked lost, standing there perplexed and cross, picking through her clutch.

She was speaking Spanish to the bartender. I could not follow the rapid exchange, but reading the bartender's face I clearly got the idea that the young woman had ordered drinks and was going to be way short on paying for them. For a moment I watched the knowing and bored expression moving across the bartender's features as he eyed the frantic young woman desperately pushing her fingers around in the tiny handbag. She was finding and dropping more and more small coins on the bar, much to the bartender's irritation.

I'm not sure exactly why—maybe because I felt sorry for the woman, though more likely because she was beautiful—but I pulled out my wallet and laid a twenty dollar bill on the bar, letting the bartender know to take her order out of my money. Startled, the young woman looked up at me and for the first time I saw how truly stunning she was. Slightly squared chin, dimpled with a small clef; full lips glossed with red lipstick, smooth, light brown skin, a gentle aquiline nose, large, dark eyes, now pointed at me in sharp surprise. The whole package was beautifully framed with shiny, raven hair that flowed like velvet curtains down her cheeks to just beyond her shoulders. While her beauty nearly took my breath away, I was a little taken aback by the hard, blank puzzlement that quickly grew around her eyes, followed by an almost involuntary shake of her head: *No*, she wanted to say to the money, but it was too late. The bartender had already snatched the twenty off the bar and gone to mix the drinks.

I was just starting to wonder if she spoke English when she asked, "Why did you do that?" without a trace of an accent.

"Just being polite."

"It's embarrassing."

I smiled. "Why?"

"It just is," and her face flushed. "I wish you hadn't done it."

"It's not a big deal—really."

She gave her head another little shake. "Yes it is," and she said nothing more before turning slightly away, letting the shiny silk hair hide her face.

The bartender returned with the two drinks. Without a 'thank you' the young lady took them and walked away from the bar. I watched her go and gave a little sigh. She was small, beautifully proportioned, dressed in that flashy, colorful and sexy way that seemed such a specialty of young Latin women. I watched until she disappeared into the crowd, shrugged off the loss, then turned back to the TV monitors.

I was just downing the suds at the bottom of my beer and thinking about heading home, when I felt a light tap on the shoulder. It was the embarrassed lady I'd sported to the two drinks. There was an easy smile playing at the corners of her generous mouth.

"I just wanted to thank you for the drinks. It was really nice of you and I didn't want to be rude about it." Her smile became wider and more confident. "I'm not a rude person. So thanks from me and my girlfriend. It was appreciated."

"It was nothing," I responded. "My pleasure. Really. I'm Brian. What's your name?"

"Teresa."

"Great. Well, Teresa, it was a real pleasure, and, please, wait just a second."

On impulse, I pulled the bartender over with a wave of my hand and asked for a pen and paper, on which I quickly jotted my full name and phone number. I handed it to Teresa.

"I'd love it if you'd call."

Teresa glanced at the scrap of paper, worried her lower lip a second and seemed taken aback again. After a moment she looked up at me, her eyes showing that she was pondering one of those womanly things so mysterious to men.

"Maybe," she said softly, almost secretly to herself, then turned away, leaving me full of confidence that the phone number would hit the trash can on her way out the door. I knew from the women I'd seen that I was thought to be attractive, but having been with more than just a few gave me the kind of worldly vision that told me I was never going to hear from this beautiful Latina from the Mayan.

It was a pleasant surprise, then, when about four days later I got home from work and found that Teresa had called. I listened to the message a couple of times, because at first I couldn't place the name, not until I heard the name The Mayan a second time. Her face came back in a rush. I immediately called the number she left. Another woman answered the phone, saying she was Teresa's sister, and Teresa would call me back. This woman sounded older and had a rather heavy accent.

My phone rang a few minutes later. It was Teresa, last name of Zapata, explaining that she did not have a cell phone of her own and piggybacked on her older sister. We chit-chatted for a few minutes, with me going out of my way to offer the basic information men need to deliver to make a woman feel comfortable and safe: where I worked as a warehouse receiving clerk—I was actually more of a loader—where I lived—a secure part of town—where I was from, my high school activities, and so on; like I said, the stuff any man is always obliged to offer before suggesting a rendezvous.

I eventually did ask for a date and received an odd response. Teresa said she was fine with the date, but she was definitely opposed to me picking her up, letting me know that her parents were controlling and strict. She suggested coming to my place and we could go out from there. I agreed, wondering if the fact that I was white could have been an issue with her parents. I brought the issue up at work with Emilio and Daniel.

"Yeah, Brian, you being white definitely might be an issue with the moms and pops," Daniel noted. "And then also you say she's young—maybe twenty-one?"

Emilio chimed in with, "*Órale, esé . . .* that's tender young, and pops is for sure thinking his *hija de dulce* is a virgin and the nasty *gabacho* is out to pop her sweet little cherry. I just know that's what's going on for pops."

"Yeah, and you way older than twenty-one,"Daniel added. "That'll have pops jumpy too."

Emilio chuckled, "Why you got to be such an old *gabacho*, dude?"

I was twenty-six.

"So it's okay for her to come to my apartment?"

"Oh, definitely, man," Daniel answered with a nod and a smile. "Definitely."

"Yeah," seconded Emilio. "You just let her handle *la famila*, and don't ask her any questions about it. Just let her deal with her shit, and just take it as it comes, dude."

Teresa arrived a bit early, acting a little anxious, which I put off to first date jitters. We didn't hang around the apartment long, but went out for dinner and a movie.

The date went smoothly. She was a real chatty-Cathy at dinner and I learned much more about her than the other way around. Teresa worked part time in a clothing store in the downtown Latin section of Houston. As it turned out I had her age about right, having learned that she graduated from high school about three years prior. She said she was thinking about going to community college in the winter, but that there were problems. She was a citizen, and had been a resident of Texas all her life, but money was a serious issue. It was then that I found out she had a two-year-old. Everything she made went to bills and supporting herself, her baby, and whatever was left over went to pitching-in for her family. Bottom line was that she didn't make much and was looking ahead at a difficult future. Teresa laughed and said she was hoping to win the lottery.

At one point during the dinner conversation Teresa looked at me straight in the eye and abruptly said, "Your blonde hair's really nice. I like it. But you shouldn't keep it so short. Let it grow out."

I smiled and cocked an eyebrow at what was for me an unusual complement.

Teresa smiled and nodded, saying almost to herself, "I've never been with a white guy before."

Unsure of what exactly this meant and how to respond, I offered only, "Well, I'm not that much different than Latin guys, am I?"

She squinted a little to show her seriousness. "Yep, you're different, Brian. You talk about different stuff and you listen differently, maybe listen more, and ask more questions." She smiled slyly. "Kinda like a cop."

"Is any of that bad?"

"Not really—just interesting."

"Well, I'm not a cop."

She took a sip of wine, looking at me over the glass. "I know."

"I can get references, if you want. I have a couple of Latin friends."

Teresa made a face, but laughed. "Please, Brian, don't go all racial on me. Latin guys will lie for their homies, even their white homies." She looked at me intently, but there was still humor in her eyes. "I know all about their guy-code, Brian. *Los hombres primero y segundo Latino.* Get real, *mi'jo.*"

I only vaguely understood her meaning. "I'm still okay, then?"

She smiled again, a little curl to her lip, making her look older than her years. "Sure." The intent look was still there.

"You're not nervous?"

"Nope."

"Even about my being white?"

She laughed. "I like you, Brian. You're good looking and you're nice. White's got nothing to do with anything, except to maybe make some things more interesting 'cause they're, you know, new. Let's bail on the movie and go back to your place." She cocked her eyebrow in a funny, knowing way, and asked with a blunt directness, "Unless you don't want to?"

I had a fairly clear idea of what she had in mind, leaving me only a little surprised with her forcefulness and the speed with which events were overtaking even my marginal control of the situation. I decided not to insult her honesty by resisting or asking questions. When women offer gifts they take a risk, and I've always felt men should be highly respectful of both the gift and the risk. I gave up control and decided to roll with the lovely Ms. Zapata in the driver's seat. I was growing increasingly interested in her and enjoying the direct way she was handling the evening.

On the way back to my apartment she produced a joint and lit it up, sucking in the smoke and offering it to me. I took it, looked around for the police, then took a hit.

"You do much *mota*, Brian?"

"No," I rolled down the window a crack and let the smoke ease out into the night air. "No, not much."

She laughed and clapped her hands. "Good. You'll enjoy it more."

"Enjoy 'what' more?"

She laughed again and took back the joint. "Brian, you're funny, but you're a very good looking funny. I think this is going to be fun. Did I tell you that I like your hair?"

"You told me."

"Good," and she sucked again at the joint. "I like you, Brian," she added happily, "You'll see."

I really wasn't exactly sure what "you'll see" meant, but I was starting to like her in-your-face bluntness, and after getting to my apartment I was not surprised when things began to move even faster. I headed into the kitchen to get us a couple of beers, but never made it to the fridge. As small as she was, Teresa backed me up against the sink and pulled me down for a kiss—a deep and hungry kiss. I was again surprised, but not shocked, as I was growing used to her taking over and pressing down hard on the accelerator; then, too, I was more than willing to let the marijuana and her wet mouth move me into the fast lane.

We seemed to push each other into the bedroom. She needed no help getting her clothes off, and showed no shyness about her nakedness. Why should she, as beautiful as she was? I couldn't help ogling her, much to her amusement. Teresa laughed, grabbed me, yanked off my pants and we rolled around on the bed, pulling hair and plunging our tongues deep into each other's mouth. I was more than a little startled, wondering where her seeming bottomless appetite might be coming from. But after a few moments I stopped wondering or caring, swallowed up in the dark smell of her skin, her hair, her breath, all tart and sour sweet with wine and *mota,* those lasting, savory, human, and base urban smells, all swirling in with the tight, hot wetness slipping and squirming beneath me, the smooth softness of the soles of her feet rubbing against my thighs urging me to ride higher on her, and deeper into her, all the while with her strong hands tangled in my hair, pulling, melding me into her, eagerly offering up all of everything that was hers to give.

It was over too fast. It seemed a blink. She lay on top of me kissing me around the eyes and saying things in Spanish I couldn't understand, but the words sounded both gentle and nasty and I felt myself respond. ~reached ✓grabed

Teresa reach down and grab me; she giggled. Then her eyes got a little crinkly at the corners and she lightly bit my lower lip.

"Can I ask you a personal question, Brian?"

"Ah, yeah. I guess so."

Still holding me, she wiggled me playfully. "Are you unusually big for a white guy?"

It took me a split second to get her meaning. "What?—No. I don't think so."

She laughed, patted my cheek, then quickly jumped off of me. "Really? I'd always heard that all you white guys are small."

I frowned, having nothing to say to that.

She laughed. "Lighten up, Brian, I was just messing with you—but I got to go."

"Where?"

She bent down and took my face in her hands. "Home, *cariño*."

"Teresa?"

She kissed my eyes then my nose. "I like you, Brian."

"Then why do you have to go?"

"I have a kid, silly—remember?" She kissed me again on the nose and let her lips brush my eyelids. "I really had a great time, Brian."

"So did I."

Teresa laughed. "I could tell," and then pointed playfully at my crotch. "You got a real fountain there, *mi'jo*."

That sparked me, anxious. "I didn't come too soon?"

"No, *loco*. You were fine—great in fact. I got off real nice." She was still bending over, holding my face, looking intently into my eyes. "I said I liked you, Brian. I don't lie. I mean it. Now, can I use your bathroom—to take a quick shower?"

I brushed her cheek with my fingertips, pushing back the black, silky hair. "Sure," I answered, admiring her full lips. "There's a clean towel under the sink, and there's shampoo in the shower."

"I don't have time to wash my hair. It takes too long to dry," and Teresa stood up and went to the bathroom, pausing at the door, again showing her directness. "I had a great time, Brian. Really. And yes, you were really, really good. Honest. I don't lie."

Smart girl, I thought. How did she know I liked reassurance? Was I alone? Don't all men? Was she that smart—and that bold to say the things even the best of us men need to hear? This woman, this Teresa Zapata, was fascinatingly young to realize so much about men, about the way I was, about the way of the world. She clearly had more self-assurance than I did, was more knowing, and that scared me a little; but it also made me want her more.

Still in the doorway, Teresa hesitated a long moment, deliberately it seemed to me, giving me a last opportunity to take one long look at her. I couldn't get over how gorgeous she was. I let my eyes flow over her body, from her shiny hair to her small feet. Seeing the expression on my face, she smiled, flashing even white teeth. I must have been drooling. She laughed, filling herself with the look I was offering her, then disappeared behind the closed door.

I lay in bed for a moment, listening to the running shower and wondering about her leaving. Teresa was in a hurry and yet wanted to take time to shower before she left. I slowly began to suspect that it was not a baby at home she wanted to get to, but maybe a man also—that she might be living with a man, her husband, or a boyfriend—and I had been a momentary whim, and that she needed to get the smell of me washed off of her body. I wasn't upset about being her whim, I had certainly enjoyed her, perhaps more than she had enjoyed me, but for a moment, laying there, listening to the water run, I felt a pang of anxiety followed by guilt, only I wasn't sure why or for what.

I believed that Teresa had a baby; she had stretch marks here and there, few and beautifully faint around the edge of her belly. I believed too that Teresa had a low paying, dead-end, nowhere job, and that her judgment was not the best, a judgment that was quick, and fed with lust and instinct. It crossed my mind that I might even be proof of that faulty judgment—and just maybe she had a live-in situation that was going nowhere but down—again, as evidenced by me. There was much about Teresa Zapata that I did not know.

On impulse, I got out of the bed, grabbed the wallet out of my pants, and went barefoot into the living room. Her coat and purse were lying across the back of one of the dining room chairs. I pulled most of the bills out of my wallet, neatly folded them, and pushed them into the bottom of the handbag. I didn't know how much it was. It was twenties and tens. It was around sixty or seventy bucks. It sounds goofy, but I wanted her to feel good about me, show her that I could help her, could protect her. I wanted her to know just how much I felt drawn to her, and her way of being smart and sharp, fully possessed of a direct and natural gift for honesty, yet stuck in a dead-end life that was sucking her ahead into an unforgiving future. I felt that I had fully entered Teresa's life and was now partially responsible for her well-being—wasn't I? Aren't responsibility and guilt those most enigmatic of anxieties ghosting all things human, especially our relationships?

I got back into bed just before Teresa came out of the shower. She hurriedly dressed, not looking at me. Almost as an afterthought, she stopped by the bed and gave me a kiss, more affectionate than passionate, then looked at me for a long moment before saying she would call, and was quickly out the door. Feeling a little weird and worried, I glanced at the clock. It was half past twelve. I was feeling deserted and empty and alone. How many women had I left feeling like this?

The next day at work it was late afternoon before I could catch up with Daniel and Emilio. Both of them had been out on the trucks working as swampers[3] and didn't get back to the terminal until just before quitting time.

I hooked up with them in the locker room where they were washing up. I quickly outlined my previous night with Teresa. Both agreed that her wanting to shower before going home was suspicious.

"Yeah, dude," Emilio confirmed. "Your suspicions are probably right-on—sounds like she wanted to get the stank off her before she got home to her old man."

Daniel stopped washing his hands and for a moment gazed thoughtfully at me. "Best be careful, Brian."

"Yeah, dude," Emilio seconded, then added with emphasis, "If you don't know what's up, be extra alert." He looked at me in the mirror. "It sounds like her shit ain't exactly right." He ripped some paper towels from the dispenser. "You got a nice pad, a nice car, a good job—yeah, most sorry-ass bitches would want to hang out, like forever, dude—even if they got a kid at home. Yeah, man, check it out—her shit ain't right."

Daniel shot Emilio an ugly look to silence him. "Lighten up, *ese*," then he turned to me, saying with in a serious tone. "I hate to put this on you, Brian. But go slow—a Latin *vato* is apt to bust a cap in your ass for messing around with his shit. Just go slow with this *chicka* and be extra cool."

Emilio was drying his hands on the paper towels, and suddenly grinned at me as he continued to eyeball me in the mirror. "But, hey my paddy-dude, check it out—even if her shit ain't right, there's some kind of cosmic law that says if a fine-ass *chicka* is offering up some righteous *culo*, and a dude don't jump on it, he's gonna burn in hell for sure."

He laughed while Daniel wagged his head in mild censure.

The situation with Teresa grew even more complicated later that evening. I was home, doing a little stir fry on my outdoor grill, when the phone rang. It was Teresa.

She was direct as usual. "Brian, did you put some money in my purse last night?"

The sharp edge in her voice caught me by surprise. I stopped stirring the vegetables and pushed the pan to a cooler side of the grill.

"Ah, yeah I did, Teresa. I thought you could use the money."

"Brian—you fucking asshole. I'm no *pinche puta*."

I knew what that meant. "Teresa, I . . . "

"You use money way too much, *chingado*! But not with me, *esé*!"

"I was just . . . "

"Fuck you, Brian. You don't treat me like one of your white-ass, fucking whores."

I had to hold the receiver away from my ear. She was shouting into the phone.

"Teresa, I didn't . . . "

"Bullshit, Brian. You're an asshole. I'm not just some piece of ass you can buy. I knew I shouldn't have been messing around with no fucking, dumb-ass *güero*!"

I knew what that meant too. I got pissed. "Goddamn it, Teresa, I didn't mean . . . "

"No! Fuck you *chingado*! I ain't nobody's piece of shit!"

"Goddamn, Teresa, I . . . !"

But she had slammed down the phone hard enough for me to wince at the other end. I stood still holding my phone, shaking, my anger almost driving me to throw the phone at the wall of the apartment building next door. I understood why Teresa was furious, even in a rage, but I also knew that thinking of her as whore would have been about the last thought in my mind. I also got it that I could never adequately explain my motives, not that it made much difference now, because I was sure that I was never going to see Teresa Zapata again.

When I brought up the exchange with Teresa, and the cause, with Daniel and Emilio they reacted with both amusement and a cynical wisdom.

"Man, it sure sounds like you stepped in the shit with that *chicka*," Daniel pronounced with a chuckle. "Not only is she maybe hooked-up, and if so you might have just turned her old man into a pimp."

Emilio had a slightly different take. "Did she offer to come by and return the money?"

I shook my head.

He shrugged. "Then maybe she is a *puta*." Then giving me a sly wink, he added, "Like that black group sings it, you just got busted by the way of the world."

The dock supervisor had put all three of us in a box car unloading cases of canned peaches. The weather was cool for late September and the boxcar hadn't heated up enough to force any of us to start stripping off our shirts.

Daniel stopped transferring the cases to the pallet and straightened up, a serious look on his face. "Don't listen to this *pendejo,* Brian. It don't have to be that way. You didn't do anything wrong, *esé*. And you know what? You're right. You pay attention to your heart. This *chicka* doesn't have jack. She's stuck in a chickenshit job and has a kid to support. Maybe she has an old man at home, and maybe not, but either way I know she can use the money you gave her. Naw, *esé*, you didn't do anything wrong." He nodded, looking a bit surprised with a sudden thought. "Giving her the money was a righteous thing to do, Brian." And he nodded again, then studied me for a moment. "Yeah, *esé,* it was way cool of you."

Emilio too had stopped working and was digging into the pocket of his freight apron for a pack of smokes. "And besides that, dude, relax. They're all *putas* anyway. We're always paying for it, dude. We pay for it on the front end or on the back end. Pussy's cash-and-carry or on the installment plan, but we're always paying. Bitches don't ever want to admit that shit, dude, and they think we're some kind of pig for saying the shit like it is, but you know what, dude? Every dude knows it, knows that we're always paying for it, one way or another."

Daniel waved his friend off. "Forget that shit, Brian, we're all *putas,*" and he tipped his head at the wall of sixty pound cases of canned peaches ahead of us in the freight car. "Aren't all us *vatos* renting ourselves out by the hour? Using what we got to make money, and getting fucked just like any whore. We're all cash-and-carry."

Emilio shook it off. "Fuck that shit, man."

"You don't got to like it," Daniel came back. "It's the world."

"That what I said, *vato*," hammered Emilio. "It's the way of the world. But you make it sound, I don't know—really fucked!"

"It is," Daniel shot back. "But it doesn't have to be."

"Woooo," Emilio swung his arms in little circles. "Big revolutionary here."

"All I'm saying," returned Daniel, showing some frustration with his friend, "is that it don't have to be that way," and he turned to me. "You just keep following your heart with this girl, Brian, and you'll do right."

Emilio shook his head. "Yeah, you follow your heart, *esé*, and I'll follow my dick, and we'll see who get to where he wants to go first."

Daniel ignored Emilio. "You were trying to help the girl, Brian, and somewhere inside of her she knows that. So forget it, *esé*. You didn't do nothing wrong."

"Yeah, maybe so, *vato*," Emilio seconded his friend. "On your part it's all righteous." Then he added thoughtfully, "But you know what, dude, you can never be sure of anything where women or money are concerned. You can't trust them, dude, money or women—and you especially can't trust women *and* money. Money can fuck up anything—make good people bad and bad people *putos cerdos*."

Emilio was far more cynical than Daniel, but both of them had tried to make the same point. In this world we all sell ourselves. The owners of this railroad were trading us for our time and sweat, but they weren't interested in helping us. That was life, straight up. Only this situation felt way different. With Teresa, I had tried to help her, not rip her off, but the money flipped it around and made it so she didn't get it—made it so she *couldn't* get it.

Things lay stone quiet for nearly a couple of weeks, and I was just getting over Teresa when I got a call from her. I was kicking-back on a Sunday afternoon joyfully watching Houston pound the Forty-Niners when the phone rang. Annoyed, I went to the phone and snatched up the receiver, still watching the game.

"Yeah, what," I snapped into the phone. "I'm watching the game. Who's this?"

A long moment's silence at the other end. I nearly hung up. Then: "Brian—it's Teresa."

Startled, I didn't respond for a second.

"Teresa Zapata—Brian—God, I hope you didn't forget me already." Her voice sounded tiny and far away, edged with a whisper of self-consciousness.

My attention immediately shifted from the television to the phone. "No. No, Teresa, I didn't forget. How are you?"

"I'm okay, Brian. You . . . ?" the faint hint of self-consciousness still there.

"Yeah. It's good, Teresa. I'm good."

I was starting to remember how she looked standing naked in the doorway of my bathroom, her smile and her expression then when she saw how much I appreciated how good she looked to me.

"I wanted to apologize, Brian. I said some mean things to you and I'm sorry."

I cradled the phone against my ear, walked to the TV and turned the game off, an awkward confusion tying up my tongue.

"I'm sorry," she repeated. "Are you still there?"

I found my voice. "That's okay, Teresa. I get what happened. I might have been wrong. I didn't mean to be, but I might have been."

"No, not really, Brian. I misunderstood. That's all. I appreciate it now." She laughed, but the laugh still held the self-conscious edge. "I actually used the money to pay a doctor bill for my baby." She paused. "Stupid isn't it. You did help me, Brian, and I appreciate it. I want you to know that."

"I'm glad, Teresa. I really am."

"You're not mad at me, then?"

"No. I get it—your reaction."

"Thank you, Brian. That's nice."

I sat down and put my beer on the coffee table. "I'm just being honest."

"Really?"

"Yes, really."

"Thank you." There was a deep breath of relief in her voice, then she was back to her directness. "Do you want to get back to your game?"

"Ah—No. No. It's okay. I can talk."

"Good. You know I meant it when I told you that I liked you."

I felt her lips, warm and soft, brushing my eyelids. "I know. I mean, I remember."

"Have you started seeing anyone?"

"No."

"Truth, Brian?"

"Yes."

"Would you like to get together again?"

I was still feeling a bit off guard, tender and sensitive—sensitive to her. I looked at my reflection in the blank TV screen. "Ah, yeah. Sure. Did you have some time in mind, Teresa?"

"Whenever you'd like, Brian. Tonight'd be okay, maybe, or tomorrow, whenever?"

I wasted no time. "Tomorrow? Seven-thirty."

"That's good. I get off work at six."

"I remember, Teresa. Want to come to my place?"

"Great."

"I'll make us dinner."

"Way cool, Brian." She laughed. This time it had the sound of relief. "You're way cool to forgive me."

I knew I was starting to love her.

On the following when day Teresa arrived, it was obvious that she had paid close attention to the way she looked. I was unexpectedly relieved, and pleased. Her hair, makeup, immaculate, all crisp and perfectly arranged; she had spent time preparing.

She was a lovely woman and I was flattered and assured, locked in my feelings for her.

The evening went comfortably and less hurried. Even though we both knew where it was going to end, we were not anxious about it.

It seemed to me that this time the sex was less about sex and more about feeling. At least that was the way I thought of it. There was more kissing, nuzzling and touching; it was less frantic, with more devotion paid to those gentle details of lovemaking that produce warm and lasting memories. Our touches were electric and magical, our whispers soft and sure. Certain that we were both sated and drawn closer to the other, I found myself gathered into a deep and comfortable fondness for Teresa Zapata. I was becoming aware of a great pressure I was feeling, a serious wanting to see much more of her, and see her more often.

At the end Teresa asked again to take a shower before returning home. I know I shouldn't have been, but I was a tiny bit surprised at her request, and felt a tiny bite of pain. I had hoped it wouldn't happen this way again, as I wanted her to spend the night with me; and here again I was stung with the thought that Teresa might have had another man in her life, a man at home she had to return to. The thought both angered me and hurt me.

Teresa stood in the doorway of the bathroom, as she had the first time, the light cast on her youth and softness, looking even more beautiful than she had before—if, I thought, that was even possible. She put a hand on the door frame to expose the gentle contour of her breast as she looked across her shoulder at me lying in the bed.

"My baby, Brian. Remember?"

"Yes."

She hesitated, then awkwardly, "Brian, that was so sweet of you—to try to help me out, like you did before. You have no idea how much I really appreciated it. I was so mean to you about the money and I'm so sorry about that. You have no idea how much you helped me."

Teresa halted for a long moment, as if waiting for a reaction, for me to say something back, respond to the quiet but direct undertone in her voice. When I didn't, she smiled shyly at me and added more directly, "Thank you, *cariño,* the money really helped me out. I wish I could tell you how much it helped and how much I really appreciated it. I'm so broke all the time, and it's so nice of you to help me out. I can really use the help."

I was completely unsure if I should reply. There was more than just a hint of urgency in her tone; her voice was slow and gentle, but insistent.

When I said nothing she dropped her arm and turned toward me. Leaning against the door frame, she suddenly looked tired and older, as though giving in to something inevitable and unavoidable.

"Brian," she said in that direct voice. "I hate to ask, but I'm really broke." She hesitated and frowned at me, as though surprised at herself, then quickly snapped out of it and went on, only her voice now a bit more brittle. "Brian, can you put some more money in my bag? God, I hate to ask, but I'm really desperate this week. It's so damn hard." She waved her hand and turned to the bathroom. I could tell that she was looking at her reflection in the mirror over the sink and not liking what she saw. "I know this is fucking us up, Brian, but my work sucks. Shit!" she stamped her foot. "My whole fucking life sucks." She was still staring at herself in the mirror, anger rising. "I'm sorry, Brian—I'm sorry I'm such a fucking worthless bitch, but I need the money . . . . Please help me . . . . " And she disappeared into the bathroom closing the door hard.

I felt a coolness wash over me. I stared hard at the bathroom door, at the light glowing around the edges of the jamb, and listened to sound of the shower being turned on.

I remembered the conversation with Daniel and Emilio, but I didn't care. I didn't care about anything except Teresa Zapata. I knew exactly what I was going to do, and I also knew it did not matter, because either way I knew I was never going to see Teresa again. The dawn of the thought brought with it a loathing—not an anger, not a hatred, but a loathing, only I could not tell at what. It was not directed at Teresa, nor at me, or even at the money she so desperately needed, but somehow a loathing at the world, that vague sense of all the things surrounding us, squeezing and devouring us, and ending us—all of us, eventually.

I sat up in the bed, swung my feet to the floor, and listened to the shower, imagining her washing herself, the soapy water running across her breasts, over her small rounded belly, down her legs, and into tiny eddies swirling around the drain. I felt both a mounting urgency to act, and a pounding ache to be still. I knew this time there would be no brush of her soft lips on my eyelids, no gentle Spanish words, just a tense leaving as she brushed past mc, followed by the echo of a desperate fury at the small sound of the front door closing.

I forced myself to stand and look at the clock, but didn't read the time, only stared at the sweep of the second hand that seemed to flow in sync with the running of the shower. Time—the insistent dribbling of life, a living that suddenly seemed an insult. As I walked to her coat and hand bag I felt weak and disgusted and angry; it was a dull fury, not so much at what I was about to do, but at being forced to confront both of our losses to the way of the world.

A Fight At Little
Annie Fanny's

Bubba Dean lifted weights. He lifted weights two, three hours a day, every day, and that was before he worked the swing shift on a freight dock—two-thirty to eleven. Bubba pumped iron, then muscled freight. Lifting and moving heavy things was Bubba's life, his whole life. Bubba Dean wouldn't—couldn't—live without it.

"Hey, Dean," shouted the dock foreman. He was yelling at Bubba from three truck bays down the dock. "You want some overtime, Country Boy?"

"Hell, yeah, Boss!" Shouted Bubba over the roar of the forklifts behind him. "I always want OT."

Nothing made Bubba happier than hefting freight and breathing the hard, warm air lightly laced with the diesel fumes that drifted from the yard and across the NorCal cargo dock. This was the best part of Bubba's life and he seemed to have nothing else to do with that life but to lift and carry, to pick and set, twist, turn, bend and move. Lifting defined Bubba Dean. Lifting *was* Bubba.

"Two, maybe three hours, Dean."

Bubba loved overtime, though what he did with the money only he knew. He was secretive that way.

"I got it." Bubba almost ripped a giggle. "Hell, yeah, boss. I got it."

Lifting gave Bubba Dean a fat and thick feeling, pumped up, with shoulders like railroad ties and arms like well fed anacondas. Lifting gave Bubba a big sense of purpose, a raw edge of dumb energy for the way he swaggered in this place of truckers and dockworkers. Bubba's want for lifting filled his chest and shoulders, soaking him with a dark and heavy appetite, but for what, he didn't know.

"Okay, Bubba, then when you're finished there," returned the foreman, "get down here to bay four and help swamp out this half-set.[4] I already got Casey on it."

Bubba gave him the thumbs-up. None of the other dockworkers were anxious for overtime. Exhausted after their straight eight, for them it was home, a cold brew, dinner and sawing zz's. But Bubba wanted the time. Bubba loved working, and with a good union job and the hours being piled on, Bubba should have had new cars, great digs, fine food, and hot women. Only Bubba had none of these. Bubba had nothing anyone could see. His life was modest—a furnished apartment in a low-rent part of town, an aging car, a few work clothes, and a gym membership. He had nothing—nothing anyone could see. So just what did Bubba do

---

4. A half-set was a short trailer (usually twenty-six feet in length) typically hooked up to a second half-set for a full set of double trailers.

with all his money? It wasn't a high priority to get this question answered, so only a few ever learned the flow of Bubba's green.

The foreman returned with a shout, "Don't thank me, Dean, no one else wanted this load."

Bubba trotted down to the bay where the foreman was standing.

The half-set trailer was loaded chest high with burlap bags full of ball bearings. Bubba knew right away why none of the other loaders wanted the trailer. The fifty pound burlap bags would tear up gloves and eventually peel the skin off your hands. A couple of hours in this trailer could put a man in the emergency room. This was careful work, not fast work. Another dockworker was already at the load, dropping bags on a wooden pallet with a solid, dull rattling of steel balls. He stopped, watching Bubba and the foreman.

Bubba smiled. "Thanks, boss. Casey and me, we got it."

The foreman walked off, letting Bubba's gratitude slide off his departing back. The foreman liked Bubba okay, but along with everyone else thought the country boy was a bottle or two shy of a six-pack.

No one noticed the quick exchange between the foreman and Bubba, no one except Wes James, who had taken a glove off and was wiping his sweaty hand on his freight apron. James watched Bubba with a tight and narrow gaze. It was as though James were studying some small and mysterious thing moving far off in a haze.

Bubba entered the half-set trailer.

"Hey, Case," Bubba let his presence be known. "Let's swamp this mother out quick. What'd ya say?"

Casey shook his head a bit sadly and took a long sideways look at Bubba, a long gaze into a country face that was broad and open, flattish and kind of smooth, shiny like a warm white biscuit that had been basted in the baking by too much butter. Plenty of times

Casey had studied Bubba, studied features which seeped out a slow undertow of simplemindedness.

"Don't you be in too big a hurry, Country Boy," Casey replied slowly. "There's always more trailers and more freight."

Bubba smiled back. "Then we'll get them too."

Casey knew Bubba, knew that this country kid from somewhere in the South could outwork any man on the dock, and he'd let Bubba do it. Casey wasn't a bad guy, but neither was he above taking advantage of the kid, letting Bubba do most of the work and saving himself, saving the skin on his hands, saving his back for another day.

"Whatever way you wanna go, Bubba," Casey replied, straightening up. "Just don't be in so big a rush to bust your ass that you get *me* hurt, Country Boy," and he walked out to the dock to collect another freight pallet off the stack in the middle of the dock.

There was often much chuckling and snickering on the dock about all the inbreeding that must have gone on in the back hills of Northern Arkansas, that dank and tangled Hillbilly Hell the other dock workers imagined had spawned Bubba Dean. Only the snickering always stopped when Bubba came near. Those chuckles became a tight cough, a sniff, a clearing of the throat, or a scuff of a boot. Bubba noticed, but he didn't get it, and he smiled his gap-toothed grin small in his big wide face.

"Get two pallets, Case," Bubba yelled after the dockworker.

All-in-all, the men liked Bubba Dean, liked him partly because of his dumb willingness to do more than his share, to push harder, lift more, take on the heavier load; and partly, because Bubba's big, unassuming nature amused them. Bubba would smile, buy them a beer, or loan out a few dollars when someone was short, then forget to ask for repayment; he'd he-haw at jokes he didn't understand and would even volunteer to be the butt of a gag once in a while, then good naturedly wave his hand and guffaw aloud at his own foolishness. Bubba Dean was a happy soul, good to have around the dock for many reasons, and he quickly became a steady fixture, always laughing, generous, smiling and willing. Even as big and strong as he was, Bubba was far from threatening. He was a soft touch on many levels.

So all the men liked Bubba—all the men except for Wes James, who did not take well to anyone, and especially not to Bubba Dean. James had good reason for disliking the country boy, a twisted reason. Bubba Dean was a special case for James, a special case few knew about, and Wes James had special needs that kept it that way.

Bubba had no friends and no family. As he remembered it, his mother had been drunk most of the time and never even noticed when he had dropped out of high school and fallen into the life of low-paid farm labor. At seventeen, Bubba abruptly left Arkansas for good and drifted west, moving with the crops across Oklahoma and into the Texas Panhandle. He followed the farm work, and was chopping cotton in the West Central Texas when he'd learned about his mother's passing, and that was so long after the fact that Bubba never learned where she was buried. Bubba did not know who his father was. His mother never talked about him; Bubba had never even seen a picture of him. His mother's brothers and cousins had all moved out of Arkansas and he had not seen them since he was ten or twelve.

Crop seasons had pushed Bubba on further west with the immigrant field workers. His blonde hair and ivory skin set him far apart from the healthy brown skin of the Mexican migrants. Bubba never made any friends among them. He spoke no Spanish and had no interest in learning. He eventually drifted north with the picking, moved up the lettuce and grape fields of the San Joaquin Valley and into northern California where he wandered into

San Francisco. It was across the bay in Oakland that
a gym. He took a bit of his picking money and joined.
that Bubba met a couple guys from the freight docks. Bi
found that in a stretch of the bay from Oakland down to Sa Leandro there were hundreds of freight docks where a guy as big and
strong as Bubba could get hired in a heartbeat.

The bosses loved the way the big kid slung the heaviest freight,
outworking any three other workers on the dock. It wasn't long
before Bubba found a permanent home at NorCal freight. It was
there, in San Leandro, after a couple of weeks, that some of the
dock workers took Bubba Dean across the street from the freight
terminal and introduced him to the life and ladies at Little Annie
Fanny's. Bubba wasn't quite yet twenty, but as big as he was,
and what with the company he kept, he was never asked about
his age.

Back then, in the late '80s, Little Annie's was only one of two
topless bars south of 'Frisco—at least before one got as far south
as Reseda, just north of LA. The outside of Fanny's looked like
a storefront in Spanish style stucco and terracotta, the windows
heavily blacked out except for the Bud and Coors signs flashing in colored neon. The entrance was a single wide door and a
heavy black curtain. Just inside the darkened interior was Chock
Arcsino, the overly bored bouncer, who carefully scrutinized
every patron. Passing Chock, the rest of Fanny's was cast in low
lights and shadows that heightened the sultry impact. Adjusting to
the light, pinched vision piercing the veil of cigarette smoke and
the nearly naked women fully seized hold of a man's hungry eye.
Little Annie Fanny's was loud—pounding out hard rock, or blues,
or sometimes old country rock, whatever the pole dancer on stage
had queued up with the disk jockey. The tempo, the din, the flashing lights—Little Annie's was a cherished oasis of release and
fantasy to the dockworkers and truckers of San Leandro.

As fast paced as it was, all glittery and jumbled and raucous, Little Annie Fanny's was a steady new home for Bubba Dean. Here, time slowed for Bubba, keeping a new rhythm with the smooth roll to the women's walk, the dancer's undulations, the slow cadence to the changing lights. To the amusement of the other dock workers, Bubba's mouth would sometimes hang open, his gaze wide, staring with an earnest but politely innocent longing. He took the beer the men offered and gawked at the women, rarely tearing his eyes off their breasts. There were big breasts with pointy nipples, and Bubba kept missing his mouth with the beer bottle, and there were small breasts glazed with large, honey pale nipples, and Bubba flushed and bit his lower lip. Bubba was a kid in a candy store where all the candy smiled and winked back.

The only man who wasn't amused by Bubba's ogling was the bouncer, Chock Aresino, who kept a wary eye on him, giving the big white kid a good measure, seeing him thicker, wider, more muscled than the other truckers and dock-men. Bubba was bigger even than Chock, and that bothered Chock Aresino.

Then there was Sahara, with her small girlish legs, muscular at the calf and soft at the top where they swelled into hips just barely wide enough to get two hands across, and oh, how Bubba noticed the way she moved, teasing out her walk with a knowing roll to those hips with a soft, dimpled squeeze to her rounded buttocks. While Sahara was hardly her real name, the image of soft, rolling dunes at sunset merged seductively with her figure, giving a full-bodied life to the moniker, Sahara.

"Hey, Country Boy," one of the men would snicker. "Don't trip on your tongue."

Bubba would hee-haw and flap his hand at the crack, but the thought that the handle Sahara was a crude fake had never crept into his mind. He was too lost in the low light glancing off the gentle slope of her shoulder, by the moist gleam of her rich lower lip as it pressed forward in a sly pout, her lowered green eyes not looking at him, as Bubba was certain, out of a blushing shyness.

Bubba was possessed of feelings toward Sahara much less than love, but much more than sex. Whenever she turned away from the bar, loaded with a tray full of drinks, the sweet smell of the short, frosted hair scorched his nose and his lower belly tightened just enough for him to get a harder grip on his beer bottle, feel the cold sweat off the glass squeak between his thick fingers. His eyes would dog her back and tapering legs as she glided between the tables toward the stage where a topless dancer would bob and squirm, floating in and out of colored lights, glowing now pink, tinted now magenta, smiling and beckoning, luring cash from the men at her feet. Only Bubba rarely glanced at the dancer, or took his eyes off Sahara. He studied Sahara's small mouth, cleft chin, green eyes, her throat that drifted into soft, perky breasts that rode out before her tan body as if offering a tantalizing affirmation that women and youth were the grandest trap yet of a wickedly conspiring universe. To Bubba, Sahara seemed so perfectly like the only woman he had ever wanted, or ever would want.

Sahara? No, her name was not Sahara. And yes, everyone but Bubba knew that. But few knew her real name: Louise. Those few in the know included Wes James, because James knew Louise better than anyone else did at Little Annie Fanny's. Louise was Wes's squeeze, and everyone knew that, too—everyone except for Bubba Dean.

"Hey, Bubba . . . !"

Bubba turned toward the dock. He and Casey had been waiting for the fork lift to remove the last pallet from the half-set. Nick and Danny, a couple of swampers from the last shift, were looking into the trailer. They gave Bubba a thumbs up.

"Bubba, you off now?" Nick wanted to know. "Let's grab a beer over at Fanny's."

Bubba glanced at the big clock over the dock office. 12:30 a.m. He'd finish the shift with two hours overtime.

"Come on, Bubba," Danny coaxed him. "We'll even let you buy, Country Boy."

The longer Bubba worked at NorCal, the more often he did the buying. Bubba smiled at Nick and Danny and nodded his head, hoping that Sahara was working.

The three of them got to Annie's just before one a.m. The bar was dusky and packed, close with smoke, laughter, voices and booming music. Both stages were working, commanded by teasing topless dancers, ringed with seated men flagging them with dollar bills. The crowd was thicker than usual, the volume higher, the air hot and heavy.

Nick leaned toward Bubba and shouted against the din, "Go on, Bubba, get us a pitcher of beer at the bar and bring it to that table in the corner."

Danny edged in from the other side. "Yeah, Bubba, it's be kind to your buddies week. Let's use up some of that good OT money of yours."

Nick added with a poke in Bubba's arm, "And Bubba, I think I see your sweetheart over there getting drinks."

Danny and Nick walked away toward the empty booth, leaving Bubba to push his way toward the bar. None of them noticed that at the other end of the room, just behind the bouncer, sitting with a few other men from NorCal, was Wes James. James adjusted his chair slightly so that he could watch the bar from a better angle. Chock Aresino saw James make this move and turned his head slightly to follow the dockworker's gaze. Chock saw that James was watching Bubba Dean. This got Chock's attention, as he was careful at his job, always ready to make sure there would be no trouble starting. Chock was proud of the job he did, of his command over the goings-on at Little Annie Fanny's.

Bubba pushed his way to the bar, not deliberately knocking men out of the way, but his size made it difficult for him to manage in tight quarters and he tended to clear a path without even trying. He did see Sahara standing at the server's station, holding a tray loaded with glasses and beer bottles. She turned toward the room just in time to face Bubba. Looking up at him, she blinked, as if to clear something from her eye, then slowly smiled.

"Hey, darl'n," shouted the lovely Sahara, a.k.a. Louise, above the music. "I'm glad you came in, hon. Have a seat and I'll be back in a minute." Without waiting for a response she slipped easily around him, balancing the loaded tray before her.

Bubba turned to the station, slapping too much money on the bar top, and got two pitchers of beers for Danny and Nick. He hurried to the table and dropped them off, saying he'd be back. This seemed to amuse the two dockworkers.

Bubba was back at the bar, standing by the server's station, when Sahara returned with the empty tray.

"Hey," he said.

"Hey, back." Sahara set the tray on the bar and put a small hand on Bubba's chest. "So how you do'n, big man? I've been missing you."

Bubba smiled.

Sahara followed the hand on his chest with the other hand on his forearm. "You know how much I miss you." She pulled lightly at the hairs on his arm. "I've been hoping you'd to come around."

"I'm here now."

"I know, darl'n, and I'm in trouble again."

"With your baby?"

"No, it's my mother, sweetie, she's in the hospital."

"Again? I thought she just got out."

"I know, but it's more serious this time."

"Can I help?"

"I hate to ask."

"Sahara, I can help."

Sahara took her hand off his chest and it made Bubba sorry. Bubba liked her to touch him. It always felt warm and gentle when she placed her little hands on him. They were soft and smooth, nails always glowing neatly with polish. She reeked of the kind of easy femininity that made Bubba's skin tingle all over.

"Can I help you, Sahara?" he repeated, genuine earnestness in his tone. "I can take you to the hospital."

This Bubba was anxious to do. Bubba had never seen Sahara outside of Annie's, and he wanted badly to do so, even if it was to take her to see her mother in a hospital. It could be a first step in taking her to a movie, or out to eat, or going for a walk on the beach, letting her know she'd be safe with him. Yet somehow just getting to see her outside of the bar was fast becoming only a remote possibility.

"No, sweetie," she answered him. "I have a car."

He hesitated a second, his throat tightening all the way down to his belly. "Do you need money, Sahara?"

She dropped her eyes in a shy, uncomfortable way. "Honey, you've already done too much for me," she said.

Bubba wished she'd call him by his name. She would always call him honey, or sweetie, or whatever, but never Bubba. It was almost like she didn't know his name or had forgotten it, or for some reason didn't want to speak it. It made him feel like he was some kind of nuisance to her, when he knew better. Sahara needed him. Bubba knew he was her friend, maybe her best friend.

"Sahara, I got maybe a hundred bucks on me, maybe more, if that would help you any?"

"That'd be too much, sweetie. You're always helping me out." And those misty green eyes looked into his. "You've really got to stop offering."

Only Bubba was deaf to her protests and was already fumbling in his back pocket for his wallet, her eyes holding his in their grip. He yanked out the wallet and fingered the bills, pulling out a fistful. He left himself a ten and a five and pushed the rest of the bills into her hands.

"Wow, this is way more than fifty," she said, letting his hand with the money hold hers. "You shouldn't be doing this, honey," she added, with an unexpected blush. "Honest, sweetie, you're treating me too good."

"I want you to have it, Sahara," he replied, "and please, Sahara, my name is Bubba Dean. Please, start calling me Bubba."

"I'm sorry. I will, Bubba, but," and she looked at the folded money, Bubba still holding her hands, closing her fingers around the money. It was close to a hundred. She looked up, some small worry in her eyes. "Don't you need some of this money? I don't need this much. I can get by okay."

"Naw," and Bubba smiled, his broad face showing the pleasure he felt that she had not pulled her hands away from his. "I make plenty of overtime, Sahara. And I want you to have it. I . . . " and Bubba blinked, surprised at the words about to come out of his mouth, the words that seemed to have a life of their own. "I like you, Sahara, I really do, a lot, and I'd like you to take it."

"You come in here almost every night and give me money, hon, I mean, Bubba. It's too much. You're wonderful."

That brought a bright smile to Bubba's wide face.

Sahara let Bubba hold her hands in his a bit longer. She had an unexpected feeling, a funny feeling she didn't like. This big country kid with the southern drawl, this Bubba Dean, really meant all he was saying, and it gave her a slight queasy sensation she could not easily sidestep. Gently, she pulled her hands away.

"Bubba," she said. "I really like your—your wanting to help me. It's nice, and I'll take it this time, but please don't offer anymore." Sahara sounded serious as she laid her hand again on his chest. "Please don't again." She stepped back, taking her hand away. "I have to get to work. It's almost closing time. You go back to your friends and drink your beer before I get into trouble with the boss."

Sahara lowered her misty green eyes in that way she always did when showing her shy appreciation and Bubba's smile grew. Bubba knew then that Sahara liked him back and he wanted to lean forward and kiss her, and he did lean. Sahara must have read his mind. She shifted her weight slightly away from him and looked at him with a sudden change to her face that stopped Bubba cold. He quickly straightened, his smile losing a bit of its bloom. He understood that she was a good girl and it was too soon. He nodded and turned back to the bar room, walked past the stage and went to the door, forgetting about Nick and Danny sitting with their two pitchers of beer. Bubba felt tense as he brushed passed Chock, not noticing him, and went through the curtains and out into the night.

Chock had watched the whole scene between Sahara and Bubba at the bar. When he had seen Bubba head toward the woman, then her suddenly turn away, it had brought him off his stool. Chock was the only thing here between these women and some mess, and there was something about Bubba. It was more than the white kid's big frame and obvious muscle. It was more how he did not notice things around him. It was like the big ol' white boy was living in some kind of bubble. In a way, it made Chock more aware of Bubba because he thought that given the right situation, the big boy would not heed anything said to him. Chock carried a heavy leather-covered sap in his rear pocket, but he had never yet had to draw it out. Chock knew that his size alone was enough to back down most men, but this white boy was bigger than he was and never even seemed to notice him, and that bothered Chock. Bubba brought Chock Aresino to feeling as close to apprehension about another man as he could ever remember. It was not a usual sensation for Chock and the foreign feeling made him irritable.

The place was just closing and Chock watched Sahara as she spoke to her dude, Wes James, a slightly built man, tall, rangy, with a thin moustache and a nervous attitude. Yeah, Chock could spot a convict a mile away, the way they rarely looked directly at you and talked out of the side of their mouth. A few well aimed questions at the men from NorCal Freight had informed Chock that Wes James had done time at Lompoc for burglary. James was now out on parole and had been lucky to land a good paying union job at NorCal. Chock had nothing against cons. He knew lots of men who had done a stretch. What Sahara, or Louise, or whatever she called herself, did with her time off, and with whom, was none of Chock's business; but knowing who these men were was part of every good bouncer's business, and Wes James was now part of Chock's business. It was closing time, and civilians had to be out of the bar. Chock decided to give James and his honey just a few minutes more before asking James to leave.

Louise was saying to James, "I kind of feel sorry for him, Wes. He's just a big, dumb-ass kid, and he just doesn't get it."

"Yeah, well he's gotta grow up some day," James responded with a tired face of indifference. "How much did he give you?"

"A little over a hundred."

"Good, I need some. I'm flat broke."

"Wes," hesitated Louise. "I feel kind of creepy about it. He thinks it's to help out my mother. "

"Fuck 'em, babe. It's the way the world works. Do you think the owner of this shit-hole feels creepy about taking money from the dancers?" James was referring to the business arrangement whereby the topless dancers pay the bar owner a healthy percentage of their tips for the privilege of dancing on his stage. "It's how the world works, babe," James schooled her again, then added with a sneer, "or maybe you want to start sucking cocks for a livin' again?"

She took no offense at his bringing up her occasional avocation as a prostitute and patted his cheek. "Only yours, Wesley darl'n."

"Then somebody's gonna have to pay."

"I can't help it. I still feel creepy about it."

James laughed, "That's why I love you, Louise. You're such a damn woman."

"Is that some kind of left-handed compliment?"

"Look, babe, the country boy don't have anybody, and you're the closest thing he has to a real girlfriend. You're giving him a dream, babe. Yeah, look at it that way and stop whining. Now let me have fifty, and think of it like we're doing him a favor."

"What do you mean, *we*," she laughingly demanded, counting out the bills into his hand. "It's just *me*, Wes. He just wants to help *me*."

"Christ! Stop feeling guilty, Louise." James folded the cash and slipped it in his pocket. "I hate it when you start that guilty shit. I told you, it's how the world works."

Louise looked behind James to where Chock came up behind him. James turned, following her gaze.

"We gotta close up," Chock said, "and I gotta see that the dancers get to their cars, okay. So you gotta go."

"We're just concluding some business, Chock," James said, looking up into the face that even in the quite light looked solidly unpleasant. "We'll be finished in a sec."

"You gotta go now," Chock said. "I don't want Oakland PD seeing you walk out of here at 2:30 a.m."

"In a sec," repeated James impatiently.

"Now, *pendejo*!" and Chock Aresino put his big hand on James' shoulder, turning him fully around so that he faced the door. "You go now!"

"Okay, Goddamn it," and James jerked the hand off his shoulder. "Don't get so fuck'n hot."

"Hot? I show your ass fuck'n hot, *chingado*!" and he reached for James, who jumped back.

"Okay—Okay, shit. Ease up, big guy," and Wes James spun and headed toward the door.

Smiling, Louise watched Wes disappear through the curtain. She reached up and patted Chock on his shoulder. "Thanks, Chock."

"*Por que*?"

She laughed. "For showing Wes how the world works."

"*Mi'ja*?"

But Louise had already turned toward the dressing room.

Bubba never missed a day—or night—at work. He was never sick, never tired, never lazy, and never refused extra time at the dock, no matter the load or the labor. The man seemed inexhaustible.

As Wes James watched Bubba from the other end of the dock, he felt something like a distant headache coming on, a pain just behind and below his right ear. He and his girl, Louise, had been milking this kid for over three months, relieving him of his money almost nightly, and the kid never seemed to catch on to the scam. Sure, Louise got tips, a lot of them, and before she met Wes those tips had led to an occasional out-call. But since she's met Wes she quit hooking and just lived on the tips, assuming that Wes would object to sharing her favors with an occasional John, no matter the heft of the remuneration. In point of fact, Wes James couldn't care less for whom the little lady threw a leg up, so long as he could peel a few skins off the top.

But both Wes and Louise knew that Bubba was different. He was giving Louise money without any expectation. He was giving her a lot of money and, much to Wes's annoyance, Louise was plagued by feelings of guilt. Her mood was turning sour and it was starting to cause a strain between Wes and Louise. James could see the gravy train threatening to go off the rails. He wiped the sweat off the back of his neck, stuffed the bandanna back in the pocket of his freight apron, and turned back with a grunt to the trailer load of sewing machines.

Later that day Chock was rounding the corner of the parking lot on the way to the front door of Little Annie's when he spotted Louise in a heated conversation with James. Chock skirted the couple, picking up an odd word here and there, nothing that made sense. These things were none of his business. People have problems and so long as they kept it out of Annie's he didn't care to know anything about it. In order to keep his life simple, Chock kept his distance.

It was just about six o'clock and Chock was a bit early, a trait the owners appreciated. The bouncer changed into his muscle t-shirt emblazoned with SECURITY on the back and went smoothly about his business, making an appearance outside the locker room, always polite to the ladies; he knocked, letting the women know he was here. He next looked into the bathrooms, then checked in with the female bartender and the DJ, the only other male, who was also the manager. Chock then went to his own locker that was tucked away in the corner of the ramp behind the curtained entrance to the stage. He got out his handcuffs and lead-weighted sap, then grabbed a comb and picked his hair. He looked into the mirror and smoothed out the natural. The natural made Chock look even bigger. He liked the look. He liked the feel. Chock liked being big.

Louise poked her head out of the ladies' locker room. "Chock, can you do me a huge favor?"

He turned. "*Qué*?"

"If you see Wesley James around, please don't let me leave with him."

"What's going on, *cariña*?"

"We had a fight and he's mad and I don't want to see him, and I sure as hell don't want to go home with him."

"You want me to keep him out of here?"

"Could you, just for tonight?"

"Yeah, I could do that."

"That'd be great."

"*No problema, cariña.*"

Chock had been a bouncer for more than fifteen years and he knew his trade well. Keeping Wesley James out of Little Annie's was really no problem for Chock. He had often kept men out of the bar—men that were full of themselves and bothering the dancers. Chock went to straighten the stools at the bar and quickly forgot Wes James.

At half past eleven o'clock it was drizzling outside and Annie's was reasonably quiet. It was Thursday, the day before payday, and most of the local workers didn't have enough cash left from the week to hit Little Annie's. But Bubba had enough cash. Bubba always had enough cash. He parted the black curtain and ducked inside Annie's. He walked past Chock without noticing him and headed for the bar. Chock frowned at the small slight.

"Is Sahara around?" Bubba asked the bartender.

"She's on the floor serving."

Bubba looked around, his eyes adjusting to the dim light. There were only half a dozen tables occupied, a few customers around one of the two stages. The second stage was not in use. Bubba saw Sahara at a far table. He sat on a bar stool and waited for her to return.

"Hey, Sahara,"

"Hey, sweetie."

"You having a good night?"

"Fair." She set the tray loaded with empty beer bottles on the bar top. "You just getting off work?"

"Yeah" he grinned and rubbed his hand together. "I got another two hours of overtime."

"That's good."

"Yeah, Sahara. How's your mother? Is she better?"

Louise hesitated and started to ask what Bubba was talking about, but then remembered the other night and the hundred dollars Bubba had pressed on her for her imaginary mother's imaginary troubles, half of which went into Wes James's pocket. What had she told this kid? She couldn't recall and decided to play it vague. Louise again felt a tingle in her cheeks, like she always did when lying.

"She's fine, much better," and she looked down. "I really appreciate the money, honey. It was a big help to us."

"Bubba."

"What?"

"Bubba, Sahara. My name's Bubba."

"Oh, sorry. I mean Bubba."

Louise looked behind Bubba when she saw the curtain to the door blow back and Wes James come through. Chock put a big hand out, halting James. There was some rapid conversation. James looking agitated, making hand gestures toward the bar and pointing at Louise.

Louise watched, no longer listening to Bubba, and unaware that Bubba's eyes had followed hers where he too was watching the small drama going on at the door.

"You can't come in tonight," Chock was saying to James.

James frowned. Chock had not gotten off his stool, yet James was still looking him straight in the eye. Chock was over a head taller than James.

"How come?" James wanted to know.

"A complaint from one of the ladies."

James looked toward the bar, looked straight at Louise standing next to Bubba Dean. "Complaints? What the hell kind of complaints?"

"You can't come in tonight."

A nasty look scurried across James's face. "Why the fuck not?"

Chock got off his stool. "Out, *pendejo*!"

For just a moment, James hesitated, angrily shifting his weight from foot to foot, his eyes bouncing form Louise to Chock towering over him. "Ah, fuck this place!" he finally popped off with a flap of his hand and disappeared back out into the rainy night.

Chock readjusted himself on the stool and folded his arms across his chest, never looking at Louise.

"You know him?" Bubba asked.

"Wes? Sure—you know, just a bit. I know a lot of guys."

"He bothering you, Sahara?"

"No, not really."

"Why couldn't he get in?"

"I don't know," Louise answered and placed her hand on Bubba's arm. "I have to get back to work."

"Can I get a beer?"

"Sure, honey. Ask the bartender."

Bubba started again to remind Sahara that his name was Bubba, but she had walked away carrying her serving tray.

The bartender set a chilled bottle in front of Bubba and he took a swig, then looked around Annie's. The dump was nearly empty. The solo woman on stage had every customer in the house at ringside. Bubba wondered what was going on to keep Sahara working. He wanted to ask her to have breakfast with him after she got off work. His watch read almost one. Sahara was nowhere in sight. Bubba finished one beer and ordered another, but this time told the bartender to have Sahara bring it to a table, along with a bag of chips.

"Hey, hun, the view is better at the bar," Louise reminded him, as she deposited the beer and chips before Bubba. "You can't hardly even see the stage from here, hun."

"I know." Bubba tossed a too big bill on her tray. "I don't care. I just want to get a chance to talk to you, Sahara."

"I can't talk with you right now, sweetie," Louise threw off carelessly, counting out his change, then leaving it on the table. "Maybe later, when things slow down."

"Damn, Sahara," Bubba said full of good nature, smiling at her. "The place is nearly empty."

Louise winked at him. "Sorry, hun, but I'm the only server," and she walked away toward the side of the room that held the stage.

Bubba stared after her, perplexed. The joint *was* nearly empty. Hell, Sahara could have given him enough time to ask her to have breakfast with him. She could have given him at least that long. He watched her go to the bar and chat with the bartender for a few moments then finally head toward one of the few customers waving an empty beer bottle above his head. After glancing at his watch again, Bubba decided to wait for her after she got off work, sit in his car in the parking lot and wait for her. There wouldn't be any reason for her not talk to him then. Bubba dropped a ten dollar bill on the table for a tip and left, with the bottle of beer hardly touched.

Chock watched Bubba leave. It was abrupt. Chock had witnessed the exchange between the kid and Louise, and wasn't surprised. Few things in this rat-hole ever surprised him anymore. Louise seemed to be having real problems with men that night. Chock yawned and shook his head. It was almost closing time. Chock had seen it all before, men not getting the kind of attention they wanted from the ladies and finishing the hoop by further upsetting the ladies and getting an unceremonious kiss off. It was old news to Chock.

Bubba watched the back door of Annie's through a rain spattered windshield. It couldn't be long now. The customers had all left, Bubba was sure of that, and there were only about five or six cars left in the lot. Bubba knew the tan VW with the dented rear fender was Sahara's. He'd walked her to her car once about a month ago. He'd noticed too that the club's bouncer had followed them out and watched them the whole time. Being watched like that had annoyed Bubba, annoyed him mainly because he wasn't about to try anything with Sahara. Bubba liked Sahara and he knew she liked him; maybe she liked him more than any other woman he had ever known. Much more important was that Bubba knew Sahara needed him to take care of her. He liked being needed by her and he wouldn't do anything to mess that up. Tonight Bubba had over two hundred dollars in his pocket to give to her. He knew she'd like that.

The rain was easing up just as a car unexpectedly entered the drive, headlights ripping the night on high-beam. The car came on fast, bouncing, splashing water from a couple of chuckholes in the gravel lot, then did a noisy U-turn at the back by the fence before pulling up to the building, close to the rear exit of the bar. The headlights remained on, ricocheting light off the rain soaked puddles and into Bubba's eyes. The patter of the drops on the wind screen picked back up and Bubba squinted against the bright headlights, but could not make out the driver, just a wavy shadow behind the wheel.

Chock turned out the lights behind the bar and hit the overheads for the cleaning crew that would be here at three a.m. He picked up a jacket left over a chair and went to the DJ's stand. The manager was gone. Chock wasn't surprised. *El jefe* was usually the first out the door at closing. Chock tossed the jacket in a pile of odds and ends they jokingly called the lost-and-found department and turned off the sound system. He heard the women in their locker room laughing. He headed to the back door to watch them get safely to their cars.

In the lot, Wes James waited, not pissed, not raging; what he was feeling had gone beyond the muted irritation he usually felt with Louise—with women. He was feeling betrayed and belittled and he didn't like it much.

James watched Chock leaning casually against the back door. Wes wasn't pissed at Chock. He had studied the situation and thought the bouncer was only doing what he was told. No big deal. James had returned to the bar intending to corner Louise when she left at closing—outside the bar, beyond the interest and reach of Chock Aresino. Wes James knew well enough what time Louise left, as he'd gone home with her often enough at 2:40. He had turned fast off the street and into the parking lot, U-turned and waited, trying to make sure that his car would not be directly in the line of sight when the back door to Little Annie's opened. He wanted this to be a surprise. James snapped off the headlights. It was raining, and James could not make up his mind if his not being seen was a problem or a help to him. James understood that Chock *might* to be an issue; the bouncer was always watching the girls as they went to their cars. James slammed the steering wheel with his fist. *Damn!* The rain might keep Chock inside, which would give Wes James time—time to do what? James was driven, but had no clear idea what he was going to say to Louise. He had been insulted, taken for granted and kicked—almost literally, it seemed—out the door and to the curb—and by a whore. He drummed his fingers on the steering wheel and waited.

The back door opened and two women darted through fast, skipping through the wet gravel, coats held over their heads against the rain, now falling in a light drizzle. A third followed, then finally Louise came out, Chock Aresino watching her as she went through the door and into the lot, not hopping like the others, but picking her steps carefully. Three or four other cars pulling around her and left. A fifth car flick on its headlights and flashed them at Louise. ⌐FLICKED

Out of the corner of his eye Chock saw a movement he should not have—on the other side of the lot, a car door opened. Even from the dark of the doorway exit, even though the haze, Chock saw the big white boy getting out of his car. Chock, lowered his head slightly, sticking it just outside the door, squinting at the kid making his way toward Louise.

"Sahara," Bubba called out.

Louise stopped, startled, turning her head in Bubba's direction.

"*Chinga tu madre,*" hissed Chock through his teeth, stepping to the doorway

"Louise!" Wes's voice shouted from the opposite direction. Startled a second time, her head swiveled around toward Wes James.

What was going on?

Chock stepped fully outside the door, a hand held above his face, eyes peering through the steady drizzle, turning his head first one way, then the other. "Hey, what you goddamn fools want?"

Louise stopped a dozen or so feet from Chock, rooted in the light from the open door way. Wes and Bubba both slowed, hesitated, not so much at Chock's demand, but at the sight of each other, with the surprised woman frozen between them.

Bubba came on first, "Sahara, I just wanted to talk to you."

"Hey, what's up?" Wes demanded of no one in particular, only now he was moving forward more slowly, confused, uncertain of this unexpected turn.

Chock bolted forward more quickly, planting himself between Bubba and the girl. "Get going, *cariña*," he snapped over his shoulder to Louise.

Bubba came up short, completely surprised by Chock, who he only dimly recognized. Bubba blinked and looked closely at the black Latino, at his small dark eyes and knitted brow. Sudden wonder lifted Bubba's eyebrows.

"I . . . I," Bubba stammered, then suddenly he spotted Wes James lurch forward and grab Louise by the arm, then yank her toward him. Without thinking Bubba knocked Chock out of the way, going straight for Wes, who started at the sight of Bubba coming at him and dropped his hold on Louise.

"Sahara!"

She turned quickly and put a hand up on Bubba's shoulder, only nothing was going to slow Bubba down.

Chock stumbled backward at the hard push from Bubba, but quickly regained his footing. He lunged past Louise and grabbed Bubba around the neck, but it barely fazed the big kid who whipped around like a snake, seizing Chock's arm and twisting, throwing up one of his own arms to encircle Chock's head beneath him in a reverse headlock. Bubba's speed and power did not so much surprise Chock as frighten him. Chock had not been frightened by another man in a very long time and he was totally bewildered at feeling small and in another's power. Chock yelped and sucked hard through his teeth, realizing that he could not loosen the thick arm around his neck. Helpless, he felt the terrible squeezing and watched his vision narrowing, growing bright white, just before everything went fuzzy and dim.

While Bubba was wrenching the life out of Chock, Wes leaped on Bubba's back and clawed at the kid's eyes with his fingers and their sharp nails.

Adrenalin had numbed Bubba's body to all sensation of pain, but the tearing at his eyes ~~like~~ Wes was doing enraged him, turning him into a snarling animal. Bubba dropped the bouncer and spun around, Wes flopping around on his back like a sack of wet sand. Bubba grabbed for the hand digging into his eyes.

Wes felt his fingers suddenly in the grip of a larger, more powerful hand, twisting his knuckles and fingers.He thumped Bubba's back with the hurt, rolled and tried to tug his hand away, but the fingers held fast. In the midst of his pain James, still clinging to Bubba, felt Louise land on his back and Bubba stumble beneath the load. All three crashed into the gravel, Bubba rolling on top of Wes and Louise, and Wes heard, rather than felt, his fingers dislocate and snap like dry twigs.

When Bubba had blown past Louise she was suddenly seized with terror. Bubba was big, strong, and she felt that someone was in danger of being killed. She saw Chock leap and grab Bubba around the neck, and Bubba spin out, getting Chock in a reverse headlock as Wes pounce on his back. She screamed loud, foul words for them to stop and when Bubba, with Wes on his back, tripped over the fallen bouncer and Wes began screaming in pain, Louise went after Bubba. She jumped over Chock, who was trying to get up, and dropped on top of Bubba and Wes. It was the combined weight of her and Wes that finally forced Bubba flat on the ground.

Wes rolled off first, pushing loose from the pile of arms and legs. Bubba shoved back on the body on his back, not knowing it was Louise, rolled on her and flattened her out, his massive body weight punching the air out of her. He turned, and was just understanding what he had done when Chock reached across the short distance between them and flattened his sap across the back of Bubba's head. Unfazed, Bubba spun to faced Chock and took a second, harder sapping, flat across his temple. Bubba went down like a stone, face in the gravel.

Wes James was yelling: "Fuck! My fucking fingers are broken. Goddamn sonofabitch! My goddamn fingers are busted. The fucker busted my goddamn fingers."

Chock went over to Louise, picking her up. She was gasping, breathing fast, eyes open, blinking.

"You okay, *cariña*?" He asked.

She turned her eyes toward him. "What happened?"

"I don't know, *mi'ja*." Chock answered honestly. "The white boy, he . . . I don't know, *mi'ja*."

Chock looked bewildered, gawking first at Wes James whining, clutching his broken fingers, then at the white boy laying still in the mud, knocked out cold, and finally at Louise standing, shaking and holding her coat together against the light drizzle. It—everything—just seemed to explode out of nowhere like some kind of perfect storm and Chock had only reacted to his tiny, narrow vision of it.

Chock wasn't the only one who didn't know what had happened. The whole intense struggle had taken less than a full minute and no one had any idea what or who had started it, or fully understood the interaction through the blur of sudden violence.

The back door of Annie's yawned open, blowing a dull light across the wet gravel. A car's headlights were on, spotlighting Bubba crumpled next to Chock, his torn t-shirt showing blood on the shoulder. Chock looked around the lot, vaguely annoyed by Wes continuing to moan about his hand.

"Fuck," groaned James, clutching his injured hand. "Fuck, fuck, fuck!"

"*Cállete!, chingado!* " Chock snapped at James.

"I got to, get to a hospital, goddamn it," Wes sputtered back, showing his hand. "Sonofabitch, this fuck'n hurts like hell."

Chock looked at Louise. "You better take him?"

"Shouldn't we call an ambulance?"

"Hell no, *mi'ja!* We'd be up to our asses in fucking cops."

"Okay," Louise replied, putting her hand on Wes' shoulder. "But what about him?" She indicated Bubba.

Chock rolled Bubba onto his back, bending forward, looking close into his face. Bubba's eyes were rolling, squeezing shut and opening, as if he were coming out of a bad dream. He stared a moment at Chock.

"Who are you?"

"Security," Chock answered.

"You're the bouncer?"

Chock nodded.

"What hit me?"

Chock waved his sap in Bubba's face, but not sure if he could see in the dim light, said: "Me jack. *chingado.*"

"Jack?"

"Yeah, *güero.* A black-Jack, asshole. A fucking sap." To make his point, Chock slapped the sap against his palm with a loud clap. "And I'll crack your ass again, you fuck with me."

Bubba sat up rubbing his neck. "Why?"

"You was tearing hell out of these people."

Bubba turned his head and saw Louise standing and Wes James whimpering over his broken hand. The turn of his head gave Bubba a stab of pain and he grabbed at his temple, wincing. He took a couple of breaths and looked again at Chock. "What'd I do that for?"

Chock stood to his feet. "Damned if I know."

"Goddamn it, Louise!" Wes shouted. "Can you get me to a goddamn hospital?"

Bubba watched as Louise pulled Wes to his feet. "What's wrong with him?"

Wes heard him. "Fuck! Asshole! You broke my goddamn fingers," Wes spat at him as Louise lead him to her car. "Hey, someone turn off my lights and engine."

Louise took Wes James to the emergency room (the story now that the hand was busted in a slammed car door). Bubba shook the stars out of his head and went back to his car. Chock watched Bubba leave the lot, then brushed off the wet gravel, put his sap back in his rear pocket, and went back inside to close up Little Annie Fanny's.

A neighbor found Bubba Dean the next day, slumped over in the front seat of his car that was parked out front of his apartment building in East Oakland. The neighbor shook his head, wondering what the stupid white boy was even doing, living in this neighborhood. He was a big kid, but not that big.

The medical examiner, following a quick autopsy, ruled it a homicide, the cause of death a blow to the temple area leading to slow brain hemorrhaging. The police were immediately involved.

As Bubba's body had been discovered miles from San Leandro, and Little Annie Fanny's, the police made no direct connection with the topless bar. The freight terminal was the only focus of the investigation. Wes, who had never exchanged a single word with Bubba Dean until the fight, could honestly say he didn't know the country boy. Wes learned from the other dockworkers that the police had nothing to go on (they suspected a botched robbery in Oakland) and had discovered no immediate kin. In a search of Bubba's apartment they had discovered a shoe box stuffed with money, a few uncashed paychecks, and a Valentine's Day card, still in the cellophane wrapper.

The police were now trying to locate some relatives in Arkansas, but were having no luck. The next of kin Bubba had listed with the company was his mother, who had died several years before. It seemed that no one alive knew Bubba Dean from anywhere except the freight terminal of NorCal, and no one there knew him very well.

Wes called Louise, who spoke with Chock, and the three of them met at Annie's after closing.

"What the *hell* are we gonna do?" Louise wondered, in a tiny, frantic voice.

They were seated around one of the tables by the bar, near the waitress's station. Wes had tried to sit close to Louise, but she pushed away from him. She did not want to give the impression of ganging up on the bouncer.

"Nothing," Wes answered, his tone anything but smooth and assuring. "We're not going to do a goddamn thing. You involve cops you got trouble. Once those assholes get into shit you don't know where it's going, and anyway, what they don't know ain't gonna hurt us."

They both looked at the bouncer.

"What about you Chock," asked Louise.

"Yeah," seconded Wes. "You're the one that killed him."

Chock looked from one of them to the other. "Fuck both you *chingados*."

Only Chock knew they were right, he had been the one who killed the big white boy.

Maybe he should kill them both—the way they was looking at him, especially the *flaco*. Ripping the head of that rat-faced fuck would be easy. Chock imagined doing it with one hand around Louise's scrawny neck. Only they wouldn't deport him for that—he'd end up in a *gringo* prison for the rest of his life.

"Hey, man," James piped up. "I'm only saying what happened. You hit the guy with the sap not me. We didn't do nothing."

"I take both you *pinche* fucks with me, *chingato*." Chock snarled, reaching for Wes who jumped out of his chair to get out of the way of the big hand.

Louise reached out and shook Chock by the shoulder. "Chock, stop, neither of you are thinking. Punching someone isn't going to fix anything."

Chock leaned back and pointed his finger at Wes. "You watch that fucking mouth, *pendejo.*"

Carefully watching Chock, Wes took his chair and looked at Louise.

Louise saw real fear in Wes' eyes. Partly because of Chock, she thought, but more at the situation in which he found himself. She couldn't afford to have Wes panic.

"Wes," she said, "we all got something to loose here. If we go to the police and they start investigating we're all fucked: you got a parole violation hanging somewhere in this shit, and I have a Utah warrant for soliciting that I skipped out on. We'll all go down for something, even if it's not for murder."

She had the attention of both men now. Chock spoke first, with a touch of angry sarcasm. "Okay, *querida,* what you thinking?"

"I'm thinking," she answered, "that the cops don't have shit right now and they won't if we all keep our mouths shut."

"Jesus," whined Wes James, "Louise, you and me didn't really do anything. It was him." James nodded to the bouncer. "He killed the guy."

Chock's chair went over as he surged to his feet. "*Pequeña perra,*" and before Louise could intervene Chock had Wes James by the throat.

"Chock, let him go—let him go!" Louise screamed hanging onto one of Chock's arms trying to pull him loose from James.

The woman might as well have been trying to pry the bumper off a truck, but she hung on yanking and screaming, watching Wes' face going from pink to purple. In desperation she jumped up on her chair, wrapped her arms around Chock's neck and sunk her teeth into the bouncer's ear, clamping down hard. Chock screamed, and letting go of James threw Louise to the ground. Cursing loudly in Spanish he looked as if he were going for Louise, but checked himself at the last minute, slapping his hand again the bleeding ear.

against

Chinga tu madre, puta de mierda," he screamed at Louise, who was scrambled to her feet and back peddling way from him. "What the fuck!" He looked the blood in his hand and snatched up a napkin from the waitress's station. "You bite my fucking ear off, bitch," he shouted at her, dabbing the napkin at the bloody ear.

"You were killing Wes," she shouted back, and turned to where Wes was leaning at the other end of the bar and panting, shaking his head to clear it. "Wes, are you alright?"

He spun around to her and Chock. "Fuck no, I ain't all right. You keep that fuck'n nigger away from me!"

Louise jumped in between the two of them and yelled a James, "Shut up, Wes! This is all going to hell if you two can't get a grip on yourselves."

The three of them stood eyeing each other and breathing hard; Louise turning from one man to the other, finally saying to Chock. "Let me see your ear."

She approached Chock and pulled his hand and the bloody napkin away from the side of his face. He bent slightly so she could see.

"You're ears still there, come with me," and then to Wes. "Wes stay here. I'm gonna bandage Chock's ear."

Louise lead the bouncer to the women's locker room and got out the first aid kit. She sat the big bouncer in a chair and started to work on his ear. It was not nearly as bad as it looked in the bar room.

"Chock," she said. "You gotta leave Wes alone."

"He's an asshole."

"I know, Chock, but we can't have him get panicky and go to the police." She bent down and looked straight in Chock's dark eyes. "You understand that, don't you?"

"He's a chickenshit."

"Chock, do you understand me?!"

Chock nodded. "I understand, *mi'ja*. I'll kill the fucker if he goes to the police."

"Chock!" Louise grabbed him by the shoulders. "You let me handle Wes. He's afraid of you and people do stupid things when their afraid. Be cool! I don't want him running off and doing something stupid because he scared. Do you understand?!"

"I understand," repeated Chock. "You handle it, *mija*." He looked at her in earnest. "*Cariña*, I only hit that white boy because I thought one of them fools was gonna hurt you."

"I know, Chock. I know. You didn't do anything wrong. None of us did anything wrong." She got the bouncer to his feet. "Let's go explain it to Wes."

They returned to the bar room where James sat at the table staring glumly at his shoes. They sat down and all three looked carefully at one another.

"Wes," started Louise. "Listen carefully. Chock did what he did because he thought he was protecting me. It was his job, for Christ's sake, and he shouldn't go to jail because of that. And you—for over a year you've been consorting with a known prostitute with a warrant out for her arrest; that's a potential parole violation, Wes—you want to go back to jail? And me, I've got at least one warrant in Utah, and maybe another in St. Louis—I can't remember—both for prostitution and I *know* I don't want to go to jail! Hell, I could be looking at up to ten years, Wes, tell me where in the hell is the justice in that? I'm living a reasonably straight life here, and have been for over two years, please don't fuck that up."

She waited, watching Wes for a moment, then turning to Chock. "It was an accident, Chock. Shit, the whole damn thing lasted less than a minute, the three of us slipping and sliding in the damn mud." She touched the bouncer on the shoulder and squeezed.

"No one did anything wrong, Chock. Not you, not me, not Wes, and no one should have to go to jail because of what happened."

The bouncer said nothing. He was watching Wes James, who was looking at Louise.

"Wes," stressed Louise. "No one did anything wrong," she repeated with emphasis. "But if the police get involved the shit will surly hit the fan."

"Yeah, okay, Louise. You're right," Wes agreed after a moment. "You get a bunch of cops and lawyers in the middle of this bullshit and everything'll go sideways for sure. They can't find right from wrong with a roadmap and a flashlight." He made a face. "Yeah, I get you."

Louise looked back and forth between the two men. "We agree then, to keep the cops out of this?"

Chocked nodded, still watching Wes, who was looking at Louise.

"Yeah, Louise—you're right. Let's not fuck this up."

Like that, all three agreed that it was in the interests of justice to leave the police and the law out of the fight at Little Annie Fanny's

Friends and Enemies

"It's all these damn Mexicans." He pronounced it *Mess-e-cans*. "They're coming over here taking our goddamn jobs and sucking off the government tit. And them fools in Washington ain't doing squat to stop it." His name was Al Covington. "They're fucking over the whole damn country." He was a heavy man wearing a thick plaid shirt against the winter cold. "You ought to shoot the whole damn mess of 'em. That'd solve most of the country's problems."

To his left sat a tall, lanky driver. He grinned and asked, "Shoot who, Al, the Mexicans or the politicians?" His name was Ted Devine, and he didn't pronounce it *Mess-e-cans*.

"*Both,* goddamn it," ripped Covington. "But start the party off with the goddamn beaners. At least that'd stop them from breeding like goddamn jackrabbits. The next time you see one of them fat beaner sows trailing a dozen kids behind her ask her how many more kids she gonna pop out? I bet she's got six, eight, or ten little beaner bastards at home and ready to pop out five more. Man, them beaners breed like fucking rabbits."

Roy Sales leaned forward slightly, pushing his coffee mug along the table, and said, "Yeah, well Al, you just might wanna lighten up a bit, 'cause you can never be too sure who's got a beaner hiding in the woodpile."

The two drivers, Covington and Devine, blanched at the familiar turn of phrase. It was Covington who asked, "What you talking about, Roy?"

"Now Connie here," Sales went on with a wink at Covington, "he's got a grandmother who's one of them damn *Mess-e-cans* you're talking about."

Al Covington, not normally a man made shy by the use of ornery and despicable language, looked aside at Connie Washington, the big black man sitting quietly at the end of the table. Oddly, Washington's considerable presence was made all the more potent by a taciturn character. It was hard to get a word out of the man, so when he did speak, one took special note of the weight it carried.

"That right, Connie?" asked Covington, his eyes getting a bit small at the corners. "Your grandmother a Mexican?"

Smiling, Sales took note that this time around Al Covington did not pronounce it *Mess-e-can.*

Washington gazed at Covington for a moment, then offered him a nearly imperceptible dip of his head.

Ted Devine sat easy, staying out of the direct line of fire. Devine didn't know either Washington or Sales particularly well and hadn't really dwelt on the possibilities, but after a second, quick glance at Washington, thought it was best to avoid any direct confrontation with the big man. Covington was a brash loud-mouth, and had stupidly used the word "beaner." Devine kept his eyes on Sales and carefully considered that this time Covington might have gone over the line by a few steps too far. These days a black man could have just about anything mixed into his blood; it made talking about race a pointless rush to a bad ending.

Covington turned away from Washington, his face changed, assuming an expression mixing somewhere between embarrassed and startled. He glanced again at Washington. "Sorry, man," he apologized. "I meant no offense. I was meaning all the illegals—that's all. You know me, Connie. You know I meant no disrespect to you or your family."

Washington waved him off, apparently unconcerned by the gaff. Washington didn't know much about Al Covington, but knew him well enough to figure that the white man was not afraid of him, and was therefore probably somewhere close to sincere in his proffered regrets. Connie decided to let the crass remarks slide aside. Anyway, he'd heard rude language all his life and was certain that popping Covington would only guarantee getting him fired from a good job. To hell with Covington. Washington looked out the window and only wanted the snow to stop, exchange trailers with these men, and get back to LA. Washington hated the snow and the cold.

Roy Sales was another matter and he wasn't going to drop the ball just yet. Roy raised his eyebrows at Covington. "Let me tell you something about immigrants, Al. You owe them a mighty big debt."

"Yeah, how the fuck's that?"

"'Cause Immigrants—many of them illegal—saved this country's ass once before, and they just might again."

Al Covington smiled at Sales. It was more like a smirk. "Goddamn, Roy. You winding up to start flinging some of your political horseshit again—your *liberal* political horseshit?"

"Nope."

"I know you, Sales—I know you're just dying to bust my chops again with some of your radical liberal crap."

"You shouldn't use those two words together."

"What two words?"

"Radical and liberal."

"Why not?"

"'Cause their . . . " Sales smiled . . . "contradictions in terms."

"Contradictions in . . . " Covington made a face. "Ah, hey, you know what, Sales: Fuck you and the damn horse you rode in on. Contradiction in terms. What the hell does that even mean? You're crazy, you know that—Nuts! Man, I sure hope it stops snowing." He gave a little chuckle. "Damn, I sure don't want to get stuck here all day listening to your bullshit."

"Come on, Al." Sales dipped his head toward the window. "It looks like we got a little time."

"You're crazy, Sales."

Earlier that morning, and right behind Connie Washington, Roy Sales had pulled into the big dark lot next to the Country Kitchen Cafe. The two of them lined up their rigs and began the process of unhooking their trailers. It was just past two in the morning, and the only light that shone on their work was from the side windows of the all-night restaurant. Together they cranked down the landing gears, then clambered up behind their tractors to disconnect the air hoses and pigtails. They worked fast. It was cold, their hands growing numb, skin stinging against the frozen metal and although the snow was floating down light, the wind and the darkening clouds promised much worse to come.

"Sure I'm crazy, Al, but crazy like a fox." Sales took a sip of his coffee and winked at Covington over the rim of his cup. "With some luck I can make you crazy like a fox too."

"Shit." Covington gave out a hoot and slammed his hand on the table. "You just like busting my chops, Roy. Why do you do that?"

Sales smiled. "'Cause I can."

The four of them were in Big Pine, California, on Highway 395 that wound its way through the Owens Valley. The small town—elevation five-thousand feet, population fifteen hun-dred—was snuggled up between the Sierra Nevada Range and the White Mountains. Roy Sales and Connie Washington were there only to swap out trailers with team of drivers that came south out of Sparks, Nevada—Ted Devine and Al Covington. The Big Pine swap had to be done because the Nevada wing of the company was nonunion, and union drivers from California couldn't operate in that state. The Big Pine swap was the company's solution to the standoff with the union, and a way to keep from offering the drivers at the Sparks warehouse a union contract.

"Shit, Roy," Covington came back at him. "You're an asshole, you know that?"

"I do, Al, I surely do," Roy returned, grinning back in the face of Al's smirk.

Covington grew resigned. "Okay, what the hell," he said. "Get it over with. What you gonna start hammering me with?"

"You brought it up."

Covington looked genuinely surprised. "What?"

"Immigration."

Al waved him off. "Goddamn, Roy. *Illegal* immigration. That's what I brought up. *Illegal* immigration!"

"Let me tell you a story," pressed Sales, "a story about an ille-gal immigrant."

"More bullshit."

"Nope."

"Ah, shit, Sales." Covington shook his head. "It's probably some Crap I've heard a million times before."

"We got time."

"We sure as fuck do," seconded Devine.

Devine's crack brought all four drivers to look out the window at their tractor-trailers. The men could barely see the glow of the running lights through the near white out. The snow outside had turned hard, the flakes no longer fluffy, but popping against the glass of the restaurant nearly like hail. The snow was sticking to the ground and piling up enough that it would prevent the drivers from pulling their rigs out of the parking lot anytime soon.

Ted Devine added, "It sure as hell looks like we're gonna be here a couple more hours, goddamn it. Maybe longer." He wagged his head. "Okay, Roy, go on—amuse us. Tell us a story Al here hasn't heard a dozen times before."

Roy settled back in his chair, looking just the tiniest bit smug. "All right," and he started off with his story: "In today's world you get off a plane or a boat here in this country and they want a DNA blueprint of every wart, canker sore and ass hair you got, but do you think they wanted that stuff back at the turn of the 1900s? Hell no. When those boats docked in New York or Boston, or wherever, those immigrants just told them their name, country of origin, and where they was headed."

Covington shook his head. "Bullshit, Roy. Them boys needed something—some kind of papers."

"Nope. You only needed two legs to come down the gangplank," replied Sales. "Today Wop is slang for the Italians, but do you know what it meant back then? Wop stood for With-Out-Papers, and I ain't making that up. Christ, Al, your lily white grandpa could have told them he was a Chinaman from Timbuktu off to see his monkey's uncle in Kalamazoo and they'd have wrote it down, handed them some entry papers, and waved him on. That was what passed for legal in those days. No one gave a shit back then."

Al frowned, turned and aped a doleful look at Ted Devine sitting next to him. Devine, elbows on the table, plucked at his moustache and shrugged. "Yeah, maybe."

"Maybe, my ass," Sales went on. "Ted, I got two bonified illegals in my family—going back to the early turn of the last century. I ain't kidding. Both my grandparents were illegals."

"Roy," Al challenged, "now you're not gonna tell me and Ted here that some of your blood comes from south of the Rio Grande, 'cause you look whiter than that snow piling up outside?"

"No, Al," Roy grunted, "I'm not. My grandfather's blood comes from a worse place than Mexico and my grandmother's from a worser place still," and he hesitated, sizing up the storyline ahead, how he was going to negotiate the twists and turns of his true, but unlikely tale. Sales was determined to make a point here. "Humph. Okay, let me dig a bit into the story, Al."

Al laughed. "I can't fuck'n wait," and he winked at Ted Devine. "I heard your stories before, Roy. Half of them is bullshit, Roy, and the other half's a lie."

Connie Washington spoke up. "Just let him go on, Al."

Al glanced at Washington, who sat unsmiling at the end of the table. Washington was a very different man than Sales. Roy Sales was the kind of guy you'd have a real hard time not liking. He had forty years of truck driving behind him, and with that came a taste for the kind of humor found in odd things seen, real things done, and the quirky behavior so often found in men on the road; his was a practical and affable humor that could both reveal and round off the harder edges in life. Where Sales was warm,

Washington was cool. Washington seemed to have no particular love of life; he appeared as a big taciturn, unsmiling man of little adventure and no sense of humor.

Covington shrugged off the sharpness in Washington's voice and waved a consenting hand at Roy Sales.

"Okay, Roy, go on," Al Covington said with a smile and a sip from his coffee cup. "Let's pass the time until the snow stops and hope your bullshit is good enough to be worth the breath it takes to tell it." Covington leaned slightly forward, his smile growing a bit testier. "Is it all about your illegal relations? 'Cause I can see by the fact of you sitting here that they never got deported."

"No, Al, they wasn't, and that's also part of the story."

"Which side of your family?"

"My mother's."

"Humph." Al took another sip of coffee. "Okay, get on with it, Sales. You got us curious now, ain't that right Ted?"

Devine nodded.

"You'll like this one, Covington." Roy went on. "It's got some real twists and turns."

"I probably heard it before, Sales," Al replied. "Knowing you as long as I have, I think I heard them all."

"Maybe, but it won't hurt you to hear them again."

"Okay, Sales, shoot."

"Let's start with my grandmother, Al. She was pure Cherokee, from right off the Missouri River."

"Well, she'd be a citizen then, Roy," Devine quickly pointed out, then frowned. "Wouldn't she be?"

"Her actual legal status? Her being Native American? Maybe. Technically. But I really don't know, Ted, really I don't." Sales made a face and shrugged. "Natives always lived in some sort of legal limbo—or felt they did. And I guess partially because of that she hated this country with a passion, hated everything about it. I never heard her, or any other native, claim citizenship, but I know she'd have thrown it out the window if she could. She never voted and never drew Social Security. I don't even know if she qualified. If you asked her, she'd never say *American*. She'd say Cherokee."

"Well, your grandma didn't hate your white grandpa, apparently," Al quickly assumed, then grinned knowingly at Ted. "Or are you gonna tell us he was an Indian too—which would make you an Indian, Roy, or at least half." He leaned back in his chair, a shrewd smile pulling at his face. "Man, I don't know where you're going with this, Roy, but knowing you, I bet it'll be damn good."

Sales chuckled. "To answer your first question, Al, my grandpa was white through and through, but never a citizen."

"How the hell did that happen?" Ted Devine wanted to know.

"That's the meat of the story."

That brought a laugh from Al Covington. "Or the horseshit."

Connie Washington was silently watching this exchange. He had heard all of Roy's stories before, and had never decided how the measure of truth and fiction played out in them. He always assumed that the better part was true, but he also figured that Roy played with the truth just enough to make the point he was intending to make. Generally, Washington had little patience for deception, but he trusted Sales enough that he was careful not to inquire too deeply into the truth of his tales. At the end of the day, Washington always figured that truth was only a thing teased from competing deceptions, but then Washington was one of those strangely cynical men who never lost much sleep over lost truth. The truth was always there; you could feel it and you could find it, if you took the trouble to look deep enough into the welter of deception they all lived in.

"You see, Al," Sales was saying, "my grandfather's name was Karl, and he was in the army—the wrong one—back in the very early nineteen hundreds. He was born in Prussia around 1891 or 92, one of fourteen children on a hog farm." He waved his hand to show that the exact date lacked importance. "Anyway, his father boots little Karl off the farm as my grandpa made up one too many mouths to feed, and at the age of fifteen little Karl heads off to Danzig,[5] the nearest big city. Short on work, he signs up with the Kaiser's army as a way to put some coin in his pocket. Then along comes World War I and he fights on the eastern front until the Russians surrender, and then he gets transferred to the Western Front. Christ, he can't catch a break." Sales paused to take a sip of coffee, studying Covington over the rim of the cup, measuring the impact of what he was saying. "As Grandpa used to tell the story he's now in France, and at twenty-six or seven is the oldest non-com[6] in his outfit. By this time the Germans are taking a real pounding by the allies and are running real short on manpower. Well, one day his commander sends Grandpa down to the rail depot to round up the latest replacements for the front. Grandpa gets there to find out that his company's replacements are kids of twelve and thirteen. They were so small, he said, that their rifles were bigger than they were, and their helmets hung down over their eyes. Well, Grandpa, gets real pissed and tells his commander that he's gonna take these kids over and surrender them to the American Expeditionary Forces that have just arrived in France. Grandpa didn't want to surrender to the French or the English since by this time the war had gotten so brutal that prisoners on both sides were horribly abused and sometimes killed outright. The Americans hadn't been in the war long enough to get that low-life, so Grandpa surrendered him and

5. A city today called Gdansk, in northwest Poland.
6. Non-commissioned officer; typically corporals and sergeants.

these kids to the Americans. Now there was some kind of law in France that said there couldn't be no foreign POW camps on their soil, so all the German prisoners captured by the Americans were loaded onto transports and taken to the US. Grandpa thought they landed in Savanna, Georgia, but he wasn't real sure, and they were all squeezed onto trains headed for a POW camp somewhere up in Montana. But before they get anywhere near there, they learn of a heavy German settlement in Sedalia, Missouri, and as they pass through Sedalia, the train slows going through a rail yard. Since the train wasn't heavily guarded, Grandpa and about a dozen other German soldiers jump off. The Germans in Sedalia hide them out and get them integrated into their community. To his dying day, my grandfather was here illegally. But unlike his Cherokee wife he voted in a lot of elections and drew Social Security, but he always lived in perpetual fear that he'd be found out and deported. But, of course, he never was."

Covington leaned forward, interested now. "So what happened to him—after he jumped off the train? How'd he live? How'd he meet your grandma?"

"Well, Sedalia was hog country, and my grandpa knew hogs— remember he grew up on a hog farm back in the old coun-try. So he ups and becomes a hog butcher and goes to work for one of THE big meat packing plants there. My grandma also worked in the plant. The way he told the story, she started pestering him one day and wouldn't stop until he took to rolling in the hay with her."

"What's your grandma say?" asked Covington.

"I asked. She smiled."

Covington slapped the table with a guffaw. "So, she made him do it."

"Something like that," Roy came back. "But I guess he didn't object too much."

"Was she good looking?"

"She was my grandmother, Al, you dick. I don't know. I never looked at her that way."

Ted Devine broke in. "So they stayed butchering hogs their whole life? How's that saving the country?"

"That's only where he started out," responded Sales. "But I think Grandpa saw some righteous kind of funny payback in that—from butchering men to butchering hogs. Grandpa once told me that in slitting the belly you couldn't tell the difference between man and hog by what rolled out."

Ted Devine looked down at the table top and jerked his head back and forth. "You could've kept that shit to yourself, Sales."

"But it kinda makes you wonder about things, don't it, Ted?"

Devine cocked his eyebrow at Sales. "Yeah, it makes me wonder, all right."

Al Covington waved his hand to quiet Devine, then to Sales: "Go on, Roy. It's a funny story, but what's your point in all this hog butchering?"

"No point in that part, but after my grandpa met my grandma they had to leave Missouri in order to get married."

"Why's that?" Devine wanted to know.

"I can see you guys don't know your history," Roy replied with a wink and a wise nod. "Remember, she was Cherokee, and at that time in Missouri being an Indian might as well have been black, and whites couldn't marry outside of their race."

"Yeah," Al commented with a stolen, half glance at Washington, then made a concession. "Well, things was fucked up way back then. I gotta admit that."

"Way back then, eh?" Roy chuckled. "Al, you got to remember that it wasn't too long ago, back in the mid-1960s, that intermarriage became legal in states like Virginia. How old was you then?"

"Okay, Roy," Al conceded. "Okay, but like Ted asked, what does all this have to do with illegal immigrants saving the country?"

"Well, Karl and Tia—that was my grandmother's name—headed north into Pennsylvania looking to marry and start a family. They ended up in Pittsburg where Karl got himself a job as a puddler with the brand new U.S. Steel Corporation.[7] US industries were just starting to get real big around that time, and shortly after that he got himself involved in the Great Steel Strike in the 1920s. The labor battles of the early last century seesawed back and forth until the Roosevelt Administration forced these giant companies to negotiate with labor in good faith."

"Yeah—yeah—okay Sales. We get it," sneered Covington. "You're gonna start up with some of your pro-union bullshit again."

Washington shifted slightly in his seat. "Yeah—yeah," he mimicked Covington. "*Unions,* Brother Covington—yeah, you remember them folks, don't ya, Al? Those folks that brought you the weekend and sick leave and vacations with pay?"

Both Covington and Devine glanced at the big man, but said nothing.

Sales waved at Washington to settle him down and went on, "Immigrants, both legal and illegal, *were* the labor movement, they were the ones that built unions and gave us all the goodies we got. All those Germans, Irish, Italians, Poles, and everyone else that came from the old country knowing from the get-go who their enemy was, and based on that knowing built the American labor movement."

"Yeah," Covington popped off, "but you said it—they was from Europe, and they . . . " and he suddenly broke off, looking vexed at the table top.

---

7. In the early days of steel and iron manufacturing, a puddler was an individual who stirred the molten iron into a puddle. This was done to prevent the natural tendency of molten iron to granulize and become too brittle to roll into bars.

Unexpectedly, Connie Washington leaned in. "And they was *white*," he said it with a small crooked smile. "That was what you were about to say, wasn't it, Covington."

"Hold up, Connie," Sales jumped in. "Simmer down. Let's not go all racial with this. It's got everything to do with people and nothing to do with race." He turned back to Covington and Devine. "And more than anything, it's about *tradition*." He paused a moment seriously regarding the two Sparks drivers across from him. "You see, those immigrants had a tradition of unity, while we Americans, well, we got a tradition of rugged individualism, which suits our bosses just fine—that way they can pick us off one rugged individual at a time."

Ted Devine was silently watching Sales. Al Covington was also silent, but showing a vaguely sour expression. There was enough common-sense in Sales' remarks that the two of them felt they could only wait for the other shoe.

"All I'm saying," Sales went on, looking directly at Al, "is that without the tradition of unity that the immigrants brought with them, and the ability to recognize their enemy and a boatload of guts, you and Ted here would still be working sixteen hours a day, seven days week. I mean, you got an eight hour work day, lunch breaks, coffee breaks, time and a half for over eight, vacations with pay, pensions, medical, the whole kit-and-caboodle. Those immigrants built your world." He paused again, then added with emphasis, "And, Al, now just how do you suppose all them good things happened?" Roy pinned him with a look. "You imagine that all the rich people in America gave up those things because they was good God-fearing Christians who just couldn't wait to do the right and charitable Christian thing?"

Ted Devine ignored the crack. "Ok, ok, Roy, so immigrants built unions, but saving the *whole* country?" He snorted, then challenged, "Come on, Roy, get real. You can only stretch this line of crap so far."

"Farther than you think, Ted," Sales came back. "Think about it. Money! Money saved the country. Unions forced these greedy companies to pay their labor enough money to buy what they were making. Hell, Henry Ford started his own in-house union so his workers could buy the cars they were making. Immigrants started unions and unions jump-started the economy. They built the middle class. They became the middle class."

Covington made a face. "That's ancient history, Sales. Ancient history!"

"He's right, goddamn it, Roy," Devine jumped in, for the first time looking a little cross. "We see where you're going with this shit. You're pro-union—we get that—but up in Sparks we have the right to work without a union. And fuck it, man, we like it that way. Nevada's a right-to-work state, man. There ain't no unions there. And we get the same wages and benefits as you guys, and without paying a union for them. I like that, man."

"Right. You're not paying for your benefits, Ted—*we are*—me and Connie. *Us* guys in California are paying union dues so you can have the same wages and benefits as us and not pay for them."

"How the hell you figure that?" Al demanded.

"The very existence of a union in the state next door is enough to scare the company into paying the same wages and benefits just to keep the union out. And it's that union in the next-door state me and Connie and a hundred thousand other men are paying for. We're paying your dues for you, Al."

Ted Devine took over. "Roy, you're sounding like the company's our enemy. They're not our enemy."

"That's it, Ted. You hit the nail on the head." Sales shot back. "Unlike the immigrants, you native born now think your enemy is your friend and your friend is your enemy."

Ted Devine wouldn't ease up. "Ah come on with the bullshit, Sales. The company's not our enemy. I like the people I work for. They give us good paying jobs."

Sales shook his head. "You see, Devine? You got it backwards. The truth is the other way around. *You're* giving your bosses good paying jobs, and that job is to make you work like a dog and make them rich."

"Bullshit, Sales," objected Devine, suddenly looking genuinely angry. "You're just jealous that we get paid good and we get good benies, and all without paying union dues."

Sales kept shaking his head. "Ted, Ted, *Ted*. You're not listening. You got those wages and all those benefits *because* of the union, because there's always a union in the woodpile. The company we both work for is bribing you men with union wages and benefits in order to keep the union out of Sparks—out of Nevada."

"That's fine with me."

"It's fine with your bosses too, Ted, 'cause they know that your attitude weakens the union, and if the union goes south, so does the threat, and so do your wages and benefits."

"Yeah, yeah, we get it, Roy," Covington said. "We get it. It was unions that gave us good working conditions, but I still don't see what this has to do with today, with *illegal* immigrants and saving the country?" he glanced over at Washington. "And I ain't saying anything racial, Connie. Okay?"

Washington didn't look convinced and Covington turned his eyes away.

Devine added, "Okay, Roy. You're all about the old days, and maybe you're right, and maybe unions being around scared these companies into treating us right, but like Al says—what does any of that have to do with the Mexicans that are coming in illegally today?"

"Okay, answer me this, Ted—why are they coming?"

"'Cause they got squat in Mexico."

"That's right," Roy agreed. "They're poor, sorry-ass bastards, just like your grandparents when they came from Europe."

"Yeah, and, so . . . ?"

"And just like the immigrants from Europe, they're poor and they're poor because they was getting fucked in the old country."

"I still don't see . . . "

"Again, Ted, that's it. You said it. You *can't* see, but the new immigrants, they *can* see. Because they're poor and getting fucked they *can* see who their enemy is—they see their enemy clearly. They grow up with the seeing and knowing the *patrón*, and they bring that seeing to this county, and that's what'll save this country again."

"So what are you saying?"

"I'm saying that they see well enough that they don't get their friends confused with their enemies. And that'll go a long way to helping out working guys like you and me."

The waitress came over to refill their cups. "You guys are getting a little loud over here," she mentioned quietly. "I guess you must be talking politics."

It was Washington who answered her. "It ain't about politics. It's about education."

"It's still a little loud." She filled Washington's cup. "And I got other customers.

Sales smiled at her and remarked, "Apologize for us, will ya, and tell them that education is sometimes a tussle." He winked and jabbed a thumb at Covington and Devine.

"Maybe," she rejoined, returning his smile. "But all the same, do your educating a little quieter. There's other people here now and they don't want to get educated."

Sales glanced around at the few people sitting at the nearby tables and laughed. "We know, sweetheart, we know. Education can be rude sometimes."

Even Covington and Devine chuckled at his remark.

"And anyway," the waitress pointed out. "Here come the snow plows out of Bishop. You'll be able to get out of here soon."

The drivers turned in their seats and looked out at the highway through the frosted window. A big snow plow from Caltrans was rapidly running the white stuff into a berm along the shoulder. The snowfall had stopped and the sun was cresting brightly over the White Mountains to the eastern side of the Owens Valley.

"I guess." Covington raised his mug. "Just as soon as we finish this coffee and we listen to some more of Roy's bullshit."

She shook her head and walked away.

"Yeah, Roy, Connie, we got to get out of here," Devine announced. "Me and Al got a longer drive than you two, and it's all heading into snow up north, but I just want to say one thing about being educated. We're not dumb, Roy. You act like we are, but we're not. We *do* see and don't think we don't. We watch the news. We read the papers. We see the truth. Maybe in the old days immigrants did some good things, and so did unions. But nowadays it's different. These companies we work for are different now. They treat us right. They're okay. We don't need unions anymore. The truth of that is right in front of you, Sales, as plain as the nose on your face. Ancient history is ancient history. These days are different from our grandfather's day. You gotta see that things are different now."

Sales grunted and said to Devine, "The truth is right in front of you—like the nose on your face—plain as day, you think. Humph. Okay, Ted, we'll break up this little party, but before we do I got one more story for you guys."

Covington hung his head and groaned. "Jesus Christ, Roy. Is there no end to it."

"Let him go on," Devine granted. "We got a little time."

"It's a quick one."

Devine nodded. "Ok, Sales, we'll be polite."

"And try not to look too bored," added Covington.

"But no more crap about unions," Devine grinned and wagged his finger. "I can only take so much educating."

"No more about unions," Sales replied, then took a gulp of the coffee and winked at Connie Washington.

"I remember this time," he started off, "when me and Mac Gamble were coming back from Korea where the two of us had been stationed in the Army. We caught this midnight flight out of Honolulu for San Fran. But before we took off we stopped at a vending machine and picked up a can of hot stew. Of course, back in those days—the late-fifties—you could get on a plane without passing through a metal detector, or a search, or any of that kind of nonsense, so I got that can and snuck it on board under my Army jacket. After take-off I called the stewardess over and told her that Mac was sick and was going to throw-up. She immediately yanked a puke bag out of the seat pocket and ran off while Mac was pretending to up-chuck, making all the fuck'n noise he could—heaving and coughing, howling, hissing and cussing, making like he was throwing the most righteous puke in the world into that bag—but what we actually did was dump the can of stew into the bag. So when the stewardess made her way back over to our section again I handed her the bag—only I handed it up to her open. The babe back pedaled, clapped a hand over her mouth and nose and told me to close the bag. I apologized to her and took back the bag and looked inside, raised my eyebrows and sounding surprised as hell. I said, "Damn, Mac, no wonder you're sick. You don't chew your damn food," and I reached in and plucked out a piece of beef. "Hell, Mac, this piece of meat hasn't been chewed at all. It still looks good enough to eat," and I up and pitched the hunk of stew meat into my mouth and started chewing with a big, wide smile on my face. Man, you should'a seen the look in this babe's eyes. She turned all white, her baby-blues getting round as dinner plates, and off she raced for the front of the plane, leaving me and Mac howling in stitches."

Connie had heard this story before. Even so he had to smile as he watched the two other truck drivers at the table roar with laughter. Humor was forgiving and the great equalizer.

"Jesus, Roy," Covington blurted out between laughs. "What an asshole thing to do."

Smiling, Sales waited.

Covington added, "I gotta remember that one." He wiped at his eyes. "Jesus, Sales, how'd you get the crust?"

Ted Devine sat forward. "And what the hell is the message in that story, Sales?" he wanted to know, a sassy grin on his face, his cheeks pink from laughing. "I gotta give you that, Sales. You always got a message. So what is it this time?"

"Just a simple one, Ted. It's that the truth is not always as plain as the nose on your face."

Ted Devine snorted and grew more serious. "Yeah, you're right about that, Sales. Truth isn't always as plain as the nose on your face."

Sales nodded. "You got to live certain things to know them—be on the inside of things to know the outside of them."

Washington spoke up, "Listen to him, Devine. Try being black a while. It might give you a whole new perspective on what it means to be a white man."

Ted Devine heard Washington, but offered no response. Instead, he kept his eyes clapped on Sales, who was quietly appraising him with a soft, understated smile.

Devine said, "Like I said earlier, Sales, we're not dumb. We get it."

Sales replied, "I know you're not dumb, Ted. You and Al are smart, maybe as smart as me and Connie." He winked at Devine. "But then so are our enemies just as smart as us. The difference is that our enemies act on smart they are more often than we do."

HOW

Mira!

I jumped from the truck-cab onto the hot asphalt at the highway's shoulder. Standing there in the heat I was sensing nothing except being vaguely lost, uneasy, and sweating out a kind of queasy sensation, something like the feeling you get when pushing through the door of a dentist's office. You know got to do it, only you don't know what to expect. ⌐ You

It was the second of May, nineteen-sixty-five. Two days ago I had been honorably discharged from the Marine Corp. I stood there on the side of the road with twenty-two dollars in my pocket and a zero image of my future. The feelings rolling around inside me were not good.

It had been worse the day before when I left Camp Pendleton. I had looked back at the guard gate, watched the MPs directing traffic, and suddenly felt like a speck of flotsam spinning away down the road toward a horizon just out of sight. The Marine Corp had been my home for the past five years, ever since I enlisted at seventeen, and now I was feeling homeless, rootless, and flecked with the kind of anxiety that only gets worse with each passing moment.

When I turned my back on Pendleton I knew where I had to go, but that was only because there was no other place to go. I took a bus from Pendleton to the Greyhound depot in Oceanside and wandered across the street to where a café sat next to a truck stop. My uniform got me a free cup of coffee and a ride north with Ryan O'Brien. A day in the truck with that driver made me feel a little better about being me, better about my future, and more at ease with this new civilian world.

I heard the gears clump as his rig pulled away, heading back out onto the northbound highway, pressing for Frisco. Ryan and I had talked and laughed non-stop for six hours. Ryan was a big guy, thick in the shoulders and neck, a long face laced with a crooked smile that scrunched up a scar on his cheekbone and twisted his left eye into a half wink. Ryan O'Brien was a Korean War Marine—one of those Devil Dogs of Chosin Reservoir fame, with a faded tattoo of *The Froze Chosen* knotting under the dark, coarse hair on his forearm. That faded smudge on his arm looked to me like the smoldering afterglow to a life forever held high by struggle and personal honor. On the other arm was tatted the fat, green insignia of the One-Five-One, *Make Peace or Die,* and below, the eternal *Semper Fi*. Ryan O'Brien, now in his early forties, had once been young Lance Corporal O'Brien. He had survived the transition to civilian life, and somewhere down our line of travel he made me realize that I could too.

I stood in the swirling gust of the departed tractor-trailer and wondered why him—why Ryan O'Brien? Why had such glory not fallen to me?

I turned my head and looked up the street.

Mojave, California.

I was born here, and grew up here. I was gone, and now I am back. What was my life? Where was it? I was staring dead ahead at Jimmy's Coffee Shop. Does nothing change here? I glanced again back at the highway. Two rigs shot passed, rolling southbound, heading toward greater LA, their drivers impassive and shadowy silhouettes against the windows. I tossed the duffle bag over my shoulder and kicked through the dust to the front door of Jimmy's.

Jimmy's Coffee Shop was old when I was young. A faded beige back in the day, it was now a sun-bleached stark white, with big windows that reflected a gravel parking lot and a filling station across the empty street. Old Jimmy was long dead. The café had passed over to his son-in-law, an owner who never made much of an appearance here in Mojave. The guy lived about eighty miles south, somewhere in Lancaster. Back then, in the early sixties, Mojave was just a place you were from.

I pushed open the screen and stood in the doorway. She wasn't there. I didn't expect her to be. She had stopped writing over two years ago. Gone off? Maybe. Probably. They did that. Women. They went away. Maybe they wrote, maybe they didn't. They were here, then they were gone.

I dropped my duffle at the end of the counter and slid into a stool. Irma looked over at me. She had not really changed much in five years. Her hair was longer and there was some more gray in it. She adjusted her glasses and looked again. Was she squinting? Then her full mouth curved upward.

"Damn . . . *qué tal, mi'jo . . . cómo estas . . . ?*"

"It's all good, Irma," I smiled honestly at her. Open and happy to see her plump arms and round face, my lips stretching across my teeth in way they had not done in a long time.

She stood in front of me, looking at me with sharp points in her eyes. "You finished, *chiquillo* . . . . You really done with all them Marines? I heard you was done?"

"I was discharged from Pendleton two days ago."

"Tu papá y tu mamá. You seen them?"

"Naw, I haven't been home yet, Irma."

"You take a bus?"

"I caught a ride with a trucker."

"You lucky."

"Not luck, Irma. Wearing this uniform? Hell, Irma, truck drivers always give a Marine a ride. We talk the same shit."

Irma was suddenly around the counter and grabbing me, pulling me off the stool, her big, warm arms hugging me.

"Eddie, bien, bien . . . . Like you say, it's all good, *Enrique.* Like you say, it's all good." She leaned this way and that, in a happy little dance step, squeezing my shoulders through my uniform blouse and looking into my face, *"Todo está bien."* She stopped and took a step back, her strong, short fingers still gripping my shoulders. She took a long, hard look at me, her eyes getting wet in the corners, threatening to spill over onto her plump cheeks. "I'm glad, Eddie. You know they just sent them Marines into someplace. Some real nasty place over there . . . . Who knows? Someplace that begins with a *V* I think. You know where that place is, *mi'jo*?"

I knew. Marines always know when Marines are sent to do what Marines do, and to die. Dying is something that Marines expect to do. Dying is their role in life's drama. Marines die to live.

I thought again about Ryan and furious glory of Chosin Reservoir and I felt a blush.

"You don't worry about Marines, Irma. We kick ass."

"Still, I'm glad." She grabbed me again, hugging me and kissing my face. "Eddie, Eddie . . . I'm so glad." I felt tears brush my cheeks. "It's good to have you here, Eddie. You stay here now, *si, mi'jo. No te vayas no más, Eddie!*"

Irma let me go, pushing me to arm's length. I could see in her eyes that she knew why I had stopped here. She asked with a small voice. "*Un poco de café, hijito?*"

"Yeah . . . Yeah, sure, Irma."

Irma had babysat me and my three sisters while my mother and father went off to the big canning plant on the other side of the tracks. My Mom and Pops worked all the night through, my Mom inside the plant, my Pops operating a fork-lift on the loading dock. Irma couldn't have been more than twenty-three or twenty-four at the time. I was six or seven back then.

I watched Irma as she walked to the coffee urn. She took her time drawing the coffee. I knew she was setting something up in her mind. It made my insides tighten. She came back, setting the steaming mug in front of me. She stood quiet, watching me, waiting.

I broke the silence. "Where is she, Irma?"

She hesitated, looking down the empty counter toward the door as if expecting to see someone walk through. "*¿Cómo?*"

"Come on, Irma." I made a face to let her know that I was disappointed with her answer. "Silvia, Irma."

"Silvia?" she questioned, saying the name, then let it twist in the still, warm air.

"Where is she, Irma?"

"She's not here anymore, Eddie. She don't work here no more."

"I know that Irma." I took a sip of the coffee, trying to be patient, knowing that Irma was only trying to protect me, protect me from myself. "Is she in Mojave?"

Irma made a helpless little gesture with her shoulders, and looked at me, sadness tugging at her face. "For a little while she left Mojave, Eddie. Left her *papá* alone, and her *abuela*. All alone. She ran off with some . . . " she started to say something then bit off the word, hesitated, then continued, "some truck driver she met . . . met here." She stopped, her eyes bouncing away from my face. "It weren't no good, *Chico.* Silvia, she just like her mother. *Es malo para Silvia. Malo!*"

"Then she's come back?"

"*Si* . . . . Yes, she come back."

"Where is she?"

"*Yo no sé.*"

I played with the mug of coffee and for a moment, watching her, feeling an uneasy little tingle in my stomach. The awkwardly formal edge to her Spanish told me to believe her. Irma didn't know. Irma liked things that way. She didn't want to know.

"Anybody know?" I asked.

"*Su hermano* maybe. You know him, *mi'jo, Chuuu* *Chuco—El gordito . . .* Maybe *Chuco* knows. He still working at Manuel's Body Shop." Irma waited a second, then added, "But maybe you shouldn't ask, Eddie. It won't do no good. I heard she was to LA. That's a bad place. You don't know what she's doing there all that time. I don't think she any good for you."

"Can I leave my duffle bag here for a little while?"

"*Si*, Eddie. Sure. A little while. You go see your family, okay. You go see them. I watch your bag."

I drank the coffee in a couple of quick swallows and left the shop. The highway leading into Mojave was narrow in those days, one lane in both directions. I walked quickly to Manny's Body Shop, less than two blocks up a gravel road leading off the main road.

I made my way through the twisted and broken cars in the yard and found Chuco sitting in the office, tipping back in a straight-back chair, his face stuck in a Spanish comic book. I banged on the door frame. He looked up and blinked. "Eddie?" he jumped up, grabbed my hand, yanking me into a bear hug. We laughed and slapped each other on the back.

"Eddie, you *pinche perro*, I was thinking you was dead."

"Naw, man, naw! No way! You know what they call a dead Marine, don't you?"

"Naw, *esé*, You tell me, what do they call a dead Marine?"

"A fucking dead Marine."

And we broke up in laughter.

"You want a beer, *esé*?" Chuco wanted to know. "*Vamos a emborracharnos.*"

I pushed Chuco back. "Maybe later *Chuey*. Right now I have to see Silvia."

An instant sober look trampled on his grin. He looked out the window at the deserted road, then quick, yanked a pack of cigarettes out of his pocket. He offered me one. I shook my head. I knew Chuco was stalling.

"Yeah. That's right. I forgot, *esé*. You don't smoke." He glanced up at the globe-and-anchor pinned to my garrison hat. "You must be the only fucking Marine in the whole fucking world that don't smoke." And Chuco fired one up, flipping the match out the door. "Silvia, man . . . you know—she's got a kid now, Eddie. She's my sister, man. You know. I'm sorry, dude."

Chuco was looking at the ground so as not to see my face. Good move. I wasn't expecting a kid. I don't know what I was expecting, but it wasn't that. I stared at Chuco. He must have felt the heat from my look because he moved away, toward the door. He leaned up against the jamb and spat out into the yard, then whispered to the flies and the warm breeze blowing past, "It's fucked up, *esé.*"

"She married?" I asked, dumbly.

"Fuck no," still talking to the busted cars in the yard. "*Pinche puta,*" then quickly shook his head. "Sorry, *esé.* She's my sister and, you know—was your girl, I know . . . *tu novia,*" and he spat again into the yard. "Sorry. I spoke it all wrong. No disrespect to you, *esé.*"

"Yeah, man. She's your sister, *Chuey.*"

Chuco turned to me, his round face suddenly a long face, and no longer easy. "She stupid, *esé.* Fucking stupid . . . a stupid ass bitch. Sorry, man. Met some *pinche gabacho.* A truck driver she met while she was working at Jimmy's. Went off with the fucking *güero* to LA and come back a year later fat with a kid in her belly and landed on our fucking doorstep."

Chuco turned around again, showing me his broad back, puffing on the cigarette, dark stocky hair curling over his blue shirt collar. He said over his shoulder. "Kid's alright, but he got blue eyes. Can you believe it*, esé*? As dark as Silvia is, and her *chavalo—que tiene los ojos azules.* Blue, *esé*! The little dark fucker's got blue eyes. Looks weird, *esé*, fucking weird. But it's alright, I guess. Ain't his fault."

"You see the father?"

Chuco sucked at the cigarette. "I seen him."

"He's not around?"

"He's never around."

"Never?"

"Ditched her, *esé.* It's fucked up, Eddie. I told you like it is. You don't want none of this shit."

I didn't care. I still loved her. "I want to see her, *Chuey.*"

Chuco wagged his head, wanting to say 'no', but he didn't. He repeated, "It's fucked up, *esé*. Really fucked up. *Sabes?* Fucked up!"

"I have to see her, *Chuey. Me entiendes? Es claro?*"

My voice sounded sharper than *Chuco* deserved. He turned and eyed me, his look distant. "You know where we live, *esé*." He took a final drag on the cig and flipped it out the doorway. "Silvia, she ain't got with nobody, Eddie—not now. Just me, you know, and *la familia.* You know where we live, *esé*. You know."

I turned to go.

"*Oye, Vato.*"

I looked back at *Chuco*.

"I love you, *esé.*" And Chuco dipped his head, looking uncomfortable with his sudden gush of emotion. "I'm glad you home, you dumb-ass Marine," and he smiled, looking lost and crooked as if caught unaware by the feelings.

"Yeah, *Chuey*, me too."

"Don't let her fuck you up, *esé*," and he shrugged and dug again for the pack of cigarettes. "Bitches, they fuck you up, man."

I went back to Jimmy's and picked up my duffle from Irma, then headed toward Chuco's house. If Silvia was there, I had a feeling my showing up on the doorstep might not go too well. We had a long history, from way back when we were in grade school. Silvia chased me back then, when we were kids, up until high school, when maturity started setting in and I started taking notice, not knowing the difference between my brain and my dick. Silvia was tall, very brown, very wild and angry, only not with me—just pissed at something private and close. She never talked about it and I never asked. I should have, but I didn't. When you're feeling love you sometimes overlook things you shouldn't.

I took some heat from my *compañeros* for her being so Indian and so dark. *Negrita*, they dubbed Silvia. At first I paid attention to their bullshit, and then I didn't. I was caught up in the mystery of her. I was never really sure who she was, not sure if she liked me, her life, herself, her way of being in the world. She took to life hard, seizing it with both hands in a throttling stranglehold.

When I left for the Marine Corp, she told me she'd wait for me to come back before she married anyone else. There would never be anyone but me; she swore it, and swore it, and swore it. Then her black eyes flashed and she popped off that she didn't think she was ever going to marry anyone anyway, so not to hurry back. A second later those hooded eyes, those *ojos de los chinos*, again shot sparksfrom that swirling dark place deep inside her and she screamed at me not to get killed because she wanted me forever and ever, and I felt she had seized my life in that death grip—my quick, dark Silvia.

It was early evening when I walked up the road to her family's small plot of land. The house was pink with white trim, a chain link fence running around the front of the small property. Before Silvia's dad had lost one of his hands at work, he raised collie dogs. Small ones. Shelties, I think they called them. Now the yard was mostly dirt—three ragged, abandoned dog houses disintegrating in front, a small vegetable patch off to the corner, everything dilapidated and sad, drooping in the late afternoon shade of the house.

I pushed open the gate. It gave off a loud squeak. There was some movement on the other side of the screen door. I hadn't gotten to the porch before Silvia pushed open the door and stepped outside, one hand on the screen door and the other on her hip. The sun washed over the front of the house, sending dusky shadows across Silvia's strong, sharp features, making her handsome rather than beautiful. She was bare foot, dressed in blue jeans and shirt, a red, spaghetti-strap pull over. Her face was expressionless, but proud in that dark Indian way. I knew Silvia well. I knew that the brain behind the still face was alive and buzzing. There was nothing simple about Silvia. That was part of the mystery.

I stopped just inside the gate, lowering my duffle onto the walk. "Silvia?"

"Looks like you got another rank."

She meant the chevrons on my sleeve. "Sergeant," I replied.

"Sergeant," she repeated. "Looks pretty good on you, Eddie."

"I'm out now."

"I heard. *Chuco* called, told me you'd be here."

"Can I come in?"

For an answer she stepped forward, letting the screen door slam shut behind her, putting both hands on her hips, elbows sharp akimbo. She looked sadly defiant.

"It's not the same, Eddie."

I stopped, my lips parted, a jumble of words ganged up behind my teeth. I had not expected this; so quick, so final.

She read my expression and repeated, "It's all different now, Eddie."

I pulled off my garrison hat and tucked it in my belt. It was an awkward gesture. It was an awkward moment. "No. It's the same, Silvia. I'm the same—we're the same."

"No, Eddie. We're not." Her words were sharp and clear-cut, but not angry. "Everything's changed, Eddie, except maybe in your head."

"Your baby. I know about your baby, Silvia. *Chuey* told me."

I saw Silvia's grandmother behind her, saying something to Silvia through the screen. Silvia listened without dropping the sad, hardened look.

I said, "You could have written me. I would've understood."

"No, Eddie, you wouldn't."

Her grandmother was still behind her, still whispering to her.

"Silvia, can we talk?" I asked.

Silvia hesitated, listening again to her grandmother behind her. She straightened, then offered, "Come inside, Eddie," but adding as a cautious afterthought: "Leave your bag on the porch."

She turned and went inside, not bothering to hold the screen door open for me.

The front room was cool, two fans whirring faintly on the dining room table at the back. Silvia's grandmother was not in the room, but I knew the old woman would be sitting close by, overhearing everything that went on, everything we said; *la vieja* only pretended not to speak English. There was a small baby swing set up by the tattered sofa and a few baby toys scattered around the rug.

Silvia was sitting on a chair opposite the sofa and front window, perched tensely on the edge. It was growing dark in the room, making her eyes difficult to see. "Eddie, I'm sorry I didn't write." She sounded sincere, the sharpness gone from her posture.

I eased down on the sofa and crossed my legs in a figure four. I wanted to give the appearance of being comfortable. I was not. I was nervous. Silvia made me feel that way most of the time anyway, anxious, only now it was worse. I was afraid of what was coming. I could see it gathering in her face, in her deep brown eyes that were unexpectedly light in the evening desert sun; they seemed to glow, almost a pale tan.

"Eddie I got a kid. *Chuco* told you right."

"I know, Silvia."

She hesitated, her face dipped slightly, as though telling me a secret. "He's coming for me."

I watched her, saying nothing.

"Randy," she offered deliberately, as if she wanted to make sure I could put a name to a shadow. "He calls me and sends me money."

"*Randy*," I slowly intoned. "Christ, Silvia."

"What wrong, Eddie?" She asked indignantly. "Yeah, he's white. So what?

The words tumbled out before I could stop them, "I'll get a job."

"Stop! Don't be stupid, Eddie!"

"But I haven't changed, Silvia."

"No, don't do this."

"Don't do what? Feel this way? Jesus, Silvia, you stop!"

"*Mira!* Nothing's the same anymore."

"No, Silvia. It's the same. I'm here now."

"Eddie, he'll come for me."

Bullshit, I thought. The *güero* wanted her ass and he's done with it now.

"And if he doesn't?" I demanded.

She studied me for a moment, then: "I don't love you, Eddie."

"Silvia. . ?"

"Eddie, I got things to do."

"I'll take care of you, Silvia—you and your son."

She looked up, her eyes twisting. "Eddie, he's not yours. I don't want you around. I don't need you. He's not yours ... I'm not yours."

The words punched me back into the sofa. My mouth must have been hanging open, my eyes wide, staring at this stranger. Was I guilty of something?

"Silvia, what did I do wrong?"

"Don't be stupid, Eddie. It's got nothing to do with you. Nothing! It's got everything to do with me."

"I can help you."

"I think you gotta go, Eddie. Things are different now. I'm different and I got things to do and I don't want you around."

I just sat, blinking. Her words were harsh, but brittle; there was no real anger behind them. My head rolled side to side. "Silvia, I don't believe you."

Her lips pursed for a long moment, her eyes narrowing before she spoke. "What don't you believe, Eddie?" she demanded. "That I have a son? That he's not yours? That I'm different? That we're different? That I don't love you anymore?" Sharp words again, but again no anger behind them. "Tell me, Eddie, what don't you believe?"

"I don't know, Silvia, I . . . I shouldn't have left."

"Eddie, stop! I told you, it's not about you. It's about me. Life's done stuff to me. I'm different now."

I had no reply to that, and after a few moments of us staring at each other she went on. "You know what, Eddie, I know what you're thinking and you might be right. Maybe Randy won't come. That's what *Chuco* says. He says he won't come. It's almost been half a year. But right now Randy's sending me money and calls. I can't be angry with him for not being here. He's a truck driver and is gone always. He works hard and he promises stuff and sends me money every couple of weeks, and he tells me he loves me." She waited a moment before adding, "Maybe that's all bullshit, but if nothing else happens, I'm going to keep taking this man's money and his promises. Do you understand me, Eddie?"

"No, I don't understand, Silvia. I don't understand what's wrong with me."

"Stop! You've got to listen. There's nothing wrong with you, Eddie. I told you. It's me."

"There's nothing wrong with you, Silvia."

"You think so?"

"Yes."

"Then why am I always afraid?"

"Afraid?" I stumbled over the word. "Afraid of what?"

"Of me—of living."

"Living?"

She smiled a little sadly. "And I'm afraid of me."

"Silvia! Now who's being stupid?"

"It's not stupid," she snapped. "Nothing is ever really stupid, Eddie. Everything just is."

"Is what?" I pressed her. "Everything is just what?"

We stared at each other again, neither of us sure what to say next, or even what my question might have meant. I was beginning to feel confused, everything drifting, going out of focus.

After a short while Silvia said evenly, "Eddie, my *abuela* says everything in the world is the will of God. *Mi papá* says everything's just a dumb fucking accident—like losing his hand. But Eddie, my life wasn't either. Not for me. God wasn't there that year I was in LA. He was never there, not for me, not ever. For the first time in my life I saw that real clear. And if everything's an accident like *papá* says, then I made it over and over. My life was one long, fucked-up accident."

"You had a baby, Silvia, that's all."

"No, Eddie. It was more. A lot more."

She studied me for a long moment. I could see that she was trying to make up her mind about something. I waited, an uncomfortable tingle in my stomach, feeling unhappy about what she might say next.

"Jesus, Silvia, what happened to you in LA?"

"Everything."

She watched me closely, tense, measuring something, then I saw her expression go to a dead calm the second she made up her mind.

Lightly, she asked, "Eddie, let me ask you a funny question: Do you remember what it was like before you were born?"

"What?"

Silvia was making no sense. *What was it like before you were born?* No one knew that. Who thought of crazy stuff like that?

The ends of her mouth lifted. It wasn't a smile. It was more sullen—a reflection of some deep ache. "You heard me, Eddie. What's it like before you were born?"

Before I could stop it the word tumbled out: "Stupid."

"I told you, Eddie: nothing's stupid. It's impossible, not stupid."

I wagged my head. "I don't understand."

"That's what I see ahead of me," Silvia went on, "That place before I were born . . . the big dark, empty hole. And that's what I see every day in my life. It's right in front of me. It's like I'm always standing at the edge of this big empty nothing place just waiting for something to push me in. My whole life. Everything I do is just trying to fill up that hole so I won't be afraid. I'm trapped, Eddie—trapped between living my life and running away from it."

"Silvia, this is crazy talk."

"Then I'm crazy!" The words cut. "Ever since I was a kid," and she halted, as if caught up, thinking back on something, poking into a thing at the back of her mind. Then she shook out her long raven hair, the black waves covering her face. She quickly reached up and brushed them aside. "Eddie, I can't live my life. I'm running away. I've always been running away."

"From what?"

"From me," she answered. "I'm running away from me."

"How long have you been thinking crazy stuff like this?" I wondered aloud. "How come you even asking yourself this kind of crazy shit?"

125

"Forever." She stopped, her shoulders sagging. "Oh, Eddie . . ," she trailed off and looked down at her hands and began rubbing at the palms. "I started asking a long time ago."

I shook my head and uncrossed my legs, leaning forward, clawing for the right thing to say.

Silvia held up her hand, stopping me. "I'm dark, Eddie. You know how dark I am—way darker than my brothers? My pops used to ask me where I came from—what Indian tribe did I belong to? He was joking, but it bothered me, Eddie. It hurt me. Why was it so bad that I was dark? Why was being dark bad?" She looked up from her hands. "I used to think I must have crawled out of that dark hole—from way down deep in that dark hole." There was another long pause, then, "You know when I was around ten or twelve I used to lay in bed and look at my arms and hands and wonder why they were so dark." She looked again at her hands. "The nails so white," she mused, "the skin so dark." She looked up at me. "You remember when everyone called me *Negrita—negrita picina?* I used to hate my skin. I kept wondering if I could scrape it off, then bleach it, and have it come back white and then I'd be happy. I used to think that if I was only born white, *la rubia bonita*, then everything in the world would be as beautiful as me and I'd be happy—if only I could be white in a white world."

She wasn't confusing me now. She was scaring me. "Silvia, kids are mean," I stammered. "They're mean, until they grow up and they learn better."

"No Eddie, that's not the point. *Mira!* When I was a little girl I used to curse God for doing this to me, for making *me parece un indio,* but when I got older I realized that there was no God to do anything and that my being dark in a white world was just a way to get me to look somewhere else besides looking at me, the real me, look some place beside that place where I was before I was born. *Mira! Mira!* My skin wasn't my problem, my living was the problem, and I didn't want to look at it. I didn't want to look at me, really see me, at my being alive, so I looked at my skin and not at my being *in my skin*. I blamed my skin, blamed *la poco chica india* for everything so I wouldn't see me—me!"

"But Silvia, it's hard on all of us—being who we are in this white world."

"Jesus, Eddie, you're not getting it. It's not about color. It's about not *looking*! Do you understand? I used my dark skin so I didn't have to *look*! Eddie, *mira!* It wasn't my dark skin. It was the dark hole I crawled out of—that we all crawl out of—and into this world and will one day fall back into, and who the hell would care? No one and there was no one to blame for this—no one anywhere, anytime. Look, Eddie. *Mira!*"

"Look at what?"

"At . . . at . . . " she swirled her arms around in a hapless waving. "At all this shit, at all of it, at everything."

She saw my face droop, settling into a frown. I wasn't getting any of this and was thinking she was drifting off the deep end. Silvia saw it and smiled.

"Eddie," she insisted gently. "I needed it—needed to be that little *negrita* in order to push me away from myself, out of sight, to keep me from looking anymore into the dark hole inside me, so I wouldn't feel lost and scared and alone. I needed to be *la negrita* to get away from the me inside my skin. I didn't hate *la negrita*, I loved her. She saved me from looking at me."

I was shaking my head, growing more afraid that she had turned completely crazy while I was gone. I pressed my hands together, full of frustration. To her I must have looked like I was praying. I yanked my hands apart.

"Silvia, you're saying things that don't make any sense."

"Eddie, you're not listening. *Mira!* It's got nothing to do with you or me. It's the hole I keep trying to fill up—fill up with men, drugs, sex, parties—and now my son. Now I'm filling it with my son, and I'm sorry for that, sorry for him. But I can't help it. That hole inside of me makes me hurt real bad, and it makes me want to ask questions, only I can't find the right ones. I got to find the right questions."

She was being deathly serious and it was scaring me. I started to open my mouth to speak, and she again held up her hand.

"Eddie, I swear if you say anything like my *abuela* about asking God for help I'll smack the shit out of you."

I realized I had put my hands back together.

She went on, "God's there so I *won't* ask questions. God's like my skin. God is there so I won't look. God's not an answer. God's an excuse not to look."

I dropped my hands. "I wasn't going to say anything about God."

Silvia waited a moment, maybe for me to reply, or maybe just to let the tidal waves inside her head roll back.

"Good, and don't ask me any more 'why' shit. *Why's* when you open up that hole and look. *Pero, ¿cómo, es diferente.* I got an answer for that—for the *how*. My son is here because of me. That's the *how*! Because of me—of how I am. But *why*?" She waved her hand in irritation. "He's also here because of *why* I am—and maybe he'll hate me for it—for not being able to answer that, to tell him *why*—why me, why him?"

"Damn, Silvia. He won't hate you. You're his mother."

It was her turn to shrug. "You're still not listening," and her voice softened. "But my son's here and now it's me that's taking this truck driver's money and his promises, and I don't know why that either, why him, why Randy, why anything. *Lo que no llego a entender es por qué.* So maybe I'm just crazy."

"It's his responsibility," I said. "He's the father."

"Randy?" A slight puzzlement flickered across her features. "Randy's not the father."

"Huh, then . . . "

"The father's gone, Eddie, *adios, chingado.*"

"Where is he?"

"I don't know, Eddie. I'm not even sure who he is. I told you, I was partying pretty hard in LA. I was running away."

"Then who's this Randy?"

"Randy is just a man that says he loves me and my son."

"Where did you meet this Randy? LA?"

She shook her head. "Working at Jimmy's—when I was three months pregnant."

"How did you meet him?"

She smiled. "The way women always meet men—*Culo.*"

That stung me, but I ignored it. "Do you love him?"

"I don't know, Eddie. I don't even know what love is . . . . *No el tipo de amor entre un hombre y una mujer.*"

"Love can be real."

Her smile changed, became thoughtful. "Yes, I think so. Maybe. For some people."

After that Silvia was quiet for what seemed a long time, her head slipped slightly to one side so that her black shiny hair covered an eye and a cheek. She reached up with her hand and swooped the thick silky curtain behind her ear.

"Randy, he's a very nice man, but no, Eddie, I don't love him; but a new life with him will keep me from thinking about me so much—maybe. He's something real and very, very different. It's a direction to move, *entender?*" She smiled at something out the window, over my shoulder. "We never feel lost when we're moving, and the faster we move, the better it is? *¿És claro?*"

When I said nothing, she went on. "Eddie! *Mira!* I got one thing to do, and only one. I got to make sure that when the day comes for my son to ask questions he won't be like me. I got to be in a place so that he can ask much better questions than I ever could. Maybe that way he won't feel so lost like his mama." She hesitated, then added, "I know if he can figure out the right questions to ask, he won't feel like me; he won't feel lost and I'll have been a good mama for him. I know it, Eddie. That's all I can really do for him. Maybe that's all anybody can ever do for anybody, help them ask the right questions"

She looked me dead on with those sharp, black, hooded Indian eyes. "And now you got to go, Eddie. I got things to do."

I slowly got to my feet. It was over. I had never heard her speak like this before. She watched me move to the screen door. Neither of us said a word. I stepped out into the shade of the porch and picked up my duffle.

"Eddie?"

I turned.

"It's not you, Eddie. You never did anything wrong."

I had no words. Silvia was someone I had known since I was five years old, but I didn't know her. Not anymore. Had I ever? I felt certain she had gone insane.

I went home, where things thankfully had not changed.

My parents were overjoyed to see me. My *papá* was especially happy. I was his favorite, his son among a wilderness of daughters. *Su hijo!* Men always favor their sons; see in them their lost youth, their abandoned dreams, a breath of life to inflate their withered desires. Daughters are always foreigners to their fathers, part of a lost tribe, never to be fully understood or fully appreciated, but always deeply loved in an honest and respectful but distant way. I hugged my pops especially hard and respectfully kissed my mother on the cheek, my beautiful Madonna, letting my lips brush off her tears of joy.

As fast as I got out of my uniform my life slid back to where I'd let it lay five years ago. The grime of Mojave filled my nostrils while the dry heat dropped my living into another, lower gear, and the feel of the time slipping by clicked my mind into pause. I went back to the canning factory, working on the loading dock with my *Papá*. The work had not changed since high school. It was heavy, dirty, and boring, the truck drivers always in a hurry to be in and out, the loaders sweating to accommodate them with their endlessly tight schedules. Among the clanging of the forklifts, the slamming of crates, the cursing of the drivers and their swampers[8] I saw my life disappearing into some swirling Mojave dust devil at the far end of the dock.

Me, Freddy and Martin always showed up at Manuel's Body Shop every Friday evening after work. Chuey would pull the three doors down tight and we'd all sit on the two broken sofas, crack open beers and pass around a joint. It was good to have a few dollars in our pockets and be done with work for the week. All four of us were living on the edge of an utter pointlessness, and secretly we all knew it, so we puffed on a dooby and drank, and waited for the turn of the card, the *mota* making the wait on chance an easy glide to a somewhere soft landing.

I asked Chuco, "How's Silvia doing?"

Chuco took a toke on the joint, sucked in the smoke, held it, and let it squeak out with a, "She's fine, *ese*," and he passed the joint to Freddy.

Freddie blew off the ash. "Forget her, man. There's a party at the end of Cypress Drive tonight. Let's hit it, homes."

---

8. A swamper is a helper that goes out on trucks with a driver to assist in loading freight. The name seems to be peculiar to the western states. On the east coast an, individual occupying the same laboring position is called a lumper.

I watched him suck at the joint and said to Chuco, "She ever ask about me, *Chuey?*"

Chuco looked at me under his thick eyebrows and I thought I heard Martin giggle, only Martin was too intent on plucking the roach from Freddy to be paying attention.

But Freddie heard my questions and chimed in. "Eddie, man, you sniffing up the wrong skirt."

Chuco shut him down. "*Cuidado, ese! Es mi hermana!*"

Freddie rolled his eyes. "*Órale, ese.*"

Chuco looked again at me. "No, *ese*. She don't ask."

"Is it the *güero?*"

"I don't know, man. She don't talk to me about shit. She only talk to our *abuela*—and her boy."

Martin suddenly asked, "Does she think she can have a better life with that *güero?*"

Chuco pinched the roach from Martin. "She said the *vato* was buying his own truck." He paused, studying the tip of the joint. "But she really don't talk to me, *ese*. I already said that. Man, I don't know shit about what's going on with her. Silvia's always been a little off, you know? She was always asking stupid questions, even as a kid. But now? Who knows. Maybe the *gabacho* will get her shit straight. The *vato* seems okay."

Freddie laughed, "For a *gabacho*."

Chuco rolled his eyes at Freddie. "You're stupid sometimes, *esé*, you know that. Stupid."

I'd left Silvia alone, and hadn't seen her in almost six weeks. That was a neat trick in the Spanish part of Mojave. Back then Mojave was a town of maybe fifteen thousand people total, with well over half being Hispanic. I deliberately stayed out of her way, figuring that she needed her space, and maybe time to get over whatever it was she needed to get past—get around what was puzzling her. I'd once told Chuco what his sister had said about a dark hole, not expecting his pissed-off response.

"*¿Como?*" Chuco spat out angrily. "*Chinga tu madre*—come on, crazy-ass bitch." He stabbed his finger into the air ahead of him and ranting to the stains on the ceiling. "Get your ass busy with something real and stop sitting around thinking about stupid shit. Get a life, bitch, and get on with it—go party, blow some weed, get fucked, but get off that stupid shit. Dark hole? What's it like before you're born? *Hijo de puta!* The only hole I want is pink and surrounded by fur. Man, who's got time to sit around and think about that kinda dumb-ass shit."

Chuco was as frustrated as I was baffled.

Then there came a Saturday when Silvia and I came across each other in the grocery store—Silvia, her son and her *abuela*.

Her grandmother hesitated, giving me the squinty eye, not sure what to make of the situation, then disappeared down the pasta aisle and pretended to read the label on a box of rice. Silvia stopped, touched her son on the soft hair of his head, and waited for me to speak.

I decided to be blunt and honest. "Silvia, nothing's going on with me. I haven't got with anyone. I want to see you."

"I know." Her dark face was turned slightly away. Was that a perplexed look I saw softening her handsome features? She said, "*Chuco's* been telling me about you."

"Chuey and me, we get together a couple times a week,"

"I know."

"Silvia, I . . . "

She stopped me with a look that went straight into my belly. "Why don't you come the around the house Sunday, Eddie."

"After church?"

She gave me a queer look. "How long you know me, Eddie?" she asked. "Since grade school. You ever know me to go to church?"

"You used go with your mom."

"*For* my mom, Eddie. I went to that place for my mom, not for God or anything else." She cocked an eyebrow. "But no more. God can kiss my ass. And my mom—she's gone—probably to hell—and I don't go to mass no more, not even for my *abuela*," and she shot her grandmother a quick look.

"I can be there. What time?"

"Nine—ten. While it's still cool."

"I'll be there."

"We'll talk then."

Had she changed her mind?

And without waiting for me to reply she smiled and pushed the cart past me, her son looking back at me, an oddly puzzled expression tilting his face. Chuco was right. The *chavaito* had Silvia's rich, dusky skin and the brightest blue eyes, sharp like Silvia's, but not hooded in that Indian way. They were big and round, like his Anglo father's, I supposed.

Sunday came around quickly. I was anxious, full of anticipation when I turned the corner to her street and suddenly hit the brakes. Parked in front of her house was a shiny blue conventional-style tractor,[9] all tricked out with chrome grill and stacks, hooded sun visor, and the winged hood ornament that perched above the circled brand of KW, for Kenworth. I drove slowly past the tractor, eyeing the chrome edging on the visor and the chrome rims on the dual drivers in the

---

9. A conventional-style is a diesel truck where the engine sits in front rather than under the driver, as in a cab-over tractor. With the driver sitting between the axels the ride is considerably more comfortable than in a cab-over, where the driver is perched on top of the steering wheels.

back. This KW was brand new. I noted something else. The driver's door was emblazoned with "R. Riverton & Son, Northridge, CA."

I drove to the dead end of the street, turned around, and pulled up behind the tractor, hesitating, eyeing the fifth-wheel that was as yet ungreased, unused. This tractor was so new it had never yet been hooked up to a trailer. I got out of my car and walked to the side of the tractor where the passenger-side door was open. I looked up into the cab. There was box sitting on the seat, and behind, kneeling in the sleeper compartment, was Silvia.She was pushing another box further back on the mattress. She turned, looking at me, her thick black hair in a ponytail.

"Eddie, *¿Que tal*?" She smiled and climbed from the mattress to the passenger seat. "Let me get this, *cariño*, and I'll come down."

¿Cariño? Silvia was happy about something, which filled me with a deeper anxiety. I was sure I knew whose truck this was, and the boxes she was muscling into the sleeper belonged to her, maybe everything Silvia owned in the world.

Silvia climbed down from the cab. She wore a white t-shirt and blue jeans. The sun was over my shoulder and shone fully on her face. There were no lines in her face today. She looked very young and very beautiful and very strong.

She put up a hand to shield her eyes. "I'm glad you came, Eddie. I'm leaving Mojave today."

"With him?"

"With Randy? Yes, with him."

Behind me, I heard the screen door to the house slam shut. I turned and saw who I guessed was Randy Riverton, together with Silvia's father, coming toward us. I must have been staring, as Randy was not at all what I was expecting.

I greeted Silvia's father by shaking his left hand, as his right was missing. I mumbled *"Buenos días, senior,"* but never took my eyes off the *gabacho*.

I was introduced to Randy Riverton, took the offered hand and we exchanged a firm grip. He had the hard hand of a working man, but other than that, Randy Riverton was a complete surprise, almost a shock.

Riverton was short, shorter than me, and just a shade taller than Silvia. He was of stocky build, maybe even pudgy, with a round face that looked to have smiled a lot. The parted lips showed small, uneven teeth, with a slight gap in the front two. His hair, which was only a horseshoe, was clipped short, very close to the scalp, and this was back in the day, way before bald was a fashion. This completely ordinary looking *gabacho* had to be in his mid-forties—almost twice Silvia's age. I dropped his hand and looked into deep brown eyes behind the glasses he wore. Silvia's small, dark son never got such striking blue eyes from this white boy. Silvia had told me true. This *vato* was taking on a family he wasn't responsible for. The thought made him look different to me.

We spent a few minutes admiring the new Kenworth tractor, which Randy said only had three hundred miles on the brand new Caterpillar engine. Randy joked with Silvia's father that the father had plenty of time to learn diesel mechanics, as the Cat would run well over a million miles without needing an overhaul. Randy completely ignored me, walking with Silvia's father around the tractor, pointing out a few features on the KW the old man might have missed.

I turned to Silvia, asking with a kind of disbelief, "This is the guy?"

She smiled softly. "It's him."

"Silvia, the dude's got brown eyes."

She watched me for a moment, her lips pursed, then said, "I told you, Randy's not my son's father. You think I was lying?"

"Does he know?"

Silvia laughed. "That he's not the father? Damn, Eddie, you *vato loco*, you think I'd lie about that? I'd never lie to a man about shit like that."

"Why's he doing it?

"I told you. He says he loves me, and that's his choice."

"But you said you didn't love him?"

"Eddie, I think you're asking the wrong questions, and as long as you do that you'll get the wrong answers."

Lost again, I could do nothing but frown and shake my head.

"There's no right answer to any of this, Eddie, only better questions," she said. "*Mira!* What I got to do to make you see? You got to look at things different and ask the better question."

"So what's the better question—with him?"

"Do I admire him?"

"That's better than love?"

"Here? Now? Lost in this crazy-ass world?" She lifted her hands to the heaven to make a point. "Yes, Eddie, it's better than love. Maybe later I'll love him." She dropped her hands. "Or maybe not. Right now I admire him. That's enough. I admire his honesty and the way he's simple and truthful, and that makes me feel good to be with him." She cocked her head to one side. "I like being with someone like that. Is that really so hard to understand?"

Randy and Silvia's dad were returning from the tour of the KW, engrossed in conversation, the father smiling at whatever Randy was saying. The two seemed happy as they glanced at us before going through the gate and heading toward the front porch. Silvia and I waited for them to go back inside the house.

I pointed to the door of the truck. "It says Riverton and son. What about *his* father, Silvia? How's *he* going to like you?"

Silvia smiled as if I were an innocent child. "Eddie, I met Randy while I was working at Jimmy's. I told you. He knew I was three months pregnant with someone else's kid—someone that he knew I'd never see again. And Randy didn't care. He took me back to LA and I stayed with his family there until my son was born. Eddie, the 'Son' on the door means *my* son—*our* son."

The single word *'why'* passed out of my parted lips in a whisper that knocked the smile from her face.

"Eddie, *por qué?* Really?" Randy bought this truck new, him and his dad, and they bought us a house in Reseda. Eddie, the guy is going to bust his ass for me and my son." She hesitated, suddenly uncertain herself. "Don't you think I've asked him—asked him 'why'? Why is he going to do this for this *Mexicana negrita* and her bastard son? All he says is that it's because he loves me. Eddie, the guy might be crazy, or the bravest man I know. I don't know which, but the man *likes responsibility,* and being around that kind of man makes me feel wanted and very, very safe for me and my son. With Randy part of me doesn't have to escape."

"What about the other part?"

"That part will always be running."

"To where?"

"I don't know, Eddie."

"You should love him, Silvia," I said.

Silvia hesitated, glancing at her house, seeming to look through the broken screen door, then back at me. "Eddie! *Mira!* I'm learning about something more important than love. I'm learning about living right and doing right. Because of him I'm starting to understand that doing right is more important than love, even though I know both right and love come from the same place. Doing right and love both come from not being afraid of searching that dark hole and never finding an answer. So don't ask me if I love Randy, because it's the wrong question and it doesn't make sense to me right now."

Abruptly, she went around me and through the gate. She stopped, hesitated, looking at the house for a long moment, then turned to me and closed the gate. "I did love you, Eddie." I could see that she was crying. "*Te he amado mucho . . . Mucho, mucho!* Very much, Eddie. I loved you hotly. I loved you until I thought I would explode with it. But now I'm different and I have to go do something else and I want you to respect me for it. I don't want you to wonder, always wonder about us, about things. That would make me very sad and very afraid. Please, don't love me. I want your respect, Eddie. More than your love, it's respect that I want from you."

"Silvia, I . . . "

"Eddie," she looked at me with begging eyes, tears flowing down her cheeks. "Eddie, I want to live my life now. Part of me will always be running, afraid of the questions I can't answer, but now part of me will be alive, and I need that, I need to feel alive—be alive."

Silvia turned and was gone inside the house to be with Randy Riverton. I stared for a terrible moment at the closed screen door, then turned and studied the rear of the tractor, stared at the tangle of wires and hoses and the brand new fifth wheel, at the sunlight glancing off the chrome exhaust stacks and the mud flaps touting the red and white KW logo.

Was that truck really going to take Silvia where she wanted to go? I didn't have an answer for that, and maybe, like she insisted, I was asking the wrong questions, but whatever the right questions, and whatever the right answers, I knew I was not ever going to see Silvia again.

Turning, I looked again at the sign on the door, "R. Riverton and Son," and felt a grudging respect for Randy Riverton. Unexpectedly, it came to me that it would be a very hard thing for me not to like this man, this Randy Riverton.

Who was I to object to her wants, her newness? It terrified me a little; mostly, I thought, because I was being left behind in the wake of her. I understood that Silvia had moved somewhere way beyond me, on her way to doing different, being different, becoming something different and possibly something new. It was more than simply leaving Mojave. It occurred to me that she was not running, not like she thought she was. I suddenly understood that Silvia was running to catch up to a new version of herself, a self that had gone on ahead.

I walked back to my car, thinking that Silvia would only catch up to herself when she was ready to be caught. Suddenly, it seemed obvious to me that whenever that time was, whenever she was ready, Silvia would at last catch up to a woman who would be of the greatest help to her in looking for the best questions to ask.

Cherry Run

Tanner didn't know Dwayne Hicks, so the first time he got a hint that he might have trouble with the man was when he spotted the snuff tin. Tanner didn't dip himself and normally didn't mind if someone else dipped. People are supposed to be grown-up and know what they're doing—so what the hell, and at least dip doesn't stink up the truck-cab like cigarette smoke. So when Tanner saw Dwayne pull out the snuff and twist a pinch into his cheek, he didn't pay close attention, except to wonder where Hicks was going to plunk his juice. Usually a guy will spit the tobacco juice in a pop can, or an empty coffee cup, but they had neither. They had just left the terminal and Tanner never saw Dwayne with anything in his hands except his overnight kit and a thermos.

Pulling the rig out of the gate, Tanner headed toward the highway on-ramp, getting more and more curious about what Dwayne was going to do with the juice. It was only about twenty more seconds before Tanner found out. Dwayne reached around into the sleeper berth and pulled out the piss bottle.

Tanner glanced over and frowned. He felt a sense of unease. The piss bottle was a nasty little trick used by truckers to keep them from stopping to relieve their bladder. The bottle is usually a half-gallon milk jug—empty of course—with a funnel stuck in the neck. Not stopping is an important consideration for long-haul truckers. Line drivers and sleeper-cab drivers[10] are usually paid by the mile, and time is money, as they say, and pulling a rig off the highway is definitely a loss in both time and miles. It didn't take Tanner but a glance to realize that Dwayne intended using the bottle for a spittoon, which makes for one of the uglier sights one would have to look at, not to mention the accumulated stink of urine and tobacco juice.

Again, Tanner flicked a look at Hicks. He had not laid eyes on the man before two hours ago. Both of them were casual drivers working out of the Newark union hiring hall. Now and then, when a trucking company gets an unexpected haul, or otherwise run through their permanent roster of drivers, the dispatcher will call the union hall for a casual driver, or in their case, a casual team, to pull the load. Tanner had worked as a casual many times and all had always been smooth sailing; and as far as he was concerned, this haul would be no different. The load they had drawn was custom pvc pipe and aluminum siding, a very light load. There was no doubt that they would make excellent time from Newark to Phoenix, about a 45 hour run, switching out seats as often as they liked. Sweet! Tanner anticipated no problems—only he hadn't factored in his unknown co-driver, Dwayne Hicks.

---

10. Line drivers are usually solo drivers, rather than team drivers, as there is no sleeper-berth attached to the truck's tractor. But typically, all long-haul drivers are commonly referred to as line drivers.

Turning their rig onto the onramp, and quickly running up through the gears, Tanner was able to avoid watching Hicks fling his dip, but he heard the juice hit the funnel and plop into the bottom of the plastic bottle.

"Hey, Dwayne," Tanner said. "How many times you run team?"

"This is my first team drive."

"So I get to pop your cherry, huh?"

Hicks twisted Tanner a funny look.

Tanner chuckled. "A joke, Hicks—just a joke."

"Yeah. Sure."

"Well, do me a favor, will ya, Dwayne. The first stop we make, pick up a can or cup to spit in. Okay?"

"Why?"

"Why? Because I have to use that bottle too and I don't want to put my dick up to where your tobacco juice is running around the funnel."

Hicks eyed Tanner a minute and plunked again into the funnel. "Yeah, okay." He replied, only he didn't sound happy about it. He didn't sound angry exactly, just irritably indifferent, giving Tanner a peek at the rather large chip the man carried on his shoulder.

Hicks was a couple of inches shorter than Tanner, and skinny—scrawny was actually more accurate. Tanner must have outweighed Hicks by at least thirty pounds, and it wasn't fat. Hicks was also a bit twitchy and nervous, worrying his jaws a lot. He was younger than Tanner, his face narrow, pinched, but unlined, smooth, callow and featureless, a blank canvas, lacking the statement that life would stamp on it. Given his size, youth and disposition, hauling around a bad attitude like Hicks seemed to be doing did not strike Tanner as a good survival mode.

It was mid-January, the air cold, but without much snow on the ground. The weather report called for heavier snowfall in

Ohio, though the driving conditions on the interstate system should be clear.

Unfortunately, the fact that it was winter was where Tanner's problems with Hicks really began. The cab's heating system operated separately from the heat pumped into the sleeper berth; the man in the sleeper could control his own heat and ventilation. Typically, this would not be an issue, as the sleeper berth was separated from the cab by a thick, insulated curtain that blocked both sound and temperature. That was under normal conditions. Dwayne Hicks was going to take the normal out of the conditions.

Hicks and Tanner had worked out a five hour rotation of driving shifts. They did a quick stop two hours out in eastern Pennsylvania, needing to fill their thermoses with coffee and pick up a few donuts and sandwiches; and, of course, Hicks picked up some Styrofoam cups for his dip juice. Tanner also asked Hicks to rinse out the piss bottle. Hicks grunted and gave Tanner a squirrely "fuck-you" look before ambling off to the men's room, the jug banging against his leg. Tanner watched him go and decided right then-and-there to refuse any back-hauls that might involve teaming up with Dwayne Hicks.

When they climbed back into the tractor-cab, Hicks slid up into the sleeper berth for a snooze. Tanner was to wake him in a couple hours for his shift at the wheel. Politely, Tanner turned down the radio and settled back in the seat to eat up the asphalt ahead. It wasn't even five minutes into his run that Tanner started to smell something like burning rubber, only more tart, like melting plastic, only not quite. It seemed to make no sense, but it suddenly occurred to Tanner that Hicks might have set the mattress on fire.

"Hey, Dwayne!"

No answer.

"Hey, Goddamn it, Dwayne! Wake up!"

"Huh? What . . . ?" and Hicks fumbled with the zipper that closed the curtain to the sleeper berth.

"What smells back there?" Tanner demanded.

Hicks poked his head through and looked at Tanner, half startled, half angry. "What the hell's the matter, Jack?"

"You smoking or burning something back there?"

When Hicks didn't answer, Tanner shot him a quick look over his shoulder. Hicks, his forehead furrowed up, was looking at Tanner like the guy had two heads. The burning smell was worse with the zipper to the sleeper pulled down.

"Man," Tanner snapped at him. "You can't smell that?"

"Smell what?"

"That, Hicks! That smell. Can't you smell it? Like something nasty burning—maybe rubber or something."

"I ain't burning nothing back here, and I don't smell nothing. Now shut up, Jack, and let me sleep." His head disappeared back into the sleeper compartment and the zipper was yanked back down.

They rolled on, the smell of burning plastic still in the air, only not as strong as before. Tanner tolerated it, but just barely, and began wondering about the condition of the engine under them. About fifty miles west of Harrisburg, PA, Tanner pulled into a rest stop and snapped on the parking brake. He had decided to take a look at the engine, maybe find the source of the smell. The line-tractor had about a dozen gauges. They tap into everything electrical or moving in the truck and the trailer. None of them showed anything wrong. Tanner was beginning to think that a careless mechanic had left an oily rag on the engine block and it was smoldering, putting out the noxious smell.

"Dwayne!" Tanner shouted at the curtain behind him. "Get up! Secure all the gear back there. I wanna check the engine."

He waited a few seconds, then when he got no response slapped at the zippered curtain. "Hey, Hicks! Roll out, man! I gotta tilt the cab.[11]"

Tanner didn't wait for a reply this time. Opening the door, he climbed down the side ladder from the cab to the ground and waited for Hicks. The night air was crisp, but not freezing, just tangy. Tanner buttoned up his Levi jacket and slapped his gloved hands together. In a few moments Hicks opened the passenger side door and clambered down.

"What the hell you doing now, Jack?" Hicks wanted to know. "Why we stopped?"

"I want to look at the engine, see if there's a mechanic's rag left in there that's making the cab stink like it does."

"Why the hell would a mechanic leave a rag on the engine?"

"I don't know, but I gotta locate that damn smell."

"Goddamn, it," muttered Hicks. "Make it fast, will ya. It's colder'n shit out here."

When Tanner didn't reply Hicks pulled the hood of his sweatshirt over his head, then shook himself. Hicks was also beginning to make some decisions about Jack Tanner. He hunched himself up against the cold as he watched the bigger man open the door to the side-box beneath the sleeper compartment and root around inside.

After a moment he started stamping his feet on the asphalt. "Come on, Jack, hurry-up. My nuts are turning into ice cubes out here."

Tanner pulled out a flashlight and a crank-bar from among the tools, then quickly released the cab hook and levered the jack, tilting the cab forward to expose the engine block underneath. He flashed the light around looking mainly for smoke. When he

---

11. In cab-over tractors the engine sits directly beneath the driving compartment and the entire cab must be tilted forward to get at the engine. This is done by cranking a jack-like hydraulic mechanism just behind the cab.

saw none he walked to the other side of the tractor and repeated the same inspection of the engine with the same result. Nothing.

He went to the front of the tilted cab, near Hicks, and shook his head. "Beat's hell out of me what it is," he said. "I can't find a damn thing."

Hicks, his face lost in the shadow of the hood, showed Tanner nothing except his warm breath puffing into the cold night air, but his voice was clear and sharp. "You know what, Jack? I think there's something wrong with your goddamn nose," he half snarled. "Now can we get back in the tractor before my balls freeze off?"

Tanner nearly fired something back at Hicks, but decided to let it pass. He could see that this trip had serious potential to go downhill fast.

With the cab back in place, Tanner got Hicks to take his turn at driving, and he climbed into the sleeper berth, more to get away from Hicks than to sleep. Hicks had the heater cranked up, heater vent low, just above the mattress. Tanner closed the vent and dialed the heater down. That seemed to immediately lessen the rank smell and caused Tanner to begin suspecting something smoldering in the heating system. For a moment he toyed with the notion that some fool had stuffed something in the heater vent, maybe trying to shut off the heat altogether. That'd be crazy, but even if it was so, why couldn't Hicks smell it?

As Hicks pulled out of the rest stop Tanner opened the two outside vents high up in the sleeper's walls and flushed the small compartment with fresh air. The outside air was cold, but smelled fresh and clean. He left the vents open for a few minutes, then closed them and went to sleep listening to the low purr of the engine as it lost itself in the steady hum of the tires.

Hicks woke Tanner thirty minutes on the west side of Columbus, OH. They were in the parking lot of a truck stop café. The sun was up over the flat Ohio farm fields, bright and cold. It was nearly two hours into morning. Hicks had done more than his five hours. Tanner yanked his boots on and followed Hicks into the restaurant. Seating was by choice and they took a booth by a window. Tanner watched Hicks as he ordered breakfast from the waitress. Hicks had a fairly thick beard, but patchy. They were both going to look real seedy in another twenty-four hours.

The two of them ate largely in silence, any friendly dynamic between them having already gone south, lost in the friction of the past several hours. Tanner only reminded Hicks to pick up another styrofoam cup for his dip juice. The request seemed to really irritate Hicks, and although he complied it was obvious that he wasn't interested in talking anymore about anything outside of driving. They climbed back into the truck, with Tanner at the wheel, and headed back onto I-70, westbound. From Columbus to Indianapolis they didn't speak, and in fact, unless Tanner was glancing into the passenger side mirror, he never looked in Hicks's direction. There was definitely no love lost, but at least the noxious smell was gone from the cab.

They switched out again in Greenville, IL. Tanner had driven over six hours to make up for the long haul Hicks had made out of Harrisburg. If Hicks was grateful for the extra time in the co-driver's seat, he didn't say so. They grabbed a few snacks and headed back out, rolling southwest on seventy-one. Tanner had purchased a couple of hunting magazines at the last stop and was buried in them. Hicks turned on the radio, but kept the volume down, so it looked as if he was at least trying to get along.

A dozen miles east of the Missouri border it started to snow again, a flurry at first, then heavy flakes, swirling with greater intensity, the darkening highway ahead gradually obscured in drifting waves of white. The CB radio was barking with truckers west of their position letting it be known that the snow was piling up toward Springfield.

They got through St. Louis, connecting up with interstate 44. Hicks slowed the rig down, dropping back three gears, and focused intently on the drifting snow ahead. Tanner looked up, switched off the reading lamp, and put the magazine away, deciding that he needed to also watch the highway. It was getting dark, which made the visibility worse. They were both praying that the snow didn't start to stick and pile up to where the highway would disappear altogether, or that the asphalt would start to ice over. There is probably nothing worse for a trucker than to be forced into chaining-up dual drivers in a raging snow storm. Truck chains are much heavier than auto chains, and numb fingers hooking the freezing metal of the links could cause the skin on the hands to stick to the links and tear, and truck chains can't effectively be handled with gloves on.

They switched out again at a state truck inspection station just on the south side of Lebanon, MO. Tanner adjusted the driver's seat and said to Hicks, "You might want to get some sleep, Dwayne. I'll run us into Oklahoma to a truck stop I know, and you can take over from there."

"Where?"

"Sheriff's—just this side of Tulsa. You know it?"

"Nope," and Hicks crawled over the doghouse[12] and into the sleeper.

---

12. The "doghouse" is the wide, flat surface between the seats in a cab-over tractor. It is a housing for the engine situated below the driving compartment, and the surface of the "house" was occasionally used as an uncomfortable perch for a third passenger. This, of course, was before seat belts were mandatory, as they are now for truckers.

Tanner was referring to one of the largest truck stops in the US—Sheriff's—just east of Tulsa. Sheriff's was more than an eatery. Sheriff's was a small city. The stop had the two restaurants, one fast food and the other sit-down. There were also couple of motels, a gym, a small movie theater, and a clothing and drug store. But Jack Tanner was more interested in the dressing facilities and the mechanic's garage. The stink had mysteriously left the cab, but Tanner still wanted a mechanic to look the engine over; and before he ate he wanted to take a shower and shave. Tanner had been in his clothes for close to twenty-eight hours and he was starting to feel the kind of crusty grime that caused his shirt to stick to his skin.

Sheriff's was only a few hours ahead, so Tanner settled in to deal with the snow and, had been driving for just about ten minutes when he started to smell the rancid burning again. It was worse than before. The stink filled his nose with a smell that was now more like rotten eggs with a sharp, penetrating edge. He started to gag and shake his head. The curtain to the sleeper was pulled down but not zipped. He reached back and parted the curtain and took a quick glance inside. The sleeper light was on and Tanner immediately understood where the noxious smell was coming from. Hicks had his stocking feet shoved under the heater vent.

"Hey, Hicks," he shouted. "Get your damn feet from outta heater."

"Huh?"

"Get your goddamn feet out from under the heater," he shouted. "That's what's been stinking up the cab."

Hicks sat up, snarling. "What about my feet?"

"They're stinking up the damn truck."

"It ain't my feet!"

"No," Tanner fired back. "It's probably your whole damn body. When was the last time you took a shower?"

"Hey, fuck you, asshole."

"No, goddamn it! *Fuck you!*"

But Hicks was having none of Tanner's mouth. "You wanna pull off to the side of the road, Jack? I'll stomp your fucking ass!"

Tanner was going to do no such thing, and Hicks no doubt knew it—no matter how pissed Tanner was feeling, he was not going to pull the rig off the highway and onto an unstable shoulder in a blinding snow storm.

Tanner knew that he had to figure something out, and fast. The cab was stinking with the smell of dirty feet and he still had well over a thousand miles into Phoenix to be stuck in the cab with THE source of the smell. A hard falling-out between the two would make the remaining twenty-four hours into Arizona more than just a little difficult. Between the stink and the attitude that now defined Dwayne Hicks, the word "unbearable" came to mind. He would end up duking it out with Hicks for sure. Tanner could guess the outcome of that, even if Hicks could not, but as such things are never entirely predictable, Tanner wanted to avoid an openly physical confrontation, if possible.

"All right, Dwayne," Tanner said. "Calm down. When we get to Sheriff's just take a shower and get some clean socks on."

"You know what, Jack? Eat shit!"

Damn! This was going nowhere fast. "Dwayne, listen up, man, we're stuck in this cab together for the next fifteen hundred miles. We got to try to get along."

"Sure, Jack! Then get along."

"I can't do that with you making this place unlivable. I can't breathe, man."

"Then open the window."

"Dwayne, that's not going to work in a goddamn snow storm."

"Then fine, asshole: eat shit!" And Hicks drew down the zipper. "Now let me get some goddamn sleep."

"Goddamn it, Hicks," Tanner shouted. "Get real about this."

"Shut the fuck up, Jack," Hicks yelled from the other side of the curtain. "Or pull over to the side of the road and take an ass whooping."

Tanner was steaming, his ears burning and his throat tight. He smacked the steering wheel with his hand, realizing that it was only because Hicks had never run team before that the man could have possibly survived his own kiss-my-ass attitude. Team driving was work that demanded not just cooperation between human beings, but unquestioning accommodation. There was no way Hicks could ever have passed through the small world of a sleeper-cab tractor and come out the other side singing his *me-first* bullshit. It was just Jack Tanner's huge misfortune to be his co-driver on this, Dwayne's cherry run.

The rest of the way up to Tulsa, Hicks had the curtain down and Tanner had the window cracked open just enough to get some fresh air swirling past his nose. It was icy, blowing past Tanner's face, but clean and preferable to the stink of Dwayne's feet.

They rolled into Sheriff's around midnight, with Tanner still at the wheel. The parking lot at Sheriff's will hold nearly a hundred trucks, with small carts going around shuttling the drivers to and from their rigs. Tanner set the air brake and switched off the head lights, leaving the running lights lit. Hicks was moving around in the sleeper. Tanner opened the door and climbed to the ground with his overnight bag in his hand. When Dwayne followed, Tanner noted that Hicks was empty handed. They caught one of the carts for a silent ride to the diner.

The problem with the truck being human and not mechanical, Tanner no longer felt the need to roust a mechanic from the repair shed, so the first thing he did was head for the showers. He bought a ticket, grabbed a towel and key, and unlocked one of the small changing rooms with a sink and shower. After a shave and shower and a change of clothes, it occurred to Tanner to make sure Hicks took a shower by picking up a second shower ticket. Not only did Tanner buy Hicks a shower ticket, he also bought him a pack of new socks before heading back out to the diner.

Hicks was eating his breakfast at one end of the counter. Tanner dropped the socks and ticket next to his plate. The fork froze just off the eggs as Hicks looked at the socks and ticket, then the fork continued on to his mouth. He never once looked at Tanner as Tanner walked down the counter and sat down. Tanner ate and watched to see if Hicks would pick up the socks and shower ticket.

Hicks breezed through the sports section of the *Tulsa World* while he waited to get his change from the waitress. He got up to leave at about the same time Tanner dropped a few bills on the counter next to his empty plate. He saw that Hicks had left the socks and ticket where they lay. Tanner picked them off the counter and caught up to Hicks outside.

"Hicks, didn't you see the shower ticket and socks?"

Hicks took a pinch of snuff out of the small tin and stuffed it in his cheek, never looking at Tanner. "I can buy my own socks, Jack." He slipped the tin back into his rear pocket. "And you know what, Jack? I'll do it when I'm good and goddamn ready."

"And the shower?"

"When I'm ready, Jack. Now fuck off!"

"Dwayne, I ain't getting back in that truck with you unless you shower."

"So fine, stay here."

"Hicks, I ain't gonna let you in that truck."

"Yeah—try to stop me, asshole."

"I mean it, Hicks, goddamn it."

"I'm warning you for the last time, Jack. Don't fuck with me, unless you want to get your ass kicked."

Their voices must have gotten a little loud. Several truckers turned and were watching them. Hicks stared back at them, hard, and for a moment Tanner thought Hicks was going to say something wise-ass to them about minding their own business.

But Hicks was smart enough not to mix words with any of them and he turned back to Tanner. "Just quit your bitch'n, Jack," he said as a cart swung around the corner. "You ain't that tough, now let's get back on the road."

It was out of anger and total frustration, but when Hicks took the step down to the muddy road Tanner stuck his foot out and tripped him. It happened fast. Hicks pitched forward, hands outstretched, hit the ground, rolled and ended up on his back in the snow and mud. Tanner didn't know what to expect after that, but it should have been what he got. Hicks clambered to his feet and came charging up the four steps after Tanner. The two of them grappled and got into a stumbling kind of bear hug, twirling and dancing before slipping off the step, both of them toppling down in the tangle and piling up at the bottom of the landing in a squirming heap of arms and legs and black icy mud.

Hicks started swinging wildly, landing fists against Tanner's ears, with Tanner under him holding his hands up against the force of the blows. Hicks was small and light, making it easy enough for Tanner to roll, grabbing Hicks by his hair, and pull him over with Tanner ending up on top. Tanner took a fist in the side of his face, but weak, as Hicks had no muscle or weight behind it, and Tanner quickly landed two rapid punches in the center of Hicks' face, causing his nose to spurt blood. By this time several of the truckers had intervened and were pulling Tanner off Hicks, who was up quick but also held back by two other drivers.

Both Hicks and Tanner were breathing hard and covered in snow and dark mud. Tanner shook himself loose from the grip the truckers had on him, and watched Hicks as he leaned forward, blowing bloody snot from his nose.

One of the truckers spoke, "You two assholes gonna calm down now?"

Tanner waved his hand. "We're cool. Right Hicks?"

"Fuck you, Jack."

Another driver spoke, "You want us to have Sheriff's get some troopers out here?"

Tanner shook his head, and waved them off again. "We don't need the police."

Hicks looked around and shook his head too—"No cops"—and then poked at his nose with one hand and took an offered napkin to staunch the bleeding with the other. "It's done, man. We don't need the cops. Let the hell go of me."

The two truckers turned Hicks loose.

After the roll in the mud, both of them had to take showers and change their clothes, Tanner for a second time. Hicks had to be run back to their rig for his overnight kit and fresh clothes and he hit the shower stall with the overnight bag and the bundle of new socks. After cleaning up, Hicks went to the first aid station about his nose, which turned out to be broken. Tanner bought a new shirt for himself, and as a good will gesture, he bought Hicks a roll of dip cans, six in all. Tanner didn't know if Hicks ever looked in the bag, because Hicks never acknowledged the peace offering, and the two probably said no more than a dozen words to each other in the next twenty-five hours, making the balance of the run into Phoenix glum and tense, locked up together in the tight little world of that sleeper-cab.

At the Phoenix terminal, Tanner pulled the rig up alongside the office and set the brake. Hicks climbed across the doghouse to pull his gear out of the sleeper.

Tanner watched him for a moment then offered, "For whatever it might be worth, Dwayne, I'm sorry I popped your cherry like this."

"Kiss my ass."

"Dwayne, I'm saying I'm sorry I broke your nose."

Hicks stopped what he was doing and turned to Tanner. "Well, for whatever it might be worth, Jack," he sneered. "That don't cut shit, and if it was the other way around, I wouldn't be sorry."

Tanner grunted. "Maybe not, Dwayne, but I just wanted you to know that I'm not happy about it and I wish it hadn't happened."

"That's damn white of you, Jack," Hicks snapped back. "And you'd better believe it'll come out different the next time."

"There's not going to be a next time, Dwayne."

"Yeah?"

"Not for us, anyway, and I'm just hoping there's not going to be another time for you."

"What the hell's that supposed to mean, Jack?"

"You planning on doing any more team driving?"

"Maybe I am. What's it to ya?"

"Then it means what it means."

Hicks opened his mouth as if to reply, only he must have thought better of what might come ripping out and closed it. Then, clutching his overnight kit, he climbed down from the passenger side.

For a second Tanner lost sight of Hicks, until he remounted the step and reached out for the bag containing the half dozen cans of dip. Hicks hesitated and took a long, cold moment to study Tanner from out of his black-and-blue eyes.

"You know what, Jack? You're not a damn bit sorry about my nose, are you—not one goddamn bit?" It was a statement, not a question. "You liked it, Jack—I know you did—and I'll bet on something else. I'll bet you think you taught me a lesson, don't you? Well, guess the hell what, Jack? You couldn't teach me squat on a sorry ass bet—not you, not a dozen guys like you—and you know what else, Jack. It'll be different the next time. It will, goddamn it. I'm way fucking tougher than you think I am, son'abitch." Hicks raised the bag with the roll of tins and shook it at Tanner. "You think you popped my cherry, Jack? Well, fuck you, asshole, and thanks—I'll keep the goddamn snuff."

"You're probably right and you're probably wrong, Dwayne."

"Yeah? What the hell's that supposed to mean?"

"About me teaching you something. You're right: I didn't and I couldn't. And you're wrong: I didn't enjoy busting your nose. I mean that, Dwayne. It's wasn't an accident, but it wasn't intended either. So like your daddy used to say: it hurt me worse than it hurt you."

Hicks glared at Tanner. "Yeah, well fuck you, Jack? I take it back. You can keep the goddamn snuff," he said, suddenly struggling for something else to say that would salvage the losing moment. Finding nothing, he tossed the bag and muttered weakly, "It's not my goddamn brand anyway."

"Look, Dwayne," Tanner came back evenly, and gestured to where the bag landed. "You keep the dip. I can't use it, and even if you don't want it, maybe you can use it to make a down payment on a hockey mask, 'cause with your attitude it looks like you're sure as hell gonna need one."

"Fuck you, Jack! Kiss my ass! The only thing I need to do is get away from assholes."

Tanner sucked his teeth a moment, eyeing Hicks as if trying to keep him in focus. "Won't happen, Dwayne."

"Yeah? How's that, Jack?"

"Because no matter where you go, Dwayne—there you are."

Sand

I've heard it said somewhere that life happens while you're busy
doing something else.

My friends call me Top. That name came about because a little
over a decade ago I spent nearly a year as the top middleweight
contender for the world title. I got close, real close, but never
got my shot. In my last fight I KO-ed Bobby Ray Curtis and was
next in line for the title bout, but that KO on Bobby Ray ended
both our careers. About half-way through the sixth I had reached
out to Bobby with faint. It had been a set-up punch, a do nothing, light jab. I never intended to do any real damage with the
punch, except maybe move Bobby Ray off balance. Like I figured, Bobby bobbed to avoid the jab, then unexpectedly wob-
bled on his stance and for an opportune second dropped his left
and showed me some daylight. The opening was like a gift from

heaven and I rocketed in with one of the hardest right hooks I ever threw. That punch smoked us both. Bobby Ray went down hard and I line-fractured two bones in my wrist. That split-second in our lives left Bobby partially blind in his left eye and me with a wrist that never properly healed. Neither of us ever got into the ring again.

Personally, I liked Bobby Ray and felt sorrier for him than I did for myself. Bobby was much younger than me and at the start of his career, while I had made my money and was at the end of mine. I believed that I could have taken the title, but that fight with Bobby forced me to look hard into the nature of a world without big paydays. Instead of taking up sparring or training or work as a corner cut-man, I hooked up with my youngest brother, Maurice, and together we bought a shiny new Peterbilt conventional tractor,[13] heading the two of us in the direction of making real decent money hauling cargo out of the Great Lakes area for southern ports. All things considered, our months and years on the road were developing into a smooth and profitable style of living.

It was just before three in a late June morning when a distant smack of lightning silhouetted a knotted roiling sky and a fuzzy drizzle started dancing off the wind screen. We were southbound on I-65, just north of Decatur, Alabama, running a flatbed out of Cincinnati loaded with bales of rags bound for the Port of Mobile, a good three hundred miles further south. A good, solid rain would soak into those bales and put us so far over the weight limit that

---

13. A conventional tractor is a long wheel base unit with the driver sitting between the extended wheel base; this as compared with a cab-over tractor where the driver sits on top of the steering wheels. Drivers generally prefer the conventional as the ride is more comfortable than a cab-over. The disadvantage is maneuvering in tight spaces.

we could easily end up parked in a state portable weight station until hell froze over waiting for those rags to dry out. We needed to stop and get canvas tarps over the bales.

A heavier sprinkle splattered across the windshield, causing me to steer off the highway at the next exit and pull down a parallel side road. I eased to a stop by a large grassy slope, popped on the air brake and slapped the curtain to the sleeper berth.

"Maurice, I gotta get you up, bro."

"Huh?" came the sleepy reply. "What up, Top?"

"Rain, brother. Rain. We gotta get tarps over the load."

I quickly hopped down from the cab so I wouldn't have to listen to him cussing. The late summer heat was a shock from the air conditioned cab and for a second I thought to take off my light jacket, but changed my mind when a gust of warm wind splashed a veil of wetness into to my face. I slammed the door of the cab and snatched a flashlight from the side-box beneath the sleeper. Moving down the trailer I went through the utility boxes located under the flat bed and opened three of them, dragging out three waterproof tarps. I began to unpack the tarps, spreading them over the wet grass, searching for the eyelets. The blackness didn't make hooking bands through the metal rings any easier. I looked back toward the cab, hoping to see my younger brother climbing down. The wind was picking up and I needed him on the other side of the load to catch the ropes I'd toss in order to pull the tarps across the bales. The only sound I heard was the traffic swishing by on the wet interstate and I was just getting ready to go pound on the door of the cab when a car came to a sliding stop behind my rig. I turned and squinted through the glare of the head lights. The car had skidded a bit off the road and onto the grassy shoulder. A second car followed the first, only it stayed about sixty or seventy-five yards back, looking to be halted by the sight of our rig.

I was putting my hand up to shield my eyes from the headlights when I heard her.

"Help me," she screamed. "Oh, God, please help me."

I was squinting through the wind-whipped drizzle when a sudden burst of lightning out of the east lit up the car. The driver side door was flung open and a figure was standing just outside on the roadway.

She screamed at me again, "Oh, God, please help me!"

"Who's that?" I shouted back, the roll of thunder competing with my voice.

For an answer the woman seemed to jump as the following car inched forward toward her. I caught sight of Maurice as he clambered down from the cab and came over. Like me, he was staring into the headlights.

"What going on, Top?"

Before I could tell him that I didn't know I heard the car door slam shut and in another flare of lightening saw a woman racing across the tarps toward us. Maurice shot the flashlight in her face. She was young, blond, and from the wild look in her eyes, scared shitless. She ran up to my left, grabbed my arm and spun around behind me.

"Please," she panted. "Don't let them hurt me."

My brother's mouth had dropped open at the sight of the girl standing behind me, clutching my arm and shaking like a wet puppy. He hollered something at her that was lost in a crack of thunder.

I grabbed the hand squeezing my arm. "Hey, girl, what the hell's the matter?" I shouted against the wind. "Who's gonna hurt you?"

"My father," she blurted, looking up at me with eyes so wide I could see white all around the irises. "Please..." and she gripped my arm harder. "Them in that car," and she let me feel her fingernails through my jacket. "My father," she repeated and started to blubber with fear, "my brothers, and fat-ass uncle."

"In that car?" I asked, nodding at the second car still inching forward toward our rig.

"Yes," she answered, digging her nails deeper into my arm. "Please don't let 'em take me."

I pried her hand loose and turned to my brother. The wind was fading and the drizzle had turned to a light sprinkle, warm and easy on my face. "Get on your cell, Maurice," I told him, "and get some cops out here," and I told him the exit number I'd taken to get off I-65.

Maurice hustled back toward the idling tractor as the second car rolled to a stop behind the woman's car. I watched. No one got out.

"What's your name, girl?" I asked over my shoulder.

"Jess."

"Okay, Jess," I said, seeing the car stop behind the one she had been driving. "Just stay behind me. We'll get some troopers out here to straighten this out."

"Please," she pleaded. "They're gonna hurt me."

"No one's gonna hurt you, girl," I assured her, then yelled toward the tractor, "Maurice, you making that call?"

"I got them on the line now, Top," came the shouted reply.

The sprinkle slowed, then stopped, and in the red glow of tail lights I saw car doors open and several men get out. They moved forward, around Jess's car and into the splash of the headlights. They stopped just ahead of the car, leaving maybe eighty to a hundred feet separating us. Even at that distance and through the night's hazy mist it was easy to tell that there was nothing remarkable about these men. There was enough red and yellow glow coming off the running lights of my trailer to see that the man standing in front was thick set, with a broad, flat face partially hidden by a camo ball cap pulled down low over his eyes; two others were younger and thinner, hatless and of average height; the fourth man I couldn't make out, except that he was built real heavy and like the man in front wore a baseball cap that put his round face in the dark. He must have seen me looking at him; he lifted his head and deliberately shot a nasty stream of tobacco juice off to the side. All four were dressed in dungarees and jackets that looked a bit heavy for the summer heat.

"Come over here, Jess," shouted the man out in front. "Jess—here—now!" He took an uncertain step forward. "Get away from that man, Jess, and come over here." His voice was deep and gravely, grinding through a deep southern drawl, with a country way of mashing his r's. He pronounced "here" something like coughing out a "hea".

When Jess didn't move, they all came forward, closing the distance to about fifty feet. The two younger men, her brothers, I was thinking, were flanking the older man. I guessed the brothers to be in their late teens or early twenties. They were both looking antsy and irritable and cross, reminding me of dogs held on a tight leash. The fourth, the big man who I took to be the uncle, was slowly easing to the front, keeping to the trailer side, acting like a man not eager to be seen, which was comical for a man his size.

Maurice came back from making the call and closed ranks with me so that the girl was now looking at the men in front of us from between both our shoulders. I shot a glance at him. My brother's eyes were blinking with confusion.

"Jessie Teal, you get out from behind those men," ordered the big man standing out front, "and get your ass over hea!"

"I don't think she wants to do that, Mister," I answered him, feeling the girl press up against my back as she looked around my arm. "And until she wants to do that, she can stay right here with us."

Like a gathering force, they all inched forward then, shortening the distance between us to about thirty feet, the two younger men flanking the father who was doing the talking. The uncle I could now see was older and looking close to obese. He wore bib-overalls like a farmer. He stayed off to the side, near to our load, looking like he wanted to hide in the contours of the trailer's tires.

"This ain't none of your business, boy," the father fired at us. "So you boys best to get in your truck and be on your way."

Those words hit my hothead brother all wrong. "Bullshit!" he snapped back. "We *boys* ain't doing shit, so you can stuff that 'boy' shit up your cracker ass."

I was reaching out to Maurice, to slow him down. That was when the fat man came out of the shadows.

"You ain't in New York now, nigger," he snarled and shot a stream of juice in Maurice's direction. "Down here we can just shoot your black nigger ass and leave you and no one will give a hoot 'n hell."

He had his right hand in his jacket pocket. Some men will bluff like that, act like they're packing. I didn't think this man was bluffing.

"*What?!*" my brother shouted back. "You think this is 1950, you dumb-ass motherfucker?" He tensed to start forward.

I yanked his coat sleeve, stopping him. "The cops coming, bro?" I questioned him loud enough for the others to hear.

"Yeah," he replied to me and shook my hand loose, then louder, "And *fuck these motherfucking crackers*!"

"Mister, all this is gonna have a real bad ending," threatened the man in front, the one I guessed to be the girl's father, "you keep up that attitude."

"Attitude? I'll show you fuck'n attitude," Maurice shot back. "Why don't you come over here and kiss my black ass."

The fat uncle inched forward. "How about if instead we was to come over there and stomp your black ass."

Maurice was turned toward him, itching to get at any of them, but again I took hold of his arm. "You be cool, Maurice."

Again Maurice tried to shake off my grip but I held tight. "You be cool, brother" I repeated through my teeth.

"That's right. You keep that boy under control," the father said, then turned his attention back to the girl. "Jess," he called out. "Get your ass over hea now!"

The girl clung tighter to me, sobbing, "Please, mister."

"We got the State Police coming," I boldly announced, hoping that the mention of the police would knock the situation down a few notches. "Let's all wait for them."

"Fuck you," one of the brothers yelled back and surged forward. "Jess," he spat at the girl. "Get your whoring ass over here."

There was another flash of lightening and the wind suddenly picked up. The father had held out his arm, blocking the boy as I had done with Maurice.

"Let's all be cool," I cautioned, "until the cops get here."

"That's my stupid little brother," the girl whimpered, still clinging to my arm.

Up closer like they were, the boy looked younger than I had first thought, maybe around fourteen or fifteen—way too young to be out here in the middle of a rainy night involved in this bullshit.

The father pushed the boy back behind him, "Shut up, Luke," then turned to us. "Mister," he shouted, "that girl you're holding there is my underage daughter and you let her go, and right now, goddamn it!" and he took a definite, menacing three steps forward, bringing him within a dozen feet of me.

I wasn't feeling frightened of them. It had been a long, long time since I had been frightened of a fight. The fat man might have had a gun in his pocket, but I wasn't at all certain of that. I knew that even in a down-and-dirty brawl I could quickly deal with two of them by myself, and I was confident that Maurice could manage the other two, at least for the few seconds it would take me to get at them.

"I'm not holding her back," I answered him calmly, watching the fat man who was again easing off to the side of us, then added as evenly and straight forward as I could, "She's standing here on her own, Mister. We're not holding her." I lifted my hands to show him. "And I don't know what the deal is here, but she's scared of you and we've called the state police. They're on their way. This girl can stay right here with us until they get here."

"You're not being smart, boy," the fat man boomed at us from off to the side. "You don't know what you're doing."

"We'll wait for the police," I said.

"You're messing with our family's affairs, boy."

"We'll wait," I repeated.

"Maybe we'll shoot both your black asses and take her."

The fat man had yanked a gun out of his pocket and was waving it, making sure we could see it in the running lights of the trailer.

The father shouted. "Put that damn gun away, James. Let me handle this."

"Then handle it, Forrest, goddamn it. Stop fucking with these New York niggers."

Anger ripped through me, breaking like a wave over my better judgment. "We ain't from New York," I cut loose. "And you'd better stuff that nigger shit before this nigger kicks your fat white ass."

"Yeah? Well, fuck you," and the fat man started forward with the gun raised.

"*James!*" the father shouted at him. "Put that damn gun down or *I'll* shoot you myself, goddamn it!"

"Fuck these niggers," the fat man shrieked, looking nearly out of his mind with frustration.

"James, I swear to God, I ain't fucking with you! Now quit!"

There were two guns out now, things threatening to cascade beyond control.

I shouted to both of them. "Just wait for the police. We called them ten minutes ago. They'll be here."

The fat man had stopped at the sight of the second drawn gun, his face wide and wet in the glow of the trailer lights. His gun hand dropped, now hanging limply by his side, the gun losing some of its potency, but his eyes stayed little and mean.

I was automatically running through a game plan on how to handle the guns when the father shouted out a new and startling piece of information: "I am the police, goddamn it," and he yanked something from his rear pocked and held it up. I didn't need the dramatic flash of lightening that lit us up to see the badge. "I'm a Limestone County Deputy Sheriff! Now turn the girl loose!"

I heard Maurice mutter through the following pop of thunder, "A white sheriff in Bumfuck, Alabama—shit, this ain't good, brother."

He said something else, but it was lost in a second, heavy drum-roll of thunder that was more felt than heard. The girl let out a strangled word that sounded in my ear like "fuck," and she tried to make herself even smaller behind my back.

"You just keep it cool, Maurice."

I knew that my plans had to be changed. Taking on a man with a badge put a whole new slant on things. There was never a way that self-defense could work with police, no matter *what the hell* they were doing to you, and that was the same whether you were white *or* black. Behind that, being a registered prize fighter made using my fists a felony in most states, and that didn't change either because you were white or black.

The new information had slowed up my brother as well. "Go easy, Top," he said softly. "This white dude can fuck us up real bad."

The girl clung tighter to me, crying little animal, simpering noises that had the word *"please"* couched in their desperate whimper.

The same as Maurice, I recognized the long reach of the past—what it was to be a black man facing a white sheriff in the rural south. What century we were in didn't seem to matter to the timeless ghosts stalking my mind. It's dead wrong to think that being black in America is about race, because it's not, and never was. Being black in America is a made up thing that has a long history of means and benefit for the few, and hell on earth for the others, a history that starts from way back there and going way out yonder to a point that reflects only the lie of race and not the people. I had firmly believed that my entire life. Yet even believing that race is only a convenient lie of utility, I nonetheless understood it to be a lie with sharp teeth, and I was now staring down the razor's edge of those teeth.

The father shouted at me. "Stop your damn stalling and turn her loose *now*, Mister!"

"I'm not sure what you are," I answered slowly and with care. "But this girl's scared of you and I'm asking you to wait a few minutes for the state police to get here."

One of the brothers whined, "Its gonna start to rain again, Pa, let's just get her and get the hell out of here."

The father said, "I'm coming to get my daughter, and if you interfere I *will* arrest you."

He stepped forward, holding the badge in front of him like a bible in the hand of God. His revolver was not raised at us, but it was clearly there, very clearly meant to be seen. Both brothers were coming up alongside of him, and I suddenly realized that I didn't know where the fat uncle was, but I suspected he was behind me and Maurice. I had no time to look.

The father pulled up in front of me, in my face enough for me to take a good measure of him. He was as tall as me and his eyes in the dark looked light, a gray color maybe. In another time and place he could have been a guy sitting next to me in a sports bar, shouting for his team and pounding me on the back when they scored a TD. Except for the fact that he was white police with a gun in his hand, he was any man, every man.

I backed up slightly and did a quarter turn. It was a reflexive movement, an automatic adjustment for punching room. It must have been the turning part that gave the sheriff pause; by the puzzled look on his face he both understood the movement and was a bit confused by it. A man with a gun doesn't expect aggression in response from an unarmed man; he had no way of knowing that my movement was more a reflection of my training than an overt signal of courage.

The girl, Jess, ducked back, stepping away, staying well behind me and Maurice. I felt her trying to make herself small.

"Jess, get out from behind that man," he said to her, his voice lower, cautious, his eyes never leaving mine, "unless you want *him* to get arrested."

I heard the girl answer, but to whom I could not tell, "Please—No."

"Look, Mister," I said while glancing at the gun in his hand. "We need to wait for the State Police."

"She's my daughter, Mister."

"I hear you, but she's staying right here with me until the cops get here."

"Damn, man, don't you see this gun—this badge?" His voice was rising in a bewildered anger and frustration.

"I see, but she's not going with you if she don't want to!"

One of the boys shouted at me, "You fucking crazy, man?"

Even in the darkness I could see the father's pale face changing color and at that moment the fat uncle made his move. He came at me from behind in a clumsy effort to pull me down with a head-lock around my neck. I was a little shorter than him, which must have made him underestimate both how strong and how fast I was. I slipped the lock and simultaneously spun, hitting him with a low body blow that was launched off my rear foot. There's a big difference between being hit by a guy in a back alley fight behind a bar and being hit by a professional prize fighter. My punch had all the spin of my weight and upper body strength in the contact. There was enough force behind my fist that I might have cracked a rib, even through the uncle's fluffy rolls of body fat. I could not see his expression as he landed hard in the wet grass and mud, but I heard him gasp and wheeze in pain.

I wasn't in any hurry to hurt anyone else and was turning around to say as much to the father when his gun was stuck in my face, the hammer cocked. It was close enough for me to see the bullets in the cylinder. They were hollow points.

"Lace your hands on your head!"

Having a gun pointed at you has a way of draining your face of all feeling and making your legs turn to jelly, with the skin on your back and chest getting all hot and tingly. In the movies the hero slaps the gun aside and beats the crap out of the guy holding it; in real life you carefully do exactly as you are told.

I did as the hollow points ordered. The two brothers, suddenly a little wary of me, were helping their uncle to his feet. He was doubled up, clutching his side, still gasping, and now cursing me through his clinched teeth.

"Pa," one of the boys said. "I think Uncle James is real hurt."

"Get your sister and we'll get out of here," the father answered, the gun never wavering from where it was pointed at my forehead.

Oddly, I didn't think the man would shoot, yet staring into the barrel of that revolver kept me rooted to the spot. Maurice stepped back and the older boy took the girl by the arm, gingerly watching me. I could see that even with my hands laced on top of my head he was afraid of me and didn't want to get too close.

It was right then that the state troopers pulled up, two cruisers, two cops, blue lights flashing, and I felt a flush of instant relief.

"Put down that gun!" I heard through the loudspeaker.

I turned my eyes and saw one trooper out of his car with a gun pointed in our direction and the second trooper still in his car and talking into the loudspeaker.

"Put the gun down now," boomed the loudspeaker, "and get on the ground."

The sheriff lowered his gun and held up his badge.

It wasn't long after all the guns were put away that Maurice and I found ourselves handcuffed and sitting in the back of one of the state police cruisers watching the troopers speaking with the girl and her father. The injured uncle and her two brothers were sitting in their car, waiting on the outcome.

"Shit," Maurice said. "They ought to be arresting them assholes instead of us. What the hell did we do, Top? It's because it's against the law to be black in Jim Crow Bama ain't it?"

"Just be cool, brother," I cautioned him. "We didn't do anything wrong. It's a problem for them troopers now, and the important thing is to get loose and get the tarps over our load and get the hell out of here. We got to be in Mobile in less than five hours. Let them cops handle it."

"Yeah, Top," replied Maurice. "Only we're the ones in handcuffs."

"They'll turn us loose."

"You sure about that?"

Rain had replaced the sprinkles, light, medium sized drops now sparkling and running in little rivulets down the windshield of the cruiser. The two state troopers waved the father back to his car, then surprising me, handcuffed Jess. They led the girl to the front cruiser, got her in the back seat before coming back to us, climbing into the front seat just ahead of a steady downpour. I glanced at Maurice and realized that he had not seen the girl being handcuffed. I didn't tell him. I knew his temper and run-away mouth. I noted too that one of the brothers drove off in Jess's car. Were these troopers arresting the girl too? Why? This was getting way too murky for me, but I had other problems.

"Hey, Officers," I said to them as inoffensively as possible. "Do you suppose you could let us put the tarps over our load? That rain will soak in quick and we'll be overweight."

The younger of the two troopers was about Maurice's age. He turned, eyeing me through the cage wire separating the back seat from the front. "When we're done with you."

He didn't sound unpleasant. It was a matter of fact comment, and I was thinking that he didn't understand the need to cover the load.

"Come on, Officer," I encouraged. "In another five minutes that load will be so soaked we won't be able to pass a scale."

"I said: when we're done, Mister Little. You're just damn lucky you're not heading off to jail, so you'd better button it up before that luck runs out."

I could see that he could care less about our problems. For police to be causing other people discomfort was so much a routine part of their job that they are often completely blind to its effects.

"Lucky?" Maurice popped off. "Jail? Just how in the hell are we lucky? We were just trying to help that girl and *we're* in handcuffs."

Both police had military style haircuts. The one with the attitude—the younger one—also sported a burly blonde moustache. It didn't make him look any older; it made him look like a kid awkwardly struggling to be taken seriously. His brass name tag announced his name in small black letters: *Lam*.

The other trooper was much older, looking to be approaching fifty. His hair was graying, his face beginning to show the lines and marks of both his age and his profession. His name tag read *Billings*. He was bent over some paperwork. After a moment he looked up from the clipboard. "I don't know what the hell you two thought you were doing, but like my partner says, you're lucky we're not arresting you." He pointed to the car that was pulling away. "That's a county sheriff you guys assaulted."

"My brother didn't hit anyone," I corrected him. "I did."

"Well, seeing as he's a sheriff, and assaulting him is a felony in this state, it doesn't matter who hit him, we can *still* arrest the both of you."

"That guy I hit wasn't a sheriff," I tried correcting him again.

"Oh, yes he was," Billings contradicted me. "A *reserve* deputy sheriff."

"That fat-ass pig?" Maurice sounded off. "That some kinda fucking joke."

"You watch your damn mouth," the younger cop, Lam, ordered, then turned to me. "Assaulting a bonafide peace officer in the state of Alabama is serious jail time, so you both better shut up and cooperate."

"We didn't know who he was," I protested. "And I only hit him after he jumped me."

"He didn't jump you," Lam said.

"What?" I shot back. "Like hell he didn't!"

"They all say it was an unprovoked assault, and it *was* an assault on a deputy sheriff."

"Bullshit!" Maurice fired back at him. "They're a bunch of lying sonsabitches. Tell 'em, Top."

Billings pinned Maurice with a harsh glare. "Put a lock on that mouth, son. I've known Forrest Teal for the best part of fifteen years, and there's no reason for him to lie, so you'd better get yourself under control and let me finish this here paperwork and feel lucky that we're even thinking about turning you loose to be on your way."

Maurice came back at him, "And that man who that don't tell lies told you the fat dude didn't jump us? Is that right? Huh?"

For a moment Billings didn't answer, but worked on his report. I was trying to figure a quick way to shut Maurice up when Billings finally answered, "One of the sons told us how it happened."

"Shit. So his kid lied. Is that it?"

Billings didn't reply, just scribbled at his report and we all got quiet for a moment. I watched the rain with a sinking feeling, then looked at Jess in the front cruiser. She sat unmoving, silhouetted against the running lights from my trailer. These troopers seemed to have everything backwards.

It was growing light outside, a cloudy gray sky climbing out of the flat farmland to the east. The handcuffs were cutting into my wrists and my hands were tingling, going to sleep, and I knew that another twenty minutes of this rain and our load would be beyond anything that we could get to Mobile by our deadline. We'd never make it past one of the state's portable state scales and there was sure to be one set up in the next three hundred miles.

"I don't suppose there's any way you can let us out of these handcuffs," I said. "I'm losing circulation to my hands."

"We'll be done here in a moment," replied Lam.

Maurice wagged his head, and asked in a low tone, "What about the girl?" he said. "You talk to her? Me and Top were just trying to help her." He evidently still hadn't noticed that Jess was sitting in the front cruiser.

"That not what her father says."

"Then he's lying," Maurice responded. "Again."

"Forrest's not a liar," Billings replied evenly. "That man doesn't lie."

"Well he did tonight. Or he let his kid do it for him."

"He said you were keeping him from taking her home."

"Did you even *talk* to the girl, asshole?"

Lam turned and snarled at Maurice through the wire screen. "Just keep at it, Mister. Around here we respect the police, and I suspect they even do that up north where you two come from. And you, Mister Alvoid Little"—he took a long second to eye-fuck me—"got a card on you from the New York State Boxing Commission saying you are a registered professional middleweight prize fighter, which makes the assault on that sheriff a *felony*-assault with a deadly weapon. Now just shut the fuck up or we'll forget that man doesn't want you arrested."

"That *man*," Maurice dug his heels in, "doesn't want me and Top arrested because he doesn't want anyone questioning the girl and finding out what was going on."

Billings glanced at Maurice, then looked at me. "Nope, you're being arrested is not up to him." He hesitated a long moment, studying me, then said with some easy deliberation, "I don't know about how it is where you gentlemen come from, but here in Alabama it's not up to victims of a felony to prefer charges or not. A felony arrest is not up to anyone but the arresting officers. So whether we turn you loose or not is up to me and my partner." He let that sink in, then asked a leading question: "Now, do you want to finish your haul to Mobile, or do you want to go to jail?"

Seeming to offer an option caught us both by surprise. Maurice just stared at them and I looked again the car ahead of us. The girl looked to be sitting quietly, waiting. Were they going to arrest Jess *instead of us*? What was going on here?

I finally answered quietly, "We need to finish this run."

"Good," Billings replied, seeming to study his partner rather than us. I could tell he was sizing something up. He finally looked at me and asked, "You know where Auburn is?"

"What? No."

"Auburn, Alabama?"

"No. Why?"

He turned and looked at me. "It's about fifty miles northeast of Montgomery, up I-85."

"Okay. So what?"

"It's on your way."

I waited, puzzled.

Billings glanced at Lam, then back at me. "We want you to take that man's daughter there."

This request from Billings came so far out of left field that for a moment I was unable to respond. I looked at both the troopers, wondering if this was some kind of joke.

I finally managed to get out, "Why?"

"Because I don't feel like arresting anyone today," replied Billings, "and that *includes* not wanting to arrest that Limestone County sheriff."

I did not understand. "What are we missing, Officer? I'm not getting any of this."

Billings seemed to settle back, taking a long look at us both in the dim light of the overhead. "That girl," he jabbed his thumb at the front cruiser. "Forrest's daughter—she's pregnant—seventeen and pregnant." Billings waited a moment for that to sink in. "And Forrest wants her to have an abortion, which is damn near illegal in the state of Alabama, except in cases of rape and incest, which means in order for her to get the abortion she'll have to swear out a complaint against the father of the baby for rape. She's refusing to do that, and right now Forrest doesn't know who the father is, and if he gets his hands on that girl he's like as not to beat her—his own daughter—until she does name the father and swears out a complaint. Then he's like as not to go after the boyfriend, and I'm not real anxious to arrest my friend for battery on a minor—either the girl *or* the boyfriend. I have to separate her from Forrest for a time and keep him from doing something stupid that'll land everyone in a world of hurt."

"Jesus," Maurice said. "Is he crazy? Just send her to another state where it's easier to get an abortion."

"She won't consent," Lam informed us.

"The girl wants to keep the baby," Billings added. "She wants to keep it and marry the father."

"Okay, okay," replied Maurice. "All that's the crazy, fucked up family shit. What's in Auburn?"

"The girl's mother," Billings answered. "And there it'll—*she'll* be someone else's headache. I told you I don't feel like arresting my friend, not today, not ever."

"Who's the baby's father?" I asked.

"I don't know and I didn't ask."

"It's some racial shit, isn't it?" carped Maurice. "She got knocked up by some black dude and these crackers don't like it, right?"

It was Lam who replied to my brother. "You know what, asshole?" he angrily fired off. "You black guys give me a pain—always screaming about racial shit, when it sounds like you're the ones up to your eyeballs in your own fucked-up racial shit. We said we don't know who the father is and we don't care." Lam watched Maurice for a second. "What? Do you think we're lying? Why? Why lie? All we want to do is unscramble this stupid shit with as little damage as possible to everyone—including you two, by the fucking way—so put the goddam race card back in your deck and count your blessings."

"Blessings," squawked Maurice. "You're asking us to drive a hundred miles out of our way."

Lam shrugged. "It's either that or go to jail."

"How the hell did we get involved in this crazy shit?"

"Because crazy shit happens," Lam shot back. "And when it does you deal with it, and if you deal with it in the right way shit goes away; if not, you go to jail."

"I don't think we have to threaten them, Cullen," the older trooper admonished the younger, then turned to me. "Because they know the right thing to do."

"Yeah?" It was Maurice who replied. "What makes you so sure we know that this is the *right thing* to do?"

The older trooper studied my brother for a moment, then answered, "Son, when a man says he doesn't know the right thing it's *only* because he's a coward."

"Says you."

"Sorry, son, but everyone knows what's right."

"Jesus," Maurice hissed in exasperation.

Billings added patiently. "We all know what's right, but most folks don't have the guts to do right."

Maurice glared at him and Billings twisted in his seat to speak directly to me. "Look, I know you didn't ask for this, Mister Little, and I'm sorry we're asking this of you—I really am—but look around—there's no one else. Just you—and that's the way it is sometimes, being the only one, so deal with it." He waited a moment, letting me get a grip on that slice of reality. "Look at it this way, Mister Little: you got wrapped up in a situation where there are two possible outcomes, one good and one bad. You can choose to help someone—help out an entire family—help people out of a jam—or you can choose to go to jail."

I was quiet, thinking, and Lam jumped back in, looking from me to Maurice. "I know this looks like a shitty deal, Little, but it's the only deal you got."

"Cullen!" Billing snapped at his, then turned back to me, saying, "We don't always ask for what comes our way, Mister Little, but we have to deal with it in the best way possible. I'm sorry about this, but like my partner says, shit happens. Now think on it, think on the right of it and help us out—help *this girl* out."

"Supposing one of them assholes reports this?" Maurice wanted to know.

"They can report anything they like," Lam responded with a smile. "Because it never happened."

I asked, "What are you gonna tell this guy, Forrest?"

"We already told him that we got the girl in seventy-two hour protective custody. He's bought it."

"And at the end of the seventy-two hours?"

"I'll tell him where she is. Maybe he's cooled off by then."

"And if not?" Maurice chimed in. "Supposing your pal goes to Auburn to find her? What then?"

"Like I said," Billings answered. "Then it's a police problem a hundred miles from here. I can't stop every bad thing in the world from happening, just what's going on right in front of me. And that's true for any of us—and this is right in front of you, Mister Little, so step up." He waited a moment then added, "I really don't want to take you to jail, Mister Little. I believe your story, so we probably won't jail you no matter what you decide, but I'm betting you'll step up and decide right and do right."

I looked out the window at the police car to the front of us. It had stopped raining and the windows of the second cruiser were steamed up. I could only dimly make out Jess in the back seat.

Turning back to the trooper, I said, "This is way out of line for you, isn't it?"

Billings just looked at me, but his eyes told me I was pushing the right button.

"You're running a risk, aren't you?" I asked him. "Not arresting us right now and turning that girl over to us could jam you up bad, couldn't it?"

"It could."

"Supposing that this sheriff tells your superiors what you're doing?"

"He won't."

"Why not?"

"Because he's my friend."

"And that'll count for him more than the law?"

"I believe so," he answered evenly. "It ought to."

"Funny cops," muttered Maurice.

I suggested, "Maybe they'll find out some other way?"

"Maybe so," replied Billings. "But everything worthwhile in life is a risk."

"What about us?" Maurice wanted to know. "We ain't your friends. Why you trusting us? What makes you think we won't just drop that girl off at the next gas station? Or report to the next cop we run into?"

"You won't."

"Why?" Maurice shook his head, genuinely baffled. "Why you trusting us so damn much?"

"Because," answered the trooper slowly. "According to Forrest and James both, you didn't want to turn Jess over to them in a situation where most men would have been real quick to buckle."

"So what's that have to do with shit?"

"So those two thought you men were crazy," Billings informed us. "But me and Cullen, we think different. We think you two men saw the right thing and did the right thing and that took sand."

"Sand?" I questioned.

"Sand," Billings repeated, pausing to take a good long look at me, then added, "I know you know what that means, Mister Little."

I did, but I didn't understand its meaning here. "What does that have to do with anything?"

"It means, Mister Little, that I respect men who got sand. I trust men who got sand."

Still confused I shook my head. "We weren't holding her back."

"Yeah, and that's kinda the point isn't it," Lam put in.

Billings seconded him, "That girl trusted the both of you—you and your brother—to stand there between her and four men you didn't know—two of them with guns—and she was right in her trust. You did the right thing and we're—no, *she's*—asking you to do it again."

Maurice gave up. "I don't get it."

"Hell, man," Lam spoke up with a slight chuckle. "You even took one of them out, and him with a gun." He chuckled in a marveling way. "Two guys with guns and you didn't shit your pants. That county sheriff thinks you're nuts, but he was also mighty damn impressed with you."

"And so are we," added Billings.

Maurice looked from one of them to the other. "Yeah, like I said, you dudes make funny cops."

I wasn't sure how it looked to them. I had just gone with the flow. Guns or no guns, my actions seemed a reflexive response to events. Part of it was my training as a fighter, but the rest of what these two claimed to see in us seemed rooted somewhere in the way we were.

"And beside that," Billings continued, "you have nothing to lose by helping her beside a couple hours' time and I think it's a small enough trade to keep this girl from getting hurt. I'm betting that you can see that as clear as we can."

"Funny cops," whispered Maurice to no one in particular.

I saw that the two troopers and Maurice were now looking at me. I realized that the decision was mine and I got it that what Billings and his young partner were asking might well be illegal, but was really no big deal, and I saw also that it was these two troopers out here in rural Alabama who were taking the real risk. They were risking their jobs—and maybe worse—to sort through a problem with some human reasonableness rather than hiding behind the indifference of the law. This trooper—Billings—said he didn't feel like arresting his friend, but I knew it was more than that, and I also knew that there was more depth to these men than I could see on the surface. It was to this depth that I responded.

"Yeah," I nodded. "Okay. Give us an address in Auburn for our GPS."

I felt Maurice give me a sidelong look, but to the troopers he said: "And get us out of the cuffs."

Billings dipped his head at his partner. "Unhook 'em, Cullen."

After it was carefully explained to her what was going to happen, Jess was turned over to us. Maurice and I got her up into the cab of the Peterbilt and on into the sleeper berth. I felt her anxiety in every glance and we went about this a gently as we could, soft talking to calm the apprehension that was written all over her.

Returning to our load we were surprised to see the two troopers already pulling one of the three tarps over the load. Quickly, the four of us worked together and had the bales of rags covered by the time a gray, dinner plate sun topped a windbreak line of pine and cypress to the east.

The older trooper came over to me and Maurice and handed over his business card. "Don't let the sun fool you, guys," he said. "Down here in Alabama weather's a funny thing—tropical like, this time of year. It's supposed to rain on-and-off today and be hotter'n hell."

I glanced at the card. His first name was Chad—Chad Billings.

"If you get stopped on a scale and your rig's overweight have them call me. My cell numbers on the back."

I stuck the card in my back pocket and for a brief moment had an urge to shake his hand. It seemed awkward somehow and I let the moment pass.

Billings nodded to Maurice, then asked me, "Mister Little, your brother keeps calling you Top. What's that for?"

I told him.

"Humph." He looked a little closer at me in the clean morning light coming across his shoulder. "I remember—or rather I remember my dad talking about it. I don't follow boxing that much, but my dad does and I remember him talking about that fight—that you'd almost killed the other guy—they had to carry him out of the ring, he said. What was the other fighter's name again?"

"Bobby Ray Curtis."

"You fuck him up real bad?" asked Lam.

"I did."

"What ever happened to him?"

"I don't know," I answered honestly. "I hurt Bobby's eyes real bad with that hook, and I'm not sure what he could do with his life after that. I'm real sorry about that. I wish it hadn't happened."

Chad Billings nodded. "Well, Top, try wishing in one hand and spitting in the other and see which one fills up first."

"That an old southern saying?" Maurice asked.

Billings smiled at my brother. "I guess. I've heard it all my life."

"It has the ring of truth." I said.

"It does," Billings acknowledged, "doesn't it."

"All the same, I wish it hadn't happened."

Billings grunted, still smiling. "Like my young partner says, 'shit happens.'"

"I just hate dealing with it," I replied.

"Don't we all," responded Lam. "But if we deal with it right, shit goes away."

"Right," my brother snorted sarcastically. "Come on, man. Half the shit in this world we're told is right, ain't right, and the other half is just plain wrong."

Chad Billings looked to him. "I hear what you're saying, son. But in all that confusion there's still right and wrong, and like my daddy used to say, when people tell you they don't know the difference between right and wrong it's only because they're afraid to put their ass on the line. Think on that deep, son, and you'll see my daddy was on to something."

Billings waited a moment, the look on his face telling me that in the worst way he wanted Maurice to understand him.

He said, "So follow me down this road, son: that girl in your truck isn't a confusion of legal mumbo-jumbo. That girl in your truck is part of the real world of right and wrong. Jess Teal's the real deal. That girl's where the rubber meets the road."

Maurice looked into the trooper's smile and slyly curled his lips in a half grin. "Like I said: you guys make funny cops."

Chad Billings glanced from one of us to the other, then stopped a moment to give Maurice a long and honest appraising look before pronouncing, "Well son, this funny cop knows you well enough, knows all he needs to know."

Maurice frowned at him.

Billings explained, "He knows you got sand."

Union Made

Spider Riley wanted to avoid the rest of the drivers. This wasn't a day he wanted. Ignoring the light drizzle, Spider went down the steps at the end of the dock and crossed the asphalt to wait in front of one of the bobtail trucks. Anywhere was better than being up on the dock. It was as if the men were hanging around, waiting for the start of a funeral. Spider pulled up his sleeve, glancing at his watch: ten-twenty. It was going to be one hell of a morning for everyone, especially him. Spider always loathed and feared finding himself in this position. He hated it every time it happened. He wasn't made for this kind of crappy situation. Some men were hard and mean and scrappy, but not Spider. So why did he do it? Why did he let himself get talked into being elected shop steward again and again? Every year he promised himself he was never going to place himself in this stupid position again, and every year he let the men talk him into being their steward for another year. It made his head ache just to wonder *why*?

Spider looked toward the parking lot and caught sight of John T. Williams crossing the wet asphalt toward the freight yard. There was not a soul on this earth that should have made a more welcome picture for Spider right now than John Williams. Only this morning Spider Riley watched John T. and rolled his eyes upward to the dark clouds overhead, feeling himself sinking into the cold quicksand of dread. Seeing John T. was always a bit like watching the hammer swing toward the anvil—exciting and ter-rifying, yet satisfying—a sure waiting for the spark from the hit. There was always the spark. John T. was that kind of man. John was a man made for his job.

As long as Spider had been driving local freight in this city, John T. Williams had been a union business agent, ageless and tireless. Year after year John T. Williams stayed exactly the same—thick shouldered, thick necked, balding head, heavy lips, crooked teeth and eyes that looked to have been a hundred years old when God was young. John T. was smart and tough, and much focused and very unbending. John T. never budged from this demanding point of view: the companies were never right, labor never wrong. Watching John T. approach this morning made Spider nervous. No matter what was right or what was wrong, Spider knew a fight was coming. That was always John T.'s way.

"This is a war," John T. would say, "a war in which we are not evenly matched. These companies got the courts, the police, the President, the army and the hydrogen bomb—and you know what we got?" And then John would hesitate, looking around, tapping the side of his head. "We got our minds and we got each other and we got winning. We got our minds to give us will, and we each other to give us unity, and if we're ever going to move forward, even a single inch against these companies, we've got to use our will to be closed to everything else but winning, and winning for each other. Winning for us and our children and our families is all there is, and that means eye-gouging, ear-biting and scratching, because winning is the only way we're gonna survive—and we will survive!

These men always knew that with John T. Williams they could count on a stand-up fight. With John T. they were never uneasy, never suspicious, never frustrated and never pissed-off, the way they'd get with the other union officers who were forever rolling their eyes and scratching their balls and wondering about the legalese and all those shades of gray that cost 'em jobs and money and self-respect. John T. was not like that. John T. was straight-ahead. Without hesitation, John Williams knew which side he was on and which side was right—*always right*—and that was what was what! John T. embodied their feelings and fought their fight, and that was that! No wavering! No matter what! From the members in the local union it won him a hard-charging loyalty.

John T. briefly shook hands with Spider and took a pack of smokes from his pocket. He yanked one loose. "Anyone go to work yet?"

"Not yet," Spider replied. "I thought you might want them out." John T. lit the cigarette and singed his tongue with the burnt out match before tossing it. He and Spider mounted the steps and walked onto to the freight dock. Williams stopped and shook a hand here and there, nodding, smiling his crooked smile and passing a greeting to an acquaintance here and there. After a moment, Williams stopped and turned to Spider, showing him that snaggle toothed grin, then looked over the yard and rolled his cigarette between his fingers.

"You ready?"

"I guess." Spider replied.

"Is Elmo here?" John T. asked.

"At the end of the dock."

John T. looked. About forty or fifty yards away, at the far end of the terminal dock, was a figure leaning against one of the girders holding up the corrugated iron roof. Elmo's hands were jammed deep into his jacket pockets, his pipe drooping from his mouth. He was staring out at a row of line tractors, now dim and distant in the winter mist and drizzle.

Spider offered, "He's waiting for his final check. He figures it's over."

John T. took a slow puff on his cigarette and said, "It ain't over," and he wiggled his eyebrows. "Not 'till the fat lady sings."

Spider took a slow look at John T., feeling unsure, unsure in that he did not know what John meant by the crack or what he had in mind to do. Spider felt something give way inside his belly, and he looked again down the dock at the hang-dog old man worrying his pipe.

Elmo Grubbs had been nabbed stealing a pair of children's tennis shoes. At least that was how the company was choosing to interpret it. In fact, the shoes were a freight overage, meaning that more of a particular item was shipped than was ordered. In Elmo's case, the receiving clerk, rather than make out the extra paperwork, has simply given the shoes to the delivery driver—Elmo Grubbs. In no way was this exchange an unusual occurrence, but back at the terminal Elmo has been spotted by one of the security guards carrying the shoes to his car. Elmo, seeing no wrong in what he was doing, patiently explained to the guard how he had acquired the shoes and that he was giving them to his granddaughter. The guard shook his head—*no way*—and he took the shoes from Elmo.

The truth of the matter was that Elmo was sixty-seven and management wanted to offload him. The years had caught up with Elmo and the company figured that a guy his age was a liability in a multitude of ways. Elmo was slower than the other workers, would certainly be more prone to industrial accidents, and frankly, steering forty tons of steel and rubber down a highway was clearly an increasingly risky business for a guy Elmo's age. Nobody at the company disliked Elmo. Nobody at the company was out to get Elmo. The company was just out to protect everyone, including Elmo. From Spider's point of view, there didn't seem to be any bad guys here. It is what it is.

When all this had gone down a few days ago, Spider had considered that maybe the company was right to use the shoes as an excuse to can Elmo. Elmo was old, wasn't he? He had a great pension coming, and certainly the company was right to fear that Elmo could get hurt, or hurt someone else? Maybe this firing was a blessing for Elmo in disguise. There didn't seem to be any downside.

Elmo, go buy yourself a traveling-trailer and have a nice life.

Spider had to inform his local union of Elmo's dismissal. John T. Williams took the call from Spider.

Williams's response to Spider's news was predictable, yet still a surprise. "Bullshit!" William's had snapped. "No fuck'n way! The only guy who gets to decide if Elmo is leaving is Elmo!"

That was the way of John T. Williams. It was the union way, and more importantly, it was labor's way, and that was just the day before yesterday.

John T. tore his eyes off Elmo at the end of the dock. He took his time, dragging unhurriedly at his cigarette, turning his gaze to Fred McDonald, who was standing to the left of Spider, then to Burgess behind MacDonald. He then surveyed the whole of the dock, the stacks of freight, the trucks back in, the dockworkers scurrying in and out of the trailers likes ants tending a fat queen that had lain the golden egg. Spider saw John T.'s eyes drawn again to Elmo at the far end of the dock.

Williams said to Spider, "Grissom here?" It sounded more like a statement than a question. Williams wanted the drivers to hear.

Since Spider was the shop steward it was his responsibility to sent up a meeting with management to determine whether the union should file a formal grievance on a driver's dismissal—in this case, Elmo's dismissal.

Spider nodded, reading John T.'s face, unexpectedly realizing that John T. was actually looking forward to this meeting with the terminal manager, Lloyd Grissom, who was also a company vice-president. At that moment Spider would have bet six months' pay that John T. did not have a snowball's chance in hell of getting Elmo back on the seniority roster. The look on John T.'s face puzzled Spider.

"John," Spider said, "can I talk to you for a minute?"

The two of them walked a short distance away from the men.

"John," said Spider, "I think they got Elmo by the shorts on this stealing thing. They got pictures—they got the damn shoes, the guard's statement and the manifest, and if that isn't bad enough, even old Elmo's admitted to it."

John T. Williams made no reply to Spider, only watched him deliberately with those tough old eyes, expressionless, knowing that Spider was growing uncomfortable under his gaze. Spider had just been caught suggesting that the company was right, and the labor wrong, a sin far worse than any of the other deadly sins.

"John," Spider blurted, suddenly embarrassed and exasperated, "we both know that they're just using this shit as an excuse to nail

Elmo's hide to the wall, but I don't see how in the hell we can stop 'em if they want to go through with it."

John T. waited, still with that gaze that seemed to probe deep into Spider's soul.

"Goddamn it, John T.," Spider spat out, feeling hot and helpless. "Shit! They got us, Goddamn it! The sonsabitches got us this time!"

The corner of John T.'s mouth curled upward and he nodded, but not in agreement. There was a deeper understanding alive in John's mind. John understood Spider. Labor had been helpless for so long that passivity had become a way of life. John ground his cigarette under his shoe. "Let's go see what makes the fat lady sing."

Spider moved his shoulders in an awkward attempt at a shrug. "You want me to tell Elmo that you're here?"

"He already knows."

Spider turned his head. The old man was facing them now, the pipe still drooping in his jaw.

John T. and Spider started for the front office.

"Now, I want you to do something," John T. said as they walked. "You do the talking at first. All the talking! I want to size this Grissom character up for a while. And .... " He held up his finger for emphasis. "No matter what I say in there, you keep a straight face. Understand, Spider? You keep a straight face!"

Spider eyeballed John T. cautiously. "Just what the hell do you have up your sleeve, John?"

John T. grinned. "My guns, baby—my guns."

They went through the terminal office door and down the soft carpeted hallway that led to the terminal manager's office. The secretary rose and awkwardly nearly bowed, before showing them into the inner sanctum.

Lloyd Grissom appeared positively tickled to have John T. and Spider walk through the door of his office. The V.P. was a lean, wiry guy, looking just this side of smug. He sported a short, athletic haircut, always wore his tie tugged loose and sleeves rolled up. Grissom tried hard to cultivate a vaguely fortyish look while shamelessly smirking a salesman's good-time Charlie smile. Spider noticed right away that Grissom was alone. No witnesses for management. Grissom must have been damn sure of himself, a thought which launched a tiny knot twirling around in Spider's stomach.

They all shook hands and sat down. Behind Grissom, on the wall, were hanging several plaques, awards of some sort. There was one from the Rotary Club, another from the Chamber of Commerce, and a few others too small to be read from where Spider was sitting. They were arranged in a stiff, uniform pattern, arrayed like troops on parade, suggesting a manicured formality that contradicted Grissom's casual appearance. Spider glanced at John T. to see where he was looking. His eyes were on Grissom.

"Would either of you like some coffee?" asked Grissom, with a smooth diplomatic ease.

Spider said, "No," while John T. said not a word.

"Well," Grissom went on, his face turning serious, "I won't waste anyone's time by asking why you gentlemen wanted this meeting, but it seems to me that the issue is more than clear." Grissom meant that he had Elmo by the short 'n curlies, like I thought.

Spider moistened his lips, afraid it made him look worried, which he was. "Mister Grissom," he began, "the issue here is not at all that clear. Not at all."

Surprise mechanically toyed with Grissom's features. "Oh?" He drew the word out, letting John T. and Spider know just how well he had this act wired. "Please, Gordy, you have the floor."

Spider hated the way Grissom so sanctimoniously used his first name; he crossed his legs, hoping the gesture would give him the appearance of confidence.

"The company's gone way overboard on this," Spider went on. "We all know that a freight overage is consigned to no one, and that taking an overage is not a completely uncommon practice with labor, either for drivers or dockworkers. It's clearly an issue of past-practice."

Grissom settled back lightly, the springs in his chair whispering. "Stealing," he replied, "does not fall under the auspices of past-practice. At least I hope not." He smiled and fixed Spider with a steady gaze. "And that, Gordy, is what we are talking about, I believe—stealing."

"But Elmo wasn't stealing," Spider responded. "It was a freight overage. You *know* it's not the same thing."

"Oh?" Grissom put a sudden interested look on his face. "Then tell me, Gordy, tell me exactly how the shoes came into Elmo's possession."

"The receiving clerk gave them to him. You already know that. Overages are overages. It's past-practice."

"No." Grissom pinned Spider with a twist of his eyebrow. "And let me repeat this slowly: stealing doesn't fall under any union contract clause I know of. And you can't grandfather stealing under some obscure past-practice notion." He eased back in his chair. "You're the shop steward, Gordy. I can't be telling you something you don't know. In fact, *past-practice* is not a term mentioned in the union contract anywhere. However, we can end this conversation right now if Elmo can prove that he paid the consignee for the shoes, then it becomes the receiving-clerk's problem."

Just like Spider expected, under the guise of being reasonable, the terminal manager was going to stonewall it all the way. Spider stole a quick look at John T., wishing that the big man would say something. It was making Spider feel lonely, hanging out there, twisting in the wind. But John T. seemed very relaxed, pleased with himself, even, as if everything was going exactly the way he had hoped it would. Spider wondered what the hell was on John T.'s mind. John did not even look at Spider, just kept his eyes glued to the terminal manager, his hands pensively before his face, as if he were casually inspecting a bug.

"Gordon," Grissom continued with an air or reconciliation and looking to have forgotten the presence of John T., "the company is not going to be inconsiderate in this matter. If Elmo would like to correct the statement he gave us, to the effect that he did in fact, pay for the shoes, we'll be more than happy to check it out with the consignee. Or if he can produce a receipt . . . "

Inside, Spider felt himself turning ugly. Grissom was actually grinning, feeling the champ, cocky as hell, and rubbing everyone's face in it, the company's victory. Spider was at a loss for words. What did John T. expect him to do now? Stealing was stealing. Period!

Almost through his teeth, Spider said, "But technically, non-consigned freight has no ownership."

Grissom waved his hand, shooing off a fly. "That's utter nonsense, Gordon, and you know it. Any and all freight overages would be returned to the shipper."

Spider screwed his jaw down until his teeth hurt. That was a lie—or rather a half-lie. What was true was that the shipper would be contacted and asked if they wanted the overage returned. But for one lousy pair of tennis shoes they would refuse to pay the additional freight charges and eventually the shoes would be auctioned off with other unclaimed freight for storage fees, yet even then it would not cover the freight company's handling costs. The stupid reality was that Elmo Grubbs had actually done the company a favor by picking up the shoes and getting them off their books and out of their hair. This was often the way it was with small overages. Grissom knew that as well as John T. and Spider. Spider was really getting into hating the smirking Grissom right now and longed to have the sonofabitch in a dark alley somewhere.

Spider glanced again at John T. The business agent was quiet as a stone. Spider could think of only one more thing to say, and he already knew it would not work. Being a shop steward had taught Spider one thing, if nothing else: appealing to management's sympathetic side was always a laughable mistake. Managers had been robbed of that piece of humanity on the way up the ladder. But try he must—it was the last bullet in Spider's gun.

"Mister Grissom," Spider started out half heartedly. "Elmo's been here twenty-seven years. Practically since the company opened its doors. Does a few bucks worth of shoes really balance off twenty-seven years of loyal service?"

The terminal manger rustled in his chair. Spider could see that Grissom had anticipated him, which caused Spider no little surprise when he realized that V.P. Grissom did not relish dealing with this point. Maybe the bastard had a heart after all.

Grissom's eyes lightly tip-toed around the office, pausing momentarily on the framed portrait of his wife and children atop his desk, then hopped back to Spider.

"It's not the cost of the shoes that concerns us, Gordon," he said. "It's the legal principle."

Legal principle? Spider wanted to jump over the desk and smack him. The only principle this asshole cared about was the profit margin. Who was Grissom trying to kid?

This seemed to be the moment John T. Williams had been waiting for. John dropped his hands from in front of his face. He made a small gesture that silenced Spider, then sat up in his chair. Spider watched John T. and waited.

"Mister Grissom," John T. said. "Since you want to bring up legal principles, may I ask you something?"

Grissom had been dealing with Spider for so long he seemed to have forgotten that the business agent was present. He blinked and gave John T. a faintly curious look, as though the business agent had just given him a friendly poke in the ribs. Grissom nodded slowly. "Of course, Mister Williams—by all means."

John T. asked, "Were those shoes union made?"

For a few seconds everything froze. Nobody moved. Spider stared at John T., or maybe gaped would have been more accurate.

Were the shoes union made?

What the hell was John T. up to?

Grissom too was staring at John T., appearing to be as dumbfounded by the question as Spider.

They all sat quiet, listening to the air hiss softly through the vent in the ceiling.

Grissom finally frowned and gave himself a little shake. "Were the shoes union made?" he slowly repeated. "Did I hear you right, Mister Williams?"

"You did," John T. said smiling, and probed softly, "were the shoes taken by Elmo Grubbs union made?"

Grissom was still blinking. "I fail to see what that has to do with anything, Mister Williams."

John T. tugged at his chin, still smiling, unexpectedly looking like a dark and dangerous wizard. "It has everything to do with it, Mister Grissom."

Grissom squinted at John T., as though the business agent were fast receding out of focus. He opened his mouth. " I . . . " and he shut it. There was slight sag in his gaze as he turned it on

Spider, looking for an ally. Spider couldn't help him. He and the terminal manager were ~~sudden, unexpected~~ *(SUDDENLY, UNEXPECTEDLY)* bonded by bewilderment. Grissom looked back at John T. "I don't see the point."

John's smile broadened. "Oh, there's a point," he replied, sounding very confident and in-the-know. "And I only hope for your sake that those shoes were union made." John T. rolled his eyes over the manager's face, then dropped the smile. He leaned forward and repeated the question, only now not so softly. "Were the shoes taken by Elmo Grubbs union made?"

The terminal manager pushed himself back from the desk as if he were going to rise. "What the hell difference does it make if the shoes are union made or not?" Grissom looked confused, a little less than certain. He glanced again at Spider as he muttered, "What are you talking about, *union made*?"

Spider remembered what John T. had said about keeping a straight face and he stared back at Grissom, solidly deadpan.

John T. said, "It makes a big difference."

The terminal manager's eyes dropped for a second to his hands resting on the desk top, then back to John T. "Okay. Perhaps you'd better explain your point, Mister Williams, because I'm not getting this."

A scorpion smile crawled over John T.'s mouth. "Mister Grissom, you can't fire a driver or dockworker for stealing non-union goods."

Spider had no idea how he did it, but he managed to batten down his face and keep it like stone cold iron. He felt his skin tingle under the strain and knew ~~this~~ *his* face was changing color—only Grissom did not notice. He was fairly gawking, bug-eyed, at John T., *his* face draining of color.

"What the . . . ?" Grissom stammered, blinking like a boxer punched off balance.

"Just what I said," John T. replied, completely in control of the sudden turnabout. "You can't fire Elmo if those shoes weren't union made. I'm surprised you, a vice-president of this company, did not know that."

The terminal manager now looked more than shocked. Grissom looked nearly horrified, as though he had just been caught with his hand down a Girl Scout's panties. For the first time in the five years Spider had known Grissom he watched the man's cool composure evaporate completely. Grissom must have anticipated about everything under the sun except this.

Spider looked from Grissom to John T., and back. John T.'s line of crap would have been almost funny, except for one thing: John T.'s face wore a damned and deadly serious cast. There was no smile on John T.'s face now. The business agent was sitting forward in the chair, aggressive, mean, his eyes little, boring holes in Grissom's bewildered face. Spider could not keep his expression still. His forehead wrinkled as he began to realize that John T. was really on to something. Christ, John T. had known this all along, but why did he make Spider do all the talking up front? Why not just sandbag the sonofabitch from the outset?

Slowly, Grissom swung his head from side to side. It was not a sign of *No*. It was a sign of confusion. Spider realized that Grissom was beginning to understand the same thing as he. Spider relished the sight of the ground swaying under Grissom; knocking V.P. Lloyd Grissom down a peg almost brought him to eye level with the rest of the world.

John T. said, "Now, there's no real problem as of yet, Mister Grissom. At present, the company only owes Elmo two day's back pay."

Back pay!

Spider nearly leaped off his chair. Now he was certain that John T. did have something. If not, he would never push for back pay.

Spider immediately saw that Grissom got the same message and there was no way to stop it: Spider's face cracked in a wide open, sunshine grin. Damn, but those were mighty big guns up John's sleeves.

Grissom eased back in his chair, now drawing a thoughtful mask down over his features. "You have to admit, Mister Williams," he reasoned, "that on the surface of it the position sounds utterly preposterous." Grissom stopped for a moment, chewing on his lower lip. "But you look serious and I know you're a man that doesn't like to joke, so educate me. Tell me what exactly this position is based on, because it sure as hell isn't in the union contract. I know that document as well any union lawyer."

John T. nodded. "The ruling grew out of an arbitration that was finally settled in a Seattle federal court, about eight months ago." John T. paused, then added as punctuation, "Try, McKay Steamship Lines vs. The International Brotherhood of Longshoremen."

Spider listened intently to this piece of official-sounding information and suddenly grew a little uneasy. Spider knew John T.—knew John T. way better than Grissom—and he was hearing something too deliberate, too calculated in John's voice. He looked at Grissom and saw that the manager had not picked up on anything. In fact he was nodding at John's credulous tone.

Grissom sat up, putting his arms on the desk. "I'll tell you what I'll do, Mister Williams." He glanced at the phone on his desk. "I'll check with our lawyers and contact you tomorrow, or the day after, and we can talk again."

"That won't work," replied John T. dryly. "I'll be leaving for New York this afternoon. We'll have to get Elmo reinstated now."

A tiny minnow began to flip-flop in Spider's belly. He knew that John T. was not going to New York, or anywhere else today—or tomorrow, or anytime soon. What was John up to?

"How long would you be gone?" Grissom asked John T.

"Seven business days," John answered.

"So," Grissom figured aloud, "assuming you are correct, it could be as long as two weeks before we could reinstate Elmo."

John T. stayed quiet.

"And you would," Grissom went on, "ask for the two weeks back pay."

"Elmo gets everything Elmo has coming," replied John T.

Spider caught Grissom looking a second time at the phone on his desk. Why didn't he just pick it up and call the lawyer right now? As Spider watched Grissom he began to suspect that Grissom was thinking he was in a lose-lose situation. Maybe the lawyers would confirm John T.'s position and that would make Grissom look like an idiot for not passing the dismissal issue up the ladder like he was supposed to before taking action; but if he reinstated Elmo today he could bury the two days back pay somewhere in petty cash. On the other hand, if John T. was totally bluffing and Grissom called in the lawyers, he stood every chance of becoming the laughing-stock of the company office for even listening to the business agent. Spider could see the wheels turning in Grissom's head. John T. suddenly had terminal manager Grissom thinking, pondering, calculating. Elmo's termination must have begun to look like it was going to be more trouble than it was worth.

"One thing I don't understand," Grissom said to no one in particular, though he sounded vaguely resigned. "Elmo has a damn good pension coming. Hell, it must be over forty years he's been driving for union shops. He's old and more lucky than . . . . " Grissom bit down on his words and focused on John T. "Mister Williams, I honestly don't know if you're right or not, but under the circumstances and Elmo's apparent desire to continue working, it is in every one's interest for me to put a reinstatement letter in." He slowed, then added, "I'll have Elmo issued a new time card *and* he'll be paid the two days back pay."

Spider slowly let his breath out. He looked at John T. Damn, it was over. Just like that. He'd walked into Grissom's office with John T. as a stone-cold loser and was walking out a winner. How the hell had that happened? They both shook hands with Grissom and went out onto the dock.

The drivers met them as they came out of the office door. Elmo Grubbs was no longer there. The old man had been too sure of the outcome and had not waited around for the official word to come down. Elmo had collected his check and cleared out his locker and left. The other men had waited, their faces long until Spider told them what had taken place in the meeting with Grissom.

Fred MacDonald was the only man there as big as John T. MacDonald bunched up his eyes and leaned toward the business agent. "*Union made*? What the hell kinda of crap is that, John?"

John T. lit up a cigarette and singed his tongue with the burnt match. "Is it, Mac? Is it a bunch of crap?"

"Is it true?" Burgess wanted to know.

John T. smiled. "You men want truth? Ok, take a good look around this railroad's trucking terminal. Go on," he commanded, "take a good, long look."

Mechanically, the drivers obeyed him, swinging their heads, eyeing the length of the dock piled high with cargo, the dock-workers loading the dozens of trailers backed in on one side, the other side of the dock lined with rail freight cars being rapidly emptied by crews of loaders, then they looked at the rain soaked yard, filled with tractors and trailers, turning their gaze next to the bobtail trucks gathered around the mechanics shed, then to the guard shack and the main office, seeing everything they had seen for years.

"You see it?" John T. asked them. "Do you really *see* the *truth* of this railroad company?"

The men looked back at John T., faces blank.

"You want truth?" John T. questioned. "Well here's the truth: Do you know how this company got to be so big—so rich—so powerful? By stealing—and worse. Look around. Do you see how people were beaten, broken and burned out of their homes, how Indians were massacred, and Chinese labor worked like dogs and died like slaves. Do you see how land was taken and people murdered, the country plundered so that this company could get so big, so rich? Now, that's the *truth*. Do you *see* it?!"

John T. waited a moment, puffing in his cigarette, only no one had anything to say. "If you want to know about how Elmo got his job back, just remember how this company got to be so big, so fat, so rich: by *stealing* land and *stealing* people's lives."

John T. turned away and headed for the stairs at the end of the dock.

Spider went after John T., catching up with him as he started across the parking lot toward his car.

"John," Spider called.

John T. stopped, turning. Was he smiling now at Spider?

"John, you never answered me." Spider said when he caught up to the business agent. "I gotta know."

"Know what?"

"Shit. I know this might sound dumb, John, but were you making that crap up in there about the shoes being union made—were you bluffing Grissom?"

John T. took a drag on his cigarette and studied Spider for just a moment then looked away, letting his eyes sweep around the freight yard. "I suppose that depends on what you mean by bluffing, Spider."

The Steward snorted sardonically and shook his head. "Come on, John, damn it. Stop fucking with me. Were you ~~were~~ bullshitting him—Grissom?"

John T. looked back at Spider, the corners of his eyes crinkled. Was it a smile? It actually looked more like a grimace than a grin. "I never bullshit anyone, Spider. Never! Remember that in that war for survival we have to win, and win every battle. Every loss in this war is a human loss. And if you call that bullshit you're in the wrong place at the wrong time doing the wrong thing."

Spider looked frustrated. "Okay, John, I get all that, but I still gotta know. Were you telling Grissom the truth? I think it's important for me to know."

John T. worried his cigarette for a moment, examining the smoldering head. "You already know, Spider," he replied cryptically. "You already know everything there is to know that's important, either that or I've been wasting my time with you." He looked up at the sky to where the sun was breaking through the clouds, then again to the shop steward. "It's gonna get muggy later," he observed, then hesitated a moment before adding, "You know damn well that Lloyd Grissom couldn't handle the truth." He suddenly flipped the butt away in an irritable gesture and watched it sputter in a puddle. "The real question is, Spider, can you . . . ?"

YA-HOO

It had been raining for most of the morning and Junior Biggs struggled to keep the logging truck from sliding off the dirt and gravel road. Up ahead the narrow tree lined passage steepened even further and disappeared into a dark green tunnel of leafy hickory and tall Georgia pine. Biggs strained, muscling the gears into a sharp downshift, as a string of nasty words tore loose from his mouth. The lower gear caught just as Biggs felt the mushiness through the steering wheel when the front tire slid off the bed of the gravel and onto the soft shoulder. He tugged, straining his left arm against the pull of the wheel and bounced the logger back onto the winding road.

Harlan Dean, dozing in the seat next to him, was jolted awake. He yawned and sat up straight, looking out the open window. It was early afternoon—one or two o'clock—but the high trees cut off the sunlight, darkening the woods to a quiet dusk. Harlan sucked in a deep warm breath and ran a handkerchief over his face.

"I hate this damn heat."

Biggs took a quick glance over at him, then looked out the driver's side mirror, watching the brown, muddy mist being blown out behind the wheels of the empty flatbed trailer.

Biggs said, "By the time we get them damn chains and binders it'll be too late to get back down to the mill."

"Suits me fine," responded Harlan.

"Well, I'm not sleeping in this goddamn truck."

The roadway widened as they came around a sharp twist, and Biggs slowed, braking, easing the rig into a large sunlit clearing. On one side of the clearing sat an unpainted wooden house, flanked by a garage with the tail end of a green pickup truck sticking out of the open doors. Directly across was a small barn. It had been painted red at one time, but now the sides had turned coarse brown.

In front of the house a blue pickup was parked and two men lounged in the shade of the porch. Biggs brought the truck to a stop in front of the barn and snapped on the parking brake. A belch of air rushed from beneath the back axles. Biggs and Harlan climbed down from the tractor cab.

"Hey," Biggs yelled at the men on the porch. "Don't nobody but me and Harlan work for a living?"

"Hell no," one of the men shouted back. "Only two damn fools allowed in Georgia at one time."

Another man lifted a jug. "Hey, Junior, don't pay no attention to Jim Bob. You and Harlan got time for a little taste?"

Junior Biggs shouted back, "Silk, now you know I don't take to no white-light'n you got."

"This didn't come from no still, boy." Silk, a man with bright yellow hair, laughed, shaking the jug at Biggs. "Bought it last night down at Davis."

"He ain't lying, Junior," added Jim Bob.

Harlan came around the front of the truck. "You get across the river okay?"

"Yep. Easy." Silk waved the jug. "You wanna taste?"

Harlan looked at Biggs. "You?"

"I'm gonna get them chains and binders first."

Harlan started across the clearing towards the house, with his hand reaching out for the jug, while Biggs went off toward the barn.

It was dark and warm inside the barn, and smelled of hay, rust and gasoline. Biggs hesitated a few seconds, letting his eyes adjust to the dim light filtering in through the cracks in the roof. Off to the side sat an old automobile, flat tires all the way around, with two V-8 engines sitting and rusting on the dirt floor just in front of it. In the back of the barn, under the low beams of the loft, sat an old man hunched over a work bench.

"Coates?" Biggs called out.

The old man jerked his head around and squinted. He was blind in one eye. His forehead wrinkled up and he blinked the good eye. "Get the hell out of the doorway, damn you. I can't see you standing there in the light."

Biggs stepped out of the sunlight and a few feet into the barn. "It's Junior Biggs, Coates. I come after them chains and binders for the mill."

The old man slid off the stool he was sitting on and came over to Biggs. He had a full head of hair, white as pressed, hotel sheets, thick and cropped close to his head. His face above his beard was wrinkled like a raisin and he was toothless. He gapped a grin at Biggs.

"What if I was to tell you they ain't here, Junior?"

"I'd have to call you a liar."

"Would you fight me for 'em?"

Coates was somewhere in his nineties and half-crazy with seventy years of mountain whiskey.

"Hell no, Coates," answered Biggs, trying to keep his face somber as granite. "I don't wanna get myself stomped."

"Damn right ya don't." Coates gave his head a little snap. "Used to whip your daddy, Junior. Guess I can whip his boy too."

"I guess." Biggs looked down on the top of the white head and grinned. "Now let's get them chains and binders."

Coates started for the door in long legged strides ahead of Biggs. "Let's get us a taste of that Davis whiskey first."

Biggs caught up with him just outside the barn, grabbing him by the arm. "No, the chains first."

Coates looked up at him, his toothless mouth parted in surprise. "You don't expect me to work without first whiskey'n-up, do you?"

Biggs nodded. "The chains first," he repeated.

"Horseshit, Junior—you dern fool," and Coates shook himself free from Biggs' hand. "Whiskey first!"

Before Biggs could grab hold of him again Coates was half way across the clearing on his way to the house and the Davis whiskey.

"Well, Junior," grinned Harlan, when they both got to the porch, "I see Coates talked you into a little taste."

Biggs shook his head, watching Coates lift the jug up to his whiskered lips. "The fuckhead mule won't work unless he's drunk."

Coates coughed and wheezed and set the jug back on the step. "Nope. You're wrong, Junior Biggs." He wheezed again. "I just don't wanna work!" And he sat down and let out a hoot and a laugh and slapped his thigh.

"Just wants to get drunk and lay in the sun," said Biggs.

"Just like any old dog," yelped Coates, squinting up at Biggs silhouetted against a sharp sunlight sky.

"Well, you fixed them chains, at least?" Harlan prodded him.

"They're fixed." Coates leaned his back against the top step. "Had to replace, hum, let's see." He paused, thinking, wiggling a couple of fingers. "About two dozen links in all—between the nine chains."

"And the binders?"

"Weren't nothing wrong with two of them." Coats answered and took the jug back from the man on the porch. "The other two just needed new couplings for the hooks."

Coats raised the jug for another solid pull, then stuck it out to Biggs. "Here now, you take this here whiskey, Junior Biggs, or I won't get you them chains, no way."

Biggs took the jug from Coates and put it up to his mouth, drawing at the liquid inside. He brought the jug down, sucked a breath, feeling his teeth on fire and his gums go numb. "Whoooo." He closed his eyes, his stomach heating up. "Silk, you say you got this shit in a real store?"

Silk nodded. "Yes'r. Over to Davis."

"Take another taste, Junior." Coates waved his hand and winked his good eye at him. "And you'll feel more like setting and less like working." He cackled, his wide open mouth looking like a little rabbit hole burrowed in white reed grass. "Go on, Junior, Gaw-dang-it. Take another little bit."

Biggs tipped the jug again, sucking hard at the opening, then brought it down, shaking his head. "Shit!" He drew a deep breath, cooling his throat. "Shit. I'd swear this was raw-ass, still-whiskey if Silk hadn't said he got it at a store."

"Take some more, Junior." Coates grinned at Biggs, his one eye getting wickedly narrow. "Just one more little taste." He held up a forefinger and thumb to show him just how little, and let out another whoop when Biggs pressed it to his lips.

"Gaw-dang, Junior Boy, Gaw...dang," Coates squeaked. "You just gonna drive hell out of that old logger tonight."

Jim Bob sat up quick and squinted, looking down the road Biggs and Harlan had come up. "Say, isn't that Tim?"

Around a twist in the road they could see a faded, twenty-year-old Ford pickup truck. The left fender was missing, and the hood tied down by a piece of coarse rope.

"Hell yeah," announced Silk. "And damned if he don't have Ces with 'im."

"Dang!" Jim Bob jumped up. "We're sure gonna need some more whiskey."

The blue pickup bounced across the clearing, followed by a cloud of dust, and pulled up in front of the house. Both doors opened and two men dressed in overalls stepped out.

Coates snatched the jug away from Biggs and waved it above his white head. "Hey, Tim. Ces. I know you boys got time for a taste."

Tim, a tall skinny man with an old railroad cap pulled down low on his head, stopped at the sight of the jug in Coates' hand. He giggled and hurried back to his pickup, popped inside and back out, holding up a bottle. It was full to the top with dark brown whiskey. "And we got this," he shouted.

"Well, come on ahead, Tim," cheered Coates, "and we'll have ourselves a fun get-together."

Biggs took hold of Coates by his bony shoulder. "What about them chains?"

Coates turned on him, hard, pushing his hand away. "To hell with your damn chains, you dern fool."

Harlan reached out and touched Biggs on his arm through the Levi jacket. "Best have a seat, Junior. We don't have to be no place. No place at all."

The whiskey was getting to Harlan. Biggs could hear it talking in his voice. It was getting to him too, making his head light and his legs heavy.

Tim set his bottle on the porch next to where Silk was sitting and suggested, "If we ask nice, we might get Silk here, and Ces, to pick awhile for us."

"Goddamn." Coates thumped his knee happily. "There's an idea, Tim. Get your banjo, Silk! Get your banjo, Ces!"

Biggs thought about the chains laying somewhere in the heat of the barn, but let the thought slither away when Jim Bob dangled Tim's bottle over his shoulder. He took the bottle from Jim Bob and drank as Silk brushed past him on his way to his pickup. Biggs held the bottle out to Coates, who shook his head, and when Ces came up the steps with his banjo, he handed it to him instead. Ces took the bottle and set it close to his leg, lifted the banjo onto his lap and thought for a moment, then started to pick—slow, timid at first, a little sad, as though he were trying to make up his mind about something important. Just a piece of a scale came out, then a cord, then another bit of scale, then he hesitated, looking up at the sky above the barn, puzzled, as though wondering about something far away.

Silk, his banjo slung over his shoulder, remounted the steps like a man among children, the pleased look on his face of a man knowing what he is about. He sat alongside Ces, and a little behind him, as if he were going to push him, guide him, steer Ces through some wilderness. He rubbed the palm of his hand along the strings, waiting, listening to what Ces was doing. Ces played a few notes and Silk copied, with an added flourish, and Ces cocked his ear, listening back and imitated, then Silk repeated, but built it onto a flourish, and Ces, stealing the sound from Silk's fingers, echoed the addition, putting in an extra note or two, and striking a rhythm just before Ces followed along with a flow into the lead given him by Silk, then Silk added a chord, and Ces added it too, only faster this time, twice, once with the flourish and once without, and Silk spread his face in a huge grin and raced on ahead of Ces, adding something else he knew just before Ces caught up, and pushed ahead, adding more, only Silk didn't need any pushing, for he plunged forward and Ces raced to catch up, their fingers suddenly hitting the same tune, each adding all that he knew, beating down the same rhythm, no longer tracking each other's heels, but now together, sailing, flying, fingers and smiles both working hard together, meeting and yet beating each other, hammering, glowing and grinning at each other, the sweat popping out in tiny crystal beads across their foreheads.

Old Coates could not hold it back.

"YA-HOO," he whooped. "YAAA-HOO."

And up he jumped and broke into a wild, thousand legged dance. The dust and flecks of mud flew up from the road in a brown cloud around him as he spun round and round, clapping his hands and shaking his head, his feet stomping and rocking. He had given himself over completely to the strong, lightening quick fingers of his friends beating on the strings of the banjos, beating out a rhythm of celebration, and he hammered the ground and threw up his legs. He laughed and waved his arms about and slapped his thighs, his eyes closed, his head back and forth, bobbing with the banjos, and he danced and danced, working at dancing as only a man with nothing in the world to celebrate can dance, with a stylish abandon, and so old Coats worked and danced to the rhythm of the his living, worked and dance to war against every ache in his wrinkled body, every fear conjured in his mind. Old Coats danced and worked, slamming and kicking. He danced to celebrate his work. He worked to celebrate his life.

One tune spun into the next, rhythm and melody swimming up, around and back under the strong fingers plucking the strings. Biggs no longer had any way to tell if Coates was following the banjos, or the banjos were following the old man, and Biggs suddenly found himself standing on the step, swinging, and banging his hands together, clapping with Harlan and the rest of the men. He threw his head back and opened his eyes wide at the long solid blue sky overhead.

"YA-HOO," he screamed at the heavens above. "YA-HOOO."

And Coates grabbed him by the collar of his jacket.

"YA-HOO," he yelled into Biggs's grinning face. "Come on Junior, get out here in the sunshine," and he hooked Junior by the arm with his own, pulling the big man off the step and onto the dusty road. "That's right, Junior Boy," he heard Coates roar in his ear. "Enjoy yerself. Enjoy yerself, Junior. Live! Live!" And Coates and Junior spun round and round, quick, together, stomping and spinning and sweaty, and Junior closed his eyes and kicked up his legs, drifting, letting the banjos grind their driving rhythm deep into the callused hide of his brain, the two of them twirling and kicked around in circles, faster and faster, throwing up twice as much dust and mud, and Biggs wanted to grab hold of Coates, hug him, and dance like that, his arms around the gray old man, and dance forever to the grandness of life.

"Don't this just beat hell out of work'n, Junior Boy," yelled Coates. "Don't it just beat all hell! Feel it, Junior. Feel it!"

Biggs closed off his mind to everything but the rapid sound of the banjos and the heavy thumping of his blood in his ears, and he felt the sweat running down through the short hairs on his head, tickling his scalp, and he felt his big boots getting soggy from the moisture soaking through his socks and he wished he would never stop, but dance on like this forever.

Suddenly Biggs felt a yank, a tug. It nearly pulled him off balance. He stumbled, nearly losing his balance, and opened his eyes. The banjos had gone silent. He planted his feet and turned around, his head spinning, his sight blurry.

Coates was lying still in the road. He was face down in one of the large mud filled ruts. Harlan was stooped over the old man, turning him over. Biggs shook his head, blinking hard, trying to stop the swimming behind his eyes.

Harlan looked up at Silk, who had come down from the porch.

"What's the matter with Coates?" Silk wanted to know.

"He's dead," Harlan answered.

Biggs stumbled a step and a half toward Harlan and Silk and laughed. "Dead fuck'n drunk, you mean."

"No, Junior," Harlan insisted. "I mean *dead*," and his blue eyes blinked. "Dead, Junior. Old Coats is *dead*."

The rest of them had come off the porch and gathered around to where Harlan had turned Coats over and was brushing the dirt off his face. Junior Biggs stepped in closer, wanting to stop what was going on, tell them they was talking silly shit, that everything was all right, that the old man had only ya-hooed himself to death and it was all right. Everything was all right.

"Get him to a goddamn hospital," Tim commanded.

"That's forty fucking miles down that logging road," Ces snapped at him. "Jesus, Tim, he's fucking dead."

"What the hell we gonna do?" asked Harlen.

"Get him outta the goddamn road," Ces answered.

They carried the body over to the porch and laid it in the shade. Biggs, not knowing what to do, followed behind and kept squeezing his eyes shut and wiping the sweat off his forehead. *"Jesus,"* Biggs thought, *"the chains, Coates'd forgot to give him the chains."*

Silk and Ces set their banjos up against the wooden slats of the house and sat down, nobody saying anything. Somebody picked up the bottle and it got passed around. Biggs took a small sip and looked at Coates and his head cleared.

Jim Bob asked, "What'll we do?"

"What the hell can we do?" replied Tim. "He's dead."

Somebody had closed the old man's eyes, but he did not look asleep. The face was blank, dreary, faded and white as his beard. Biggs thought it looked like someone had painted a face on the washed out side of a barn, or pasted it on like Halloween mask, or something; it didn't look like Coates.

"What'll we do," Jim Bob repeated, looking for something around him, mystified.

"Get a blanket," Ces advised. "Cover him."

Junior jumped in. "Hell no," he barked. "We ain't hiding him under no blanket. Not Coats! Leave him the way he is."

Harlan and Ces watched Junior close, but no one countered him.

"Damn fool," Biggs said.

Silk too glanced at Biggs, wondering at the big man for a moment, then reached out and took the bottle from him. He hesitated, then set the whiskey down next to the body.

Silk said, "Old fool ain't got nobody."

"'Cept us." Ces added.

"What'll we do?" Jim Bob asked again. "He's dead."

Harlan answered, "Put him in the back of the pickup truck and take him down to Davis—to Parker's funeral parlor there." And he frowned hard at Coates, then looked over at Junior. "But we gotta wrap him in a blanket first, I guess."

"Jesus," Tim whispered. "Parker'll want money."

"Then by God we'll give him some, goddamn it," Biggs snapped, and looked around at the others. "Jesus, we can't just leave him here. He's got to be buried."

Silk reached behind him to where he had rested his banjo and picked it up, slinging it over his shoulder again. "Old Coates don't have nobody except us."

"Jesus," mused Jim Bob as he watched Silk poke at the strings of the banjo for a moment, making sounds quiet and sad. "Parker's," he said softly. "We'll get him to Parker's. He'll know what to do."

Tim sat down on the lower step next to Harlan. "Damn, I can't believe it. Ol' fool danced himself to death. What the hell we gonna tell the undertaker?"

Harlan tore his eyes from Coates and looked at Tim. "Just that, I guess. He danced himself to death."

"Dern'd old fool," Tim pronounced.

"Hell, might as well put that on his damn gravestone," suggested Jim Bob. "Coates! Danced himself to death."

"Could'a been something worse," added Biggs.

"Yeah," echoed Harlan. "Dying ain't the worst thing that can happen to a man."

"Living can be worse," pronounced Ces.

"Except when you're dancing," Harlan pointed out.

Silk kept poking and plucking, looking at Coates lying stretched out in front of him, and then he let his fingers pick up, moving faster, stroking out another quick dance tune, and he closed his eyes, his body still except for his head which bobbed faster and faster, keeping up with his swift fingers.

Rooted to the spot, Junior Biggs stared at Silk, the banjo player's eyes closed tight, his head cocked, bobbing, listening to the picking of his fingers.

"Coates, he weren't no dern'd old fool, Tim," Silk cried over his picking. "No sir. Coates weren't no ol' fool."

Ces grabbed his banjo, too, and he and Silk played together with the old man's body lying between them, lost themselves in the music, like they had before, only now they played faster than they had before, and then they played faster than that. They played swift, they played hard, they played deliberately, pointed, and then played so quick that Biggs thought the banjos would both break in two, playing fast, then faster, the sweat running in streams down the deep creases folded in their cheeks, played faster until Biggs could see the pain gathering in their faces, and they went right on playing the pain, like they would never stop, played on and on, twisting and pressing their features to keep the hurt in their arms and hands from stopping their fingers moving, so fast now that Biggs thought only the devil or God would play faster.

"GODDAMN IT," screamed Silk, his eyes closed tight and his face a dark and heavy beet red. "Goddamn it all to hell if it ain't YAAA-HOOO!"

In Plain Sight
A Novella

This is Friday night, and as on all Friday nights Sully's Saloon is jamming with the righteous babble of voices and laughter and the pop of peanut shells snapping on the floor beneath the soles of work boots that shuffle around pool tables where cue sticks gesture in the lazy cigarette haze then drop, aim and strike pool balls with the crack that starts a weekend break out. The eagle soars on Friday, and on the wings of this hard-charging, green dragon rests the power to whip the world of Sully's Saloon into a raucous swirl of lights, shouts and laughter, all fueled by cold beer, chiliburgers, pounding country music and the freedom bought by the eagle that is the green dragon.

Sitting at the bar is Archie Daniels. He quietly swallows from a cold long-neck and watches the clock behind the low row of whiskey bottles opposite him.

The red digital numbers wink at Archie: *8:19*. He glances into the smoky mirror above the clock and sees a man in his early thirties looking back at him, a man shaved bald, his face long, thickly mustached above a tight and darkly stumbled jaw. Archie's eyes are pointy and bright. You cannot stop watching Archie's eyes. They are a virulent pale blue, intense and alert and old. Looking, they seem to pause, hesitate, frown, then penetrate, piercing through you and off into a far distance some thousand years behind you. It is as if Archie sees you, but does not really see you, but only because he does not seem to care, or has learned not to care. The eyes are sharp, penetrating, and cold.

There is a sudden blast of laughter behind him and the alert eyes quickly shift down the mirror.

At the edge of the raucous swirl Archie sees a big man wearing a plaid shirt, waving his cue stick around. The big man is drunk and not happy. The laughter and ribbing are coming from the men around him. Something is going on at the pool table that does not sit well with the big man. He is a thick-set man with short, dark hair. As he ducks in and out of the shadow cast by the pool table's light, Archie sees that his face is twisting. He is yelling something ugly. Archie can read the angry expression without hearing the words. The music in the bar is much too loud for hearing, but the body language is unmistakable. Detached, Archie watches with a lazy ease. Archie is well versed at reading body language. He knows that the man in the plaid shirt, while heavy in the arms and shoulders, is not dangerous. He is yelling for effect. He isn't a punk, but neither is he a threat to anyone around him. Archie's brain is always lost in study, always absorbing, always calculating, always judging.

"Hey, Arch!"

The voice snaps Archie back from his study and he turns to the face that appears next to him. It's Cleo, one of the helpers at the moving and storage company where Archie works: DWW— Denver World-Wide Moving. After Bekins and North American, it's the third largest moving company in the Mile High City.

With a glow, Cleo smiles at Archie. "I'm thirsty."

Archie stares at Cleo for a moment, saying nothing.

"So, what I got to do, Arch?" Cleo nudges him, is insistent. "I can't leave you here sitting all by your lonesome? If I know you at all, Arch, I know you can't wait to buy me a beer."

Know him? What does Cleo, or any of them, know about Archie Daniels? Almost nothing, for Archie Daniels is all that was the frozen place, the place where the Archie's *then* was a time and place that had sopped and stamped him with a harsh reserve, a careful and practiced sense of focus, and a mean hunger for personal security that has become the real *now* of his personal cross to bear. More than any single event, the eight year stretch at Colorado State Penitentiary, up in the crisp, clear air of Fremont County, had sucked the life from him, drained Archie into a half man, then slowly filled the half-man with emptiness and pointlessness.

And the *now*, is all that it is.

"Is that right, Cleo?" responded Archie, but not lightly. "You really think know me? Know I'm lonely? Know I want to buy you a beer?" His face didn't change, but his voice grew easy and comfortable with himself.

Cleo smiled.

Archie had carefully considered the draining of his life, the factoring and canceling of his personal worth by prison life. Archie sensed the loss; he felt it; he stopped resisting it; he got it that life was a pointless thing to bear, a weight put on him by an impersonal fate he could only know as a cruel and accidental reckoning with the aimless indifference around him.

"Yeah, Arch." Cleo answered. "I know you, dude."

Archie turned back to his reflection in the mirror over the bar. "Then tell me why I'm gonna buy you a beer?"

A single mother, an unknown father, drugs and alcohol and the police, a judge telling him to join the army or go to YA, or fight a war, or be unemployed, or go to prison. Life was nothing. You didn't fight it. You let it happen to you.

Cleo winked. "'Cause you drivers get all the big tips." Cleo's smile grew, "and you're particularly generous with them tips, Arch. All the helpers see how you are."

Archie knew that he survives and that was all. But survive for what? Survival was a reflex, not a meaning. There was no point or purpose to anything, not even survival. Not really. Living was its own distraction. The irony of the thought that living was a distraction from itself was not lost on Archie. He watched Cleo in the mirror.

"Do they?"

Cleo blinked. "Arch?"

"Do they think I'm fair."

"Hell, yeah."

"Do they know why?"

Cleo blinked again. "Arch?"

Archie pulled the hard time at CSP because he had two priors—criminal assault and resisting arrest—though he'd never done any time for these. So now the judge figured that Archie had graduated from a petty-ante life and needed to learn the harsher lessons the penal system had to dish out, and Archie did learn, quickly and with great reverence for the teaching.

"I do what I do for me, Cleo."

"It sure don't seem that way, Arch."

"That's because you're not looking close, Cleo, or maybe you can't look close enough."

Archie learned to walk the prison walk at CSP, a crookedly learned straight-and-narrow that had tweaked him hard, burrowing a certain kind of ugly mastery deep into the belly of that beast part of his human spirit.

"I'm not?" puzzled Cleo. "What'd you mean, Arch—that I'm not looking close enough?"

"It's called the forest for the trees, Cleo."

"I don't get it, Arch."

"I do what I need to do, Cleo. You don't see that."

"But you're fair, Arch."

"Because that's what I need to do."

At CSP, Archie had learned of the special need to study men and their ways, their pride and their loss, their value and their habits. He learned quickly to determine who was dangerous and who was harmless, who was cruel and who was just another punk, who to owe and who to avoid. This learning developed a reflexive, acquired sense of people, a grasping of humanness, both in its pointlessness and in its stubbornness; Archie's was now an instinctual understanding, which in Archie's world, had so often been central to his survival. This now habitual study had become a primary focus ingrained by his gray and cloistered prison past, and now had wrapped and insulated the thread of Archie's life after CSP. The survival focus had taken up a permanent residence with who Archie Daniels had become in this world.

"Jes' Arch," chuckled Cleo. "You don't think like other people do, you know that."

"Yes I do."

"How"

"I think about surviving, Cleo."

"By splitting even up with everyone?"

"Everyone survives that way and everyone's happy." Archie put the bottle down, turned and looked at Cleo. "If everyone's happy, everyone survives."

"Jes' Arch, I don't know where you get this stuff . . . all I know is that you're fair about things. And we all see that. You ain't like some of them assholes, like Bender. I pulled a big move with that fool today."

Archie had worked with Cleo now and then. He was not Archie's first pick as helper. Archie had nothing against Cleo. The guy worked hard, hustled fast, only his hands lacked the strength to grip a triple dresser for a long-carry. Cleo continually had to rest a heavy piece on his knee to let the pain drain out of his hands before moving on. Cleo annoyed the other drivers. In the back of their minds they worried that Cleo depended on their strength too much, or worse, that he would drop the piece of furniture. That could get them *both* suspended, or worse, fired. Cleo's hands were just weak.

Archie waved the barmaid over and ordered two beers, then said to Cleo, "If you're on the work roster tomorrow, Cleo, you'll work with me."

"Thanks, Arch. I appreciate that—you taking care of me. I don't wanna work with Bender no more."

Mike Bender was one of the senior drivers at DWW. He was none too popular with the helpers. From their point of view, Bender truly qualified as an asshole. He would stand off to the side, passing the harder pieces to his helpers, while silently pocketing any tips without splitting them up. This could add up to a couple hundred bucks at the end of the week—for Big Mike

Bender. None of the helpers ever said anything about it. Not to Bender anyway. Bender was big—six-foot-three, two hundred and thirty at least, and all that size wrapped up in a nasty, eat-shit disposition that nobody wanted to test.

Archie said to Cleo's image in the mirror. "Don't thank me, Cleo. I'm not taking care of you. I'm taking care of me."

"Yeah, but you're taking care of me too, Arch."

"I'm taking care of myself, Cleo."

Archie thought it sucked and honestly felt sorry for Bender's helpers, but it was none of his business. If Bender's helpers could not get Big Mike to pay up, then it was on them, their issue, their problem, their weakness, and they paid for it; you always paid for your weakness. Survival was about strength and the smarts to apply strength correctly, in the best possible way. Archie's taking on Cleo, by using his strength to shield Cleo from his weakness, meant that Cleo would owe Archie. To Archie, his offer meant nothing more than a debt to collect. At the end of the day, taking care of Cleo was a benefit.

"You make everything sound like you're being selfish, Archie. But you're not, You're a good guy. We all think so."

Archie knew better. He watched himself in the mirror. He wasn't a good guy, but a safe guy, a calculating guy. Archie didn't hold it against Cleo or any of the helpers that were afraid of Big Mike. Everyone has something in the world to fear.

"Forest for the trees, Cleo."

Cleo chuckled again and took a sip of his beer. "Man, I don't get you, sometimes, Arch." He took a little nervous pull from the bottle. "Thanks for the beer, by the way."

"You owe me."

Cleo hesitated, not understanding, and took another swig from the icy bottle before wanting to know, "Arch, I don't understand you sometimes. But I know you're smart. We all know that. That's how come I gotta ask—if you don't mind. You gonna sign, Arch?"

Archie pretended he did not know what Cleo meant. "Sign what?"

"The union pledge card? I know you got one. We all did."

Archie placed his bottle on the bar and turned to Cleo. "I think I'm going to mind my own business."

"Yeah, Arch. I know. It's just that I—we—well you know."

Archie rolled his eyes at the ceiling above the bar, wishing he was home taking a shower, cleaning himself of more than just the grime and dried sweat. He wanted to be clean of the people around him.

Cleo went on: "We need protection, Arch. The union can do that."

"Forget the *we*, Cleo—there's just you."

"But if we band together, Arch. Unite—like they say."

"I think I'll mind my own business."

"Jesus, Arch . . . " the disappointment was heavy in Cleo's voice. "We need you."

? What he begging?

Archie pinned Cleo with a thousand yard stare. "Leave me the fuck out of it, Cleo. You understand?"

Archie got it, that the scales were never fully aligned. Everything was out of balance. Only Archie had learned to put a thumb on the scales.

"You leave me out of it and we'll be even."

Cleo watched Archie for a moment, then asked, "You worried about getting into trouble with the parole board—if you don't mind my asking?"

"Yeah, Cleo, I do mind you asking and I also think you'd better mind your own business. That way everyone stays out of trouble."

"Yeah, Arch, yeah. But a union, man," Cleo replied. "They could really help us—look out for us."

"That's not the way things work, Cleo. No one ever helps anybody—for nothing. Never was like that, and never will be."

There was just enough frost to the Archie's words that Cleo looked the other way from the blue eyes, making wet rings on the bar top with the bottom of the beer bottle. "Man," he said after a moment. "Shit. I don't know, Arch." He seemed to flounder; he was looking for a direction to take that would not offend Archie. He timidly repeated, "I don't know, Arch. I don't know."

For about three weeks now, organizers from the union had been coming to the moving company. They had been standing at the gate, just outside the yard, handing out pledge cards, trying to talk to the drivers and their helpers. They wanted to organize the place, bring in the union. Archie did not trust them. They said they'd be looking out for you, the men in the yard. Archie knew that was crap. No one ever looks out for anyone but themselves. It was the way of the world, and Archie knew well the way of the world.

Cleo gave his head a little shake, making his mind up. "I need better pay—no, I mean *we* need better pay. The company's making plenty of cheese off us, Arch. They ought to split it up better, give us a bigger slice. That'd be fair. I mean, we work our asses off, but it'd mean a strike for sure," and he shook his head again in that little knowing way. "We'd probably just get beat, though. I guess that's what you mean, right, Arch? That's why you won't sign, right Arch? We'd just get beat?"

Archie grew uncomfortable. He knew that Cleo was looking to him for something. *What?* Was it guidance? Reassurance? Leadership? Archie knew that the other men in the yard also looked up to him. He knew why. He knew it was because he he'd done that stretch at CSP. A fact they loved remembering and a fact he wanted to forget.

"We might get beat, we might not," replied Archie. "But that's not the point, Cleo. If you wanna pick a fight, make sure it's your fight and not someone else's. The union's another boss. We don't owe them anything, so why fight their fight for their benefit?"

"Yeah, Arch." Cleo stared dejectedly at his reflection in the mirror. "I guess you're right."

Archie knew that there was something about doing hard time—his being able to talk-the-talk because he had walked-the-walk, lived life at its lowest common denominator—that made the other men look up to him, listen to him. Archie Daniels, they imagined, had lived and survived life in some dark, outer dimension, another world, another universe, a universe that was ugly and dangerous, but also tantalizing and mysterious for the curious, alluring for the faint of heart. To the other men it looked to be something romantic; their imagined survival game must have made Archie seem tough and dangerous. Only Archie knew that he is neither tough nor dangerous. He had done something stupid, a harebrained armed robbery and got caught. It was all like some weird trick of fate. *Fate?* Archie knew better. Dumb choice, was all. Archie knew he had survived prison, not by being tough, but by being smart, by keeping his own counsel and avoiding other people's problems. That was all. Archie survived by strictly tending to his own business and shining-on what wasn't a part of that. He never committed. He never borrowed. He never owed. Archie got all that, had done all that. *Did they really want him to talk-that-talk?* Looking up to him was stupid thinking and it made him feel guilty of some further crime, the exact nature of which was unknown to him because he could not trace it to a debt—where, he wondered, were the scales so out of alignment? What did his withdrawal from these others subtract from the equation? Where was the debt? Who did he owe? Yet even in his rejection of the mysterious guilt at mere being alive, he felt a deep sadness for the men he worked with. MERELY

Cleo said, "Well, at least let's talk to these guys."

Archie looked in the direction Cleo had nodded. Two of the union men had come into Sully's and were walking down to the bar toward them. Archie rarely betrayed any thought or emotion with a facial expression. Now his eyebrows rose slightly.

Cleo added, "Maybe there's something in it, Arch. It doesn't hurt to listen, does it?" Cleo ran his thumb around the rim of the beer bottle and repeated, "Does it, Arch?"

One of the two—the big blonde headed guy—approached Archie and stuck out his hand. He was about the same height as Archie, square shouldered, with a sharp, clean face, handsome in a severe sort of way.

"You were tough to find, Archie Daniels."

Archie accepted the hand. "Apparently not tough enough."

That man ignored the crack. "Sten—Sten Rivers, President of Local 352." Rivers introduced himself with a sense of smoothness, then jabbed a thumb at the dark, heavy guy next to him. "This is Bob Valladez, one of our business agents with the local. Can we buy you another beer?"

Archie quietly turned and watched them in the mirror. But not Cleo. "Sure, man, we're always thirsty." Cleo greedily shook hands with both of the union men. "Me and Arch was just talking about you guys."

Rivers took a fast measure of Cleo, then said to Archie, "We need you Archie. It's guys like you that will make or break that yard."

Archie knew himself better than anyone. He knew he was not the guy Rivers was looking for.

Rivers moved in and sat on the bar stool next to Archie. "There's no one that can do what you can do, Archie. I can't even get close to these men. But you can, Archie. And if you can't get those men on with us, no one can. You got something, Archie, and it's something we need—something they need."

Archie listened to the pool balls clicking behind him. He didn't look anymore at Rivers. He looked into the mirror behind the row of bottles, taking in the scene in the wide bar room. The big guy in the plaid shirt who had been waving the cue stick was gone. Now there were two women playing, one wearing a ball cap pushed back on her head, and the other graced with a long, flowing ponytail. Archie could tell they weren't taking the game too seriously.

Sten Rivers said, "I want you to listen to me, Archie. Just listen," and he signaled the barmaid and held up four fingers, indicat-ing a round of beers for all of them. "You know what I hear from the men when I hand out the pledge cards?" Rivers asked. "They all want to know, 'What's Archie Daniels gonna do?' That's all I hear. 'What's Archie gonna do?'"

Bob Valladez reached around Archie and picked up a cold beer. "You got what it takes, Archie."

Sten squeezed Archie's shoulder. "Man, I don't know what you got, Archie, but these men will listen to you."

Valladez said from the other side of him, "You can help them help themselves, Archie. We need you, man."

Ignoring Valladez, Archie turned and looked straight at Rivers. "Yeah? Well, you can stop blowing smoke up my ass. Because, believe me, I'm not part of any world you wanna know."

"If I'm blowing smoke, Archie," Rivers replied, not intimidated by Archie's response, "then your brothers are blowing smoke up mine, 'cause they talk plenty about you and you know what—I think they got a real good instinct about you."

Archie turned back to the mirror and watched the two union men in the reflection, the blonde with the narrow face and the thicker, shorter man with the dark moustache that hid his upper lip. He then looked at his own reflection. Archie saw nothing there of what these men seemed to want, or to see. He saw a man silent, careful, and alone.

"I don't think they can do this without you," said Valladez. "You got something, Archie. Everyone can see it. The men in that yard, they look up to you."

Archie felt his ears turning red. He turned and snapped at Valladez, "This bullshit's getting deep. Everyone can see *what*? You don't know me, so stop slinging shit and trying to get me caught up in your game."

"It's no game, Archie," Rivers replied. "It's the lives of thirty-five men. They need your help. I know you got it to give."

People had everything backwards. Archie gave nothing. In prison Archie had learned to steer clear of the gangs, the drugs, the queers, the hacks, and anyone else that could stir the quiet rhythm of doing his time, his life. He survived the curse of his living by retreat, not by giving, not by charging into unknown territory.

Archie put down his unfinished beer, turned and looked from one of them to the other. "I have an early move tomorrow."

"Pick up your money, Archie," Valladez said. "We got the beer."

Archie dropped some bills on the bar and gave Valladez the kind of look intended to shut the man down, then brushed past him and headed for the door. Valladez watched Archie's back for a moment then glanced at Rivers, looking for a sign. Unable to interpret the blond man's pensive expression, Valladez shrugged Archie off and dropped some more bills on the bar top.

Cleo reached for a beer. "Man, I hope he changes his mind. You guys are right. We need Arch, we need him real bad."

The next morning, when Archie went to the dispatcher to get his paperwork and truck keys, he knew something was going on. Bob Moreno, the dispatcher, did not stand up from behind his desk, but waved Archie off and leaned back in the chair, saying in a relaxed, but tired voice, "Get on out to the yard, Arch. There's a meeting with Giles this morning."

Archie didn't ask what about. Archie never inquired too closely. He walked out of the office and into the yard. There were thirty plus men gathered in a circle around the owner of the company, Madison Giles, who was flanked by three other men Archie did not recognize—only it did not matter that Archie did not recognize them, because Archie knew them—knew their type. Archie knew the three men well and the knowing put him instantly on edge.

The owner glanced at Archie when he joined the circle, then nodded. "We know who you are."

Archie blinked back at the owner, for a moment not understanding that Giles was not speaking to him, but merely passing a comment off to the entire circle of drivers and helpers. It was Archie's studied habit of keeping his face immobile and expressionless and that saved him many times from the tell-tale look of apprehension. His face was still now as he stole a quick glance at the men standing with Giles.

"And don't be surprised when we find you out," Giles was going on. "Because we *will* find you."

Archie studied the men flanking Giles. Yes, he knew them, alright—knew them by their look, the way they stood, the way they studiously pretended not to see into the faces surrounding them. They had that look of prison guards—the hacks always striking a careful pose that was quiet, but alert—distant, but in the know and in control. There was something in the eyes of a hack that was little and narrow, the way they would hold their hands clasped in front of them, casual, yet deliberate and cool—easy in their sense of themselves, yet projecting a presence harsh and tight. There was a look about them that told you there was a *line*, and the two sides of that line crossed only when things in your life went real bad. These men had that look.

Giles shifted his sharp gaze around the circle of drivers and helpers. "We know there are union men in this yard—union organizers and we'll find you. You union men are finished." Giles waved his hand to the three men beside him. "These men with me are private detectives."

Archie looked again. *Detectives, my ass*. Muscle, Archie thought, goons hiding behind a cheesy state license. Prison wisdom: *what you think you see, you see.* They're the new hacks, bent on keeping the world safe from anyone crossing that line. Prison doctrine: To survive, trust your instincts. *What you think is happening, is happening*. Everyone knows everything. It's all about trusting your instincts.

"They will find out who you are," Giles went on. "If you men really want a union job, go get one. They're out there. Go and get one. But there will not be any union here at Denver World-Wide. I mean that, goddamn it! You sign with those union men outside that gate and I'll fire you. I will, by God, then go see what they'll do for you. Nothing. They won't do nothing because they can't do *nothing*."

Archie saw a dozen men turn their heads and look out beyond the back gate to where there were gathered eight or ten of the organizers. Archie didn't look. He didn't have to look to know he'd see the blond head of Sten Rivers and the thick set body of Bob Valladez. He knew they were watching the meeting through the fence, just as Giles intended that they should.

"Don't look at them," Giles snarled, and pointed to the gate, wanting the union men outside to see the drama they could not hear. The gesture had the definite feel of a threat. Giles kept his hand raised.

"They won't do a thing for you," he shouted for emphasis. "You men do your job and you'll get good pay. I treat you well! I pay you real well! You get paid as good as any union house. I make sure of that. They won't do anything for you that I won't. You go with them and you'll only end up with two bosses." Giles raised his voice for emphasis. "Me *and* them! And believe me, it's *them* that'll pick your pockets clean."

How desperately awkward were the lies Giles slung about while standing with both feet in the middle of a counter reality. Union wages? Here they were on Saturday morning, working on straight time, not overtime. Archie got it that to understand the lie you had to understand the liar, and to understand the liar you had to know who benefits from the lie—always *who benefits*. Still, it puzzled Archie that Giles could possibly think this crew was so stupid that they did not recognize the outright horseshit coming out of his mouth.

Madison Giles waited a moment, then wound up with a flourish. He opened his arms with generosity oozing from every pore. "You men cooperate with these detectives when they interview you. Help us find the union spies. You won't be sorry. I promise you. There will be a reward in it for any man who steps forward. Life here at DWW can be very good, and will only get better for any man who cooperates with this investigation."

Often, Archie knew, the liar believed his own lies, and was freely allowed the belief because the grunts living at the bottom of the pile, Archie included, had lived most of their lives at the mercy of arbitrary demands for discipline, and they had long ago learned to shrug off the lies as merely part of the world as it was. To be lied to was insulting, but for those like Archie Daniels the world as it was had always been an insult.

A driver next to Archie turned to him and whispered, "Who are those guys, Archie? Are they cops or something?"

Archie adjusted his face slightly and spoke out of the corner of his mouth as he had learned to do in prison yards. "Keep out of this shit, keep your mouth shut, and it'll go away."

Giles finished up: "Now helpers find your drivers and go move some furniture."

Archie grabbed his paperwork from the dispatcher and hustled up two helpers, one of them Cleo, the other Johnny Gaynos, and headed for his truck. This was to be a medium size industrial move. There were to be two trucks, both city tractors and trailers. Archie backed his tractor under the trailer, locked the pin and got out to quickly attach the air-line glad-hands and pigtail.[14] He climbed back in the tractor and studied the paperwork for a moment.

"Shit," said Cleo. "Man, Giles was sure worked up."

The second helper, Johnny Gaynos, added. "Yeah, what's up with them detectives?"

Archie said, never looking up from his paperwork. "They're not detectives, and you guys stay away from them."

---

14. Glad-hands are a nick-name for the air connection fittings that come out of the trailer to which air hoses from the tractor are coupled in order to unify the tractor and trailer braking systems. The *pigtail* is the electric line that runs from the trac-tor to the trailer and charges the trailer's lighting system.

Gaynos ventured, "Giles said they was detectives."

Archie put the truck in gear and pulled out, heading toward the open gate. "Just stay away from them," he told Gaynos, then repeated, "They're not detectives."

Johnny Gaynos and Cleo passed a look between them, then Gaynos asked, "What'll we tell them when they interview us."

"As little as possible and look out for yourself."

Rolling slowly out of the gate, Archie looked down from the cab window at the union men, at Vallades, then at Rivers. Archie kept his face impassive—as always.

Rivers jumped on the running board. "Archie, don't listen to Giles," he said through the closed window. "We can protect you."

Archie looked in the tractor's mirrors to see what the three "detectives" were doing. Two were watching, same pose, from the safety of the yard. He could not see the third. Archie answered Rivers by picking up speed and the union man jumped off the running board.

It was a two trailer, six man office move—heavy filing cabinets, heavy furniture, heavy everything—big and heavy. Four pieces so big they had to be lowered out of windows by pulleys. When they broke for lunch Archie dropped the trailer and he and his crew hopped in the tractor, bobtailing[15] it to a burger stand.

When Archie sat down with his sandwich and soda he could see that Cleo and Gaynos had been talking. Archie was sure he knew what about and he did not want to be drawn into any conversation about it.

Gaynos said. "Archie, wha'ya think we outta do?"

"About what?"

"Those detectives," Gaynos replied. "You're right, man, they don't look much like detectives."

15. A common expression used to indicate rolling in a tractor separated from any trailer.

"They're not."

"Then who are they?" Cleo asked.

"They're meant to keep out the union."

"How?"

Archie looked at Cleo around the edge of his cup. "Sign a pledge card and find out."

"Yeah. Shit. Right."

Gaynos asked, "Can they do that?" He made a hapless little gesture with his hands. "I mean, ain't that illegal or something?"

Archie thought about power and the prison hacks. "They can do any damn thing they want," he answered Gaynos. "They'll beat the living shit out of you and leave you bleeding in an alley. You just stay clear of them guys."

"Jesus, Arch," whispered Cleo.

Gaynos ventured, "What about the cops?"

"What about them?"

"Can't we get them arrested?"

"For beating your ass? Maybe—maybe not—but you'll still have a few broken ribs and missing some teeth."

"Then what are we gonna do, Arch?" Cleo wanted to know.

"About what?"

"Them guys."

"I don't know what you're gonna do. But me? I ain't gonna do nothing. I'm gonna stick to my own business and keep out of other people's business. I'm not going back to lock-up, and I'm not going to get my face busted.I'm just gonna work and mind my own business"

"Naw," Cleo protested and making his eyes crinkle up. "They sure as shit couldn't bust your face, Archie. No way, man."

Archie almost told Cleo to stop sounding like some kind of a dumb-ass, but he kept silent.

"What the hell does Madison Giles have to be afraid of anyway," asked Gaynos.

"Us," Archie replied

"Why?"

Archie crumbled up his napkin and stuffed it in the cup. "Because there's more of us than him, and he knows the union will be the end of his one man kingdom." He stood up and brushed the crumbs off his overalls. "And he'll fight like hell to stop it. You just stay clear of those gorillas he hired."

"But if he's afraid of us . . . " Gaynos raised the point.

"That's what makes him dangerous."

"Maybe the union's right." Cleo said. "Maybe we need them."

"You and Johnny do what you want to do about the union," Archie replied. "Sign pledge cards. Vote. Do anything you like, but stay clear of those three hacks."

"Okay, Archie," Cleo said. "We'll do like you say."

Archie did not like the sound of that. "I'm not your boss, Cleo; you be your boss. You and Johnny do what you want, but don't look to me. I'm not your boss."

"But you know more about this shit than we do," Cleo returned. "If you tell us not to sign with the union, we won't."

Archie liked the sound of that even less. Why did he look ten feet tall to these men? Prison did not make anyone taller, any more than it rehabilitates—it makes people smaller, more hardhearted and cynical, and many a man it turns into a coward and therefore mean and shirking. If prison gave any special kind of deep knowing, it was the knowing of ferrets which gives a man the courage of a snake.

"You do whatever you want to do, just leave me out of it," Archie snapped at them, a little hot now. "What you guys do is none of my business and I want to keep it that way. Now, let's finish up this move."

Johnny Gaynos looked as if he were getting the message, but not Cleo. It wasn't that Cleo was stubborn. He was needy.

"Damn, Arch," Cleo said. "I wish we could be as sure of stuff as you."

The only thing that Archie was sure of was that everyone already knew everything there was worth knowing. If prison had taught him anything, it was the rule and role of instinct, and especially the instinct for self-preservation. Everything that one needed to know was all around a man. All he had to do was stop being afraid to open his eyes and see. Just *look*, damn you! Off-load your safe, cookie-cutter ideas and *look!* Ask yourself one question: *Who benefits*—then *look*! Trust yourself and stay in tune with your survival instinct. There, in that question—*who benefits*—is found the truth of survival.

He didn't have to be inside to trust the prison doctrine for survival: *What you think is happening is happening.* Everything is out there in plain sight, and always has been. All you have to do is *look* and trust your instinct for survival.

———————————————

Three nights later Archie found himself on his usual barstool at Sully's. It had been a shitty day, really shitty on two counts. The dispatcher was giving Archie one industrial move after another. Only this time the move was big enough that there were two trucks and two lead drivers; Archie was one lead, the other lead was Mike Bender. Nothing had gone right that day. Big Mike had seen to that.

There had been half dozen pieces that had to be lowered off balconies. It had been difficult and Archie, along with several of his helpers, had burned their hands on the straps they'd used to lower the heavy desks. Their hands were going to need careful cleaning tonight and a good, cold soaking—if not, they'd be swollen and useless tomorrow, and tomorrow was another industrial move. Nothing had gone right.

At the end of the move, the client gave a nice tip to the two crews. Three hundred bucks! Big cheese! Only the client gave the tip to Mike Bender. As always, Big Mike had been loud and pushy and the client figured he must have been the boss. Both crews saw the money disappear into Bender's pocket. Gaynos and Cleo immediately looked to Archie, who swore under his breath. He had to do something about Bender, and now. He, Archie Daniels, was not about to get punked. Archie had learned in prison that if you once got punked, you'd be somebody's—everybody's—bitch forever.

"Bender," Archie had called to the big man and wiggled his finger for him to come over to him. It was with a mild surprise for Archie that Bender immediately complied and closed the distance between them until he stood looking down at Archie, frowning and puffing himself up.

Archie stuck out his hand. "My crew's part of the tip!" he demanded.

Mike Bender was nearly a full head taller than Archie, and a good forty pounds heavier, almost all of it in the chest and shoulders. Size made no difference, as Archie deliberately drilled his gaze dead into Bender's gray eyes, burrowing deep into them. Bender finally broke and looked away to the rest of the crew.

"I'll cut it up back in the yard," Bender answered.

Only Archie had seen Bender break eye contact under the guise of looking to see who was around, who was watching. When Bender broke eye contact, Archie knew he was carrying the push.

"You'll cut it up now, Bender," Archie prodded him softly, but through his teeth. "Not later, Bender. Now!" Archie shoved his hand out a bit further, palm up.

Bender glanced at Archie, his eyes bouncing off Archie's iron gaze. Archie noticed the beads of sweat just below Benders dark hair line. Bender was the big man in the yard, and as the big man he suddenly had to make a very careful decision.

Big Mike blinked a couple of time, and frowned, then: "Okay, Arch," and he reached, pulling out the bills. He counted out half. "Here, this is for your crew," he said, handing over the money, sounding magnanimous.

Archie took the cash, then for some reason that Archie could not fathom he broke a rule.

Mike Bender was big and he was strong and Archie had the cash in his hand for him and his crew. Archie had refused to let Bender grind him. He had saved face, kept the scales in balance. Nothing more was called for or needed, nothing more should have been of any interest to Archie Daniels. That should have been the end of it.

Prison had taught Archie to never be punked. That could never happen—not if you wanted to live with yourself as a whole person. But prison had also taught Archie to never punk another man—for that drafted a silent and dangerous debt—without having the most selfish and self-serving of reasons. To punk another man, without gaining some serious benefit, and without first knowing the outcome of any physical contest, held dangerous consequences of the most profound type, and Archie Daniels was not at all sure of the outcome of a squab with Bender.

So when Archie turned slightly aside and saw that Gaynos and Cleo were watching him, their eyes narrowed with vex and need, he swore at the sudden weight he felt in his chest. Something rose up in him that made Archie quietly swear again, swear at himself and swear at his crew for the look on their faces.

Archie turned back to Big Mike. "Now take the rest of the tip and cut it up with *your* crew," and he blanched at hearing the sound of his own words. It was as if someone else was pulling his strings, pulling strange words out of his mouth.

Bender gawked at Archie in a kind of disbelief. "What? Hey, goddamn it." Then he got a real nasty look on his face. "Hey, Daniels, I'll take care of mine, you take care of yours." He took a half step back and turned sideways. "You stick to your own, Daniels, and I'll stick to mine."

Archie caught Bender's pose and wondered for a second if he was pushing this past a safe place. Archie did not want to squab with Bender. He was lighter than Bender, though maybe as strong, and he had behind him prison yard experience that substituted a whole new book covering the rules of engagement. Archie was sure that Bender, despite appearances, still carried the gloss of civilization, some civil hesitation, some civil reflective process that would slow him down.

Archie had abandoned those civilized facilities through a process of dumb animal learning. *Still*, Archie could not safely predict the outcome of a squab, and that was never good. And then too, in the back of Archie's mind was a parole violation—always he lived with the thought of a parole violation. Fighting was a parole violation; if reported there'd be a brief court appearance, no lengthy explanation, no review, no hesitation—Archie'd be violated and sent back to CSP to finish out his jail time. There was no benefit to any of this, yet he was propelled beyond that safe place.

Archie felt the need to be cool. He said slow and even, "We'll take care of it now, Bender—pay off your crew now."

There was movement now, as if a stiff breeze had come up and worked the two crews around them. Out of the corner of his eye, Archie saw the helpers like tall grass, swaying their heads easily first this way and then that way, as they looked puzzled at each other, waiting. Only Archie and Mike Bender were not going with the breeze, each man steady, eyeing the other, each in his own way dumbfounded by Archie's words.

Bender suddenly surprised everyone. "Okay, Archie—fuck it," and Bender stuck his hand back into his pocket and pulled out the remaining twenties. "I'll cut the split now, but poking your nose into my business ain't the best way to stay on my good side," and he turned to his crew, quickly counting out the divide.

Both crews were stupefied at the sight of Big Mike backing down, but not at all surprised that it had been to Archie Daniels. Some thought for sure that Bender would squab before backing down to anyone, even Archie Daniels. Others were less shocked, sensing that Bender had been smart not to tangle with Archie; but the looks on all their faces was worth the price of admission.

Bender stuck the remaining few bills back in his pocket and snarled at Archie, "You'd better learn to mind your own business, Daniels."

Bender quickly got his crew into the tractor's cab and climbed in himself. He turned over the engine and looked down at Archie through the window, a promise in his gaze. The semi rolled out of the lot and down the street.

"Goddamn," hooted Cleo. "Goddamn, Archie! Shit! Did you see that," and he slapped Gaynos the shoulder. "I mean, shit, did you see that, Johnny?! Archie owned Big Mike. He fuck-*ing owned him*!"

Cleo was laughing and gawking at Archie, only half listening to Johnny Gaynos, who asked, "You did a good thing, Archie, but what'd you do it for?"

Archie shook his head. "I don't know."

Archie's face did not betray a thing he was feeling. Inside he was unexpectedly pleased with himself for making Bender pay up. The heavy weight had disappeared. Turning Bender blessed Archie with a soothing feeling of completeness, not a painful thinking process. He didn't think, and so the why of his actions eluded Archie.

Gaynos said, "I don't get it, Archie."

"Don't try," was Archie's response.

It was as if Bender had owned everyone for a decade, and now it was Bender who had been owned and had to pay up. Only one thing still troubled Archie: why had he, the careful Archie Daniels, done it?

There was no benefit. It ran counter to everything that world as-it-is had taught him—so why, and why him? It seemed he had done it almost automatically, a spontaneous act that rose from somewhere deep inside of him to roll over and crush his very careful learning, and the *why* of it would gnaw at Archie for a very long time.

Gaynos nodded reflectively and added in a serious tone: "You better watch your back, Archie," he said. "I don't think Big Mike's finished with this."

Cleo was still happily popping off. "Goddamn, Arch." He was almost dancing in the street. "Who needs a union with Archie Daniels here. You're a one man union, Archie."

Archie turned sideways to Cleo and shook his head again, slowly. He was still feeling the sense of soothing satisfaction at making Bender pay up, pleased at the loss of the weight in his chest, if only the feeling wasn't clouded over by the bewildering "Why"?

A few nights later Johnny Gaynos and Archie had dropped into Sully's Saloon looking for a burger and a couple of cold beers. The first thing they noticed was that Mike Bender was sitting at the bar. Archie and Gaynos had seen Bender at the Saloon a few times, but he was not a regular, so it was natural that after the other day they gave Bender a good once-over as they walked past him to the other end of the bar and pulled out stools.

The bartender took her time getting to them and Archie had a long while to watch Big Mike. Both Archie and Gaynos thought that Bender had seen them, but Bender was acting like he had not noticed them come into the bar. Gaynos was puzzled, but Archie was not. Archie knew; Bender was pretending to look away with such a studied casualness that Archie had to crookedly smile. Archie's acquired sense of people was active and always in tune to his human environment, and it now told him that Bender was here for something mean and deliberate and very calculated, and it involved Archie Daniels.

What you think is happening, is happening.

In Archie's mind, the certainty of it wrapped around Bender like a dark halo and unexpectedly Archie's smugness began to be forced out by a slight unease. Archie wasn't afraid of Bender, not by any means, but there was something ugly growing in Archie's acquired sense of people.

Out of the corner of his eye he saw Cleo approach from the pool tables. Cleo was carrying a pool cue.

"Hey, Archie," Cleo greeted them, nodding to Gaynos. "Can I buy you guys a beer?"

Gaynos answered with a question, "How long's Big Mike been here?" Gaynos nodded down the bar to where Bender was sitting.

"That prick," Cleo replied. "About an hour." He shrugged. "He hasn't said boo to me. Probably doesn't even know I'm here."

"He knows," Archie corrected him.

The bartender got to them and Archie ordered two beers. Cleo was quick to drop some bills on the bar top. "I got this."

"I wonder what he wants?" Gaynos was still looking at Bender, frowning as if studying a cockroach trying to hide in the corner of a broom closet.

"Maybe he wants to come over here and kiss Archie's ass," snorted Cleo with a chuckle, then winked at the two of them. "I got to get back to my pool game." He waved his cue at the pool tables. "I got me a real sucker there. I'm taking all this fool's money."

Gaynos tore his eyes off Bender and laughed. "How the hell you do that, Cleo? You can't shoot pool worth a shit."

Archie took a sip of the beer and watched Bender push some money over the bar top, get off his stool and leave Sully's through the front door. Archie did not feel any better watching Bender leave. It made him feel even more uneasy. His stomach tightened. He knew that Bender had seen them come in. He knew that Bender had not stopped in for the burgers and the big legged waitresses. He knew Bender had been in Sully's for a reason, and that reason had to do with him.

What you think is happening, is happening.

Archie knew that Big Mike's walking out of Sully's was just the opening bell. There was something on its way.

Archie looked around the bar room. Nothing stood out. Yet everything was fuzzy and somehow wrong.

Archie watched Cleo shoot pool for a moment. There was nothing out of the ordinary. Cleo took a stroke, stood up and walked to the other end of the table. Ordinary. Yet it seemed to Archie that everything he was seeing had faded into stark black and white and was tugged, distorted at the margins, everything faintly blurred at the edges of his vision. There was something real wrong with the scene, or maybe there was something wrong with the way he and Gaynos were arranged in the scene.

Then Archie got it. He saw how small things drew his attention. The back door? It was ajar, cracked open to the parking lot behind Sully's. Archie had never seen that before. That door had always been closed and locked. And there was something he spotted in the mirror. Behind them, off in a corner, was a booth with a shaded light hanging over it—only the light was out. There was a solitary figure seated at the booth, cloaked in darkness, unseen but for the dull glow of a cigarette. There was something wrong with the darkness and the pinpoint glow. And Cleo? Gaynos was right. Cleo could hardly tell one end of the pool cue from the other, and he was beating some guy out of a lot of money? Somebody wanted to keep Cleo occupied, keep him busy, keep him there.

What you think is happening, is happening,

He turned and looked at Gaynos, about to wonder if they should leave Sully's, but Gaynos' mildly cut, big featured profile stopped him. Arch decided not to ask. He knew that Gaynos would not understand the question. Even if Gaynos had noticed the same things that Archie had, he would not understand what he saw. That kind of understanding takes a glance first through the prism of instinct, then a deeper study through the tinted glass of harsh schooling.

The wait was short. From the dark booth at the back of the pool room one of the private detectives that Giles had introduced to the yard those few days ago stood up and came forward into the light. He was looking at Archie, and Archie knew everything—why Mike Bender had been there, why the back door was open, and why Cleo was winning at pool. Archie quietly studied the man in the mirror, worked his eyes over the short black hair, the thick shoulders and neck, the hard, deliberate eyes, and felt his bald scalp tighten.

From the pool table, the man Cleo had been shooting with tossed his cue on the table and backed away from the game, leaving Cleo looking stupidly at him. Archie glanced and took in this second man, and he knew him too. He was not one of the men in the yard with Giles that day, but it made no difference. Archie knew him and understood the meaning in the purposeful eyes of the hack that were now narrowed at him and Gaynos.

Gaynos eased up to Archie and nodded at the approaching man with the black hair. "Hey, Arch, ain't that one of the detective dudes from the yard?"

Archie looked down at his beer bottle, and like he had learned in prison, spoke out of the corner of his mouth. "Take one of these beers over to Cleo and tell him to watch the guy he was shooting pool with. Watch him close."

"What's wrong, Archie?"

Archie thought: *There's at least one more, maybe two.* These guys weren't going to take him on, just the two of them. Archie knew well their type—hacks—knew there would be at least three or maybe four, and then he realized that the others were outside in the parking lot, waiting.

"Just do it, Johnny. And keep your eye on me."

"Do you want Cleo to come over here?"

"No. Just stay there with him and watch me. If I go out through the back door you come running—*both of you*—and fast!"

"Shit," Gaynos muttered. "Fuck me," and he grabbed the beers off the bar and took them into the pool room.

Archie did not watch Gaynos walk away. He trusted Johnny more than Cleo. Johnny would do the right thing, but Cleo? Archie couldn't be sure. Only he had no time to wonder.

Archie kept his eyes on the bigger of the two men. At first the guy did not move. Archie thought he saw a faint smile on his lips, but when the man finally took a slight step forward Archie saw it was only the light playing tricks. His face was flat, his nose slightly twisted, and there was no smile. The man's lips were as a slice in a spud, razor thin, set, and unmoving.

In the mirror Archie saw the second man leave the pool table and come toward him. This man quickly approached the bar and perched on a stool, a second stool away from Archie. He was just out of reach, turned slightly on the stool, looking dead at Archie.

"Hi ya doing, Archie?"

Archie did not turn. "Do I know you?"

"Not yet."

"They why don't you get the fuck out of my face."

"You're not being polite, Archie," said the man. "I'm not in your face and I asked: How are you doing? You're supposed to answer me: 'Fine, Charlie.'"

"That your name—Charlie?"

"It is for tonight."

"Okay—then I'm fine—Charlie Shithead-For-Tonight."

"Yeah, I heard you thought you was some kind of hard ass."

"And you're itching to find out."

"Yep, me and my friends."

In the mirror Archie spotted Gaynos and Cleo. They were together, riveted to the scene playing out at the bar. The second man was standing just behind them, but completely unnoticed by them.

"Archie, we know who you are." Charlie went on.

"Yeah," Archie replied, taking a nonchalant sip from his beer bottle. "And who am I?"

"You're the union organizer."

For a moment Archie was caught off guard, then he got it, understood why Bender had been here.

"And just where'd you hear that, Charlie Shithead?"

"A little birdie—and you'd be wise not to really piss me off, Archie. This can hurt a little, or it can hurt a lot."

"Your little birdie got a name?"

"Maybe."

"Like Mike Bender?"

"That'd be a big birdie, Archie."

Archie thought to deny it, that he was a union organizer, but he knew that more than anything else Charlie would read denial as a sign of weakness and any sign of weakness now would mean capitulation, getting punked, and would have offered up an edge. Archie stayed silent and let the silence draw the man out.

"You have these men all stirred up, Archie, getting them to wanting a union and all."

Archie countered. "It looks to me like you're the ones who have everything stirred up."

"You got that wrong, Archie. We're here to quite things down."

Archie turned his head slightly, looking at Charlie. The man sitting a few feet away, gazing at the bottles lined up behind the bar, showing Archie his profile—a profile that was sharp and well defined, clear cut against the light coming from the kitchen doorway.

"How much you getting paid, Charlie?"

"Enough."

"No, Charlie, it's not enough," countered Archie. "Whatever it is, it's not enough."

Charlie frowned, not understanding, then snorted, "We need to talk to you, Archie."

Archie spun on his stool. "So talk."

Charlie turned and looked into the pale eyes. "Not here, Archie. Out in the parking lot."

Archie looked straight back at him and smirked. He said, "You're about a real dumb-ass, aren't you, Charlie Shithead?"

Archie could see that his words had the intended impact. Being called a dumb-ass was about the last thing the hack expected to hear. Archie knew hacks, knew how easily they could be knocked off balance.

For a moment Charlie looked baffled, not uneasy, not worried, just faintly puzzled. In his line of work, the man was used to seeing fear or anger or stupefaction, but never condescension. Momentarily, the man lost focus; looking confounded, Charlie unexpectedly drifted into curiosity.

"Yeah, Like I said, I heard you was some kind of tough guy, Archie." It wasn't a question, but a statement that was edged with approval. "Done time, huh?"

"Yeah, I done time." Archie's gaze never wavered. "You?"

"Nope."

"Didn't think so."

Charlie was not sure what Archie meant by that, but he was sure it wasn't a compliment, but an unreadable slight. Charlie's look slid back to annoyance and he repeated, but in a tone just a hint less certain, "Archie, I can see we're not going to get along."

"Well," Archie grinned, "You aren't as dumb as you look."

Charlie rose higher on his stool and jabbed his thumb toward the rear exit. "Outside," he ordered.

Archie took a closer measure of the man. Charlie was about thirty-five, stood over six foot and had the neck and shoulders of a weight lifter, but he also looked as if he had consumed his share of prime rib, potatoes and beer. This mattered little, Archie knew, because this one man was not the only one working tonight's gig.

Madison Giles had hired these guys to do a job, and that job definitely did not include getting hurt themselves.

Archie took another sip of his beer, then studied the bottle for a second before asking, "How big's the party, Charlie?"

"Just you and me, Archie."

That drew a chuckle out of Archie. "That wouldn't be your style, Charlie Shithead." For a moment he thought to follow up with asking if Mike Bender was waiting outside, but decided against it. Bender had already announced to the world that he was a coward.

Charlie looked Archie over. "Daniels, I gotta say that I think I'm gonna enjoy showing you my style."

Archie knew he was looking at a stomping and about the only chance he had was to cause enough anger in Charlie to dull the man's professional edge, make it personal enough that working the routine by the numbers was lost somewhere in Charlie's personal heat.

"I don't think you can measure up, Charlie Shithead."

"You know Daniels, I'm really starting not to like you. You think you're tough, asshole—well, you're gonna find out you're not so fucking tough, and I'm thinking I'm gonna enjoy turning you into a whiney little bitch."

"Well, this little bitch only has one little question." Archie turned and looked straight at Charlie with a lopsided smile shadowing his face. Then he winked at Charlie, and blew him a kiss. "Did you bring the lube? 'Cause it's gonna hurt if you didn't. I know a bottom when I see one"

Charlie lurched off his stool, planting his feet flat and square and off center. "Yeah, fuck you, Daniels . . . "

That's as far as Charlie got. Archie swung hard and quick. He had the beer bottle clutched tightly in his hand, hitting the man in the side of his head with the hard bottom of the bottle. The glass didn't shatter. It was too thick, but it rocked Charlie off his balance, stumbling him backwards, his feet tangling in the legs of the barstool, tripping him onto the floor.

Archie knew better than to stop. He quickly stomped his foot into the man' face, feeling things break under his heavy work shoe. He had time to land one more kick before turning to face the man he knew would be moving up behind him.

This second man was fast, faster than Archie, and Archie took a set of lead knuckles hard in the side of his head, pitching him into the bar stools and he hit the ground, darkness and pinpricks of light blinding him. He felt a kick land in his midsection, then another. Only they were far away, the pain winding down the trail of lost consciousness.

Archie was on parole, and even though the union had stepped in and ponied up for a hot-shot lawyer, there was no bailing him out. His court appearance was short, almost to the point of comedy, only no one was laughing. Archie had gotten way out of line. Assault and battery was the charge. Archie had broken a man's jaw, kicked out a couple of teeth, and caved in the man's eye socket, possibly costing him his sight. Archie Daniels would be going back to prison. Never mind who the man was, or what the beef had been about. Legal justice never plumbed deep enough to find human justice. The law has no humanity and therefore no real appetite for right and wrong.

But at least it was level II, minimum security this time. Arrowhead Correctional Center, just outside of Canyon City, and compared to CSP, a country club. There were extenuating circumstances, after all, and the union had paid for a top lawyer who worked out a plea deal with the Denver prosecutor's office for second degree assault and violating parole. Twenty months—six suspended.

Archie got three visitors in the time served. The first two were Cleo and Johnny Gaynos. They came all the way out from Denver together.

"Hey, Arch," Cleo said after shaking hands in the free yard. The three of them sat down across a picnic table under the shade of one of the half dozen trees. It was minimum security, after all.

"We're sorry that we didn't get to that guy before he clocked you with that brass." Gaynos apologized. "We were just so fuck'n startled. I hope you're not pissed."

Archie appraised Gaynos for a moment, then shook his head. He understood. "No, John, I'm cool with you two."

"Thanks, Arch, we appreciate that," Cleo replied with some relief. "But we managed to hold him down until the cops got there and the cheesedick got his dumb ass arrested for them knuckles." Cleo laughed. "Not for using it, Arch, but for being in posses-sion of. Brass knuckles are illegal in Colorado, ya know. Pretty funny, huh?"

"He go to jail?"

"No. He was fined."

"Giles probably paid it."

"Probably."

"And speaking of Giles, you'll never guess what, Arch." Gay-nos said, trying to conceal his excitement.

Archie shook his head, waiting. Gaynos glanced at Cleo and winked before turning back to Archie.

"We went union," he said, grinning. "Denver World-Wide went union, thanks to you, man."

"Me?"

"Yeah, man. You're a fucking hero."

"Hero," Archie echoed, then repeated: "*Hero?*" An incredulous expression blanketed his face. "What the hell did I do?"

Cleo explained. "Well, Arch, after the cops arrested you, and Giles heard about how you busted up that goon, he signed with the union. There was media all over the place. The cops and a couple of city councilmen got involved—even the Feds—something about interstate commerce. Man, it was a circus. They even had to close Sully's for a couple nights, for security reasons they said. Afraid fights would break out, I guess, but I don't know why—everyone's happier'n shit at going union. But hell, over at Sully's they didn't know what was going on, and Arch, you can still see the blood stains on the floor where it soaked into the wood when you kicked the shit out of that guy." Cleo was still grinning, his eyes shining. "And man, did you ever kick the shit out of him."

Gaynos added, "I guess Giles ain't such a bad guy after all. He was real upset about everything. I mean it. Not pissed, Arch. *Upset!* He was *really* upset. Turned the whole business over to his son. And kid's really a good guy—young and smart. We like working for him, don't we Cleo?"

"Yeah," Cleo said happily, "and we all got you to thank for it." Archie could not stop the bewilderment from creeping into his face. He hadn't done anything, except try to keep himself in one piece *and* get thrown back into lock-up. There seemed to be little enough to thank him for.

Gaynos went on, "And that asshole Bender. We figured he was the one that put those goons on to you at Sully's. We wanted to get his ass canned, but the union said no. Can you believe that shit, Archie? Bender put them anti-union pricks on you and he gets protected now just like anyone else. But we tried, Archie. We really tried."

Archie did not say anything, but he understood the weighing of the scales better than Gaynos imagined; must keep the scales in balance.

"The union's got rules," Archie reminded them. "Everybody's got rules."

"But Bender's better now, Arch," Cleo said. "He doesn't try to fuck with us anymore. Yeah, he's okay with his crews."

"Thanks, Archie," Gaynos offered again. "We owe you big time."

The sense that he, Archie Daniels, had balanced the scales eased into his thoughts and he realized whatever debt they owed him, it was one he didn't want to collect. There was a sensitive, private feeling of satisfaction at being owed that was too rich to give up—and there was another feeling he couldn't identify.

A week later Archie had his third visitor: Sten Rivers.

"Archie, you did a hellofa job for us."

Archie smiled facetiously and repeated, "A hellofa job."

"Hey, Archie, you're smiling," Rivers rebounded, seeming not to notice the sarcasm in Archie's grin. "I never seen you do that before. You must know."

"I heard," Archie replied, his smile becoming more genuine. "That DWW went union."

"Damn straight. You took out that asshole union buster. Messed his shit up real bad, Archie. And you did it publically and that got the media on it and pushed the Denver PD into nosing around. They got all over World-Wide. Your case lit everything up and we were able to get the state labor board in there, and because of interstate commerce even the Feds got into the act, and then everyone suddenly wanted to look over Giles' books. Damn, the shit really hit the fan then. Giles couldn't sign up with us fast enough. I mean the man wanted nobody, but nobody in those books. And you know the topper?

Archie waited.

"Giles. The fool got his ass arrested a few weeks ago—arrested for racketeering." Rivers laughed. "The books, man! First, we found out that the immediate reason Giles didn't want us snooping in the company's books was that he was supporting a mistress and hiding it in the books. Okay, so that pissed the wifie off, but that wasn't all, Arch, not by a long shot. Giles was also transporting stolen goods and drugs in his interstate trucks. So it wasn't just the little woman, but the Feds and the local Denver cops that got all excited and rounded up the lawyers. Ain't that a hoot? His son is running the place now, and he's okay with us. He's a college boy—real smart. The kid's clean and he knows that he can work with us so we can help him run a smooth, profitable business with a stable and happy work force. Man, it's smiles all around."

Archie eyeballed Rivers, then said cryptically, "Yeah, I guess it came around to almost everyone."

Rivers studied Archie for a moment, measured, wanting to sort the parody from the sarcasm, then observed, "Well, Archie, whatever good you had coming around went around, that's for sure, and for everybody's benefit." Sten hesitated, then added in a less certain tone, "I guess if you were ever feeling guilty of something, Arch—and I'm not saying you were—you just paid it off in spades."

Archie wasn't real sure how to feel about this victory. He was not even sure he wanted to analyze it too closely. Archie suddenly did not want to chance the possibility of losing the strange feeling. Archie didn't feel like a hero, nor did he feel that he'd done the right thing; it led to an inexact feeling. An enigma, and behind the puzzle was something more like a mood rather than a feeling. It was a mood like a farewell, a departing, only more like a sense of *relief* at the parting, not sad, but smooth and gentle, and Archie was afraid that if he solved the puzzle the relief would disappear somewhere into the solution.

He watched Rivers, waiting for the other shoe.

Sten Rivers did not disappoint. He put his hand on Archie's shoulder. "Soon, Arch, things are going to be different."

"How so?"

"You've got a new life."

Archie smiled again, commenting with a sarcasm more obvious. "Yeah, in the joint."

"A few months," Rivers chuckled. "Minimum security," and he nodded at the picnic tables, the families, with their children, visiting the prisoners, at the single unarmed guard looking around himself, doing little to disguise his boredom. "Do the time standing on your head, Arch. Then you got a really good job waiting."

"For who?"

"For us."

Archie frowned. "Moving furniture?"

"Hell no!" laughed Rivers. "You're done with all that, Arch. *Organizing.* We want you for a full time organizer."

"Rivers, I just want a job."

"Sorry, Arch, you can't go back to hiding. We all know who you are now."

Archie looked straight at Rivers, saying now with something less than conviction, "Rivers, what makes you think I'm an organizer?" He shook his head. "If you want to do something for me, just help me get my old life back."

Rivers looked back at him, just as straight, only now fully amused. "Sorry, Arch. It's not your life anymore."

"What the hell's that supposed to mean?"

"I mean, you're out in the open now, Arch," and Sten's hand on his shoulder squeezed tighter. "You're a hero now, Archie Danels, and heroes owe people, and you owe us now."

"Owe?" Incongruously, Archie grinned. "Why do I owe you?"

"Because you got caught out in the open."

"Jesus, Rivers, I got no idea what you're talking about. I'm just a nobody trying to survive."

Rivers threw his head back and laughed. "So go on surviving, Archie. You got a good instinct for it. Just go on doing what it is you do and being who you are. Like I said, Arch, you've been caught out in the open now, so go on being Archie Daniels."

"Rivers, Archie Daniels is a nobody."

Sten nodded, only now he wasn't smiling. "Then aren't we all nobodies, except that the rest of us nobodies don't trust what we feel, and you do, Archie, and far more than that, you act on what you feel."

Archie slowly shook his head.

"That's right, Arch. It all seems like a big accident, unintended by you, and that's the beauty of it all. You trust your natural instincts while the rest of us don't. That's why it looks like an accident, why it looks unintentional, because it is."

Rivers hesitated a moment, studying Archie, then added, "It is what it is, Archie. You don't think, you feel. It's in your nature to feel. The only difference between you and the rest of us nobodies is that special feeling you got for your instincts."

He dropped his hand from Archie's shoulder and turned, showing Archie his profile. Rivers was smiling again.

"Everyone's got a survival instinct, Arch, only you trust yours and we don't trust ours; its that difference that makes you the hero that's hiding in plain sight."

Equal Pay
A Novella

The big clock over the dispatch office door showed five-fifty a.m. Evidently, she had been there some time before any of the men arrived. Her hair was short, sandy in color, and pushed back out of her face. The men could see that even without makeup she was pretty, in a rough and big-featured sort of way. It was her eyes that drew the most attention. They were set wide apart, round, open, and pale blue, that innocent blue of a mountain sky in the early morning. The straightforward eyes would have given her an honest, cute look, nearly guileless, were it not for the large, vaguely aggressive mouth and high cheekbones that framed her face in a manner more handsome than girlish. She looked to be about five-five and weighted in at around one hundred thirty, edging toward the stocky side, but firm, well proportioned, not fat.

The men did not know what to make of her being there. She was dressed like them: Frisco jeans, lace up work boots, and a plaid shirt—decked out as they were, right down to the insulated vest worn against the damp and cool Northwest winter, only the heavy work clothes did little to hide the femaleness inside of them. One of the drivers said she looked like a dyke; another said she was kinda sexy, and he wished she wore blue jeans rather than Frisco's, and tighter, much tighter.

From the other end of the dock she watched the men staring at her. She understood men so she understood the stares. Even so she grew more and more sensitive to the men, fighting a growing urge to walk away, get out from under the looks, get away from this trucking company, go back to before driving school, before her move to Oregon, before her two boys, make different choices, walk a different walk to live a different life. Only she wouldn't, couldn't take even one step backwards because she realized that there were no do-overs for her. This was her life as she had played it, and she got it that she had to do this, tough out this first morning, turn this one day of work into this week of work, into this year, into this life. She shifted slightly to avoid their stares, but she would not walk away from Portland Truck and Warehouse.

Alvin Jones came out of the office. To the increasing curiosity of the men, the dispatcher walked over to the woman and handed her a stack of papers, spoke to her briefly, then smiled and laughed at something she said in return. She smiled back at Jones, bright and warm, and he patted her on the shoulder.

The drivers watched Jones turn away as the woman jumped from the edge of the dock to the yard and walked toward the line of city tractors. To their amazement she stopped before one of the tractors, momentarily checked her paperwork, then climbed aboard and fired up the diesel engine

Bill Marquez stepped out of the crowd of drivers and greeted the dispatcher with, "Hey, Al, who's that?"

Jones studied him for a second, a wicked twinkle in his eye. "She's a new driver, Bill. The front office put her on a few days ago."

Roger Madden asked for many, "Yeah, what the hell kind of license she got, Al?"

"Same as yours," Jones answered him. "Commercial."

"How'd the hell she get that?" Jake Tennyson followed up.

"I don't know," replied Jones. "Why not ask her?"

Tennyson shook his head and grunted, "Yeah, I don't think so," and he looked out across the yard at the woman sitting in the tractor a heavy frown creeping over his features, as if seeing something he didn't want to see. "Women just talk in circles, ya know."

"To you maybe," said Madden with a wink. "I don't have so much trouble with them."

Tennyson looked at Madden. "Ya know, Roger, maybe that's because you got a dick for a brain."

The drivers had all heard of such things as lady truck drivers, but only a few had ever seen one. It was something new and felt odd, out of place, like a shadow seen out of the corner of their eye.

"Well, if they hired her," Bill Marquez said hesitantly, "I guess they know what they're doing."

Tennyson looked dead at Marquez, his eyebrow raised in a testy rebuke. "Marquez, these bosses can't find their asses with both hands and a flashlight. They wouldn't recognize a truck driver if he walked up and bit them. That girl doesn't belong here."

Madden nodded half in agreement. "I kinda agree with you, Jake," and he chuckled, mostly to himself. "I mean, a woman looks more natural on her back than in a truck."

"Best think again, Roger," Al Jones admonished. "The times, they are a'changing on all you roosters."

Marquez ignored the banter and ambled away from the little group of drivers, going over to the edge of the dock where he watched Marylyn Perski bobtail the tractor toward the other end of the warehouse.[16] She slowed before a row of half-set trailers,[17] rolled the tractor forward a bit, stopped, and moved on until the number on the trailer matched the number on her paperwork. After that, and with no more hesitation, she pulled forward and backed up under the trailer for the hookup. Marquez grunted to himself as she swung up behind the tractor to attach the air and electric lines. It sure looked to him like the woman knew what she was doing.

When Marquez got back to the little knot of drivers, Jones was handing around the day's paperwork. When he got to Marquez he asked, "She meet with your approval, Bill?"

"I don't know," Bill replied, trying hard to give Jones a serious look. "She might know what she's doing. It'll take a while to figure it out."

"Oh, I'll know," Madden cut in with a salty laugh, "just as soon as I see her in her underwear."

"Come on, Roger," Jones popped. "Stop being a dick."

Madden laughed again walked off toward the yard.

Marquez took the bills of laden Jones handed him. "How'd she get the job, Al? Just walk in and ask for it?"

---

16. Bobtailing a tractor is common expression for driving a tractor without a trailer.

17. A half-set trailer is usually a 24 or 26 foot trailer, to be hooked up to another half-set to make a full set of double trailers pulled by a single tractor. In some states, three half sets can be hooked up together to made a set of triples. Triples (or trips) are only allowed on highways and in nearly all states and Canada are illegal on surface roads except for brief connection routes between terminals and the open highway.

"That's a pay-grade question," Jones replied with a wry smile. "And it's above mine. Why not ask personnel if you're so curious?"

"Yeah. Right." Marquez knew the limits of his pay graded too. "I'll be sure and do that," and slapping the papers against his leg, Marquez went into the yard to hunt up his tractor.

He looked around only once to watch the woman roll past where he stood by the front wheel of his cab. Perski glanced in his direction and nodded ever so slightly, then went on her way out of the yard with the half set trailer, stopping momentarily at the guard shack to check-out with security. She leaned out of the window, handing her paperwork to the guard. Most unusual, Marquez thought, seeing her blond hair shining in the morning sunlight. He smiled to himself; she sure didn't looking like any trucker he'd ever met. Marquez knew that he was probably wasn't the only man in the yard considering this, and he realized that he wanted to have to get a closer look at this lady truck driver.

Marquez got his chance two mornings later when he came an hour earlier than dispatch for a load that had three delivery stops in Bend. He parked his car and started walking down the driveway toward the yard when the guard at the entrance leaned out of the window of his shack and motioned for Marquez to come closer.

"That lady truck driver," the guard said to Marquez. "She got here about an hour ago. I gave her the paperwork—got a long run up to Seattle. I don't know what's going on, but I think she's having some kind of trouble in there."

"What kind of trouble?"

"Don't know. It's too dark and foggy for me to see the other end of the yard. I can hear the tractor idling, but that set of doubled ain't hooked up yet.[18] I can't leave the guard shack. I thought

18. Two half-set trailers hooked together by a converter gear to form in a single unit.

I should tell someone. Maybe you can take a look, Marquez?"

"Okay. Thanks." Marquez hurried into the yard.

It was getting light enough for him to make out the tractor at the far end of the warehouse. It was sitting still, idling, like the guard had said, and he could see Perski standing behind it looking at one of the trailers. A converter gear was set before the trailer, the tongue tilted upward, which was typical for a parked gear. Marquez immediately guessed her problem.

"Hey, what's up?" he shouted to her as he drew closer.

She turned, looking upset. "The converter gear,"[19] she answered. "I can't get it down."

That was what Marquez had guessed. He came up to her. "How much you weigh?"

"About one-twenty-five."

"Yeah, well you have to weight one-sixty or better to tip the gear."

Marquez put his gloves on, went over to the gear and jumped up, grabbing the eye of the tongue. Hanging there for second, his weight slowly counter balancing the tilted gear, he brought it down, landing it on the wheeled front peg.

He took off his gloves and looked at her. "I weigh a buck-eighty and it's still a little tough for me to tip the gear. You think you got it from here?"

"I think so," only she didn't sound too sure of her answer.

"I'm Bill Marquez."

---

19. When two half-sets are hooked together, the separate, rolling fifth-wheel unit that links the trailers is called a converter gear—i.e., the gear converts a single trailer to a set of double trailers. In the situation described above, gears are often stored with the tongue tipped upward to save space. The tongue of the gear, from fifth wheel to the eye of the coupling, can be as long as twelve feet. Storing the gear with the tongue tilted upward eliminates this extra length and allows for twice as many gears to be stored in a single location. In the situation described in the story, the gear is set before the half-set with the tongue tiled up to get it out of the traffic flow in the yard. This is a common practice in truck terminals.

"Marylyn," she took his extended hand. "Marylyn Perski."

"Russian?"

"My family's Polish."

"Well, mine is Salvadorian, and let me know if I can be of any more help."

"Thanks."

Marquez walked back up the yard to the row of tractors and got into his. He pressed the start button that shook the engine awake, then waited a few moments, turning on the wipers to knock the drizzle off the glass and letting the diesel warm up. He leaned forward, resting on the steering wheel, and followed the woman's actions, frowning. She was still struggling with the gear, only this time trying to move it, push it into position in front of the rear trailer so she would finish the doubles hook-up. Marquez watched as her feet continued to slide on the wet asphalt, the gear not budging.

"Hey, Bill, what's up with that shit?"

Marquez looked down at another driver, a tall, rangy guy they called Looper. He was leaning against the door of Marquez's tractor and was watching Perski. Several more men had now entered the yard and had climbed onto the dock. At the end of the row of trailers, the dispatch office light had come on. The woman was starting to draw an audience.

"She's having trouble with the gear," Marquez replied. "She's not heavy enough to push it around."

"You think we outta help her?" Looper wondered.

"I don't know. There won't be anybody to help her once she leaves the terminal." Marquez saw her feet slip out from under her and she fell to her hands and knees. "Ah, shit! Maybe I'd better," and he put his tractor in gear and bobtailed over to where Marylyn was getting back to her feet.

"You all right?" Marquez asked, looking down at her.

She dusted the dirt off her pants. "I can't move the damn gear."

Marquez noted the more than marginal bite in her voice and climbed down from his tractor. "They might have to give you a tractor with a gear hook[20] in the front," he said. "We got one city tractor like that." He put on his gloves. "Come on, the asphalt's a little slippery—I'll help you with the gear." And the two of them muscled the gear into place before the trailer.

She pulled off her gloves and examined her red hands. "Am I supposed to do this by myself?"

"Yeah, we're all supposed to," Marquez answered her. "It's a matter of swinging your physical weight more than anything else. Get in your tractor. I'll help you finish the hook-up."

Perski climbed up into the cab and backed the first trailer up to the gear. Marquez lifted the eye of the gear onto the hook at the rear of the trailer, then wrapped the safety chain around the tow loop.[21] He stood up and glanced over to the dispatch office as she slammed the gear under the second trailer. A knot of drivers had gathered and were watching the little drama at his end of the yard. Marquez was pretty sure he knew what they were thinking, because he was thinking the same thing: Marylyn Perski could never handle this job without help.

---

20. Some tractors come equipped with a recessed hook in the front bumper that allows for a converter gear to be attached at that point and be pushed around by driving the tractor rather than manhandling the gear. This devise is more often found in local, city tractors than line tractors (over the road tractors). These are specialized pieces of equipment and not common. Often, there are gear hooks mounted at the rear frame of both city and line tractors, but this is for towing as maneuvering the gear in reverse from this position is usually a blind operation making it nearly impossible to use the towing hook for proper gear placement.

21. In the event that the gear hook fails there is a safety chain wound through a steel loop firmly attached to the rear of the towing trailer.

When they finished attaching the hoses, Marquez asked her, "Where are you headed with this load?"

"Seattle. A warehouse at the harbor—got shrink wrapped rolls of paper."

"That's a sweet run," Marquez observed. "About six hours of windshield time." He backed up a step and waved at the trailers. "It's all palletized and'll be loaded on the trailers by fork lift. But you're still going to have to break up the set and re-hook it."

She didn't answer, but by the expression on her face Marquez could see that she was worried and upset by the prospect.

"Look," he added. "Up there you'll be at a Longshoremen facility. They're pretty clannish union guys and won't be too happy about getting into Teamster business, but you can probably get a couple of them guys to help you push the gear around. Try smiling and looking pretty," and he immediately saw from the flash in her eyes that this crack didn't sit well with her. He quickly changed course and added, "I'll see if Jones can assign you the city tractor with a gear hook."

None of this was making her happy. "I don't want to be treated any different."

Marquez chuckled. "But you are different. You don't weigh enough to manhandle these gears. That's not your fault, it's the way things are."

"But what happens to men working here that weigh what I weigh?"

Frowning, Marquez looked genuinely puzzled. "I don't think I've ever seen a guy working in trucking that was as small as you."

"But what would happen if the company did hire a man that small?"

Marquez didn't want to tell the woman the truth, that if the guy couldn't do the work as assigned he would probably be let go before his thirty-day probationary period ran out. That was all according to the union contract which allowed the companies to assess a driver's performance before permanently attaching his name to the seniority sheet. The union clearly understood the companies' position on the issues of trial work performance and was more-or-less in complete agreement with it.

Knowing that this woman was not up for hearing any of that, Marquez simply said, "I don't know."

The two of them stared at each other for another second or two before Perski repeated defiantly, "Well, I don't want to be treated any different," and she returned to her tractor, climbed in and pulled the set[22] out toward the gate.

"Did you get her straighted out?" the dispatcher, Al Jones asked when Marquez returned to the front of the office. "'Cause whatever was going on down there between you two, it got you late on your run, and her almost three hours behind. What the hell happened?"

"I don't know what to tell you, boss," answered Marquez. "She couldn't move the gear by herself."

The dispatcher frowned at that, but said nothing.

"Ah, shit," Roger Madden piped up. "Aint't that bitch'n. How in the hell is she going to do the job."

Marquez answered Madden's question, but did it while looking at Alvin Jones. "Assign her the city tractor with the gear hook?"

"Bullshit," sounded off Jake Tennyson, the driver mostly likely to object to any change in equipment and work load assignment. "That'll mean taking my tractor, ya know, and my city runs. How in the hell is that gonna work?"

Jake Tennyson was at the top of the seniority sheet, and the oldest driver on the company payroll. He was a man well into

---

22. Shorthand slang for a set-of-doubles (two trailers).

his sixties and looking at retirement at the end of the year. Jones recognizing Tennyson's age, had begun assigning him the local light deliveries. On top of that, Tennyson had the seniority to bid for his equipment, and he had a bid-lock on the lighter city tractor with the front-end gear hook. Until now it looked like a non-issue. As no one wanted to see Tennyson ruin his back in his last year on the job not a peep was heard over him getting the city tractor.

"Don't even think about trying to take my city tractor," Tennyson went on, "or I'll have a fat grievance stuck up this company's sorry ass."

"Ah, come on, Jake," Looper cut in, grinning and winking. "Give the little lady a break—hell, you might get laid, Grandpa?"

"Bullshit, Johnson," Tennyson shot back at Looper. "The only break anyone gets around here is by seniority, ya know, not by being a pretty girl—and fuck you too, Johnson, just by the way."

The other drivers watched Tennyson, knowing that if any driver was going to have a difficult time with a sharp shift in work assignments, it would be Jake Tennyson.

"I'm not giving up my city loads," Tennyson followed up. "That girl ought to start out like any junior driver, ya know, taking the heavy loads. That's fair, and its the contract. If she can't cut it, then the girl's gotta go, and that's all I got to say."

"Jake," butted in the Shop Steward, Carl Heinz, "you bid your starting times and equipment, not the runs or the loads. You get your loads by the grace of Alvin Jones and if Jones here starts giving her light loads instead of you there's nothing you can do about it."

Tennyson stuck his face out with an ugly twist. "So far as I remember, Carl, that city tractor I bid comes with city deliveries, ya know, so I get the light loads this last year here. It is my last year here—you remember that, right?"

"And so what do you want Al to do with her?"

"Shit, I don't care, Carl. Fire her ass."

Heinz threw up his hands. "Spoken like a true union brother."

"Hey, fuck you, Heinz," Tennyson fired at the steward. "She ain't in the union yet, by the way, and I was in this union when you were still kicking the slats out of your crib. What the hell did they ever hire a girl for? It's crazy. They're fucking crazy."

Alvin Jones quickly recognized that this was a conversation that was going nowhere good, and cut it off. "Okay, okay, you two—I'll take this up with the front office. Now you guys get your loads out of the yard," and he waved his hand in irritable dismissal. "Let's go deliver some freight."

Marquez lagged behind, watching the drivers heading for their trucks. He turned to the dispatcher. "So what *are* you going to do with her, Al?"

"*Me?*" Jones shook his head. "Me?—or you guys?"

"It looks like a family problem to me."

"Since when did I become a part of your family?"

"You started out as a driver here, Al, and I don't think you ever left us—not really."

Jones studied Marquez for a moment. What Marquez had said was true, after a fashion. In fact, Jones has started out at Port T&W as a loader, then graduated to driver after some years and an aborted attempt at community college. His roots were working class and his recent elevation to dispatcher had always left him doubtful and clouded with hazy misgivings surrounding loyalty.

"My personal feelings aside, Bill, it's gonna end up a union problem if Jake figures he's getting screwed. Jake's not gonna mess around. So either you guys are gonna get him to cool his jets, or fix the problem, or the union will—they'll deny her a card—'cause, Bill, I don't think the company's even close to letting her go, and please don't ask me why 'cause I don't know why."

Tennyson knew his stuff; all driven equipment was assigned by bid, and being the top man on the seniority list meant that his tractor could not be taken from him. This, and Perski's inability to handle multiple trailers, created a cloud of controversy—and what felt to the men like increasingly random, unequal work assignments.

Without the city tractor and its front end gear hook, Marylyn Perski was only given half-set deliveries, which translated to working half loads. By the middle of the third week, over half way through her probationary period, it seemed clear to the men that even though she was often doubling back to the yard for second trailers, they were often picking up additional loads, causing each man feel like they were doing a small share of her work. On top of that, she was being given light freight runs because it was quickly discovered that she could not pull pallets off the trailers with a hand-jack.[23] Since by OSHA regulations, forklifts were not allowed on trailers that lacked reinforced steel beds, dock workers at her delivery and pickup points frequently had to get into the trailers and help her with the jacks. This wasn't real popular with the clerks and dockmen at her stops, a fact that had fast gotten back to the Portland T & W. Perski was looking too light-weight to do the job.

With Jake Tennyson looking on, a furrowed, but unreadable expression masking his thoughts, several of the drivers began to get on the steward, Carl Heinz, about the change in their work assignments. Heinz felt obliged to bring this lopsidedness up to

---

23. A hand-jack operates on the same principle as a forklift, except that it is manually operated. The jack is run under a pallet and then cranked up to lift the pallet off the bed of the truck. After that the jack and the pallet must be pulled by hand to the end of the truck bed and off via a short ramp. The operation of the jack is not complicated, but pushing or pulling it requires ample body weight and leg strength.

the dispatcher and was informed by Jones that someone high up in the front office was intending to keep Marylyn Perski on the payroll—no matter what. The order had rolled down to the dispatcher that he had to make what adjustments were necessary to see that Perski continued with the company. Heinz felt a mounting frustration.

Heinz asked Jones, "What is it about her, Al, that they're so determined to keep her on? Shit, she's not doing the job, so what the hell."

Jones looked around his shoulder at Heinz. "I honestly don't know, Carl. And to be straight with you, I didn't ask. Not in my job description to wonder about these things."

"Then tell me this," Heinz pursued him. "Why'd they want to hire her in the first place? Why'd they want to start this kinda mess anyway? Somebody up there must have been smart enough to see where it'd lead. And please don't tell me shit happens."

"Carl, I am absolutely *not* going to tell you that shit happens, because shit never *just* happens." Jones put his pencil down and turned to face the union steward. "There's a reason for everything. And just because you—*we*—don't know the reason doesn't mean there isn't one. So Carl, *no*, I'm not gonna tell you some random shit happens, but I am gonna tell you I don't know why Perski was hired on here. That decision, like most of the others made around here, happens up there where only eagles fly and the air gets thin. And Carl, those eagles don't ever tell me squat. So don't ask me the why of anything, much less why they hired a woman to do this kinda work, 'cause I don't know. But I do know that shit just doesn't happen."

Marylyn Perski was born in Brooklyn into an orthodox Jewish family of Polish ancestry. She early tacked hard against the conservative cultural winds and ran off with a Sergeant of Marines, staying with him long enough to be blessed with a son of mixed heritage. Rejected now by her family—or at least by her father, the Cantor of Congregation Beth Shalom, for whom the sudden reality of a *schwartza* for a grandson was a hard smack to his cantankerous Jewish pride—an unexpected presence worthy of a heart attack, which Saul Perski promptly had, followed by a pain-issued string of loud and decidedly unorthodox curses. Marylyn Perski suddenly found herself and her son out on their own in the world.

After assuring herself that her father had not been killed by his grandson's innocent arrival on this earth, Marylyn hit a long and hard road that took her and her baby boy nearly everywhere in the lower forty-eight, supporting the two of them through Manpower casual gigs and stripping.

Marylyn rather enjoyed life as a dancer, for the generous and often fawning attention men offered her, not to mention the easy money, and she stuck with it for a time, working her way across the southern states, zigzagging from New Orleans to San Diego. It was there in San Diego that she took up with a young, good-looking Mexican truck driver. She and her now three-year-old son traveled with the trucker through Mexico and Central America, staying with him long enough to have a second son, and Marylyn presented her family with yet another little person of mixed heritage, but at least not a *schwartza*—the boy might even pass for a Jew someday, albeit a dark one, with hair a bit too coarse and thick in the godly view of her father's pious orthodoxy—however, by the slim grace of a lighter skin tone and straighter hair, a second heart attack for Saul Perski, the Cantor of Congregation Beth Shalom, was avoided.

During her travels south of the border Marylyn was taught to drive heavy-duty rigs by the handsome Mexican trucker. He did this so that Marylyn could take over the wheel for him while he slept. This arrangement was satisfactory for a time, but Marylyn knew she had to get her oldest in school so she and the Mexican truck driver parted ways, with Marylyn heading back to California. After several of years of agony, Marylyn struggling to support her two boys first as a coffee shop waitress, then a department store clerk, she finally returned to dancing. This felt comfortable, the easy comfort of living a recollection of bygone days, but with memory also comes with the uncomfortable weight and drag of years. The mounting anxiety of getting old in a young woman's trade, of seeing her growing children watch her wrestle with the life she had chosen—a choice that was suddenly ganging up on her—slowly filled her with a desperate and angry energy. So while Marylyn could still remember what the Mexican truck driver had taught her she decided to get her CDL,[24] and because she knew of no other way to get that license, and the good paying jobs that came with it, she ponied up the dough for a San Francisco truck driving school. This looked to Marylyn Perski to be the best route to the promised land of financial security for her and hers.

Getting the CDL was easier than getting the job. The San Francisco school taught Marylyn one or two the many gear systems she would encounter, and the basic maneuvers necessary to pass the driving test, but she learned nothing of the day-to-day practicality and complexities that ruled a trucker's life. The thousand details of work world credibility were left untaught, ignored or bypassed; Marylyn had no experience in the real world, and terminal

---

24. Commercial Driving License

dispatchers knew it. But below the conscious level there lurked in these men a more powerful fetish, an unspoken wrinkle in the vast social hinterland, a cultivated and stubborn way of feeling one's way through the world. As they saw it, Marylyn was a woman, and truck driving was not a field ready for women. To the typical personnel manager, such a hire felt—as the drivers at Portland Truck and Warehouse had immediately felt it—an impossibly awkward fit. Women in trucking felt plain weird. So confronted with closed doors and a barely disguised condescension, Marylyn resorted to an alternate path in the landscape bequeathed to her: Marylyn Perksi walked into a San Francisco synagogue and spoke to a Rabbi, who happened to know a guy who knew a guy, who knew another guy, who knew yet another guy up in Portland, and this guy happened to own a trucking and warehouse company, one of the largest and oldest in Oregon. Marylyn traveled north. Life wasn't easy. Not ever. But a woman had to do what a woman had to do.

Perski was aware of the rancor building in the yard. She knew men, knew when they were hurt, when they were vulnerable, knew when they were threatened. Perski knew she was a problem and she did her best to keep her head low, hunker down, and take a shine-it-on attitude, until one day it caught up with her.

Bill Marquez met up with her at a downtown Portland warehouse. He climbed up onto the dock and found her finishing off a pallet for the forklift idling at the end of her trailer.

"Hey, Marylyn" Marquez shouted at her. "Meet me at Frank's Café when you're done here."

Marquez was bent on trying to find out a few things about Perski without telling her why. Much of this was personal, a curiosity itch, but Marquez also knew that her future at Portland Truck and

Warehouse was wrapped up in how well she managed her relations with the other drivers. If Perski was going to stay there were needed changes. Even if Port T & W kept Perski on the payroll, the drivers could make her life there completely unbearable, quite likely forcing her to walk away from the job. Marquez knew that such things had happened before, only for other reasons.

Sitting across from each other over sandwiches and coffee he tried to draw her out. "You're an unknown to these guys, Marylyn. You keep everyone at arm's length."

"No one's been real friendly with me, Bill, now have they?" She worried her lower lip a moment. "What's on your mind, Bill? I know you yanked me here for something besides lunch."

"Ease up, Marylyn." He smiled. "I won't bite. But, yeah, we'd all like to know something about you that would make you out to be something besides a mysterious pain in the ass."

"Is that what I am, Bill? A mysterious pain in the ass?"

"Maybe not mysterious." He hesitated, thinking, then deciding to be candid. "Unusual'd be more like it. You're something that's rocking the boat and these guys don't understand it. I think if we knew more about you it'd take the unusual out of things."

"But not the pain in the ass part?"

Bill shrugged. "I don't know. Maybe that too. You don't have to talk to me if you don't want to, of course. But you gotta make friends with someone, right?"

"And you want to be my friend?"

"Maybe."

"You know I know men."

"I'm sure."

"I know what *friend* usually means."

"Christ, girl, give me a chance, will ya?"

Perski considered Marquez for a moment, watching him cautiously, finally figuring that she had to start somewhere with someone. She began slow and calculated.

"Bill, I'm used to living my life on my own terms," she said. "Only now with my kids things are different."

"How so?"

Perski reflected another moment, watching his roughly handsome face carrying a look that was more than simple curiosity; she read in it genuine concern.

"I'm used to making good money," she said. "So I never had to lean on my family, but now I'm getting a bit old to make money the way I used to."

"How was that?"

"Dancing."

Marquez toyed with his cup for a moment. "You mean stripping?"

Perski smiled. "Exotic dancer," she corrected.

He smiled in return and nodded his head. "Exotic dancer," he corrected himself. "And your family didn't know."

"Oh, they knew, Bill. I was never ashamed of anything I did. My problems with them are different—at least my problems with my father."

"Your kids."

Perski nodded. "They're mixed race."

"And your family can't get past that?"

"My mom is okay with it. But not my dad—he doesn't want anything to do with my kids—or me."

Marquez dropped his head. "Jesus, Marylyn."

"It's the way the world is, Bill. I've accepted it. I don't hate my dad. He's wrong, but I don't hate him. But now I have to protect my kids—from just about everything—and that means being completely on my own, making good money with a steady job."

Bill shook his head as if to clear it and was silent, blinking at the crumbs on his sandwich plate. He finally shook his head again and changed the subject.

"From stripper to truck driver," he forced a little chuckle. "That's some kind of change-up. I gotta say, though, you don't look much like a truck driver *or* a stripper."

"What does a dancer look like, Bill, when they have all their clothes on," Perski asked with a smile. "If not like any other women standing in the checkout line at the supermarket."

Marquez snorted. "No, Marylyn, not like every other woman."

"You'd be surprised, Bill—and what about being a truck driver? Where's it say in the book of rules that a truck driver's gotta have a dick?"

Nodding, Marquez conceded, "I get your point, Marylyn," then added vaguely, "But I don't know. It looks kinda strange to us, unless you're a lesbian, maybe." Perski made a face at him and he quickly changed the subject. "You ever think about going back to stripping? It's good money, I hear."

She took a sip of coffee and shook her head. "I don't want to raise my kids that way."

"There's nothing illegal about it."

"I know. But I'm almost forty, and time isn't as kind to women as it is to you men, and besides that dancing is still part of the sex trade and kids get confused easily." She paused and smiled again. "Especially boy kids."

"About the moral stuff?"

"It's about more than sex and morals."

"What?"

"The kind of men I attract as a dancer I wouldn't want to bring around."

"They can't be all bad."

"No. I met some really descent guys, but things are what they are, you know, and even the decent guys I've met leave a bread-crumb trail. And like I said, I'm raising two boys."

"They might understand better than daughters."

"No they wouldn't. I know how quickly men get confused."

"You think so?"

"I know so."

"Confused about what?"

"Like about how I got the job at Port."

Grunting, Marquez suddenly realized that this woman seemed always a step ahead of him, and not shy about making it known.

"You're dying to know," she added. "Aren't you, Bill—all of you?"

He chuckled. "Sure we are. All of us—me included. I mean it wasn't through Alvin Jones, 'cause he's as confused as the rest of us."

"Nope," Perski said slowly, watching Marquez carefully. "It wasn't though Alvin."

Marquez shrugged and tried his best to look indifferent before revealing, "We hear that someone in the front office has got the job sewed up for you."

"Wow," she nearly whispered. "That didn't take long."

"Take long . . ?"

"Yeah, to get to the sex part."

"Marylyn—Jesus," Marquez protested, "that's not what I meant."

"Maybe not, but it's right where you guys go when you get confused."

"Not confused, Marylyn—curious."

"It comes from the same place."

"Not sex, Marylyn."

"But you still want to know if it's about sex?"

Her continued blunt probing kept Marquez off guard. He rolled his eyes, shrugging his shoulders again, realizing that Perski was sharp and unafraid. He raised his hands in a small helpless gesture. "I don't know. A boyfriend in the office, maybe," he finally admitted.

She put her cup down and forced the issue. "Let's cut out the bullshit, Bill. I didn't fuck anybody to get the job. And you can feel free to repeat that to every guy in the yard."

"Not every guy's thinking that." He felt his skin flush with the lie.

"Sure they are, Bill. You don't think I know men, know the way they think?" Perski waited, irritated, waiting for Marquez to say something, but when nothing came, she added, "A smart woman survives in this world by understanding exactly how you men think."

"And how's that?"

"Too much in straight lines," she answered, the irritation still present. "Usually, because you're not thinking, you're feeling—straight from your dick to your brain—Christ, you're the biggest gossipers in the world." Marylyn watched as Bill smiled crookedly at the sassy conviction in her voice. She went on, "I can't help how any of those guys are feeling, but you can tell them for me that I'm not fucking anybody in the office."

"Damn," he observed. "You're something else, Marylyn."

Perski fidgeted her cup for a moment and wondered for a moment if she could tell Bill about the Rabbi in San Francisco and the networking he had done for her, but decided against it. She did not want to throw in the fact that she was a Jew who had worked a network of Jews—not into this situation. Perski knew all too well where that truth might lead: an inconvenient slide down into conspiracy theories and Jew baiting. No thank you!

She finally added, "There's really nothing confusing about it. I got the job through a friend."

"At P-T & W?"

"No, it was just somebody who knew somebody," she replied vaguely, then clarified: "I don't know anyone in the office, Bill. My contact came from somewhere else—South— the Bay area—Frisco. And no, nobody I was fucking there either. And, anyway, I don't want my job sewed up except by my own work. I'd like that to be real clear."

"You know you're getting all light loads and single trailers?"

"Tell me something I don't know, Bill."

Marquez unexpectedly realized that Perski was free of anything underhanded. He got the message in her tone, in her body language, he got it because he realized that she was a calculating woman, not a conniving one. She was a survivor and was being straight ahead with him and he liked it.

"Bill, look," she went on, "I have no rich-man's education from NYU or UCLA—I'm a high-school drop-out, for Christ's sake. I got no rich parents, no rich husband. My mother's a secretary and my dad owns a small bakery shop in Brooklyn. I'm broke and I need to support my two boys and I can't do that working some shit job at a department store and I'm not going back to dancing for a whole bunch of reasons. I need the money and benefits I get here, so you tell me, Bill—tell me how to I fix this with the men in the yard? I really want to fix it, Bill—I *need* to fix it. I need these men to want me there on my terms, not forced on them by the company's terms." She hesitated, then added, "only I can't stop being a woman, Bill—sorry."

"It's not about your being a woman, Marylyn."

"Sure it is, Bill, and it's just as big a problem for me as it is for you and the other men in the yard." She puffed up her cheeks and made an exasperated sound expelling the air. "I work as hard as any man in the yard—Harder, I think, than some. It's all about me being a woman."

Marquez was stumped. In a way he knew she was right. Tennyson complained more than any of the other men, yet even he was not able to do the job like he did even five years ago. Everyone knew it and everyone cut Tennyson some slack. Yeah, Perski was right. It was because she was a woman, but he'd be damned if he could figure out exactly what it was about her being a woman; it wasn't her, it wasn't the sex; Marquez knew there was a something beyond the simple, upfront stuff. He could feel it, yet could not identify it.

"Bill," she said. "You men can't get past seeing me as a woman and there's no fixing that because being a woman's not the problem. The problem is the way you're seeing me, and maybe that can't be fixed either because being a man isn't the problem either."

Marquez understood her. He knew that tall or short, fat or skinny, old or young, when he heard a woman's voice he heard it in a different place than when he heard the voices of men; when he looked at a woman he saw her in a different place than the place where he saw men. Both these different places caused him to act and think differently about and around women. He couldn't explain it. It was like some kind of imprint, in the center of the way he was—and in the center of where all men had been planted in their universe; their feeling place for a woman was different than their feeling place for another man. Perski was dead on. There was no fixing this because it wasn't about being rational. It was something different that thinking. His being a man made him *feel* about women more than think about them.

Seeing a thoughtfulness in Bill's face, Perski asked. "Can you do something for me?"

"What?"

"Help me get past some of this bullshit."

"I don't know, Marylyn. I'm not sure what I can do."

"Will you try, Bill? You want to be my friend. Okay, I'm telling you, I need a friend."

Marquez dropped his face slightly, lowering his gaze, letting his look rest on the crumbs littering his plate. "Jesus, Marylyn, you being here shouldn't be so big a problem."

"Well, Bill, it is a problem, at least in this world. But you know what . . . ?" She waited for him to look back up at her. " . . . It's a problem women get used to, at least as much as we can, and once we get used to it, it makes us smarter than the average bear. I've learned to make the problem work for me, not against me, but this—this is way different. I can't find a way to make it work for me." She hesitated, struggling to find the words. "I can sense the resentment, Bill, the annoyance, or something—I don't know what it is—not exactly—but I feel like I can reach out and grab it, only I can't, but I think you can. Get beyond the stupid rumors and the sex shit. I think you can, Bill."

"Fuck, em," he replied. "You stay, Marylyn, and they'll have to get used to you."

"No they won't, Bill."

It was late Friday of the following week before Carl Heinz caught up with Jones. "Al, you know you're forcing the men to pick up Perski's heavy loads." There was a slight edgy bite behind his words, Heinz sounding as though it were somehow possible for the dispatcher to overlook what Heinz thought was obvious.

"Really, Carl?" Jones responded with an equally sharp edge to his voice. "Didn't we have this settled?" He jabbed his thumb at the front office door. "Shit rolls downhill today—just like it did yesterday."

"Come on, Al. Is 'shit rolls downhill' a good enough answer for making these guys pick up her work?"

Jones turned fully to face the steward. "What would you like me to say, Carl?"

"You can start by admitting that it's not fair."

Jones looked steady at the Steward. "Carl, show me where the word 'fair' appears in the union contract?"

"How about being fair in life?"

Jones gave the steward an incredulous snort. "That's even more stupid. I can't believe I'm hearing a *black* man talking to *another* black man about being fair in life."

"Who else has a better right?"

Jones smiled sardonically. "Righteous, brother Carl—and slick, but don't be too quick to tie that can to my tail."

"What's that supposed to mean?"

"Fair, Carl—fair. I mean I'm talking about being fair. All you guys do is bitch—bitch about nothing—about squat. No one is doing Perski's work for her, Carl. No one! It feels that way to you guys because you're seeing her only pulling half-sets, but she's making far more delivery stops than anyone else in the yard. That girl is busting her ass, brother—busting her ass."

When Heinz stayed silent, Jones added, "Fair means something different for everyone, Carl." He studied the steward for a second. "And for your information, if anyone's working harder around here, brother, it's me. I'm spending a hell of a lot of my time shifting the work load so that our little miss Perski is getting all the pain-in-the-butt, chicken shit deliveries and pick-ups you guys want nothing to do with. You ought to be buying that girl flowers rather than trying to bump her off." He made an exasperated face at Heinz. "And by the way, buy me some too, while you're at it, because that girl's changing the hell out of my life, too. And I'm not sure that's fair either. That woman is changing everything around here, but fair or not, isn't change the nature of life?"

For a moment Heinz continued to remain silent. The steward liked Al Jones, even admired him a bit, and knew the man's loyalties were mixed; Jones had *management* written on his forehead, but *worker* tattooed on his ass. He knew that Jones would do his job for the company, yet keep to a code of equal treatment of all the drivers.

"Al, damn it, I hear you, but these men are up my butt with this," he said, pressing the issue. "What they see is what they see and my being steward means I gotta see what they see. I got to tell them something, Al."

"Then tell 'em to lighten up, Carl. Lighten up on her—and you. Nothing gonna change here, Carl. Nothing. Perski's staying."

The door to the dispatch office opened and Jake Tennyson came in followed by Roger Madden. Tennyson looked agitated.

"Where the hell's my flatbed for Bendix Machine?"

"Perski took it," answered Jones.

"What she do that for?" demanded Tennyson.

Jones gave him a squirrelly kind of look and asked with more than a hint of sarcasm, "I didn't know you wanted the OT, Jake?"

"I don't," Jake shot back. "I hate overtime, but that's not my question. Bendix Machine is my run. Why'd you give it to the girl?"

"So you could go home, I guess," replied Jones.

"Bullshit!" snapped Tennyson, angrily. "She wanted to make me look bad."

"How's that working, Jake?" Jones demanded. "Bendix is crane loaded."

"By getting in here faster than me," Tennyson answered him. "I tell you that girl's got it in for me."

"Whoa, Jake," Heinz stepped in. "Ease up."

"Ease up, my ass." Tennyson drew a breath, subsiding slightly, then asked, "I mean, why didn't *she* want to go home. I thought she had a couple of kids and needed to get home herself?"

"She does, Jake," Jones replied, "but I think she knew you wanted to go home too."

"Oh, bullshit, she ain't doing me any favors," Tennyson snapped, then repeated, "She's trying to make me look bad."

"The other reason," added Jones, "is that having two kids is a damn good reason to take the overtime you didn't want. Anyway, I made the call. It was my decision, Jake, not her's"

"This just feels all wrong, ya know," Tennyson proclaimed loudly. "All wrong." He shook his head and looked at Jones. "Doesn't she feel wrong to you, Al?"

"I think you ought to punch out and go home, Jake," the dispatcher replied, turning back to his paperwork. "And give us all a break."

Tennyson frowned at Jones's back, muttered an expletive under his breath before stomping out of the office.

"That sure seemed to frost his nuts," observed Madden, peering through the office window and watching Tennyson march down the dock.

Jones, glancing at Madden, thought for a moment, wondering how deep he could go with the young driver. He finally replied, "I guess it's hard to get cranky old guys used to how things are changing around them."

Madden turned away from the window and snorted. "Shit, boss, he ain't the only one, and I ain't a cranky old fart."

"You can't stop change, Roger." Heniz spoke up. "You can only get used to it."

"Damn, Carl," Madden snorted. "Who's side you on?"

"Everyones," Heinz shot back. "What the hell's your problem with her—your real problem?"

Madden started ginning. "It's goddamn confusing."

"What is?"

"Perski," replied Madden. "Every time I see her ass climbing down out of that truck I can't figure out if I want to kick it, or kiss it."

Jones, snorted and observed, "I think I can answer that one for you, Madden."

Madden laughed, misinterpreting Jones's crack for a compliment. "I guess you know me, boss, but at least I'm not crazy with her shit like old Jake. Man, *I* bet that old guy's wife must be a peach."

Jones looked up from his paperwork. "Roger, both you and Jake see Perski as not belonging here—that her being here messes with what you know. The only difference between you and Jake is that you're working your way through the shit in a different way."

"Yeah," Madden retorted. "How's that?"

"Because you're both dealing with her the way you've *always* been dealing with women," Jones answered him. "At least that's what I guess. You're trying by looking at her as a piece of ass and Tennyson's looking at her as a sassy-ass. But neither way's gonna work—not with this woman. She's too smart for that."

"Come on, Al," Madden looked hurt. "That ain't fair."

"Carl and me were just talking about that." Alvin Jones smiled, but at Heinz, not Madden. "About life being fair, and all."

"And what'd you come up with?"

"The same old tired shit."

Both the front and back doors were propped open, and all the fans spinning; still, Jack's Place across the street from the terminal was baking like an oven. It was unseasonably warm for Portland.

"Hey, Carl," Marquez greeted the Steward as he took the bar stool next to him. "I heard about Perski taking some of Jake's over runs, and one of Roger's too."

"Yeah," Heinz answered. "She did—been doing a bunch'a extra everywhere."

"Good." Marquez signaled the bartender, holding up a single finger. "Glad to see it."

"Why?"

"Why—what? You don't think she's doing enough?"

Heinz turned and looked at Marquez. "I don't know what enough means. But I still want to know why you're glad to see it?"

Not understanding the accusing skepticism in the steward's question, Marquez hesitated, then answered, "Kids—no other family—no place to go."

"I got two kids myself," Heinz replied dryly. "So do half the men in the yard. Hell, Big Jim Harden has five kids. What's new about that?"

"Yeah, but we can go get other jobs—she can't."

"Bullshit," Heinz exclaimed. "She's got places she can go."

"Damn, Carl," Marquez leaned back. "Ease up on her. Where'd that bug up your ass come from?"

Letting the tension drain from his shoulders, Heinz took a slow sip of his beer. "Pressure, Bill. I'm just pissed at my being a steward right now. You should try it sometime. Politics—you can't make anyone happy, so you end up looking like an asshole to everyone."

"What's going on?"

"Perski."

"What'd ya mean?"

Heinz stalled a second, ~~talking~~ TAKING a long swallow from his beer. He finally said, "I'll bet she could find herself another good paying job. Get her off my plate."

Marquez caught something in his tone. "What's up, Carl?"

Heinz shrugged and stared at his beer bottle.

"Carl?" Marquez probed. "What's going on?"

"I hope she finds herself another job," answered the steward.

Marquez still sensing an undertone to the stewards voice, asked, "Where, Carl? A chickenshit job in fast food? Where else can she go and get a good paying job? She's got ambitions for her kids and herself. Where the hell else is she going to go, Carl?"

"Someplace else, Wild Bill. Anyplace else."

Something was wrong. Marquez could sense it. "Come on, Carl, she's trying. You know she's trying."

Heinz wagged head. "Jesus, Bill, I'm getting all choked up."

"Be serious, Carl." HIS

"I am being serious, Bill." Heinz turned and looked straight into Marquez's face. "Wild Bill, everybody's getting way too involved with this—with her situation. I mean, it ain't a normal situation."

"Because she's a woman?"

"I mean the way she's doing the job."

"Doing it differently, you mean."

Heinz nodded. "Yeah, Bill, that would be what makes the situation not normal."

"Can we change it?"

"What, her being a woman, or her not exactly doing the job?"

"She is doing the job, Carl, just differently."

"Try explaining that to the men in the yard, Bill."

"Can't you?"

"That'll be an uphill run."

"For you too? You against her because she's a woman?"

Heinz spun on his stool and quietly watched Marquez for a second. "Bill, don't start any shit with me, okay—just because I'm black doesn't mean that I'm all gone crazy liberal on this."

"That's not what I meant."

"I know what you meant, Bill, and I'm just like the rest of those men, and I feel like they do. It feels like I'm pulling a little of her share of her work every day and it's irritating as hell." He shook his head. "Jones swears no one is pulling her work, but that's not the way it feels. I honestly don't know if what I'm seeing is real, or I'm not seeing it right. All I know is that things are different and damn it, I'm trying not to be an asshole about it either. But there does seem something unfair about this, don't you think? Doesn't it seem that way to you? Christ, Bill, there are good union jobs with the Retail Clerks. They get good pay and bennies, maybe not as good as we got, but good enough. Maybe she should go get on with one of their union stores." He stood up off the barstool and reached for a napkin. "Look, Bill, I like Perski. She's a real nice lady, and I get it that she's got a couple of kids and wants to get ahead for herself and them." He used the napkin to wipe the sweat off his forehead and cheeks. "Damn, when's Jack gonna get this dump air conditioned." He leaned forward and tossed the napkin at the trash bucket behind the bar. "Bill I get it. Perski's just like us—got the same problems, needs the same money, but there other ways for her to go so, yeah, women don't belong doing our job, and so, yeah, I think humming her sad song to me is an uphill move with me too."

"So where does it go from here?"

"Nowhere, Bill," the steward answered with a dip of his head. "Nowhere at all."

"So she's just fucked?"

"Jesus, Bill." Heinz laughed at Marquez. "You really got to start tapping that shit. Get it out of your system."

"Carl," Marquez cracked. "You say that again and I'll knock you off that fucking bar stool." The crack wasn't friendly.

The steward turned to face Marquez, a stern glint to this eyes. "Okay, Wild Bill, okay, I got you—where you stand—so I gotta tell you something that's not gonna make you happy. Not one damn bit happy. Hell, it sure doesn't make me happy." The steward took another pull from the bottle and set it deliberately on the bar, studying it, for a moment not wanting to look at Marquez. "Nobody knows this, yet, Bill—nobody. I just found out about it last night." He finally turned and looked at Marquez. "The Local's gonna file a grievance on Perski against P-T&W."

"For what, Carl?" Marquez exploded. "On Perski? Port hasn't broken any clause in the contract with her. Alvin Jones has held tight to the contract in work assignments. He's been real careful about that. What the hell they gonna file on?"

"Arbitrary work assignments and favoritism."

"Jesus," muttered Marquez. "What the fuck?"

"The Local might even get OSHA involved."

"OSHA? Why?"

"Dangerous work conditions."

"That's crazy. The union's really gonna do that—sic OSHA on her?"

"They gotta cover their ass, I suppose," answered Heinz indifferently. "Everybody's gotta cover their ass these days."

"Who's filing the favoritism grievance—Tennyson?"

Heinz shook his head and looked at Marquez. "No, not Tennyson. Not anyone. It's being filed by the Local as a general yard grievance. In certain situations the Local is allowed to do that—step in as a third party to solve problems where no one else wants to take the hit. Look, Bill, lots of guys have come to me, but none of them wanted their name on the grievance." He shrugged. "I don't care how hard she's working, but a bunch of the men want her gone, but they're still trying to find a way out of thinking about themselves as assholes for doing it."

"That's gonna take a lot of deep thinking."

"Bill, none of these guys want to think of themselves as beating up on a woman with a couple of kids, but this shit's just too deep an adjustment for them."

"So they're hiding behind the union."

"Politics are funny goddamn thing, Bill," the Steward observed. "Sometimes you can live with things as a group that you couldn't live with solo."

"Yeah, and that makes it fair for Perski, right?"

"Nobody ever said majority-rule was fair, Bill. In fact democracy is probably the most unfair thing there is. The idea of it is fair, not the reality—ask any black man."

"Or woman."

"Or woman," Heinz conceded. "Shit, even *white* women—but how in the hell are we gonna live in an everyday world without some little taste of unfairness? Answer me that? Sure, we ought'a make room for someone like Perski. But you know what, Bill? I'm living in the real world, not in some goddamn social experiment."

"Yeah, but where would you be, a black guy, if no one was fair enough to make room for someone different like you."

"You know why you're wrong there, Bill? You think because I'm black that I'm different than you. Well, you're wrong. I ain't different than you. You think I *look* different, but I'm exactly the same as you, and you know what, you expect me to be the same as you, do the same as you, work the same as you. If there's anything unfair about this situation it's that's she *is* different than us, but we don't expect her to *work* different than us. We want her to do the same work for the same pay and she can't. This *ain't* about being equal, Bill. It's about being different, and there ain't a scale in the world you can put *different* on."

"What about Jake?" objected Marquez. "He's different. He works different."

Adamantly, Heinz shook his head. "You're wrong again, Bill. Jake's an *older* version of us, not a *different* version. He started out the same as us, but like we'll all do, he got older. Perski is different right from jump-street. Damn, Jake is sixty-five. Can you imagine Perski trying to do this job when *she's* sixty-five?"

Marquez was quiet.

"Bill," Heinz went on, almost gently. "You're adjusted to Peski, want her here, and I think I know why. It sounds crazy, but I think it comes from the same place that makes these other guys want her gone. You want to protect her, and that's great, but it's only because of the thing that makes her different."

Heinz waited. When Marquez stayed quiet, he added. "Bill, don't you get it, what's making her different is the work, not the men. Who knows, maybe someday the world we work in will change and being different won't matter anymore. Don't blame these guys, Bill, they didn't make the world, they just live here. So let the union and OSAH do their job. Let them be the assholes in this and let everybody else off the hook—me included." And suddenly he turned to the bartender at the far end of the bar. "Hey, Jack, get this dump air-conditioned, will ya, damn it?" he fired angrily. "Or I'll be drinking my beer someplace else."

From down at the other end of the bar Jack raised his middle finger.

In a little over a week, Perski lost the single trailers, lost the light loads, lost the short runs. It seemed to Perski that her working life had gone to hell in the blink of an eye. The first morning when she got to the yard and saw her bills of laden, which indicated a full set of doubles, she took a fast double-take on the paperwork. Pulling the set didn't bother her. In a straight line, two trailers act like one; they follow the driver round. It was the splitting-up of the doubles and the necessary muscling of the converter gear that grabbed her attention. She remembered one of her first days at P-T&W when Bill Marquez had to help her hook up.

"I don't think I've ever seen a guy working in trucking that was as small as you," Marquez had said.

And what was someone as small as her to do, except push the envelope. So Perski sucked it up, stuffed the bills on her clipboard, and went to work. That was when things really went to hell. To anyone looking down the road it was predictable, only no one was looking down that particular road. All eyes were on the road to equal work for equal pay, but that was not the road Perski was on. Perski worked as hard as any man, maybe harder. Yet that wasn't enough, couldn't be enough. Perski still worked different and that put her on the road with more twists and turns, steeper ups and sharper downs.

"You are a hell of a lot to get used to," Bill Marquez had announced way back then, recognizing the newness about her, pointing out the difference that was her.

Perski was anxious about the difference, but satisfied with it, adjusted to it, even when she chose to think about her lonely place with these men—a little proud of it. Yet the difference set her apart. In the crowd she moved and worked in, Perski was alone. It seemed that no individual could help her. It was relief from the way of the world she needed. The men at Port T&W, like nearly all people everywhere, lived unconscious in the way of the world.

No more than fish noticed the water they swam in, did any man question the sea of ideas into which he had been flung at birth. That the men hardly produced an equal output was never questioned by them, just as Perski's increased effort seemed to be noticed by none. The fact that she was different, that she was a woman was all that was seen.

It is what it is—Marylyn Perski hatred that expression more than any other she had ever heard, yet—*it is what it is.*

Confronted with myopia, Perski redoubled her efforts to overturn the idea of her, and the windy road she traveled became a shorter road. It took less than two weeks for it to happen. If blame was to be assigned, it must go to the armada of inherited ideas rather than the heads they had invaded.

Alvin Jones got off the phone and returned to the men in the dispatch office. "You guys better start figuring something out."

"What do you mean, Al?" Marquez asked.

"It means I want out of the loop on this one," he replied with a bite. "This isn't company business—not anymore."

Looper asked, "What you talking about, Al?"

"I'm talking about Perski," answered Jones, rocking slightly in his chair and eyeing the drivers in the dispatch room. "It looks like now that you guys have the union and OSHA involved in this shit, things are going sideways."

His avoiding a glance at Jake Tennyson was noticed.

Tennyson spoke up angrily, "Hey, Al, don't be starting any shit with me, because I didn't go to OSHA."

The biggest man in the room, Jim Harden, stepped up, immediately taking the heat out of the potential exchange. "What do you mean, Al? What went sideways?"

"It means that I want two of you out to Ryerson Wire and Cable and pick up Perski's rig. The girl hurt herself on a converter gear."

"How?" Looper wanted to know.

"The gear started rolling on her, and to stop it she dropped it on its front stand," replied Jones. "Only the stand didn't land on the ground, it landed on part of her foot. She says nothing's busted, but this is some kind of wake-up call. The company's keeping her, so you guys better figure out what to do about her."

"Where is she now?" Marquez asked.

"Paramedics went and got her," replied Jones, drumming his pencil on the desk top. "They took her to OSHU. What I want to know is how the hell did that gear start rolling on her?"

Marquez answered him. "When you unhook the second trailer over at Ryerson you have to pull the gear out of the way by muscling it catty-corner on a small incline. The incline isn't much—but for her..." Marquez dropped his eyes to the floor and shook his head. "A gear can get away from you, if you're not careful."

"What you mean is," interrupted Harden, "if you're not heavy enough to push it."

"Okay, okay," Jones shortstopped the debate. "Whatever caused it, this accident is sure gonna ramp up OSHA's investigation here." He tossed his pencil on the desk. "You guys better figure out something. Nobody wants OSHA crawling up their ass."

"Maybe the job just figured it out for us," observed Madden.

Jones looked hard at Madden. "Yeah, Roger, the next guy that says something stupid like that I'll make sure he's first in line to be interviewed by some even dumber bureaucrat from OSHA."

Al Jones let that hang for a second, then followed up with,

"Okay, Marquez, I want you and Big Jim to go get her rig back here. Take one of the company cars to get over to Ryerson;

then Johnson, take a second company car and go get Perski from OSHU—the emergency room. I'll call her and let her know you're coming."

"Give me one of the big four doors," Looper said. "In case she has to sit in the back seat."

"Forget it, Johnson," Tennyson suddenly stood up, butting in. "I'll get her."

Tennyson's surprise move got everyone's attention. A half dozen eyes locked on him.

Looper was first to speak. "Damn, Jake, you wanna get her?"

"I do."

Looper laughed. "You gonna break her other leg?"

"Button it up, Johnson," Tennyson snapped at Looper. "I don't want to hear any of your smart-alecky shit right now."

Looper backed up a pace, holding up his hands in mock surrender. "I got nothing to say, Jake," Looper replied easily. "It's all good, Old Timer. It's all good."

For a flash it looked as if Tennyson might take a swing at Looper. Then he hesitated, nodded, and looked at Alvin Jones. "And I'll use my own car to get her."

"Yeah, sure, Jake," responded Jones, also a bit startled that Tennyson was taking a positive hand in this. "And take an accident report—top drawer behind you. Get whatever info the hospital and paramedics have on the accident—and call me—let me know how's she doing."

It was Roger Madden's turn to chuckle. "Why—you want to find out if she can work tomorrow?"

"Shut up, Madden," cracked Jones. "You're not half as funny as you think you are." He turned to Tennyson. "Take her home, Jake. She can't drive—but get that report filled out and call me. I want to know when we can send out one of the insurance agents."

The dispatcher was not uneasy about sending Tennyson after Perski, but he was curious. Tennyson's move signaled that something had changed for him—good or bad, Jones didn't know.

Harden, Marquez, and Tennyson left the dispatch office.

Madden glanced at Looper, then asked Alvin Jones, "What's up with Jake? His conscience bothering him?"

Jones studied Madden for a moment, then replied. "Sometimes people just change their minds, Roger, and that's okay, brother—it usually means a step forward has been made."

"With Jake, it's likely to be one step forward and two steps back."

"Or the other way around, Roger."

Her two outside toes were green, shiny, puffy, with a bluish tint. It was an ugly clash with her bright red toe nails. Tennyson was surprised at how small her foot was, nearly disappearing into the ace bandage and hard plastic half-boot. Her foot was not much bigger than the steel stand that had landed on it.

The emergency room orderly wheeled Perski's chair over to Tennyson's car and helped get her into the passenger side. Tennyson watched, then tossed a clipboard with the completed accident form on her lap.

"You might want to read this over and sign it. Jones will want it as soon as I get back."

"You taking me home?"

"Yep."

She looked up at Tennyson, hesitated, then said, "Thanks, Jake—for getting me."

"No problem, ma'am."

Perski watched Tennyson go around the front of the car. She decided that the "ma'am" wasn't meant as a wisecrack. When he got in behind the wheel she offered, "It's Marylyn, Jake. Not ma'am. Okay? That's more friendly."

"Okay," answered Tennyson evenly, starting the car. "Just trying to be polite, ya know."

"I know," she replied. "But you don't have to feel sorry for me."

"I don't."

"I fucked up."

He gave her a frown, possibly at her language, she thought.

"Maybe," he replied vaguely. "Maybe not."

They drove out of the parking lot in silence, Tennyson feeling only slightly more awkward than Marylyn Perski; she was aware of his unambiguous animosity. Tennyson had never spoken directly to her, which aggravated her suspicions and increased her unease.

"So, the foot's not broken," Tennyson ventured after a couple more blocks.

"No, but the bone and ligament bruising is bad enough that I'll be off a week, or even a couple of weeks. They don't know yet. But I'm hoping not ... When you get to the Freeway, head north."

Tennyson nodded. "The gear got away from you?" he said, not so much as a question as a statement of fact.

Perski was quiet for a moment, not certain where Tennyson wanted to go with the comment. She was worried for her job, and not certain why Jones had selected Tennyson to come to come pick her up from the hospital. It looked like a strange choice for the usually smooth and diplomatic Alvin Jones.

She finally offered Tennyson's statement a vague reply. "The slant to the yard was bigger than I thought. Yeah, it got away from me."

"Yeah," Tennyson replied sympathetically, "that shit can happen."

Perski was quiet for a moment before wanting to know, "Who went to get my rig?"

"Big Jim and Bill Marquez."

"Did Bill . . . ?" she started, and her voice trailed off.

Tennyson glanced at her, wondering at the rest of her question. His interest was going to go unanswered, and before they approached the on-ramp he unexpectedly turned down a side street, driving into a residential complex.

Perski looked around. "Where are we going?"

"I want to talk."

Tennyson pulled over to the side of the street, parking his car under a broad leafed sycamore.

"I feel like I gotta talk," he repeated.

"What about, Jake?"

Turning the engine off, Tennyson leaned back in the seat and stared at the tree lined residential road ahead. Perski watched him, waiting. Marquez had spoken to her a few times about Tennyson's objections to her working for Portland, and the way the man felt it unfairly impacted the general work load. Of course, Marquez had explained, Tennyson's probable primary objection was not to the general impact, but to the impact on him—or so was Marquez's take on the matter. Tennyson was a one-way guy, was Marquez's observation, and that was also the general feeling around the yard; Tennyson was guy approaching retirement and feeling tired and overworked, and sensitive to any threat.

"Talk about what?" prodded Perski again.

"I'm not really sure," he said quietly. "Just stuff I think I got to say."

With Tennyson sitting quiet, Marylyn continued to study his sharp profile. Tennyson's hair, gray turning white, was cropped short, uncombed and thinning. The skin stretched over his features was taut, lined, and tan. Marylyn thought it was remarkable that for a man in his sixties, his features could look so firm and distinct. Tennyson was not handsome—the years of labor had made him too rough, but he did have a look both defined and solid. She had always thought that when you got older your features got soft and droopy, almost sad—a blurry sad look. Tennyson's face was anything but sad. It was worn, but hard, He turned to her, his penetrating blue eyes riveting her.

"I gotta say some stuff," he said again.

She nodded warily, "Okay, Jake—talk." The strain in her voice was light, but obvious. Perski was certain that Tennyson did not like her, or respect her, that she represented something he couldn't recognize and didn't want to see, didn't want to consider, or be around or grow accustomed to.

For a second Jake waited, looking like he could not figure out which of the thousand things he wanted to come out, would come of him first. He finally settled on a benign observation: "You got two kids I hear?"

"Two boys."

He nodded approvingly and glanced down at her foot. "Your foot feeling a little better now?"

"A little," she answered, uncertain at his sympathy. "The painkillers haven't worn off yet. They told me to take a couple Tylenol when I get home."

He joked, "Messed up your polish."

She laughed back, embarrassed, but tense. "It'll give me something to do tonight . . . What do you want, Jake?"

"I'm sorry," he said, dipping his head toward her foot. "It shouldn't have happened to you."

"Why?" She felt a flash of irritation. "I dropped it on my own foot."

"No," objected Tennyson, a bit more forcefully than he intended. "I mean I feel like we all dropped it on your foot, ya know."

That sent a ripple of confusion through her. "What do you want, Jake?" she repeated.

Tennyson looked out the front window again. "I want you to know that I didn't start any of the crap that's going on."

Perski waited, wondering what was coming next. Nothing good, she suspected.

"I promise you," he added. "I didn't have anything to do with what's going on."

"I believe you, Jake," and she did. "I do, but I . . . " She closed her mouth.

He turned, his sharp blue eyes on her again. "You got hurt, and it's partly my fault," he said, then corrected. "*Our* fault—all of us, if you can't work here anymore."

"Jake," she said sharply, as if trying to wake him up. "What's going on? You're mixing me up."

"No," he objected. "You're mixing us up."

"How?"

"I don't know," he replied. "You're being a woman, I guess."

"Sorry, I can't help you there."

Tennyson chuckled. "I know," then hesitated, finding this increasingly difficult. "I sorry, Marylyn, that's all I wanted to say, sorry that this happened, ya know, and that you'll be knocked outta work."

"I'm still gonna be able to work, and nobody dropped the gear on my foot but me."

Tennyson went on as if he hadn't heard her, "I want you to know that I know you need the job and I know you're not responsible for a lot of stuff."

"What stuff?"

"For the way the job is, ya know—for how hard the job is for you."

"Jake, don't feel sorry for me. You're not responsible for the way the world is, the way the job is. The job is the way it is and I took it on—maybe not knowing how hard it was going to be, maybe not exactly, but now that I got it, I do know it; it's my responsibility, all of it, not yours or any other man. I make my own choices."

"That's not it." He shook his head. "I don't mean your choices." He looked genuinely perplexed. "That's not what I mean. I know you work as hard as any man at P-T & W, and maybe even harder. I mean, the job *is* harder for you than for us, so maybe you worker harder. I'm not that smart, so I don't know how to say a lot of stuff—I don't know what I mean—not exactly. Damn, I wish I was smarter."

"But you *do* mean to get me fired, *exactly*?"

"Shit," he hissed out a puff of air and waited a second, then again looked directly at her. "No. I told you I ain't doing that stuff. That's other people, other things getting into the way of . . . " and his voice trailed off.

"Getting in the way of what?" Marylyn's voice carried more than a hint of impatience.

"I mean getting in the way of us making room for you."

"No one should have to *make room* for me, Jake. That's not the way things should be. I should have to do the adjusting to the work—not getting the work to adjust to me. That's not the way things are supposed to be."

Tennyson turned his gaze again to the tree lined street, measuring the small, tidy houses that lined the working class neighborhood. He went on again as though he had not heard her. "Things are different when you know someone up close," he half muttered to himself, then licked his lips nervously. "When you don't know someone it's a principle, and you can feel all smart-alecky and cocky, but when you know someone up close it's a responsibility, and you can get to feeling guilty."

"I don't want anyone to feel guilty, and I don't want to be in the way of anyone's *principles*." She spat out the last word. "But if you want my opinion, fuck your principles."

Tennyson gave his head a shake. "That's what I mean, Perski. It's not you—not really. You've changed things at P-T, ya know, dropped a pebble in the water, changed everything, and those other things—principles, the union contract, *rules*—everything is getting in the way of us guys being us—all of us—it's not letting us be ourselves, ya know, so we can make everything right."

"What things, Jake? What things are getting in the way of making things right?"

"Things like the way we see things, the way we feel about things."

She could see that Tennyson was struggling, and not only for the right words, but for the right ideas.

"I'm sorry, Jake," she said. "I'm not getting any of this."

He looked at her again. "I'm sorry too. I can't explain things real well." Thinking, he pressed his lips together tight enough that they grew white at the ends. "It's the way we been looking at things, Marylyn. We got it wrong and we got to adjust, ya know. We all got to make room for you—no matter what you say—it's us that's got to adjust to the new way things are, that's all."

"I already told you, Jake, I don't want you feeling sorry for me, Jake—or making adjustments, you or anyone else there in the yard. Crap, you're gonna make me feel guilty. No one is supposed to feel guilty about anything, but you keep feeling sorry for me and I'll feel guilty and get mad as hell."

"And I told you, Marylyn, I don't feel sorry for you." His blue eyes seemed to change. They seemed to grow lighter. "Damn it.

I really don't, ya know. If anything, I feel sorry for myself." He shook his head as if trying to knock something loose. "It's confusing. Life just ain't fair sometimes. Things are confusing as hell."

Perski watched Tennyson silently struggle a moment, feeling for him, then said softly, "You're right, Jake. Things are confusing." When he gave her a questioning look she added, "Life being unfair is confusion. I mean why the hell should it be unfair?" Perski took her eyes off Tennyson and looked away, off to somewhere down the street. The dull late afternoon sunlight filtering through the sycamores and pepper trees was making the street slow and lazy.

Tennyson watched her for a second, then offered, "Sometimes there's no good reason for things—they are what they are."

"Bullshit," Perski snapped. "Nothing is what it is without any reason. What I'm thinking is that living being unfair is built into our lives by something we can't ever get away from."

Peski felt Tennyson, eyeing her, studying her. It felt prickly on her cheek. "I mean," she went on, fighting to explain something that was only a feeling, "right from the start we think about one thing: ourselves. And we can't help it, Jake. It's built into us, like part of our DNA, or our survival instinct, maybe, but something inside of us—and because of that we're never gonna really get along, never gonna look out for each other, or ever really help each other—not even close. We're not meant to trust each other, to like each other; we're meant to fight each other—step on each other." She looked over at the older man and smiled. "That's why when, every once and a while, we do help each other it's called a miracle and it ends up on the six o'clock news. But it's also because of those small miracles that pop up now and then that we understand the idea of unfair. We know how it ought to be and at the same time know it can't that be that way. It's not fair."

Tennyson waited for her to say something more, but when she did not he uttered, nearly to himself, "I never thought of it like that."

"Sure you did, Jake," she countered. "We all think of it like *that*, or something like that. We got a brain that tells us that it's not right to be the way we are—one-way, self-centered. We know it's wrong to be all about me, but at the same time we also know that doing something—*anything*—about being self-centered is damn near impossible."

Tennyson shook his head. "Damn it, no," he objected, his features screwing themselves up in bafflement. "You gotta be wrong, Marylyn. I know you gotta be wrong."

Perski rolled her eyes. "Am I, Jake? How do we get around it—how do we get around being us? Sure, one person here and there, now and then, but as a whole, get around being who and what we are, no way. Yeah, Jake, you're right about being confused, but you're wrong about who and what we are."

Tennyson looked away. "What you're saying has a bad ending, ya know? Where's it lead?"

"It leads to being trapped inside who we are, and what we are—and at the same time knowing that what we are is just as wrong as it can be. But there is nothing we can do about it." Perski laughed to herself. "You want to hear something really fucked up? That survival instinct—our *individual* survival instinct is the monkey wrench that'll wreck the survival of all of us, and that's sure as hell gonna be a bad ending."

He drew a deep breath and looked back at her. "Jesus, Perski, you gotta be wrong." He raised his big hands and rubbed them against his face. She heard the grating of his whisker stubble like sandpaper against the callouses covering his hands. "I hear what you're saying, Marylyn, and I hear that you're sure smarter than the average bear, but you gotta be wrong."

She grunted. "I know, Jake, it's ugly—its fucked up, but what's really wrong is that it's so goddamn stupid what with us being smart enough to know about our being trapped, but not smart enough to do anything to break out of it, and Jake, that's the real ugly unfairness of life."

Tennyson tugged at his ears and rubbed his neck as though he had pulled a yoke off his shoulders. "My head can only handle so much, Marylyn, and right now that's what's right here and now. I gotta work with what's fair right now, what's fair right in front of me. I like you, Marylyn, and I respect you, and I keep thinking, like I said, that you work hard, harder than most of us, maybe, and maybe that ought to be enough. They say it's equal pay for equal work, but you know what? That's stupid—real stupid. There ain't no such thing as equal work. I mean, nobody works equal. That's one of those dumb ass principles." He hesitated, then added, "Look, Marylyn, I can't do everything I used to back in the day. There's plenty of times Big Jim Harden's come over on the dock to help me when my back's acting up, and that big, dumb ox don't complain, or wants me fired just cause I'm getting old—or gets OSHA involved enough to run me into a retirement home. Big Jim—he's a truck driver like me, I guess, and he ain't the sharpest knife in the drawer either, but when I need help I see him do some quick figuring and hustle on over." Tennyson chuckled. "Man, I love Big Jim, ya know, but does he ever look like thinking hurts his head. His face gets all scrunched up like he's getting a tooth pulled." Tennyson pointed a finger at his own head. "Even so, Jim sort of works things out in his own way, and it's not going along with some survival instinct. It's not some rule he's follow-ing—it's the way Big Jim naturally is, ya know. He goes along to get along. He lends a hand according to what he see's going on, usually with me. It's like he doesn't think about it, he just does it, almost like he makes adjustments automatically. Big Jim, he don't talk much. It's natural—like I been saying—the way I see him do things. All those rules and principles—they're what you learn, not what comes to a guy naturally."

He waited for Marylyn to say something. When she didn't he added, "I mean we all got to make room, don't we, Marylyn—for other people? You know what I mean? I can't lift what Big Jim can—hell none of the guys can—not one of us—but that's not important; what's important is the effort you put out, ya know? I guess the question we all should be asking ourselves is: do you pull your own weight—and stop asking: does Perski pull anybody else's weight too, and I think you pull your own weight, Perski. That's all I wanted to say, ya know. I think you pull your own weight."

Feeling relief, Marylyn said, "You're saying a lot, Jake. Thanks. I appreciate it. I try to pull my own weight. I really do."

"I know you do, Marylyn," Tennyson repeated and nodded in agreement. "In your own way, a different way, you pull your own weight. And there's another thing. The bottom line is how much you need the job. Hell, you need a job here as much as anyone, maybe more than anyone here, except maybe Harden—he's got five kids and one on the way. Hell, Looper, Marquez, and a bunch of others are single guys and got no kids. If everyone got paid according to what they need, you and Harden would be at the top of the list, and no one works less equally than you two." Jake laughed. "I guess that's what they call some kind of irony, don't they—but you two—you and Harden—you both work just as hard as the other, in your own way, only neither one of you works equal." He pulled a red bandanna out of his front pocket and wiped at his forehead. He chuckled. "Damn, that was more talking than I done in a long time, ya know, and it *was* work."

He chuckled again. "Shit, or maybe not. I think it was more *thinking* than I done in a long time. Damn—it makes me nervous—you make me nervous—but seriously, Marylyn, you throw everything you got into it, so we all got to adjust to that and get off your ass. I just wanted to say that."

For a long moment, Marylyn said nothing in response. She watched Jake's profile a bit longer and then looked out the window at the small houses running down the residential street. She let her mind go blank, releasing the stress she had been feeling for a long time.

She finally said, "Thanks Jake, I appreciate it."

"Don't thank me," he snorted. "I don't think I can help you. I don't even think you need any help—at least not from me."

She remembered Bill Marquez saying something similar to her. "You just did, Jake—Help me. Big time."

He smiled at her. It was genuine. "Thanks, Marylyn. I don't know what I did for you, but thanks, 'cause it sure makes my head hurt. I guess I'm more like Big Jim than I thought."

"In more ways than you know."

He smiled. "Hell, I try, ya know."

"Thanks, Jake, for saying what you said."

Tennyson nodded. "I'll talk to Jones—he's really one of us—and the other guys. We'll see, ya know. We'll see."

Tennyson hit up Al Jones right away. He wanted Perski to have his city tractor so she could more easily control the converter gears. He kept his short city delivery runs, but he talked the dock men into loading an electric hand-jack on the back of Perski's trailers. That was a tough one. Even though Jones would not make note of it, the absent jacks would eventually be noticed by the warehouse supervisors. But Tennyson got the dockworkers to list the jack's keys out with a repair tag, down for maintenance, and then rotate the jacks so the supervisors wouldn't catch on. For the dockworkers, this was a humorous game; they enjoyed anything they might do to put one over on their supervisors. On the part of management, only Jones would know, and like Tennyson had thought, Jones was one of them. Next, Tennyson got with the senior drivers and argued them into releasing their trailers that had lift gates, so that most of Perski's pallets would not have to be broken up and the heavier freight muscled by hand. They understood what Tennyson was doing, and though they didn't like it much, they shrugged and went along, their grumbling part show, part deeply felt at the new normal. Tennyson got other small changes instituted, nothing extraordinary, just minor alterations in delivery schedules that would allow for Perski to handle more fork lift loads and schedule top freight[25] more conveniently.

Everybody noticed, yet hardly a man said a word. They grumbled to themselves and accepted the new normal in their work life.

The only supervisor that saw and got what Tennyson was doing was Alvin Jones, but he diligently practiced the rule of the three monkeys and let the men sort events out by themselves. He did marvel, though, at witnessing the impact of the senior man's moves, at Tennyson's push for a go-along-get-along attitude; and it was a push, as it was increasingly obvious that the changes were an awkward fit, with adapting to a new normal bringing with it

---

25. Top freight is freight that is light and easily damaged, almost always going on top of heavier, less fragile cargo. Dispatchers are usually careless about the order of their pickup , figuring that drivers can continually handle and re-handle the freight as heavier cargo is loaded. This is redundant work and slight changes in scheduled pickups and ease the work load and reduce chances of injury.

the inevitability of tension. Jones watched the men chafe in their adjustment to the new normal, but accept it as one accepts the shouldering of a new and irritating burden.

But the biggest adjustment was to Tennyson's about-face.

"Hey, Jake, hold up." Looper ran up to Tennyson outside Frank's Café. "What going on. You sure got everyone confused."

"About what, Johnson?"

"About everything, Jake. About what you're doing for Perski—giving up your city tractor, and city runs, and everything. What the hell's up with that?"

Tennyson continued toward his truck, Looper tagging along like a puppy. Reaching the door of the cab, Tennyson reached up for the handle, then turned and looked at Looper.

"I changed my mind, Johnson. That okay with you?"

"Yeah, we get that, but how come?"

"On account of I'm not sure anymore, ya know." Tennyson released the handle. "Look, Johnson, that's a lie. I'd like to say I don't know, but it'd all be a lie. The fact of the matter is that I just started to see things different."

"Different how, Jake?"

"When I figure that out good enough to explain it, I'll let you know, Johnson." He reached again for the handle and opened the cab's door. "Right now, let's just say the old dog is trying to learn new tricks."

Looper laughed. "Maybe you just fell in love."

Tennyson climbed into the driver's seat and looked down at Looper. "I wish it was that simple, Johnson. Maybe I just got tired of being me, Jacob Tennyson, of being an old, cranky sonofabitch who's full of shit."

Looper closed the cab's door on Tennyson. "I gotta disagree with you, Jake." He smiled. "You're not a sonofabitch."

He smiled down at Looper. "You're an asshole, you know that, Johnson?"

"I heard that before."

"I just got an urge to be different, that's all."

"You're different, all right, Jake."

Tennyson pressed the starter button and the diesel fired up. "Maybe what I mean, Looper, is make a difference, if that doesn't sound too corny."

"It does, Jake—corny as hell—but not stupid, if that's what you mean," and Looper slapped the door of Tennyson's tractor and walked away toward Frank's Café.

The immediate beneficiary of these changes, this shift, this difference, was Marylyn Perski, who saw and understood at some level known only to her. She had the advantage now, yet this new normal made her strangely uneasy around the men in the yard. Nothing was said, there were no gestures, no sign, and certainly no hostility, nothing tangible, yet it was as though she walked in a bubble of wariness, but not a bubble constructed on the outside. It was a vigilance coming from the inside.

"Al, how is this working for everyone," asked Perski, as she watched Marquez and Jim Harden at the other end of the dock wrestling with a couple pallets of washing machines.

"It's working out, Marylyn," replied Jones. "They're getting the hang of it," then added slowly, "of you being here."

Something in the inflection of his voice when he said "you" caught her attention. It wasn't malicious or sarcastic, but an inflection that called up her being different.

It flooded out of Perski. "I hate this, Al, that there's all this adjustment to me, to my being here, to my being something different they got to make room for."

Jones dropped his pencil and swiveled in his chair to look at her. "Look, Marylyn, your being different isn't a crime, it isn't something bad, but it is different, and that takes some getting used to."

"Jesus," she breathed. "Everybody says that."

"Let everyone work it out," Jones said. "Life goes on."

She just gazed at him, an unreadable expression on her face, but the fact that it was unreadable caused Jones to push on.

"Marylyn," he said. "Most of these guys here get it that you put out as much effort and energy as they do, that you often work smarter than they do, that the changes in their work life are small ones and you're not to be blamed for them, but Marylyn, they *are* changes, and it's not only the work load." Jones stood up and pointed down the dock. "Look down there, Marylyn. There's a bathroom down there. A man's bathroom. When you have to use the restroom you go upstairs into the front office. Is that bad? No. It is wrong? No. But it *is* different, and noticeable. Now when you go over to Jorgensen Steel and have to use the restroom, you have to go into a whole n'other building." He made a small, tight lipped grimace at her. "Yeah, I heard about that. I got a call. Sure you moved your truck out of the way, but you parked it in front of rolls of forged rebar. You were gone long enough that a forklift crew sat idle for ten minutes until you got back and moved the rig. Did you do anything wrong? No. Sure, everybody understands. I mean, how could you be expected to know that rebar needed moving at that point in time? You couldn't, and everybody understands that. But it is *different* and it takes getting used to, by lots of people." He sat back down. "And there's other stuff."

"What stuff?"

"I don't know." Jones hesitated. "Emotional stuff, maybe you'd call it. Stuff that nothing can be done about."

"What stuff?"

The dispatcher looked ~~pointed~~ POINTEDLY at her. "I won't be specific about who—I can't—but some of these guys were making cracks about you're—ah—body parts and some other guys raised objections to the comments. A couple of times the words got a little ugly. There was nothing physical, but some damage got done; I don't know how permanent, but some animosity in the yard is bound to linger." He hesitated again. "Look, Marylyn, the world's a changing place, but in this place, at this time, you being the tip of the spear of some of those changes, is well . . . It's bound to cause issues. Marylyn, I'll do my job. The company says you're here to stay, and that's become part of the changes in my job. I can get used to it, and so will most of the men around here—hopefully without a lot of collateral damage. *Your* job—if I might give you some advice—is to do the job as best you can and ignore the friction the changes are going to cause. Most of these guys *will* adjust —they'll have to—and those that can't—well, there's always the front gate. It swings both ways, Marylyn."

For a split second Perski was not sure who Jones was talking about. Who could hit the front gate. The tips of Jones' mouth were curled up, but was it a smile? Perski wasn't sure. She wanted in the worst way to have Jones on her side and the ~~uncertainly~~ UNCERTAINTY left her feeling hollow.

"What'd you think, Carl?" Marquez asked the Steward. They were sitting at the bar in Jack's Place. "Can we stand Perski—can we stand all this change?"

"We got to." Heinz looked at Bill and winked. "Time stands still for no one."

"It's got to be more than just time."

"And people." Heinz added. "People change."

"Not always for the better, Carl."

"For the better when it's voluntary."

"You really believe that?"

"Yes."

"Why?"

"Because people are people," replied Heinz. "You leave them alone and they'll work things out for themselves."

"For the better?"

"Most of the time. I trust people."

"Funny to hear you say that."

Heinz looked at Marquez. "Hey, you doing that black thing again, Bill."

Marquez shrugged.

"Well, don't be doing that black thing too much, Bill, because being black ain't *always* the first thing on my mind. Believe it or not, being a steward is."

Marquez nodded and changed the subject. "How do you think Marylyn's taking this?"

"Perski?" Heinz wondered, finally taking a long swallow of beer. "Why not ask her, Bill?" The steward nodded to the door.

Bill Marquez twisted around on the bar stool and faced the doorway where Marylyn Perski had stepped inside Jack's from the street. She stopped, adjusted to the low light, then smiled across the bar room.

"Go on, Bill, ask her," repeated Heinz. "I mean, the lady sure as hell's not smiling at me."

"Maybe I will."

Perski approached them and asked Marquez to move over a stool. She wanted to sit between the two men.

Heinz waved at Jack for another beer for her while Marquez watched her profile; her well-defined features looked softer in the quiet light of the bar.

After the beer was set in front of Perski, Marquez asked. "Carl and me were just asking ourselves how you're taking the changes in the yard. I told you everyone would get used to you eventually, if you just kept plugging away."

Her eyes darted to his, then away. "I just quit."

That caught both the men by surprise.

"Huh??" blurted Marquez.

"*Quit?*" snapped Heinz.

"I quit?" she repeated.

"What the hell you talking about?" stammered Marquez.

"I quit the job," she said for the third time. "Ten minutes ago. I went into the front office and resigned. And you know what? No one argued with me."

"But why, Marylyn?" Heinz demanded.

"The union's out of it now." Bill said.

"And OSHA's packing their bags," Heinz said.

"This is fucking nuts," Bill said.

"You've finally getting people used to you." Heinz said.

"Yeah," Marquez came at her. "You got Jake tying himself in knots to get everyone on board with you. And I think he did it."

"That's what I mean," she answered them. "Jake, tying himself in knots." She took the beer from the bartender. "Everyone's tying themselves in knots to make the world a right place for me isn't the way it should be."

She took a sip from the bottle while Marquez and Heinz looked at each other, both making faces of bafflement.

"This isn't a joke, is it?" asked Marquez.

"Nope," she answered. "I'm not ready for this and this is not ready for me."

Marquez said, "I don't get it."

"Well, I get it," she added. "To go-along-to-get-along works in both directions."

Marquez and Heinz looked at each other, neither man fully understanding what she hinted at.

Perski went on, "Here's what you don't get. You don't get the way things are." She took a small sip from the bottle and explained. "Bill, maybe someday they'll make converter gears with little motors so that rather than push them you can drive them around, and everyone will have an electric hand jacks in their trailers, and all the heavy lifting will be done by robots, and we can all take showers together and no one will notice, but until then this isn't the place for me."

"Shit," responded Heinz. "Knock me over with a feather. What you going to do?"

"I'm not sure. I'm versatile—maybe wear dresses and high heel shoes for a while."

Marquez grunted, "What the hell changed your mind?"

"Jake."

"Jake?"

"Yeah, I like him. He's a good guy."

"Yeah, yeah, Jake's a good guy," pressed Heinz. "But what the hell does Jake Tennyson have to do with you quitting? He's the guy busting his ass to keep you here."

"Maybe that's why." She turned and made eye contact with Heinz. "Jake's a neat guy, that's all."

"What the hell does that mean, Marylyn," wondered Marquez.

"Yeah, damn . . . " Heinz shook his head. "After all that we've been through, this doesn't make any sense at all."

Perski kept her gaze steady on Heinz. "I'd like to stay friends."

"Man, I sure hope so."

"I'm sorry."

Heinz nodded. "Yeah, me too, lady. I'm just sorry the job didn't work out for you."

"You got it backwards, Carl, and that's the problem here. It's not *the job*, it's *me*. I'm the one that didn't work out for *the job*." She read the steward's confusion. "If the shoe fits, wear it—you've heard that old saying, right? Well in this case the shoe doesn't fit, and no amount of tying everybody in knots will make it fit. Everyone's trying to do the right thing—I get that—but it just won't fit, and pretending that it does fit is just gonna get more people hurt and pissed off. Maybe no one will say anything, and maybe we can all pretend that it's all okay, knowing deep down inside that it's not okay. Only I can't pretend, not anymore. I think Jake made me see that." She reached out and put her hand on the steward's arm. "Carl, I'll wait until they make converter gears with motors and robots to do the heavy lifting, then I'll be back." She took another sip of beer then turned to Marquez. "And Bill, I'm not leaving here without making you promise to keep in touch with me."

Marquez cocked his eyebrow in mild surprise.

"Will you, Bill?"

Marquez glanced at Heinz, who rolled his eyes and picked up his beer bottle.

Perski ignored the exchange of glances and stated bluntly. "I want to see you, Bill."

Heinz cleared his throat. "Excuse me, you two," he said. "I think I'm gonna take this here beer and go throw some darts, or something," and he eased off the stool and wandered away, further into the bar.

Perski waited a moment then said to Marquez, "I know you're not going to say no to me, are you?"

"No, I'm not."

She winked at him. "See, I know men."

"Better than I know women, I guess. This is a surprise."

"My quitting, you mean?"

"Well, and everything else."

Perski smiled. "Yes, I'm sure—sure of everything."

He grunted. "Christ, Marylyn, I hate to see it, you leaving after we've all made room for you."

"That's what I mean, Bill. You guys making room for me means I don't naturally fit."

"Maybe I shouldn't have put it that way."

"Then exactly how should you have put it, Bill? There really isn't any other way to put it is there? Like I said, we can all pretend that I do the same job as you, in the same way, but we know it isn't so, it's different—*I'm* different. That's not something bad; it's not wrong—just different, and there's nothing wrong with owning up to that, that I'm different. I finally had to wise up to the fact that the difference was making it so that I didn't fit." She gave her head a small shake and touched his hand. "No, I won't be back, Bill, not until they redesign the job so that my being different won't make a difference to anyone."

"You won't change your mind?"

She shook her head again. "Not until I don't have to cram my foot into a shoe that's too small." She took her fingers off his hand and picked up her beer again. "It's not my fault that my foot is too big for the shoe and it's not likely to get smaller. I'll have to wait until the shoe gets bigger, and that'll happen, Bill." She smiled again. "When they make converter gears with motors and robots to do the heavy lifting. When that happens me, or someone like me, will be back, be here, and there won't be any need for everyone to pretend."

Marquez nodded, but could think of nothing to say.

She added, "But at least I never had to pretend that you were always on my side, Bill, and that meant a lot to me." She crinkled her nose at him. "Remember, I know men, right?"

"I always knew you did."

"And now you also know that I want to see you and I'm not afraid anymore to say so."

"You're not afraid of very much, Marylyn."

"And you have my number."

"I do."

"And you'll use it."

He smiled. "I will."

"Promise?"

"Promise."

She put her half-finished beer on the bar top, slid off the stool and stood on her tip toes to kiss him lightly on the cheek. "Good," she whispered into his ear. "You won't be sorry, Bill Marquez," and she went around him toward the door of Jack's.

Marquez watched her pass out of Jack's and disappear into the sunlight. Silently, he made himself a small bet and turned to see Heinz standing behind him.

"You sorry she's leaving P-T, Bill?" the steward wanted to know.

"I'm not sure," replied Marquez. "But probably not. You?"

"I honestly don't know either, Wild Bill." Heinz answered and drew a deep swallow from the bottle and set it on the bar. "I like Perski—I really do—but I sure hope the company doesn't hire any more women. The next one might not be as smart as this one."

Martinez shot Heinz a facetious look and added, "Or maybe *we* won't be, brother."

"You gonna see her?"

"Yeah, I think."

"She's got to kids." two

"I know. Two boys."

Heinz gave Marquez a healthy appraisal. "Yeah," he said at last. "It might work out."

"For me?"

"I was thinking about the kids."

"You think?"

"Yeah, Wild Bill, I think."

"We'll see."

Heinz grunted approval and turned back toward the other end of the bar. "Hey, Jack, when the hell are you going to get this dump air-conditioned?"

From down at the end of the bar Jack raised his middle finger.

Contact information

Other books by William F. Pray

Green Fields, Apollo Publications
What Can I Do? Rhino Press

William Pray lives in Reno, Nevada

You may reach him at:
Bill.Pray@Firebirdpublishing.com

Proof

47045011R00202

Made in the USA
Charleston, SC
27 September 2015